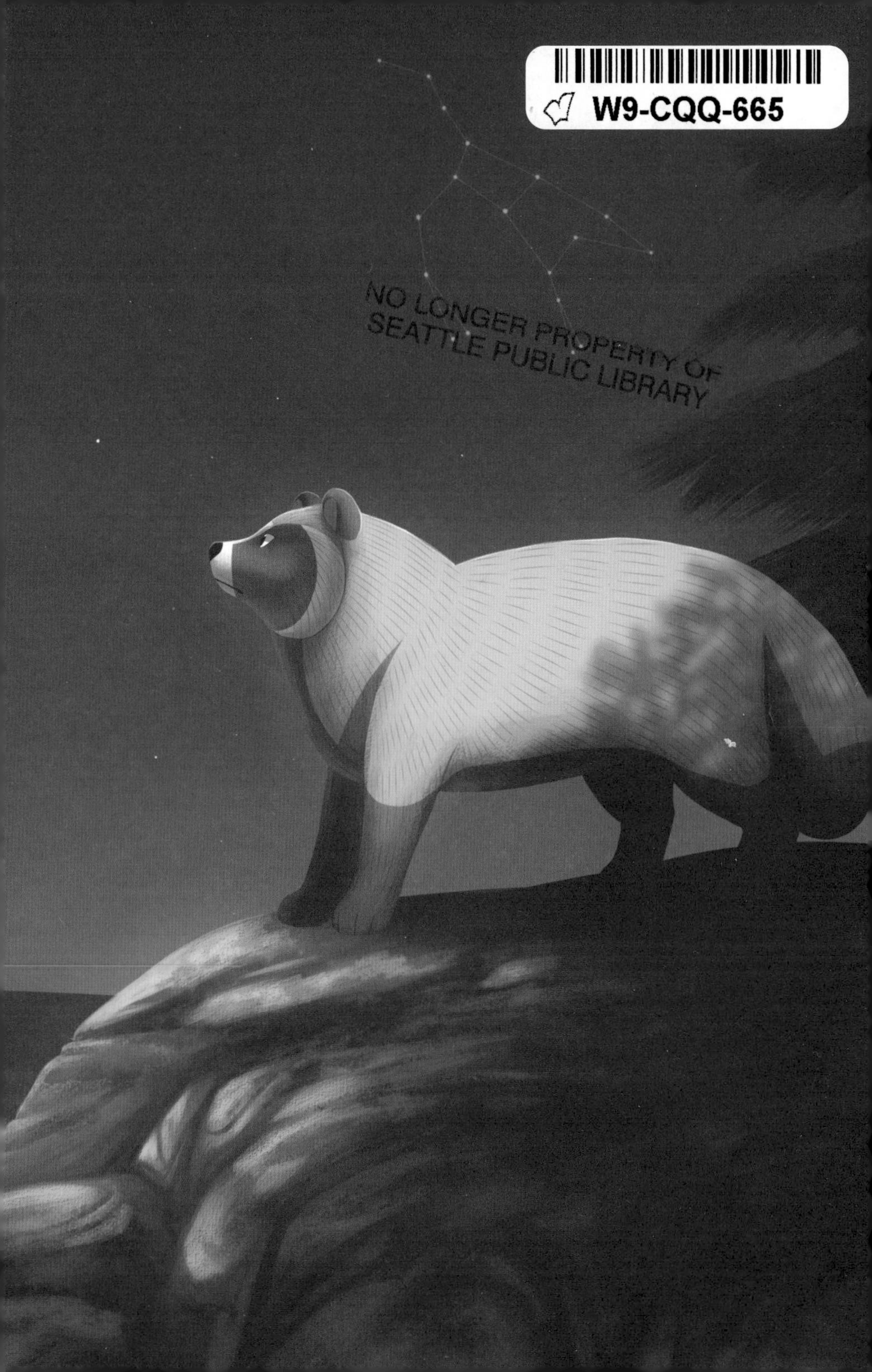

FOX FIRES

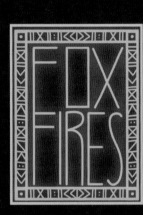

Book 1

by Emilia Ojala

Rocketship Entertainment, LLC

Tom Akel, CEO & Publisher
Rob Feldman, CTO
Jeanmarie McNeely, CFO
Brandon Freeberg, Dir. of Campaign Mgmt.
Phil Smith, Art Director
Jed Keith, Social Media
rocketshipent.com

FOX FIRES VOLUME 1
ISBN: 978-1-952126-08-6

First printing. June 2021. Copyright © Emilia Ojala and Rocketship
Entertainment LLC. All rights reserved. Published by Rocketship
Entertainment, LLC. 136 Westbury Court. Doylestown, PA 18901. "Fox
Fires", the Fox Fires logo, and the likenesses of all characters herein are
trademarks of Emilia Ojala "Rocketship" and the Rocketship logo are
trademarks of Rocketship Entertainment, LLC. No part of this publication
may be reproduced or transmitted, in any form or by any means, without
the express written consent of Emilia Ojala or Rocketship Entertainment,
LLC. All names, characters, events, and locales in this publication are entirely
fictional. Any resemblance to actual persons (living or dead), events, or
places, without satiric intent, is coincidental. Printed in China.

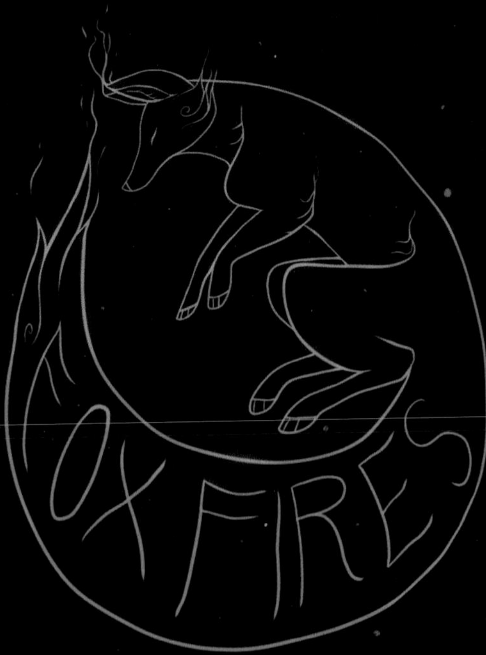

Table of Contents

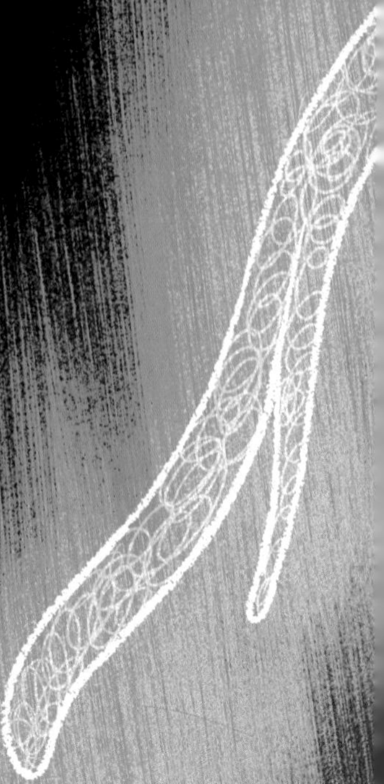

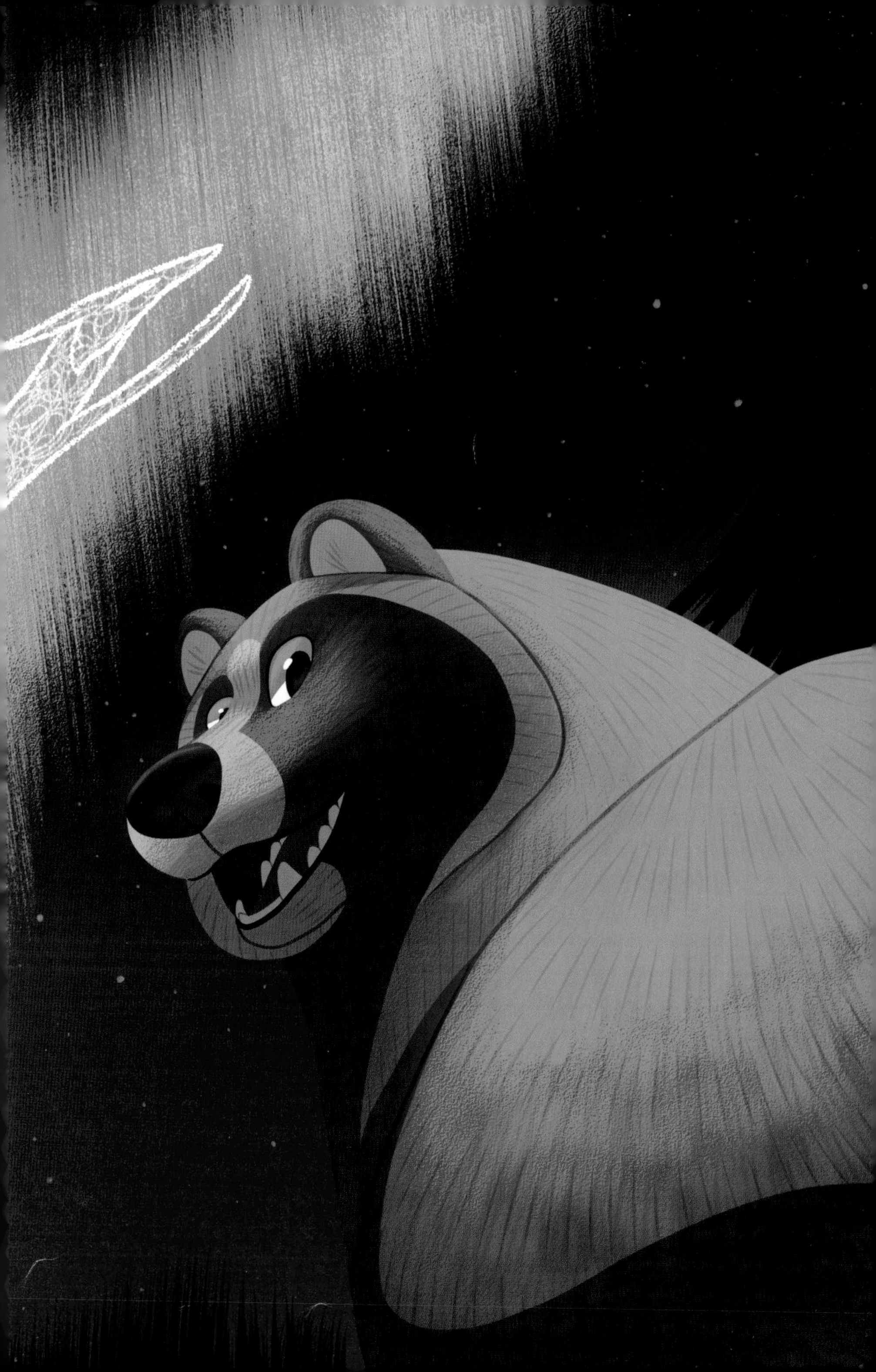

Chapter 1

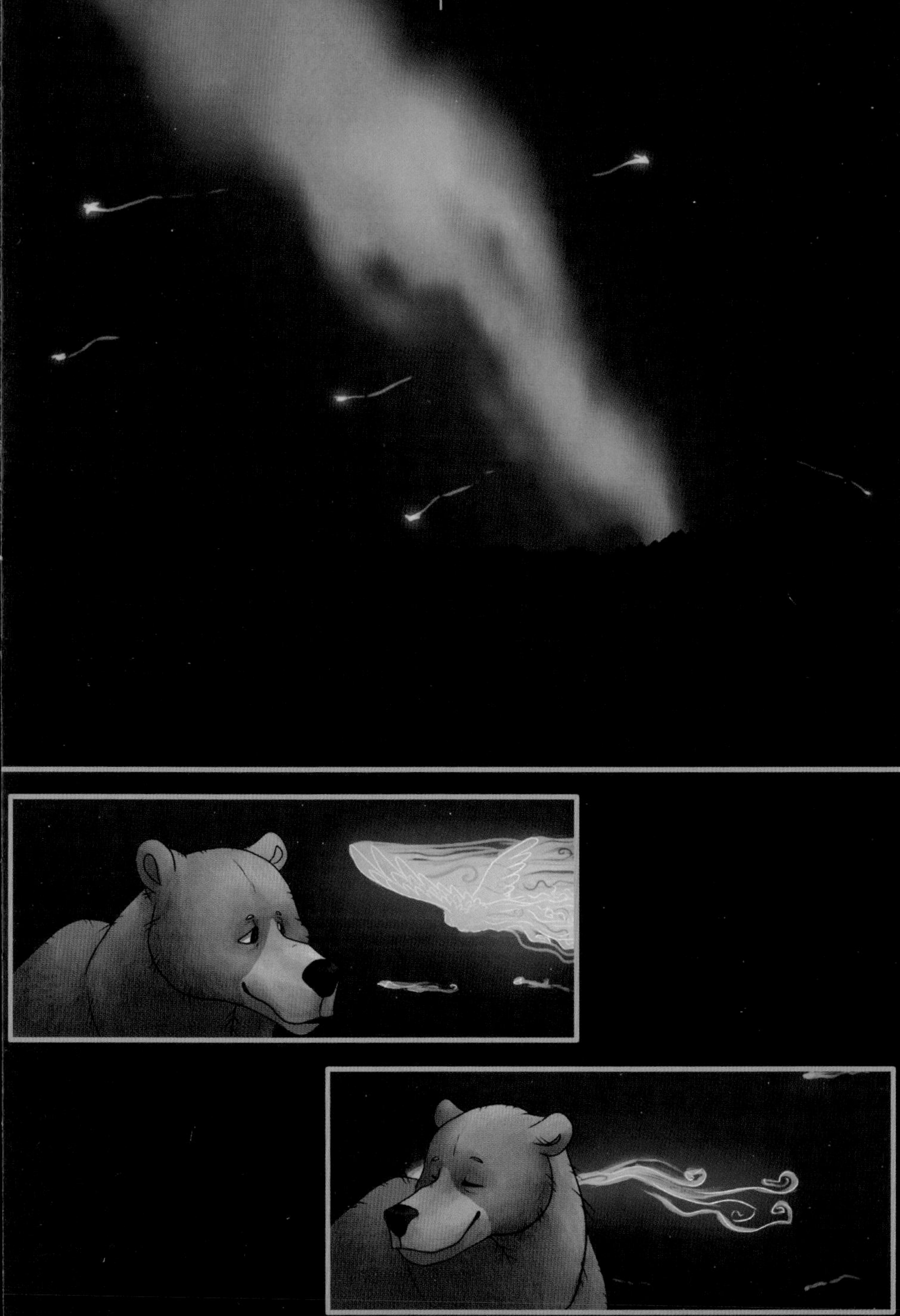

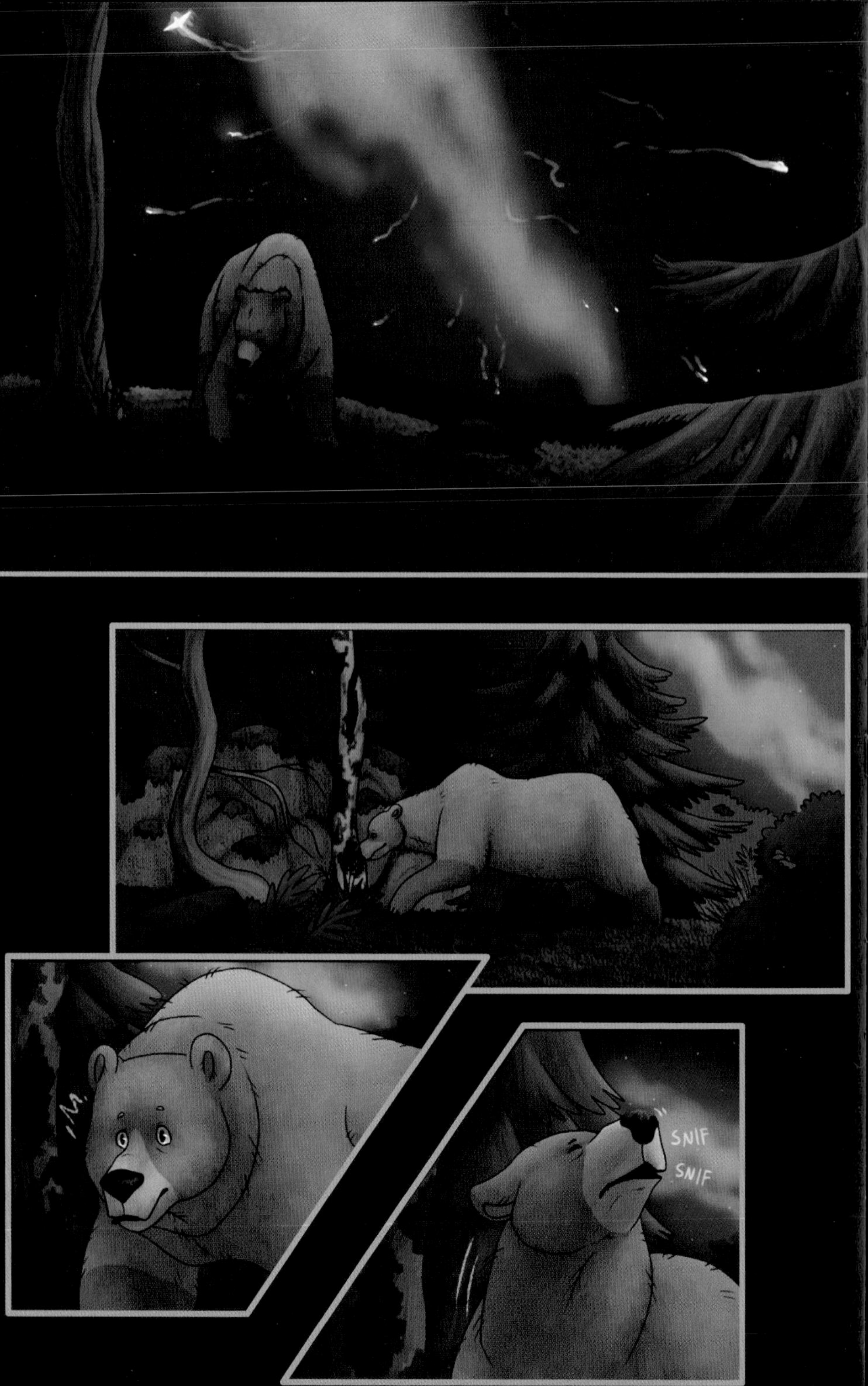
SNIF
SNIF

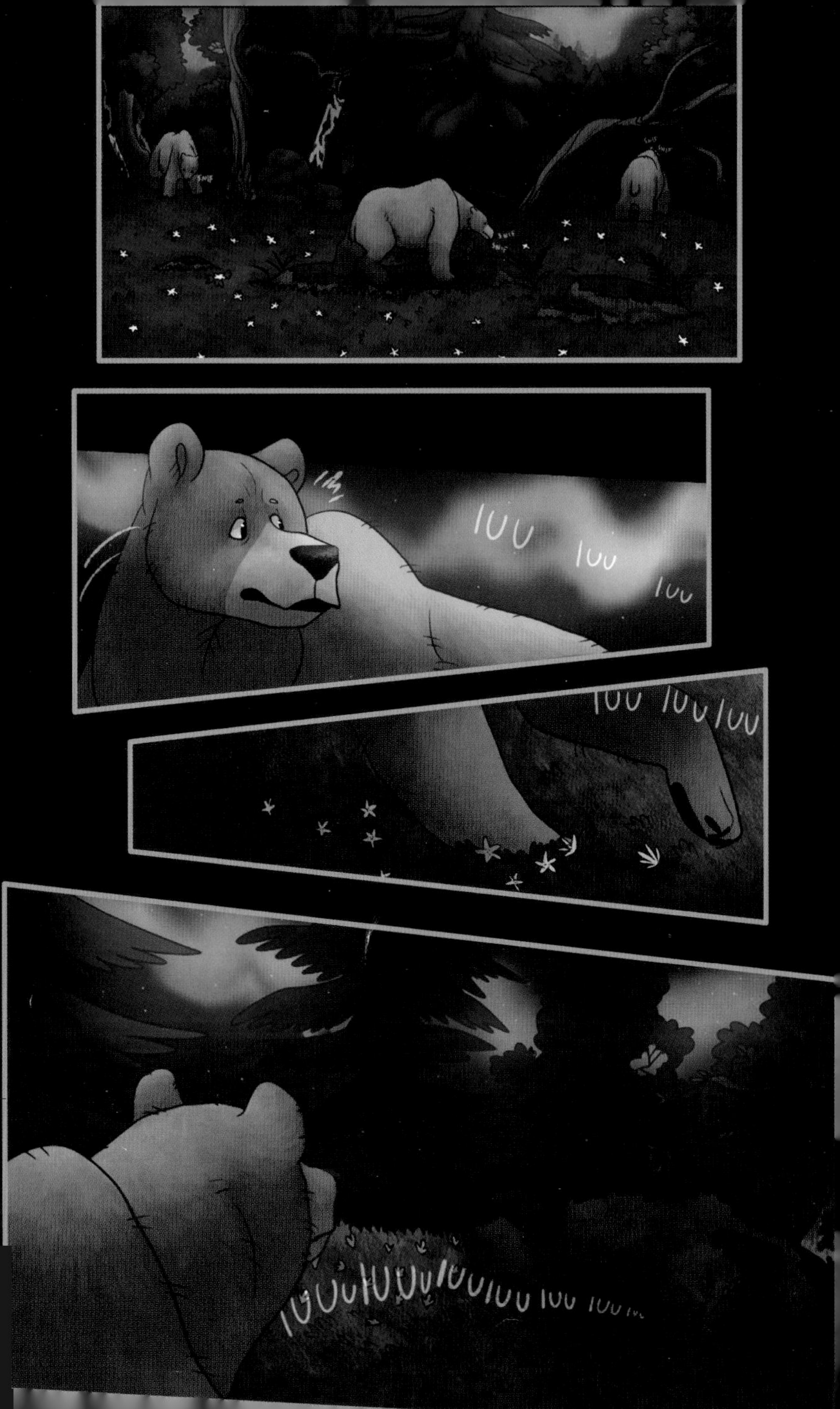
IUU IUU IUU
IUU IUU IUU
IUUUIUUUIUUIUU IUU IUU

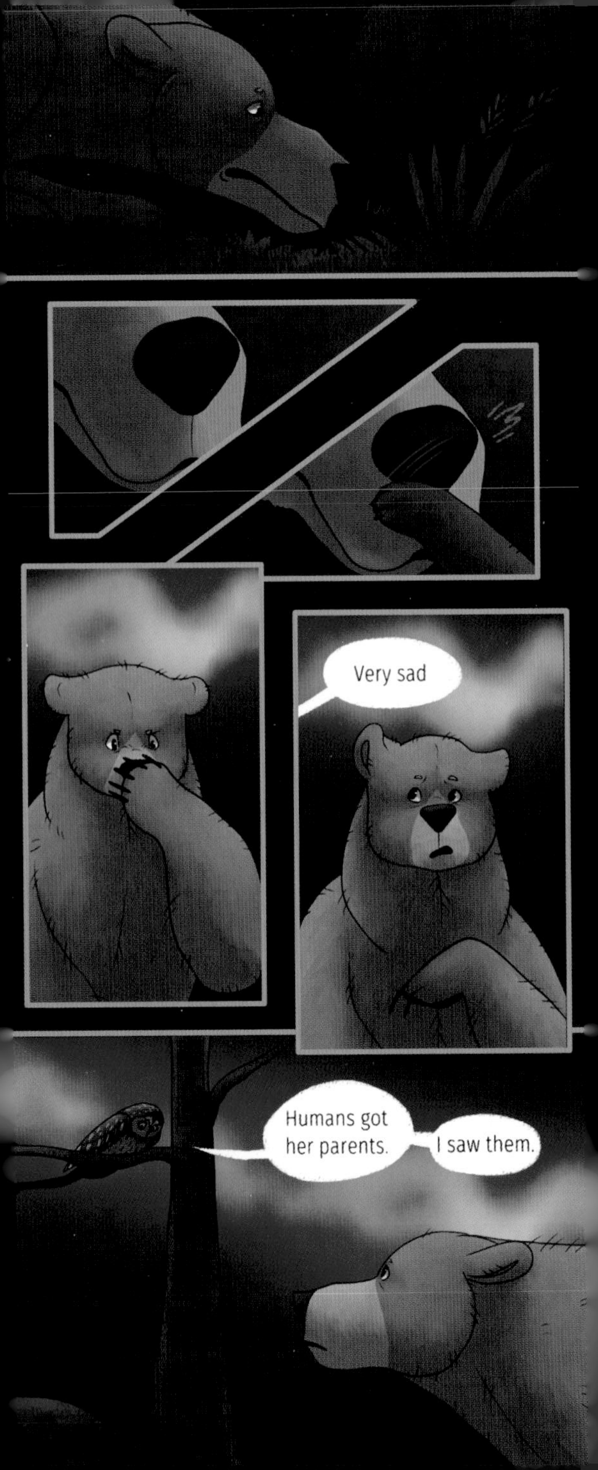

Very sad
Humans got her parents.
I saw them.

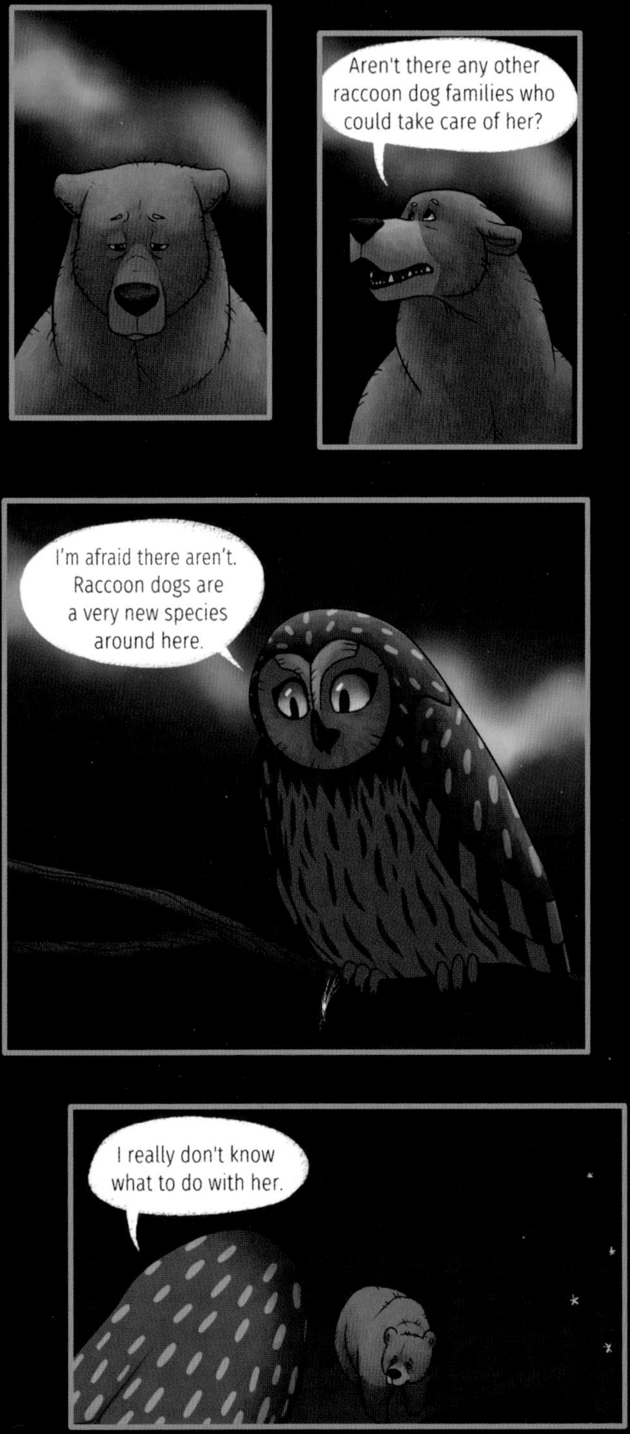
Aren't there any other raccoon dog families who could take care of her?
I'm afraid there aren't. Raccoon dogs are a very new species around here.
I really don't know what to do with her.

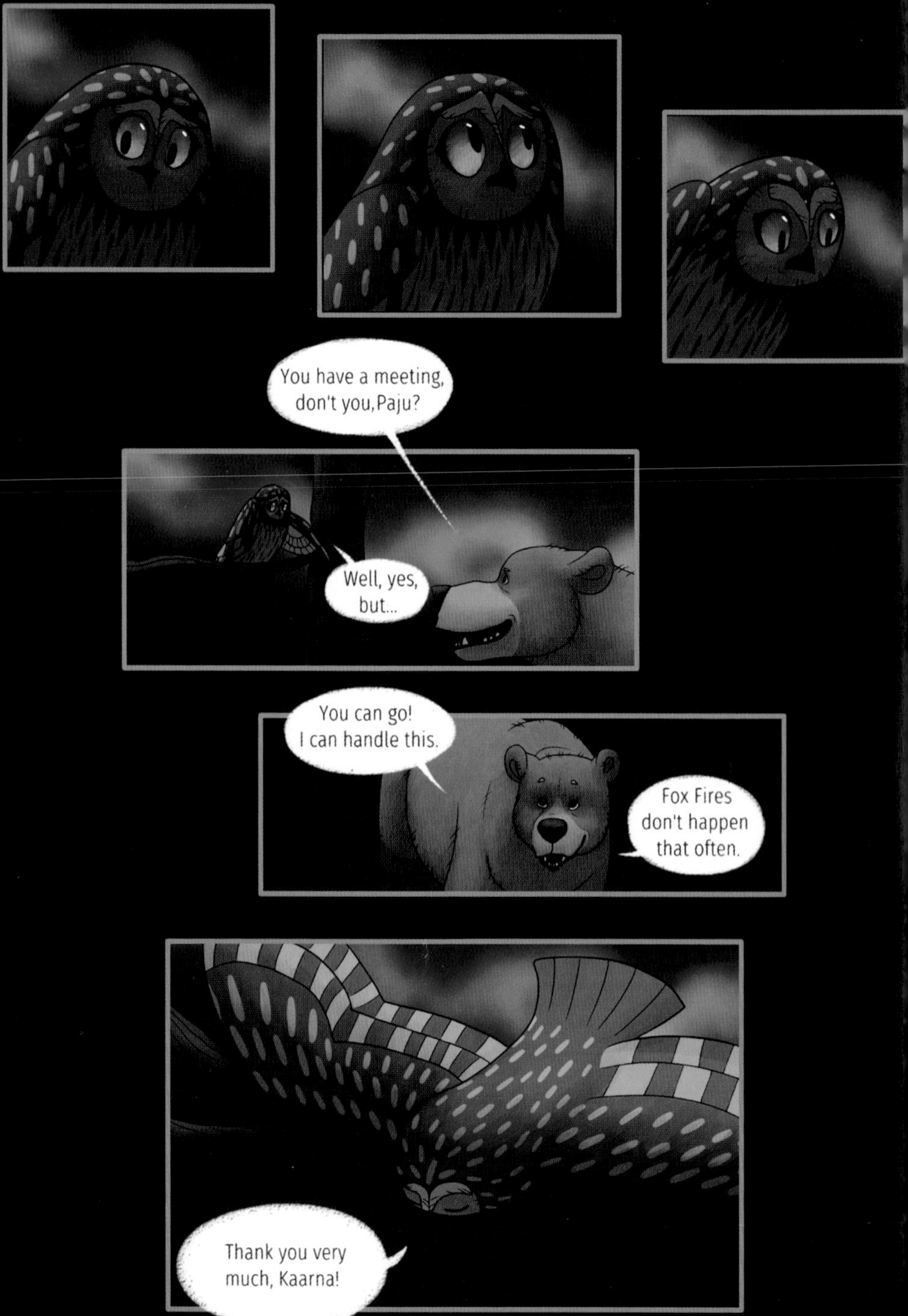
You have a meeting, don't you,Paju?
Well, yes, but...
You can go! I can handle this.
Fox Fires don't happen that often.
Thank you very much, Kaarna!

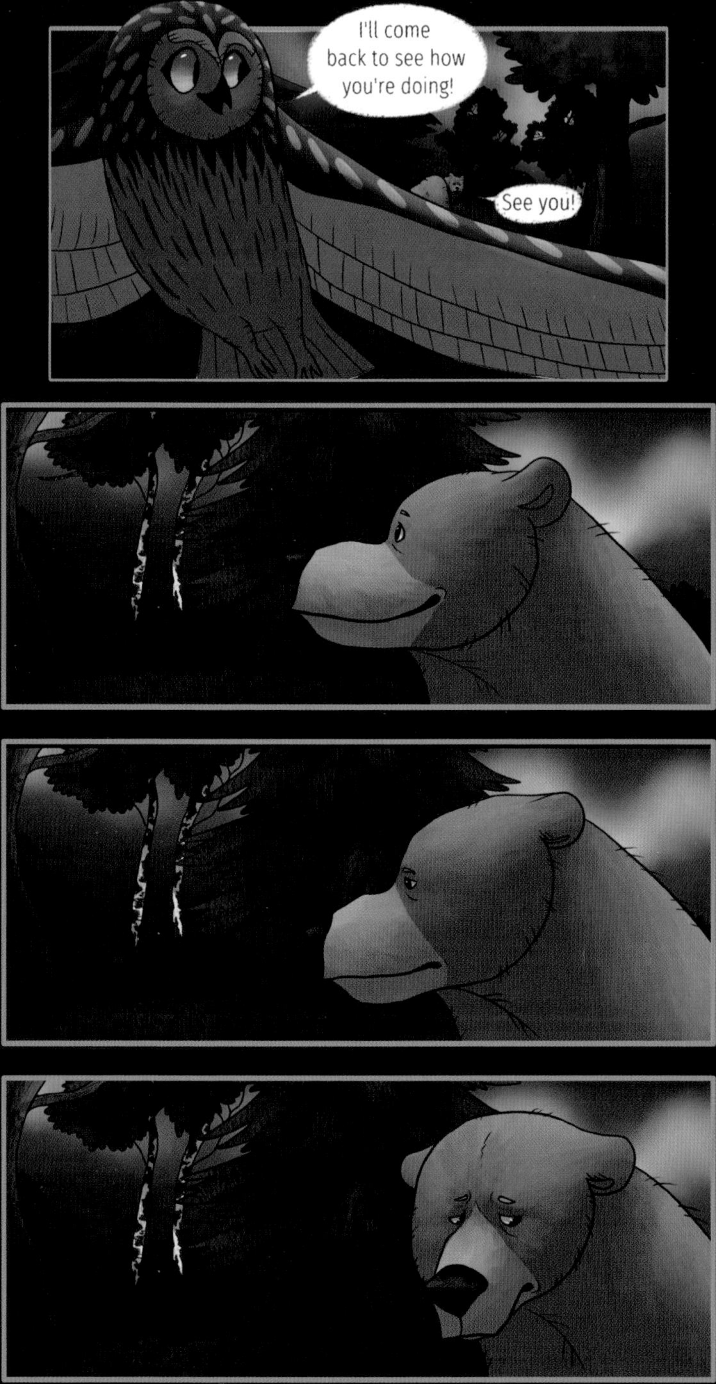
I'll come back to see how you're doing!
See you!

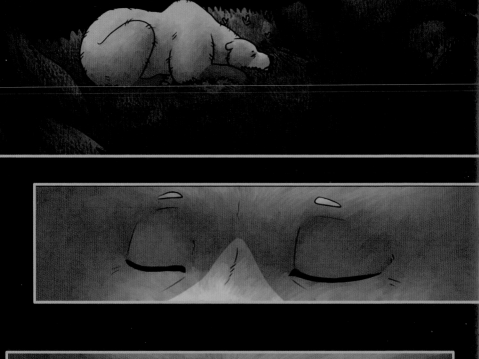
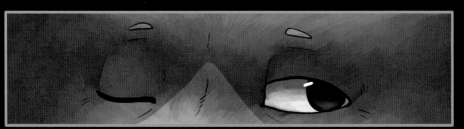

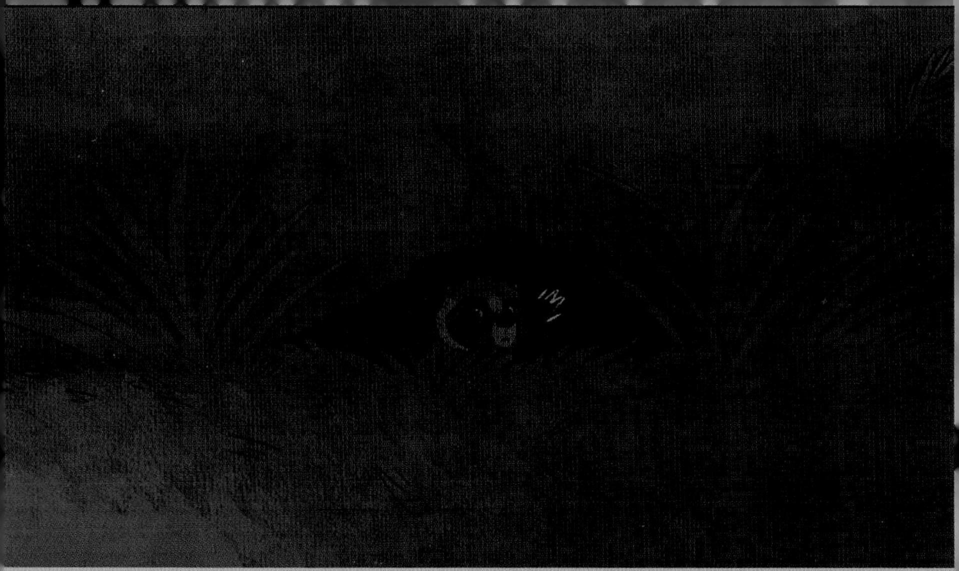

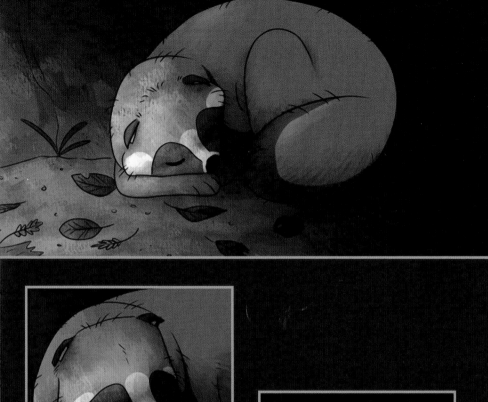

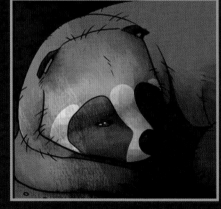

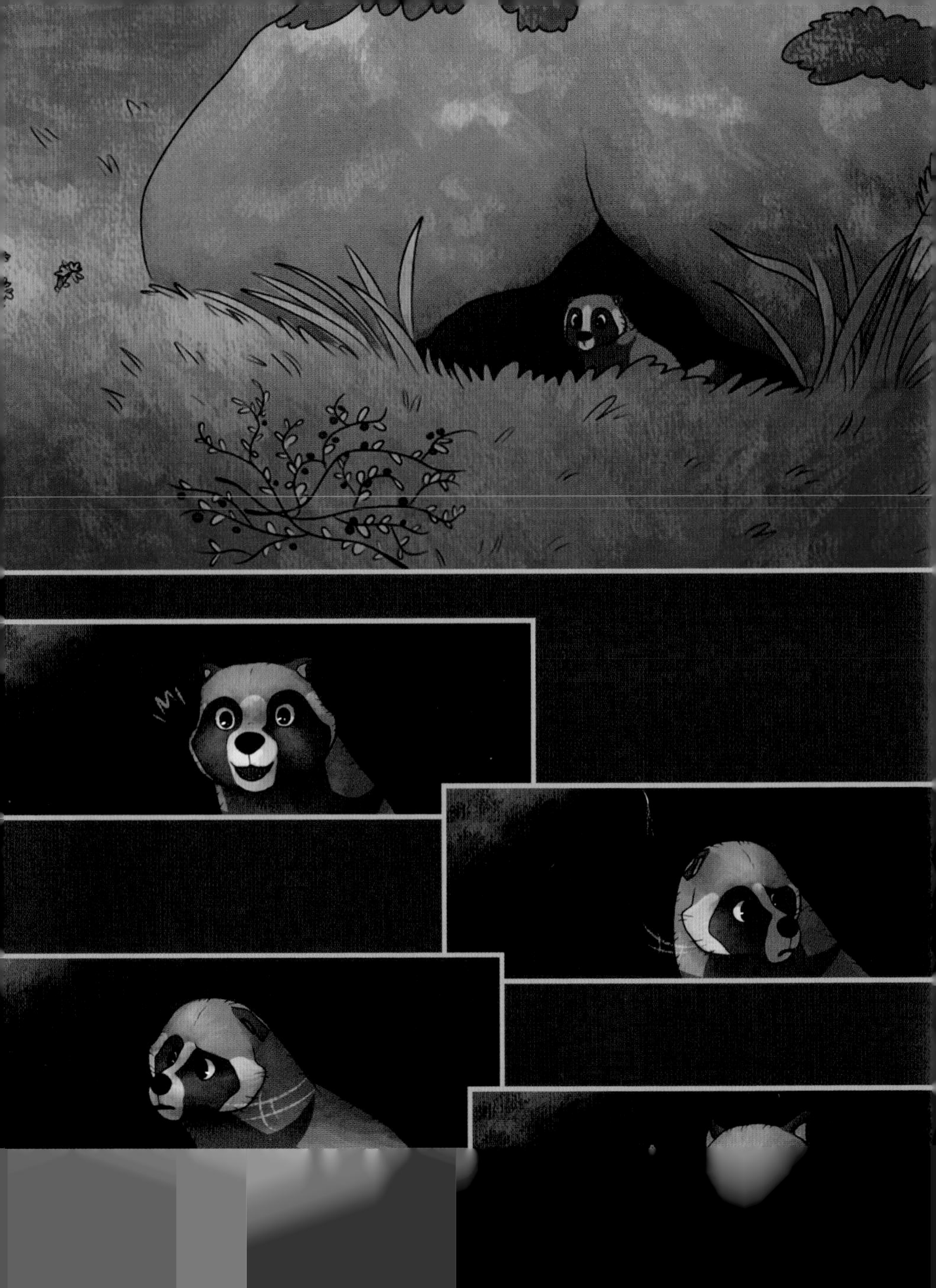

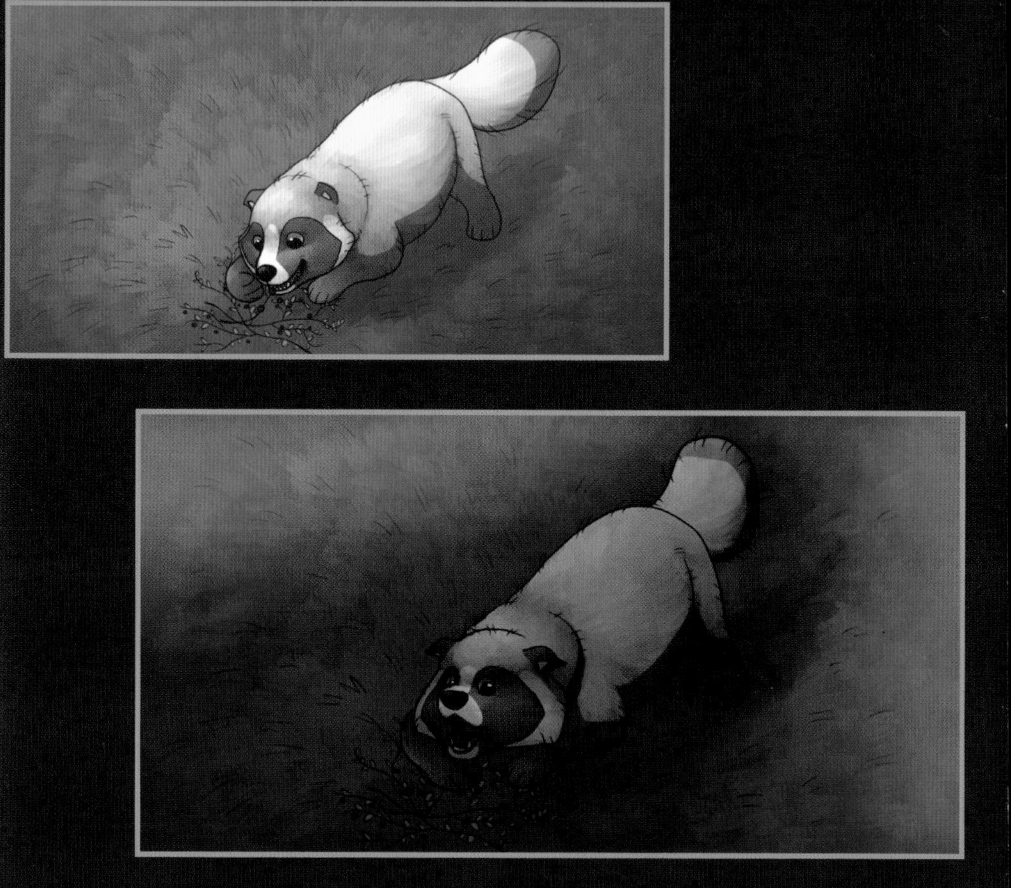

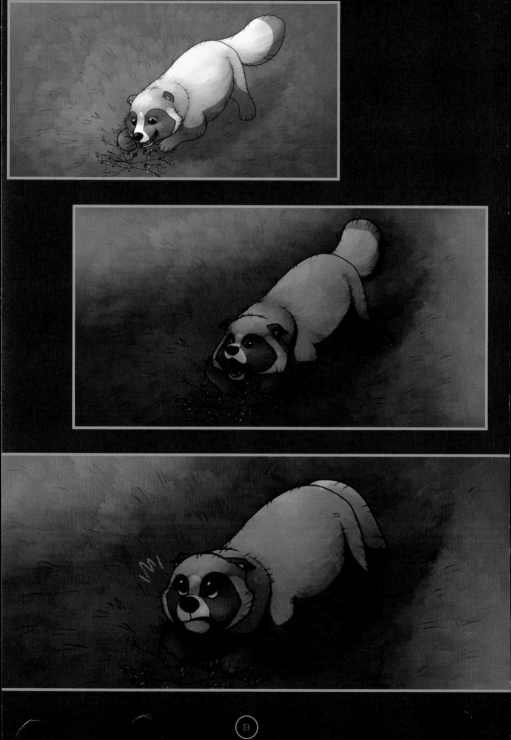

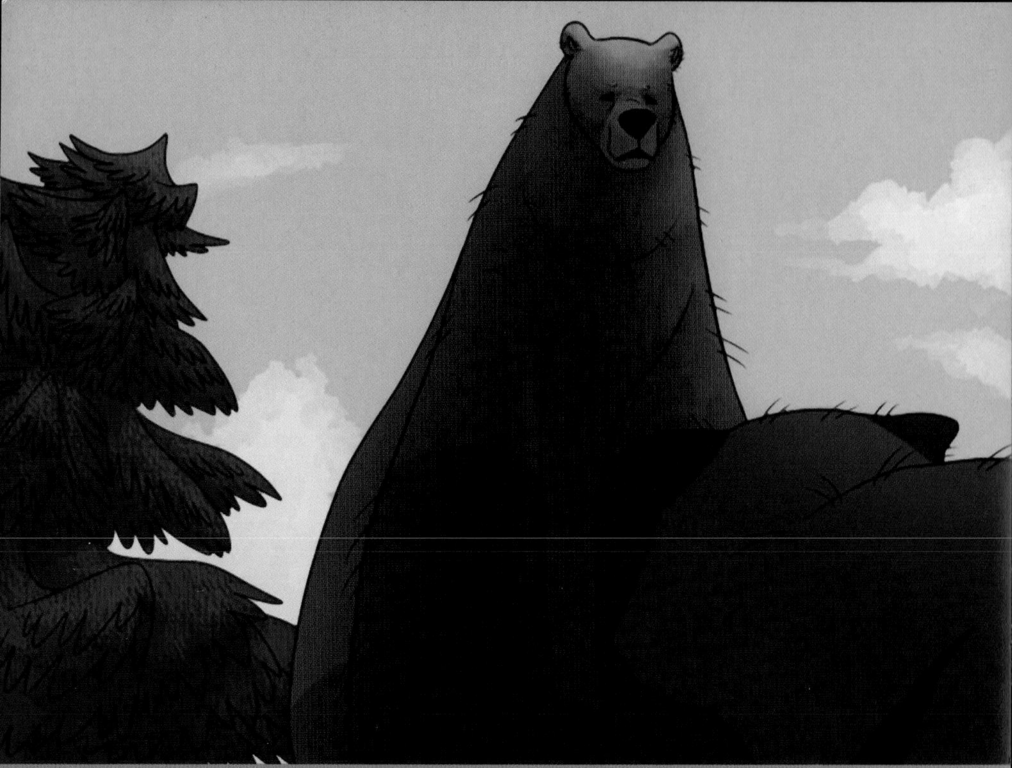
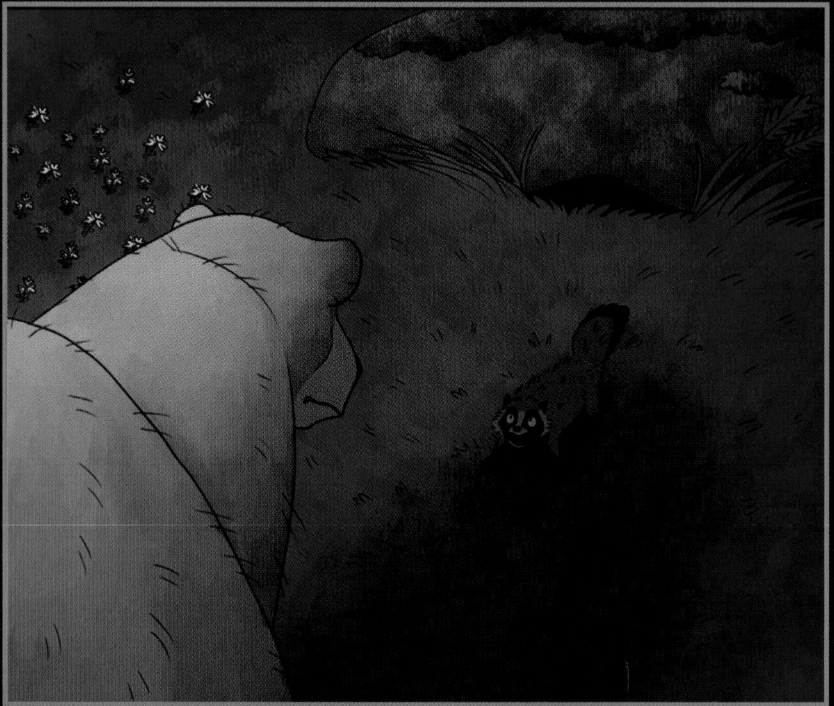

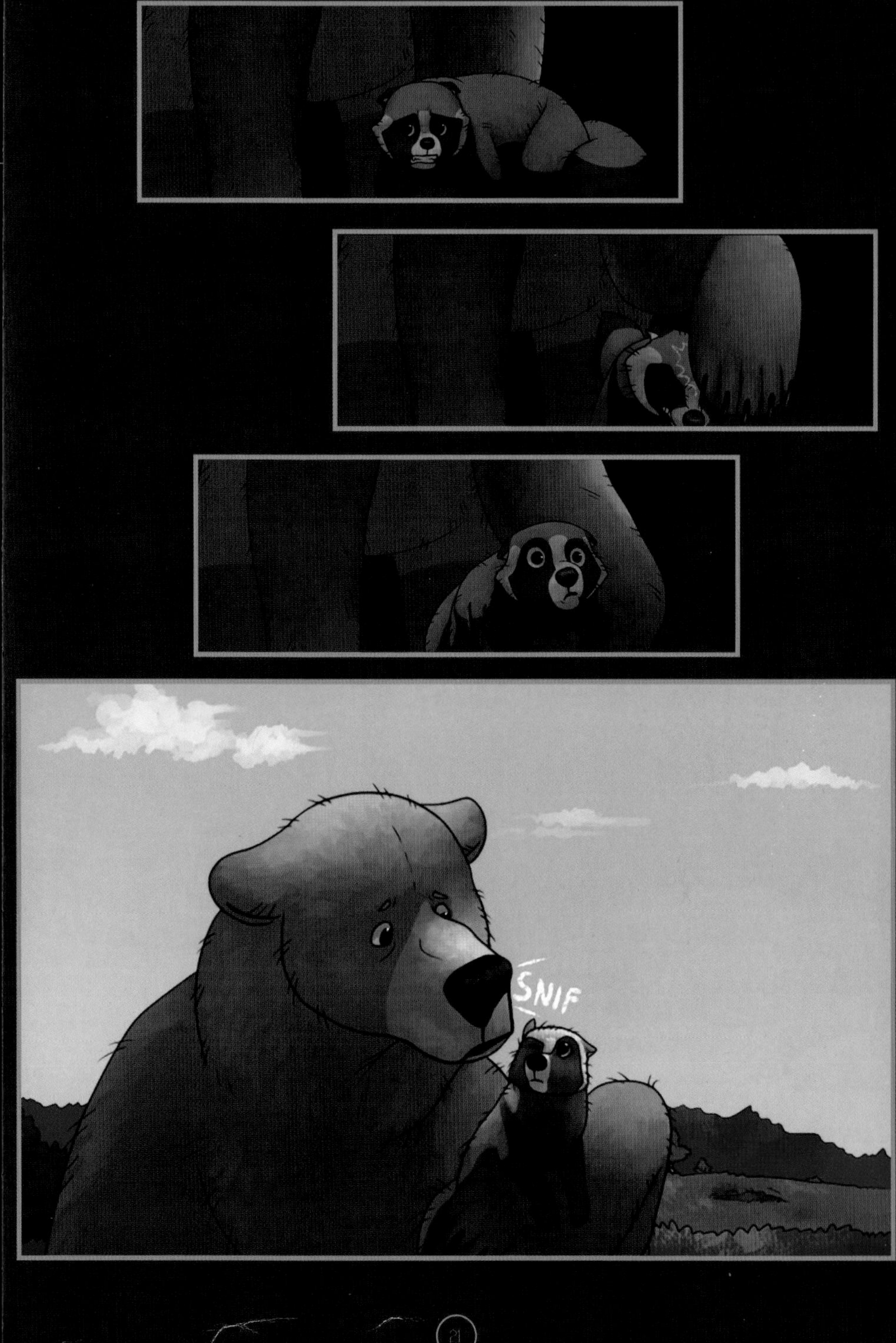
SNIF

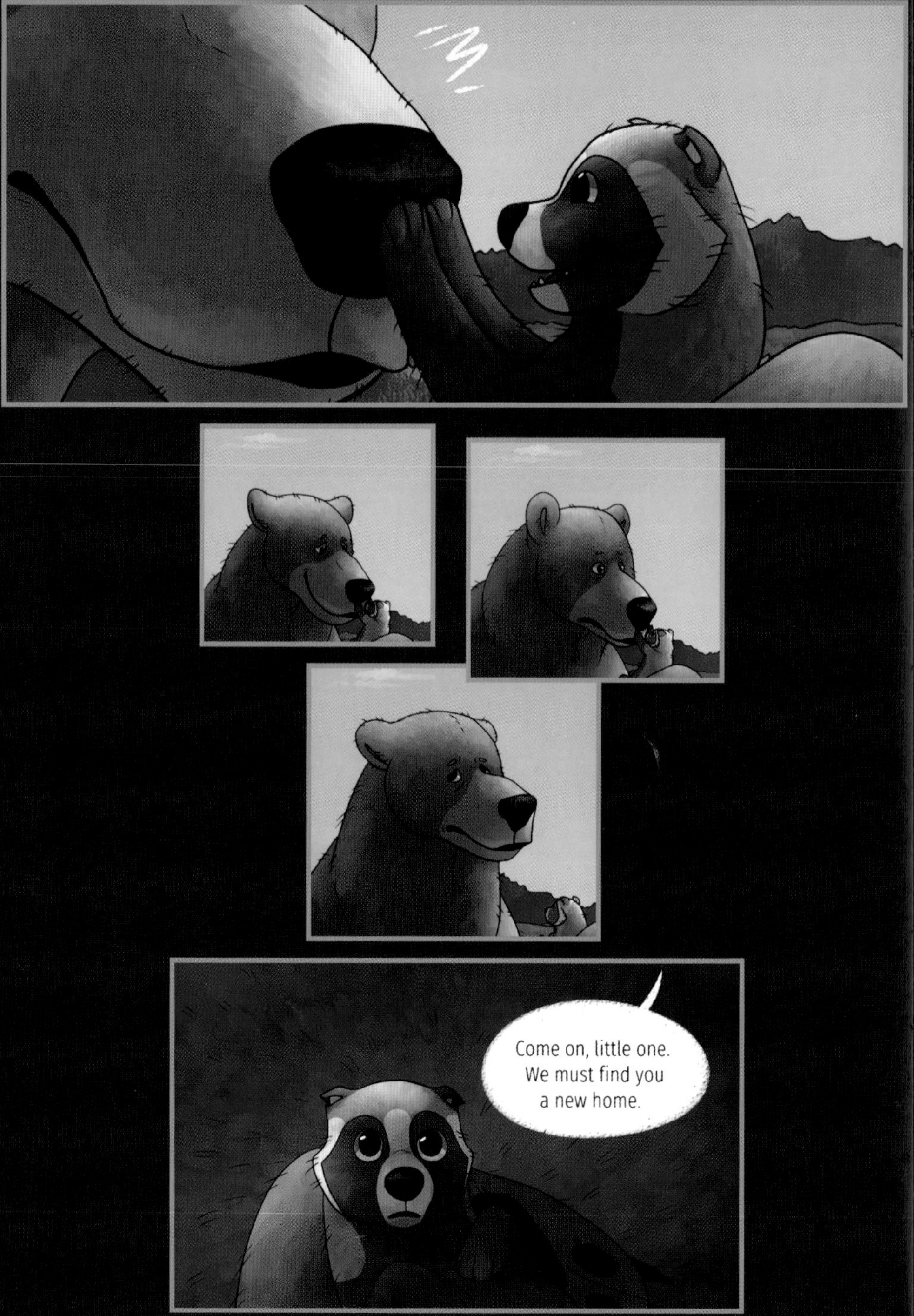
Come on, little one. We must find you a new home.

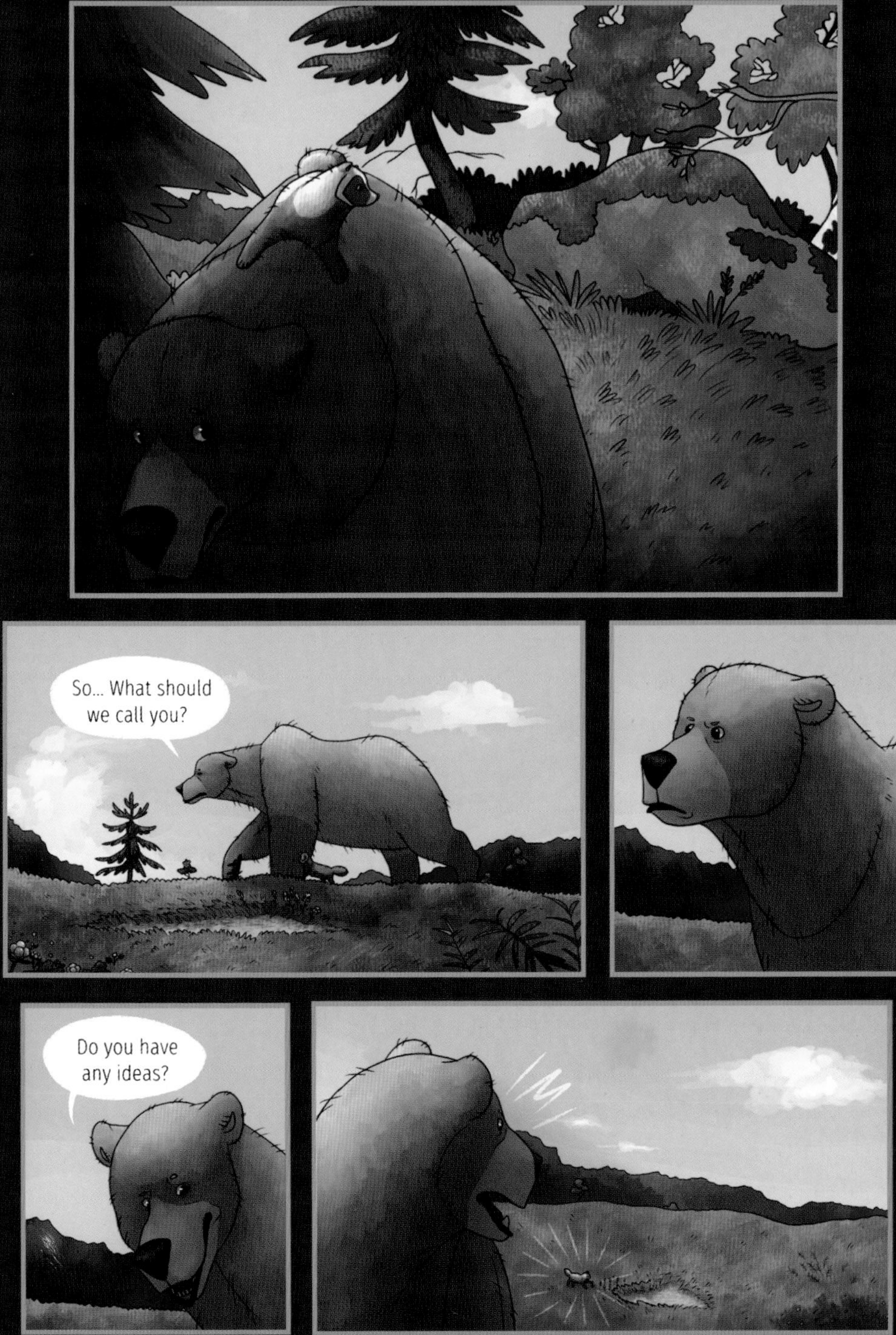
So... What should we call you?
Do you have any ideas?

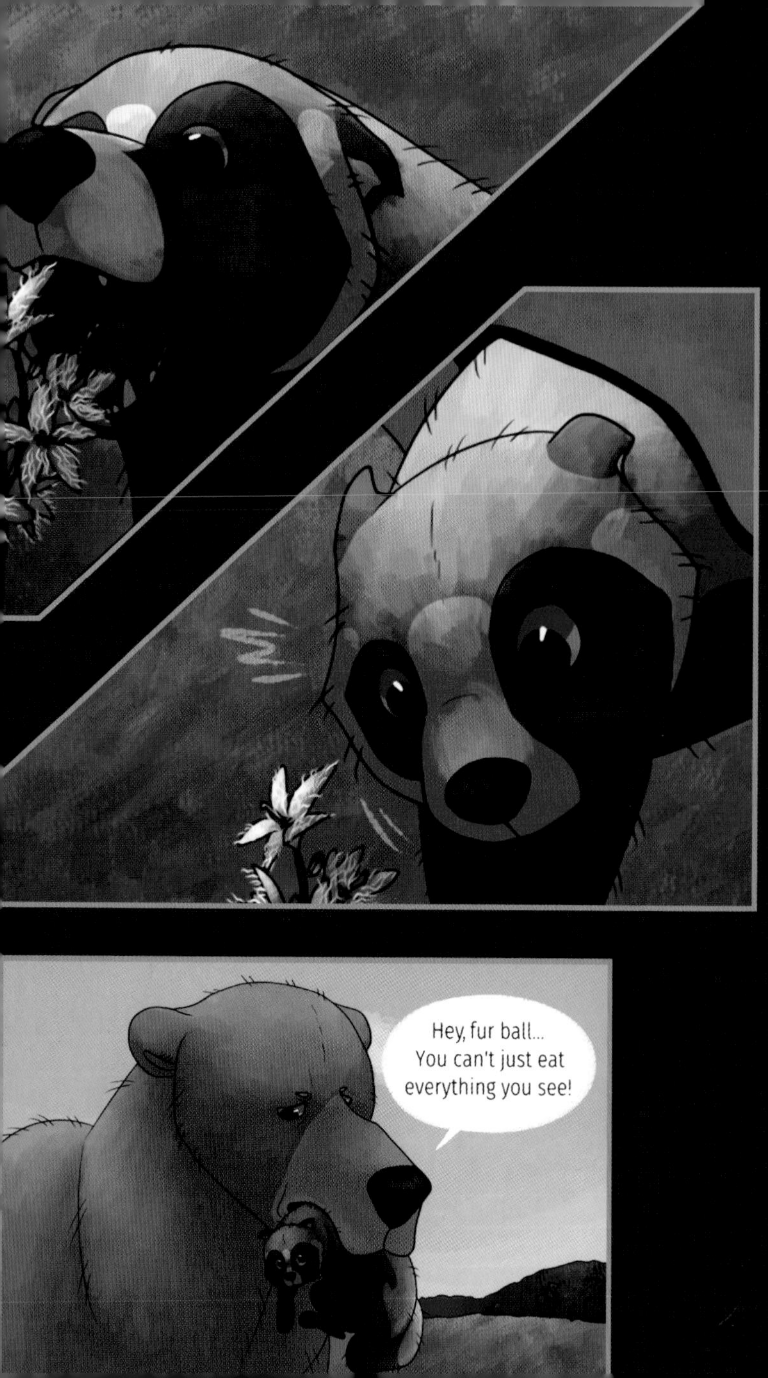
Hey, fur ball... You can't just eat everything you see!

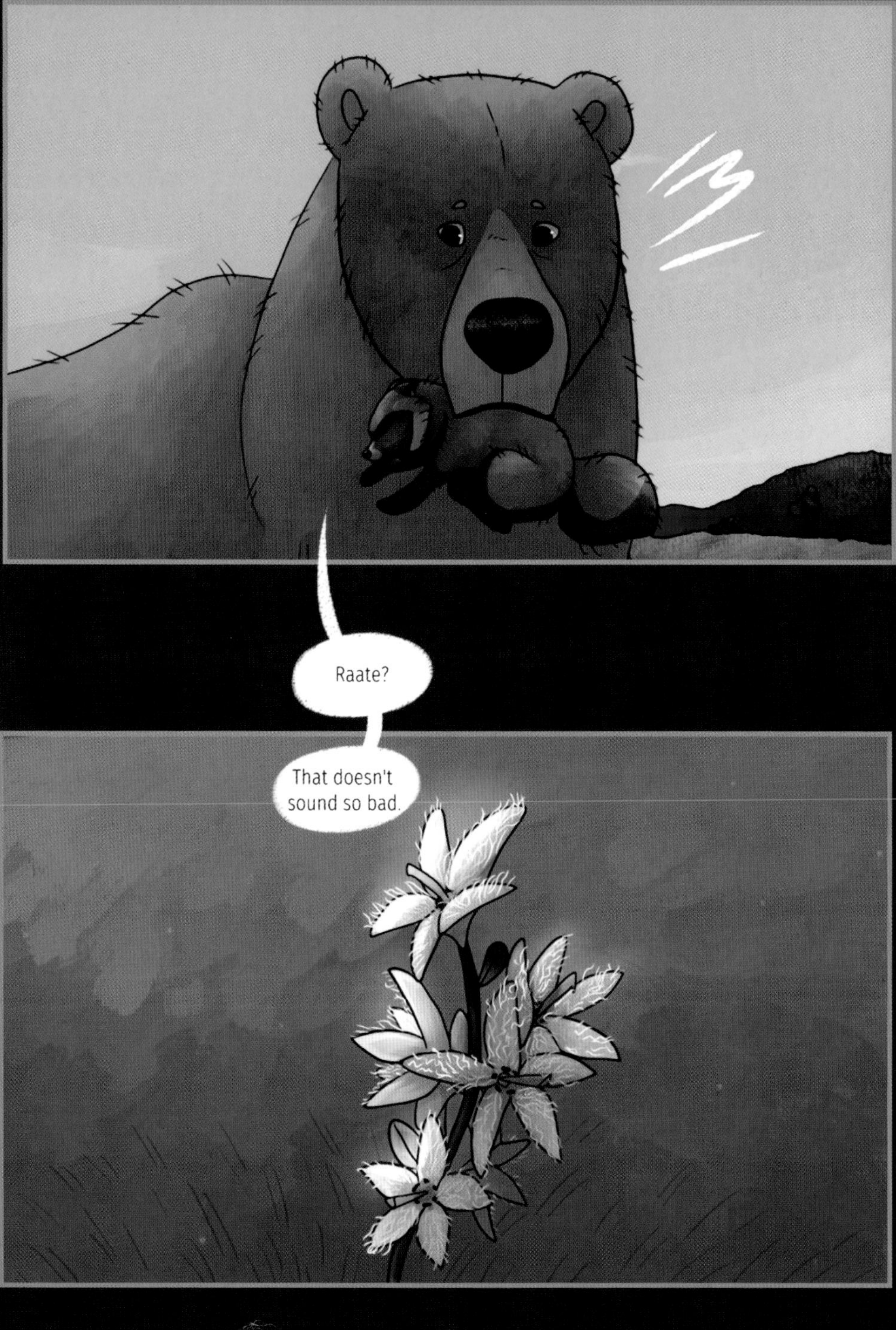
Raate?
That doesn't sound so bad.

Chapter 3

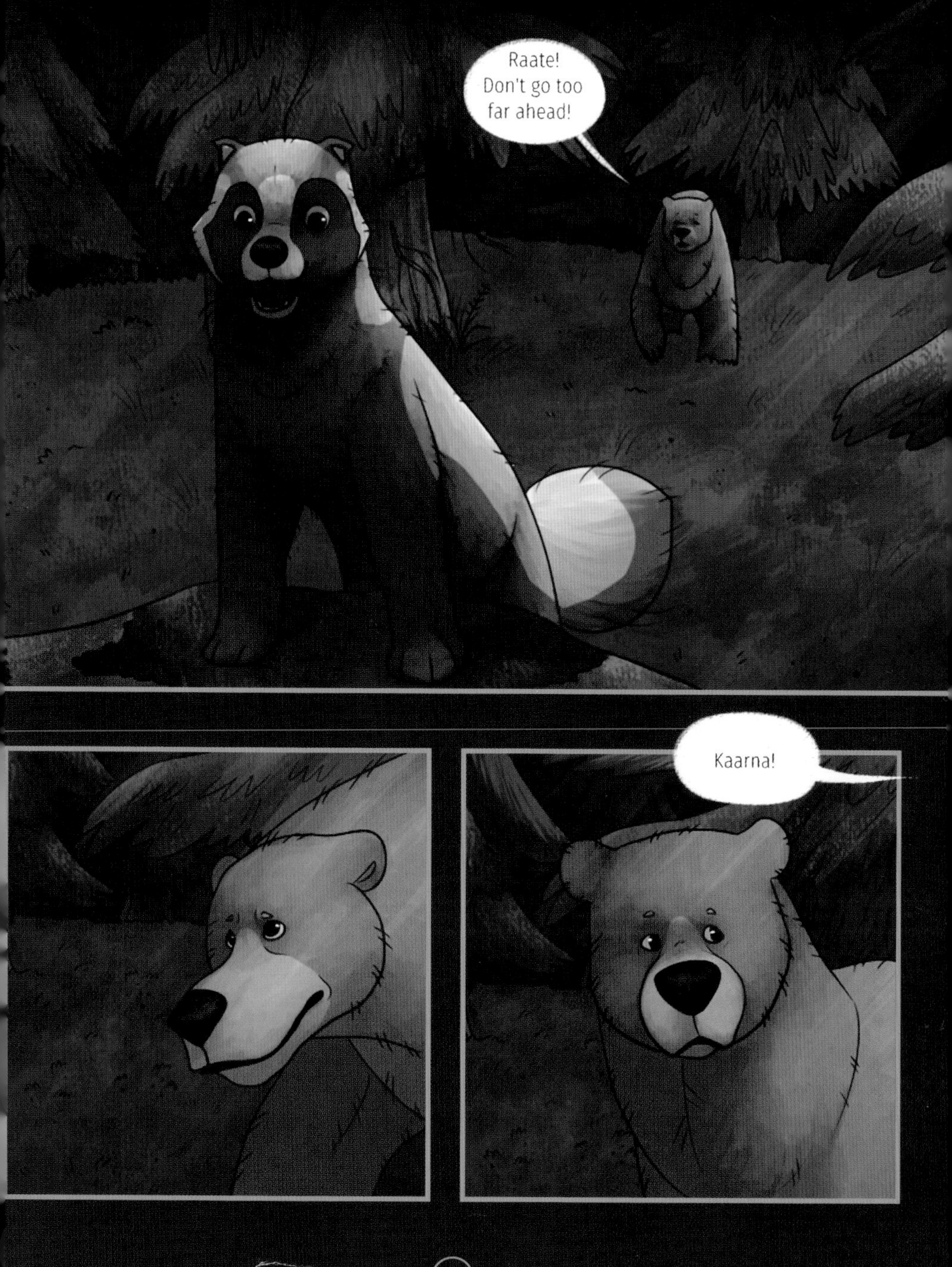
Raate! Don't go too far ahead!
Kaarna!

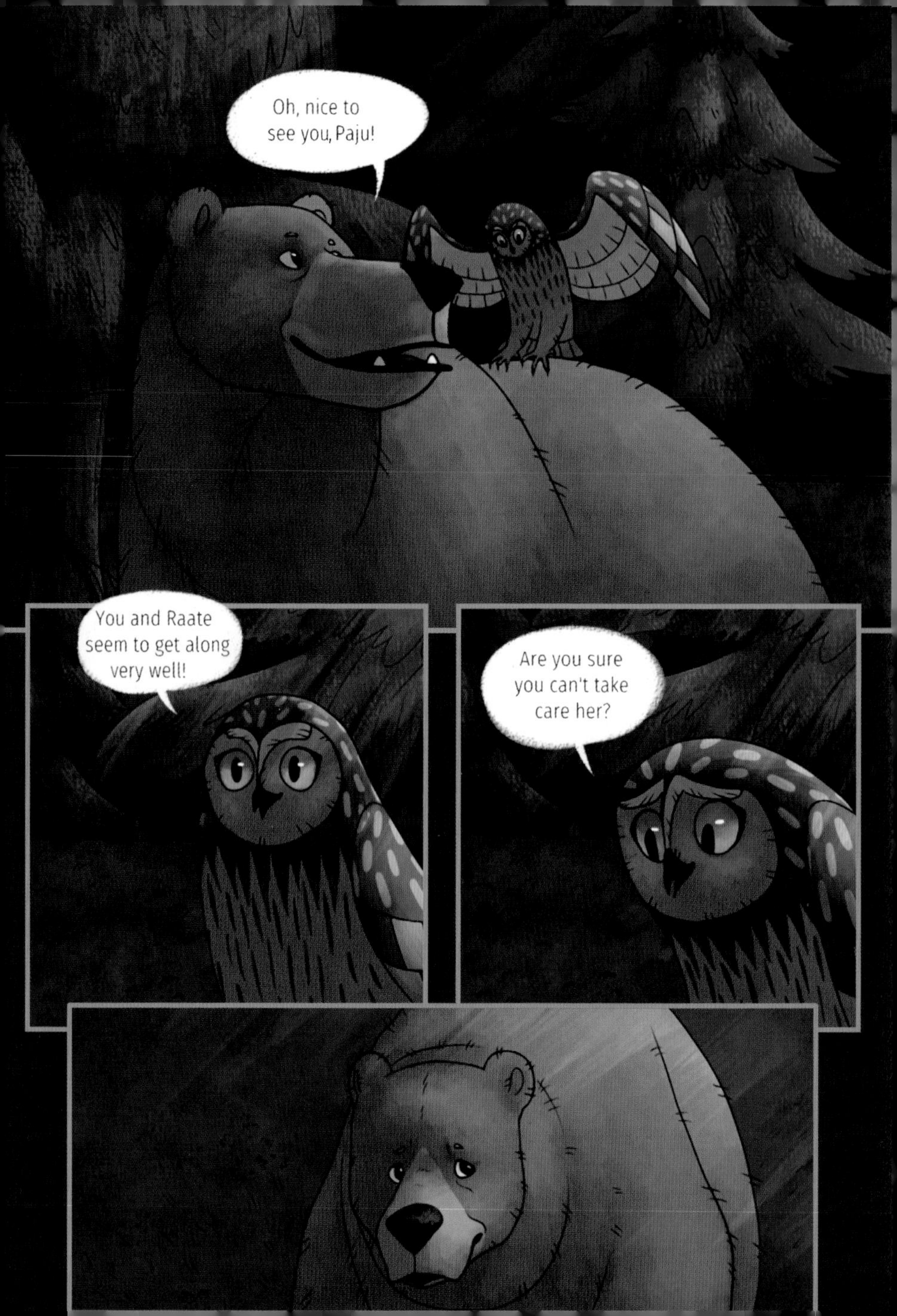

Oh, nice to see you, Paju!
You and Raate seem to get along very well!
Are you sure you can't take care her?

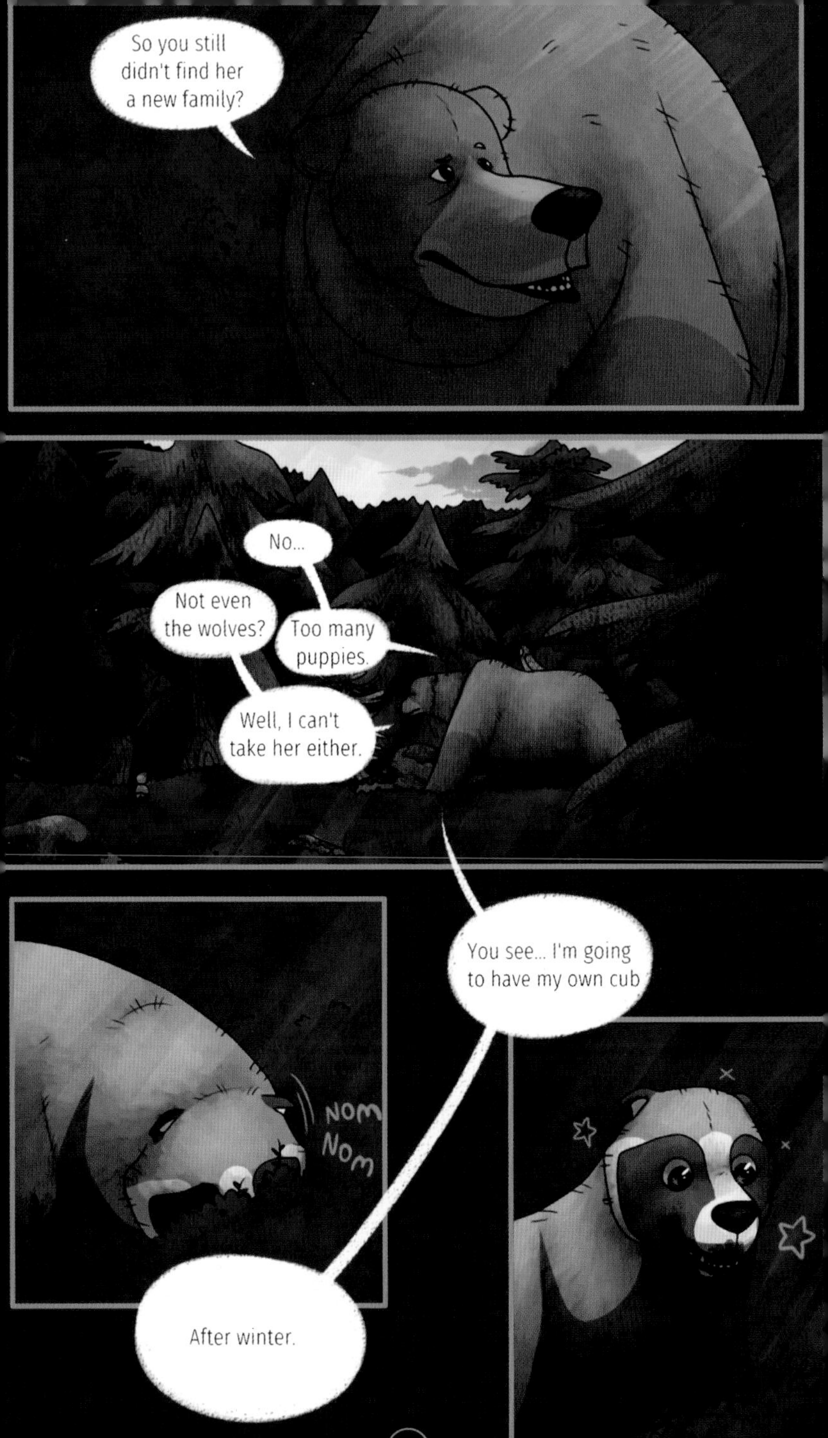
So you still didn't find her a new family?
No...
Too many puppies.
Not even the wolves?
Well, I can't take her either.
You see... I'm going to have my own cub
NOM NOM
After winter.

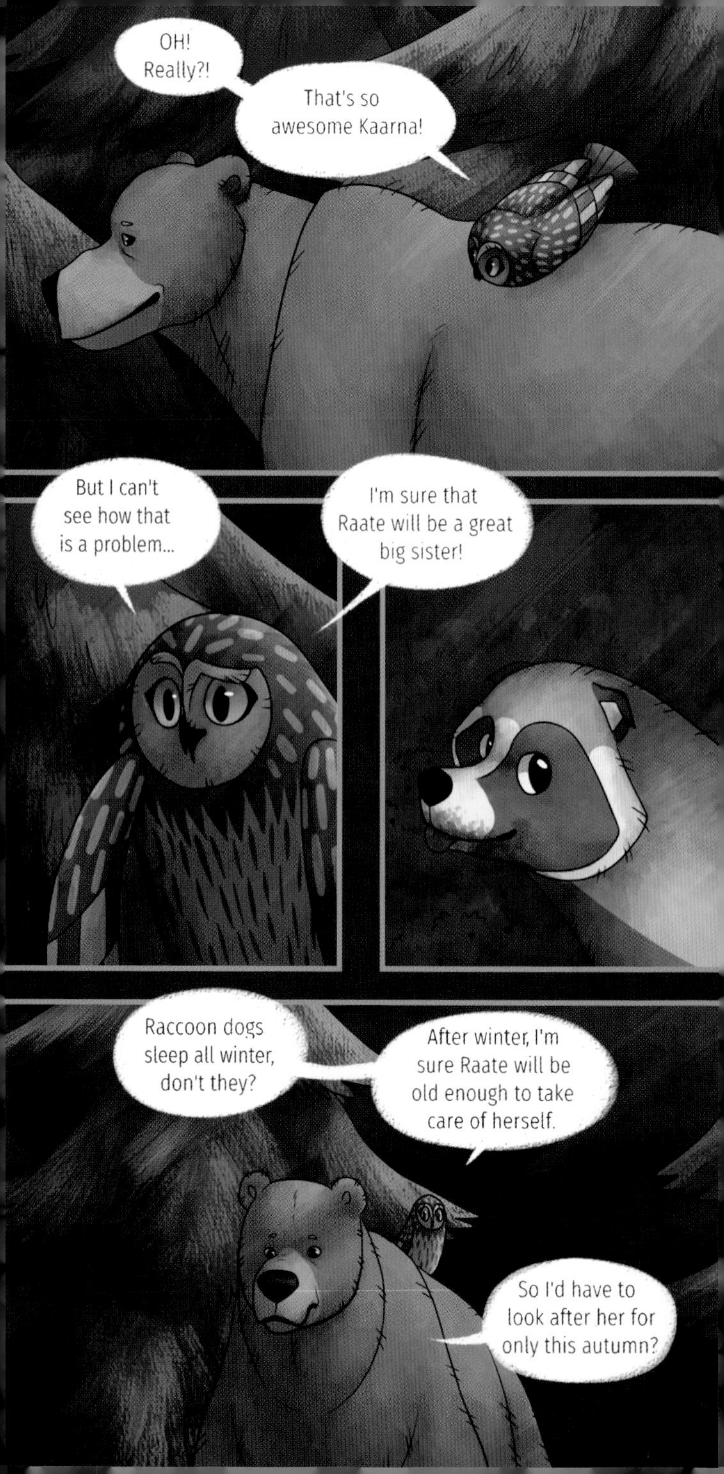
OH! Really?!
That's so awesome Kaarna!
But I can't see how that is a problem...
I'm sure that Raate will be a great big sister!
Raccoon dogs sleep all winter, don't they?
After winter, I'm sure Raate will be old enough to take care of herself.
So I'd have to look after her for only this autumn?

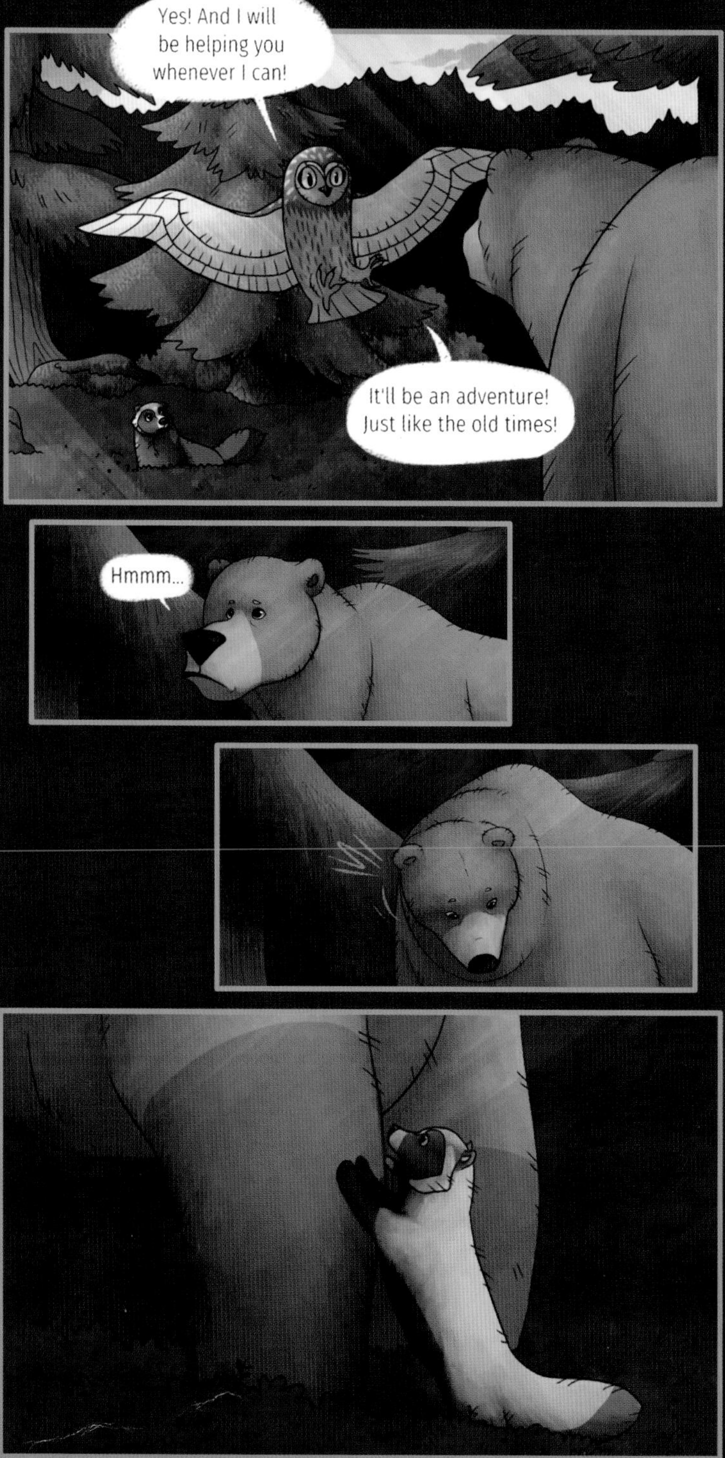
Yes! And I will be helping you whenever I can!
It'll be an adventure! Just like the old times!
Hmmm...

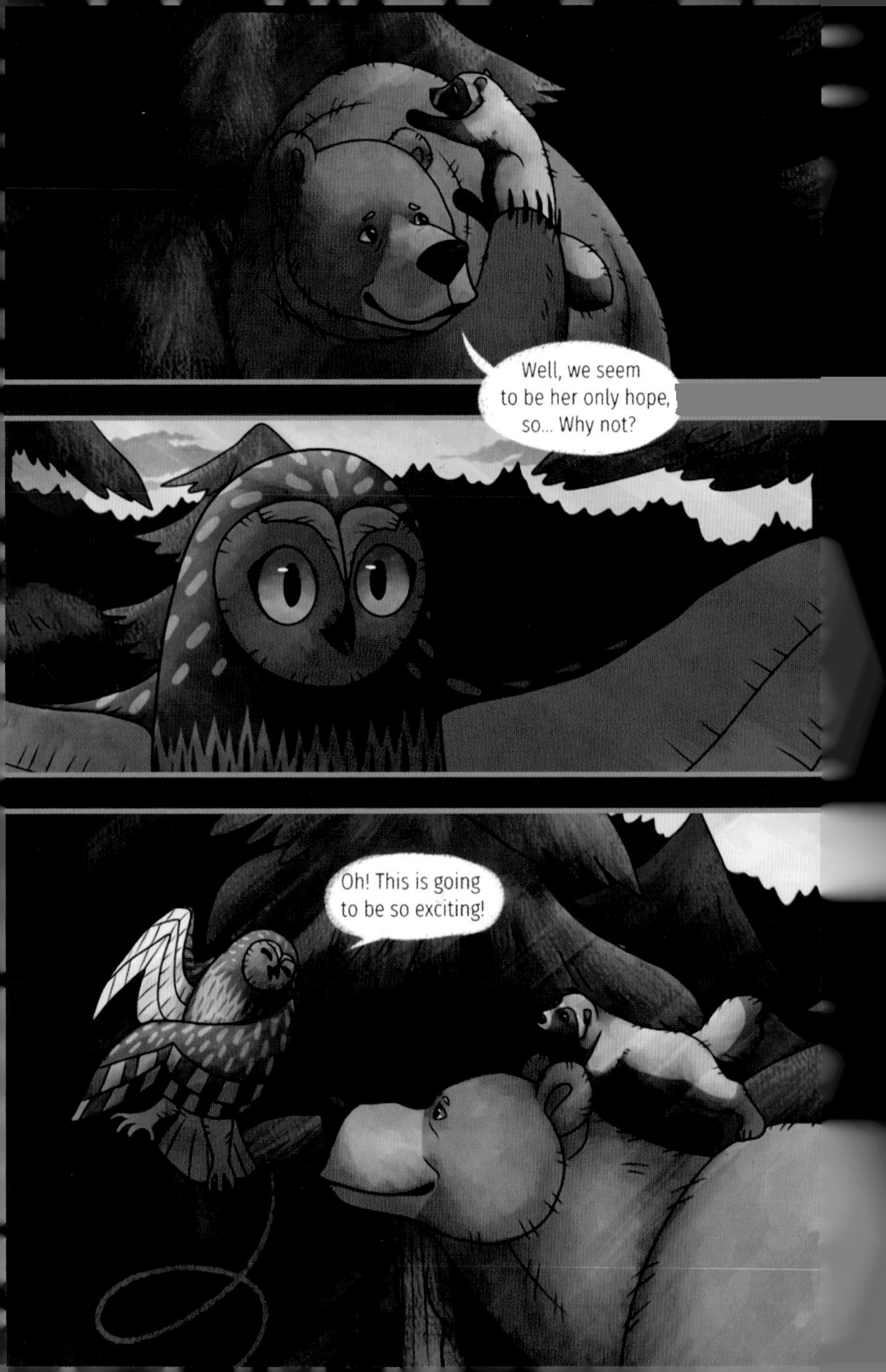
Well, we seem to be her only hope, so... Why not?
Oh! This is going to be so exciting!

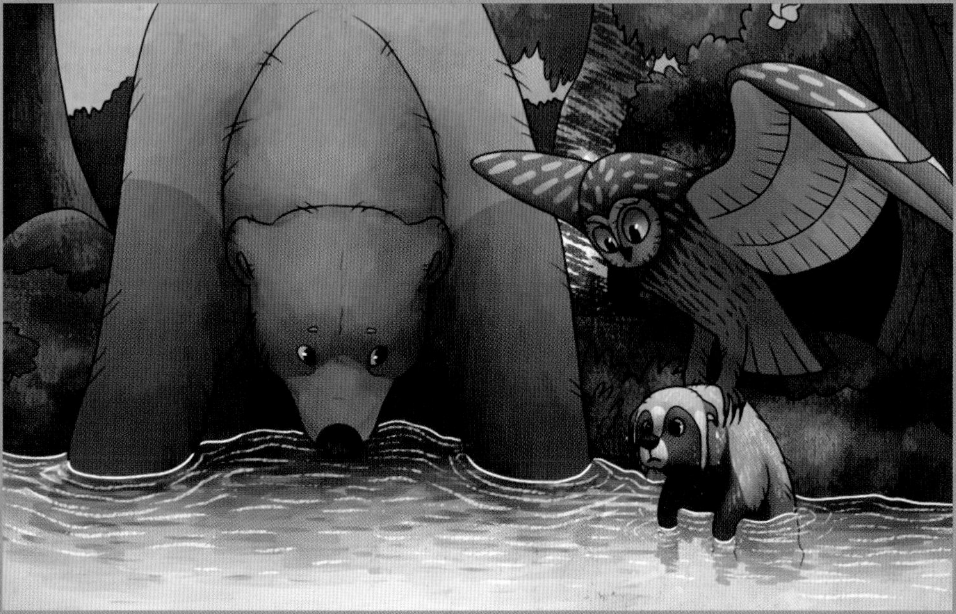

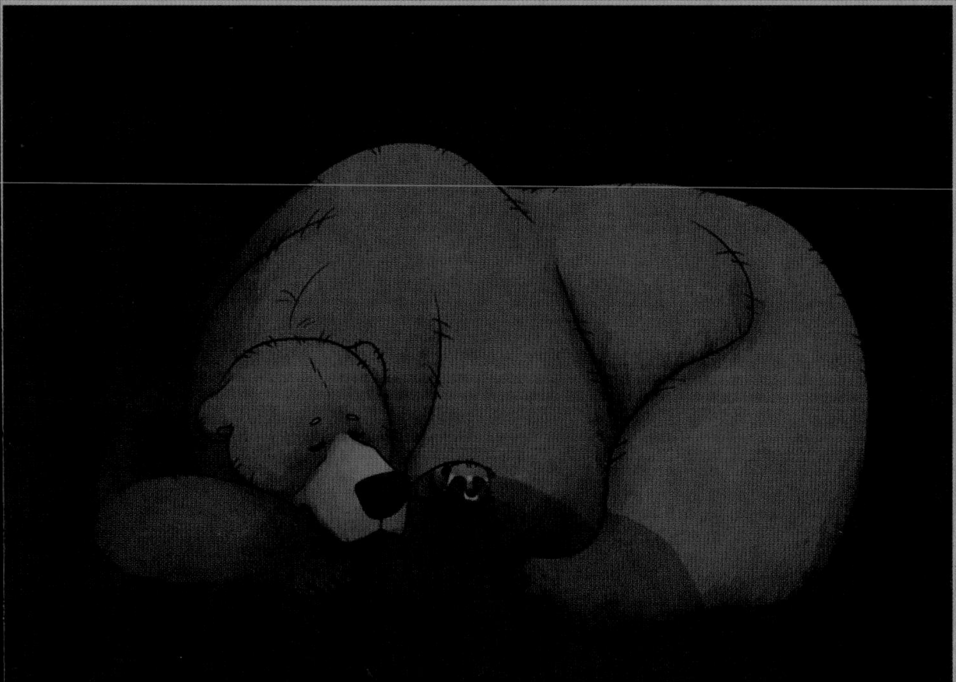

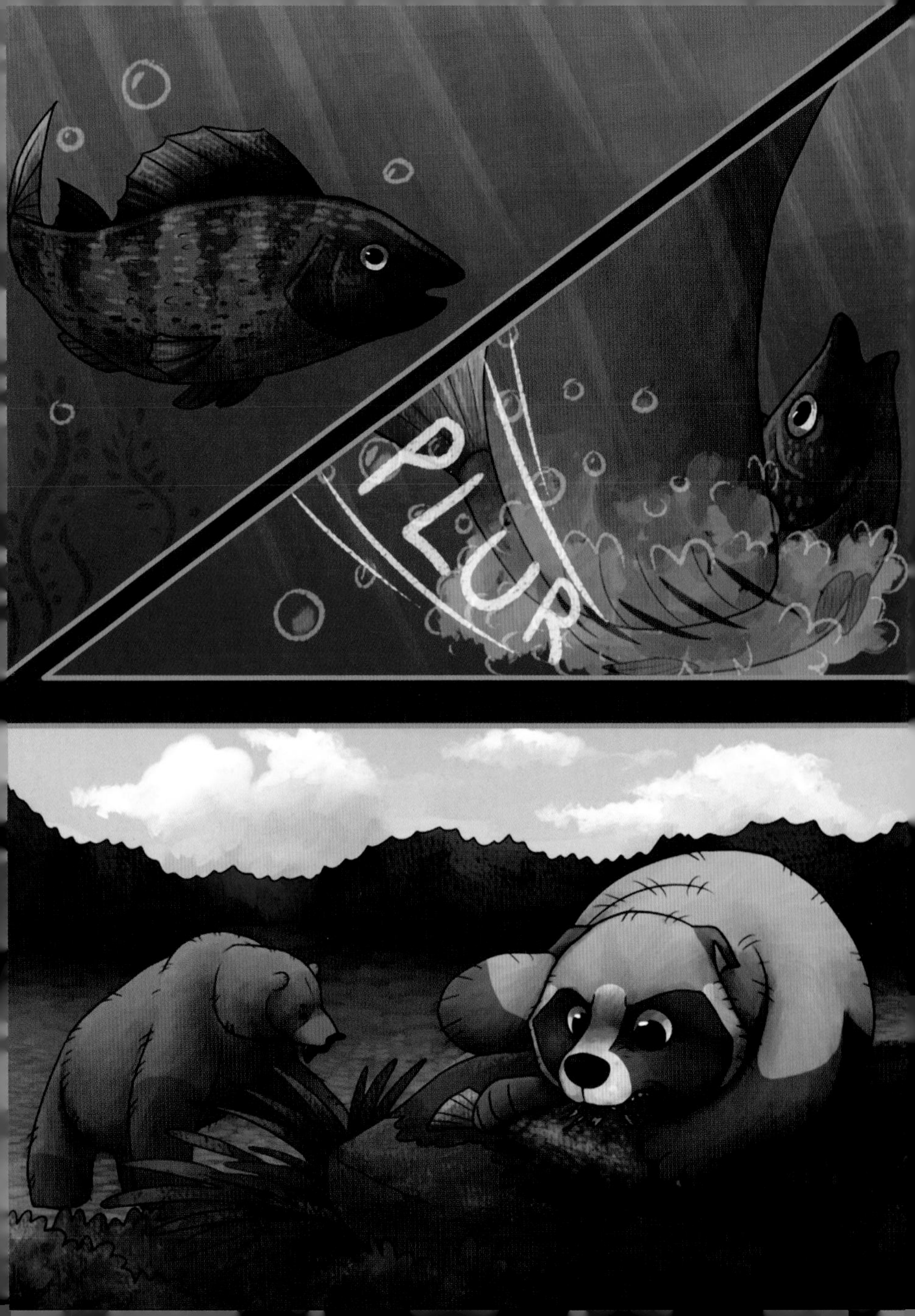
PLUR

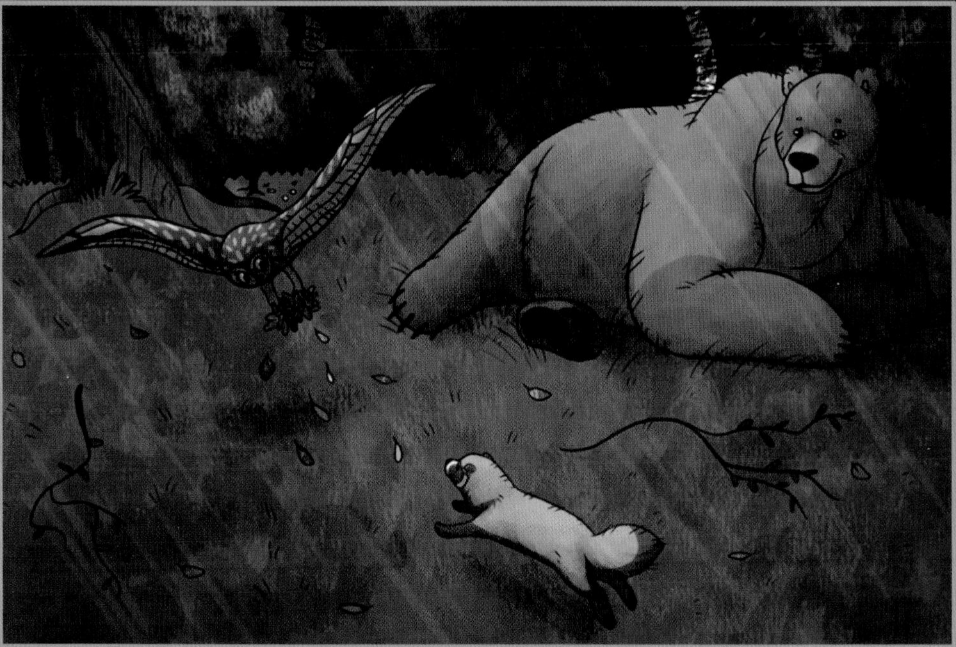

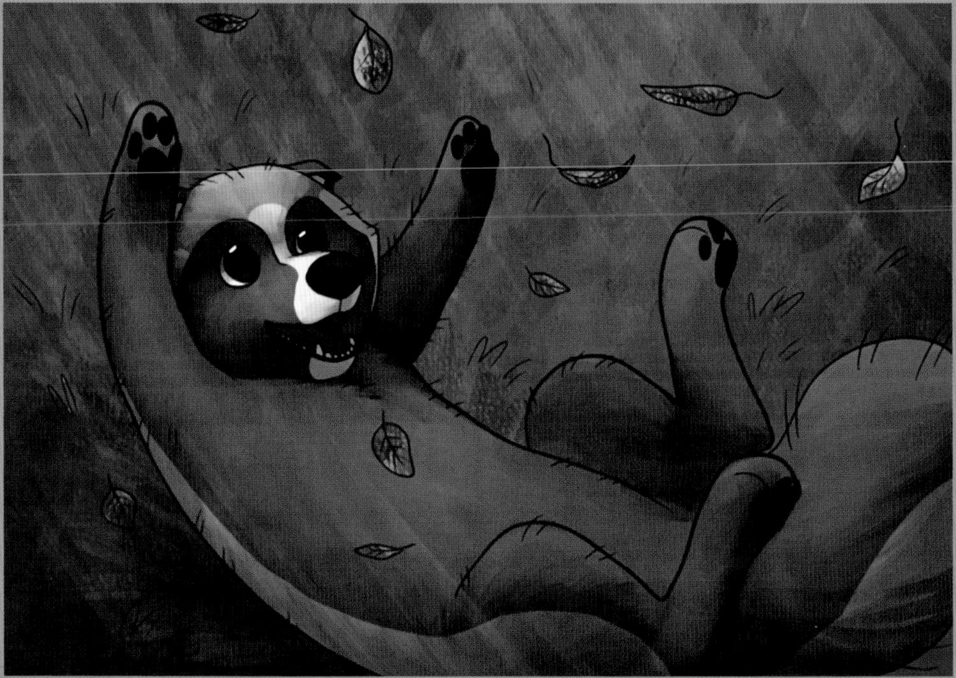

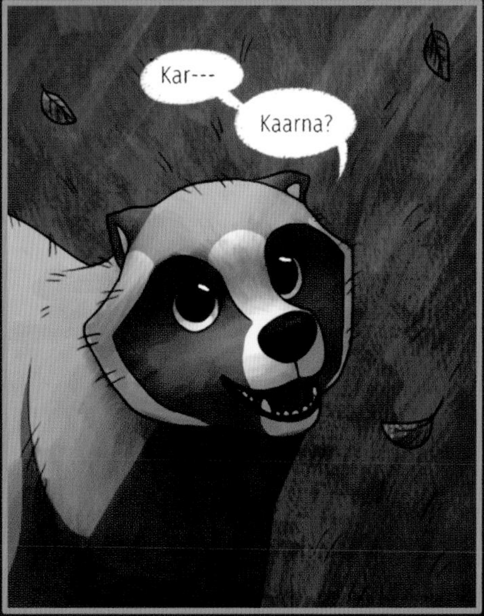
Kar---
Kaarna?

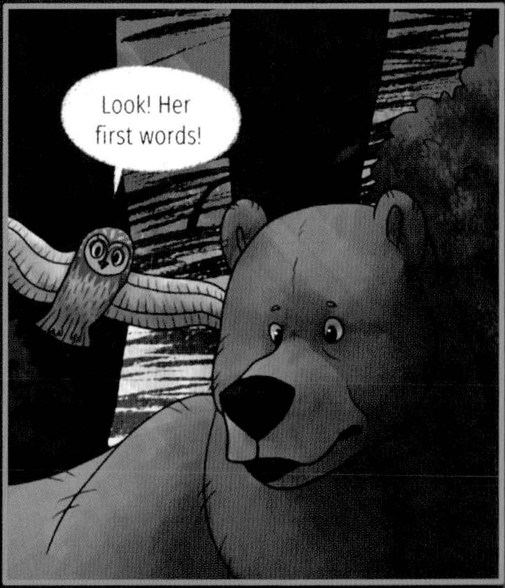
Look! Her first words!

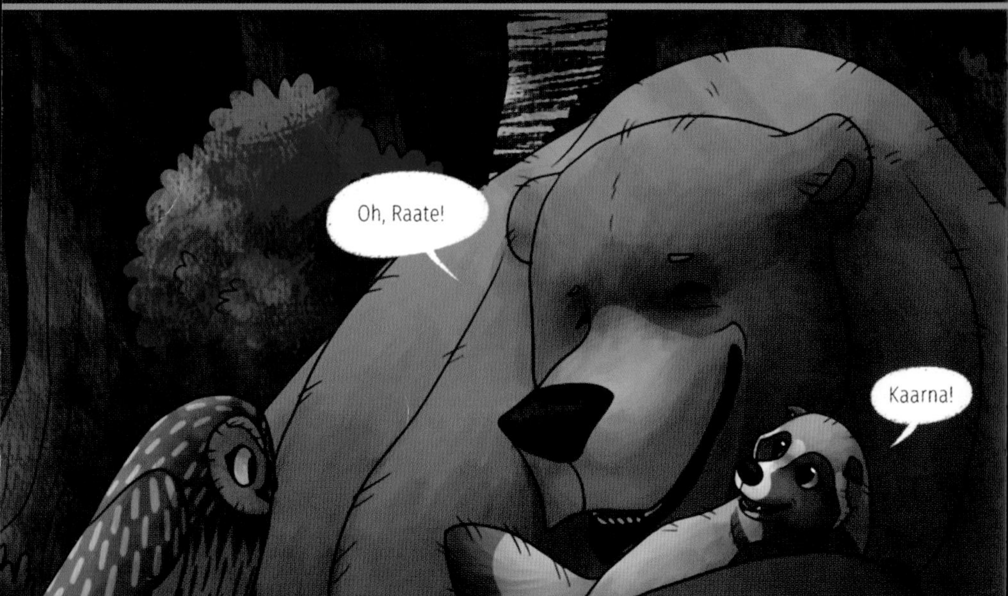
Oh, Raate!
Kaarna!

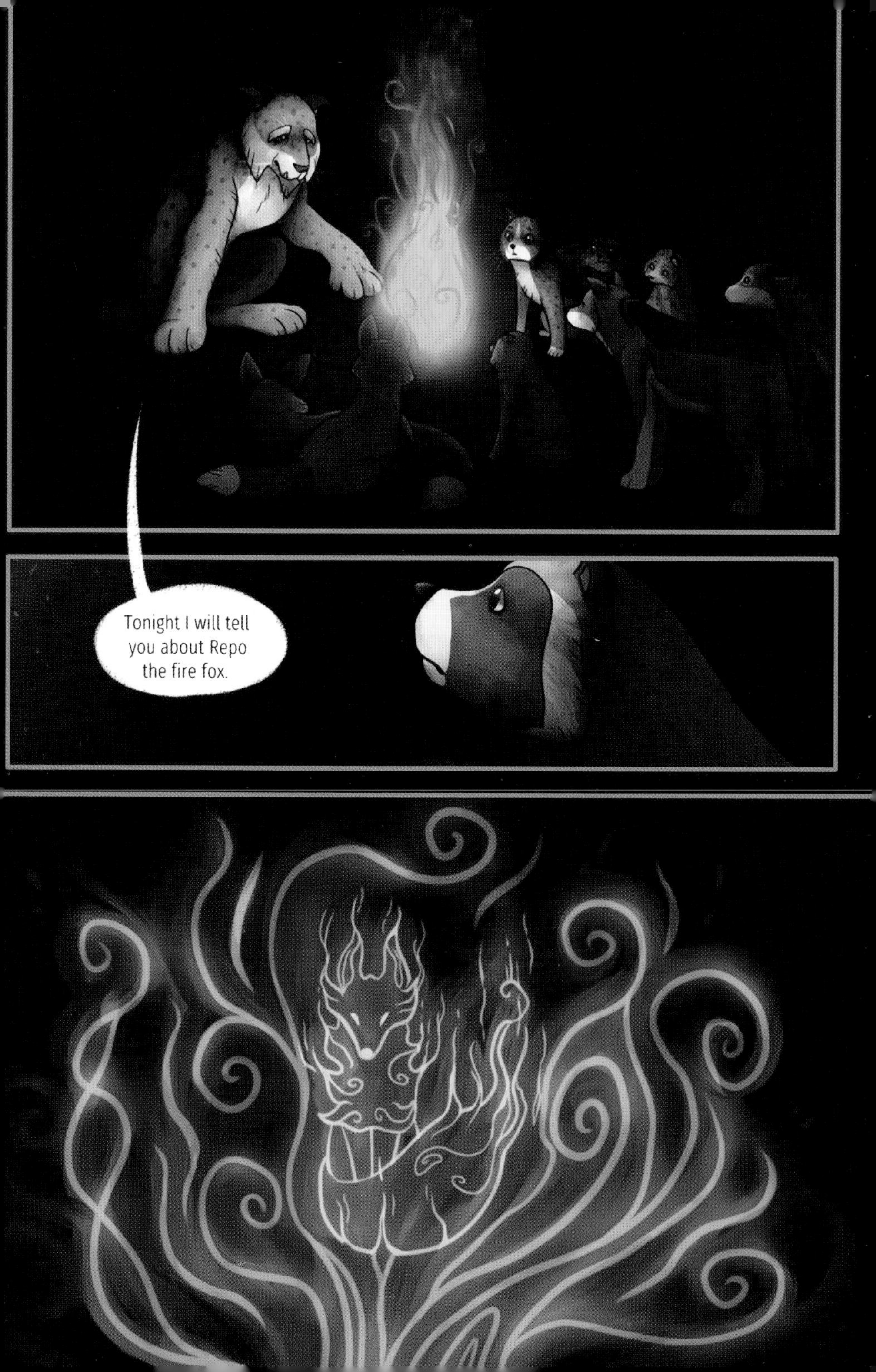
Tonight I will tell you about Repo the fire fox.

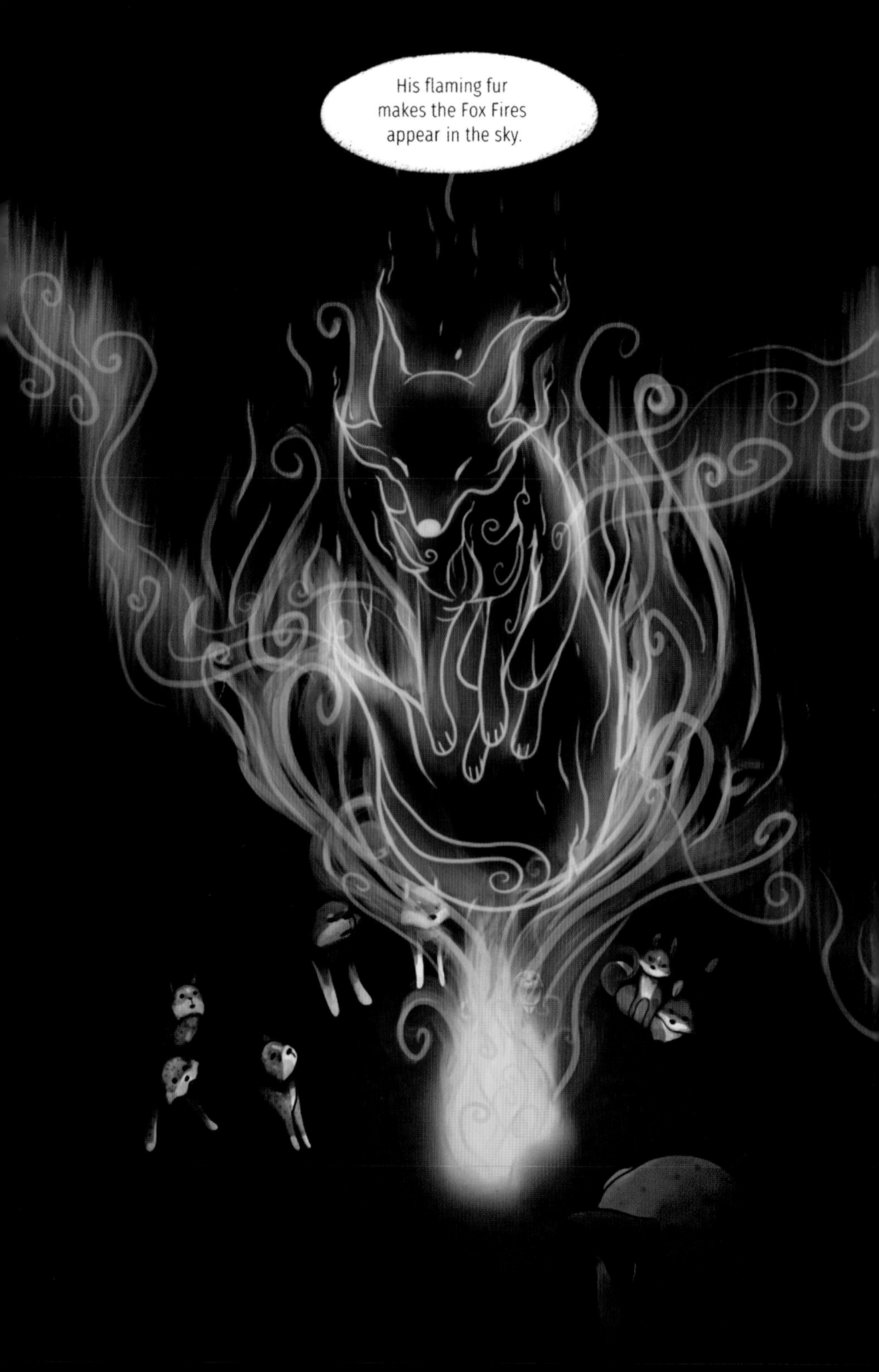
His flaming fur makes the Fox Fires appear in the sky.

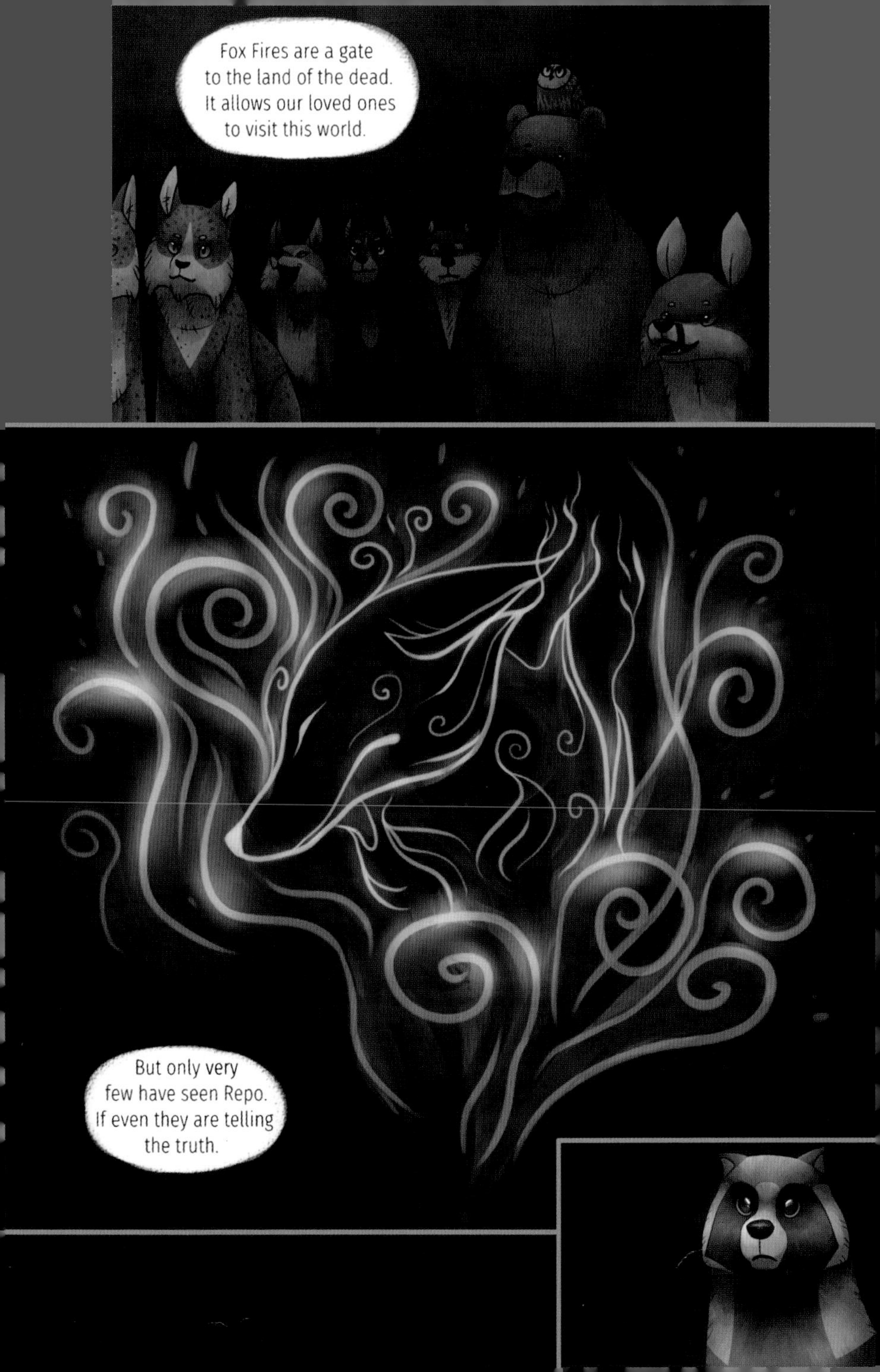
Fox Fires are a gate to the land of the dead. It allows our loved ones to visit this world.
But only very few have seen Repo. If even they are telling the truth.

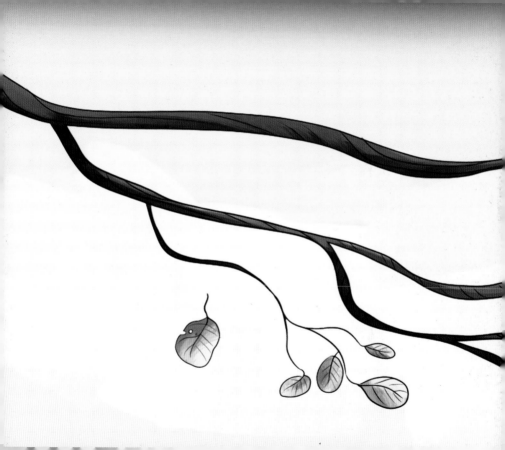

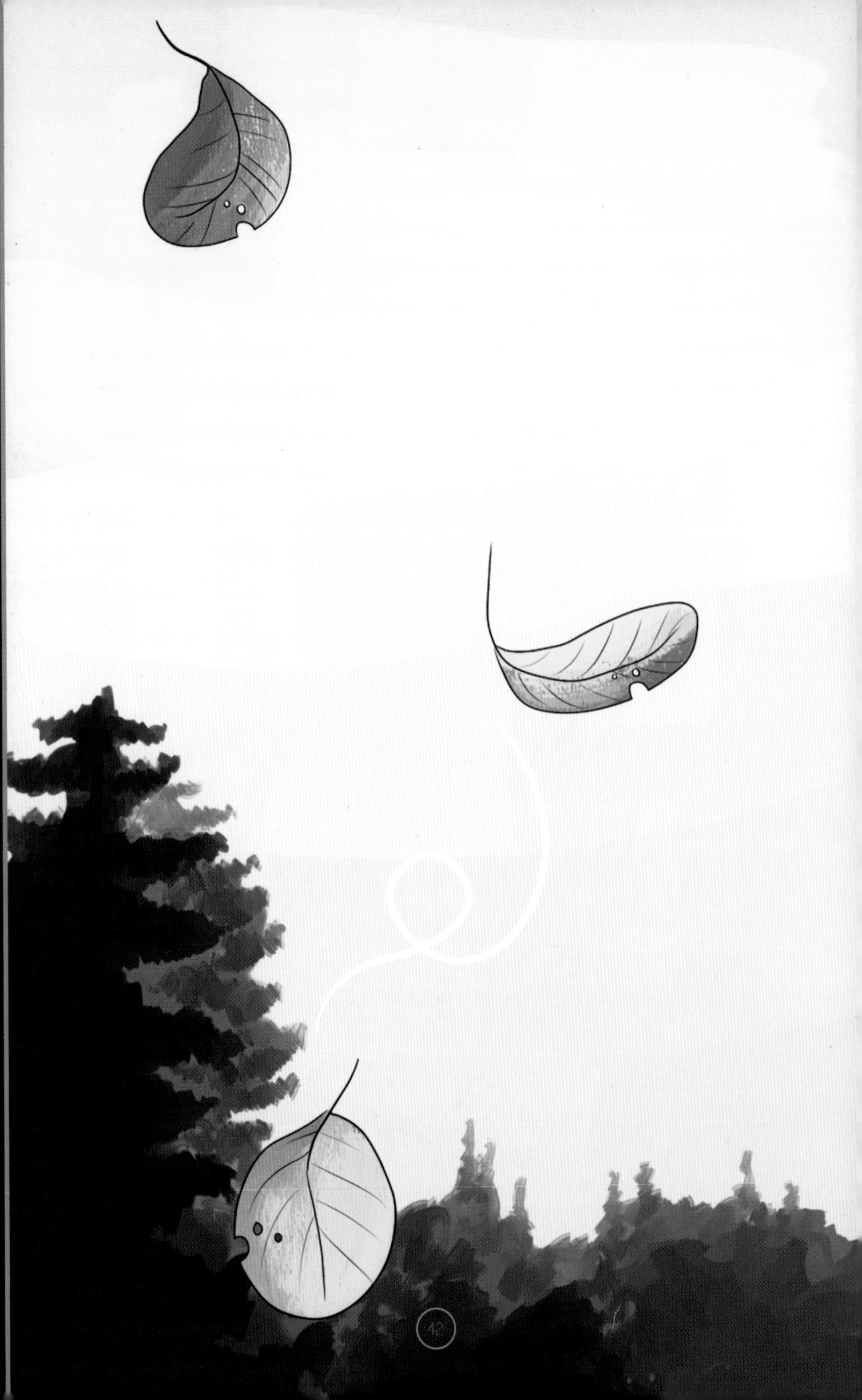

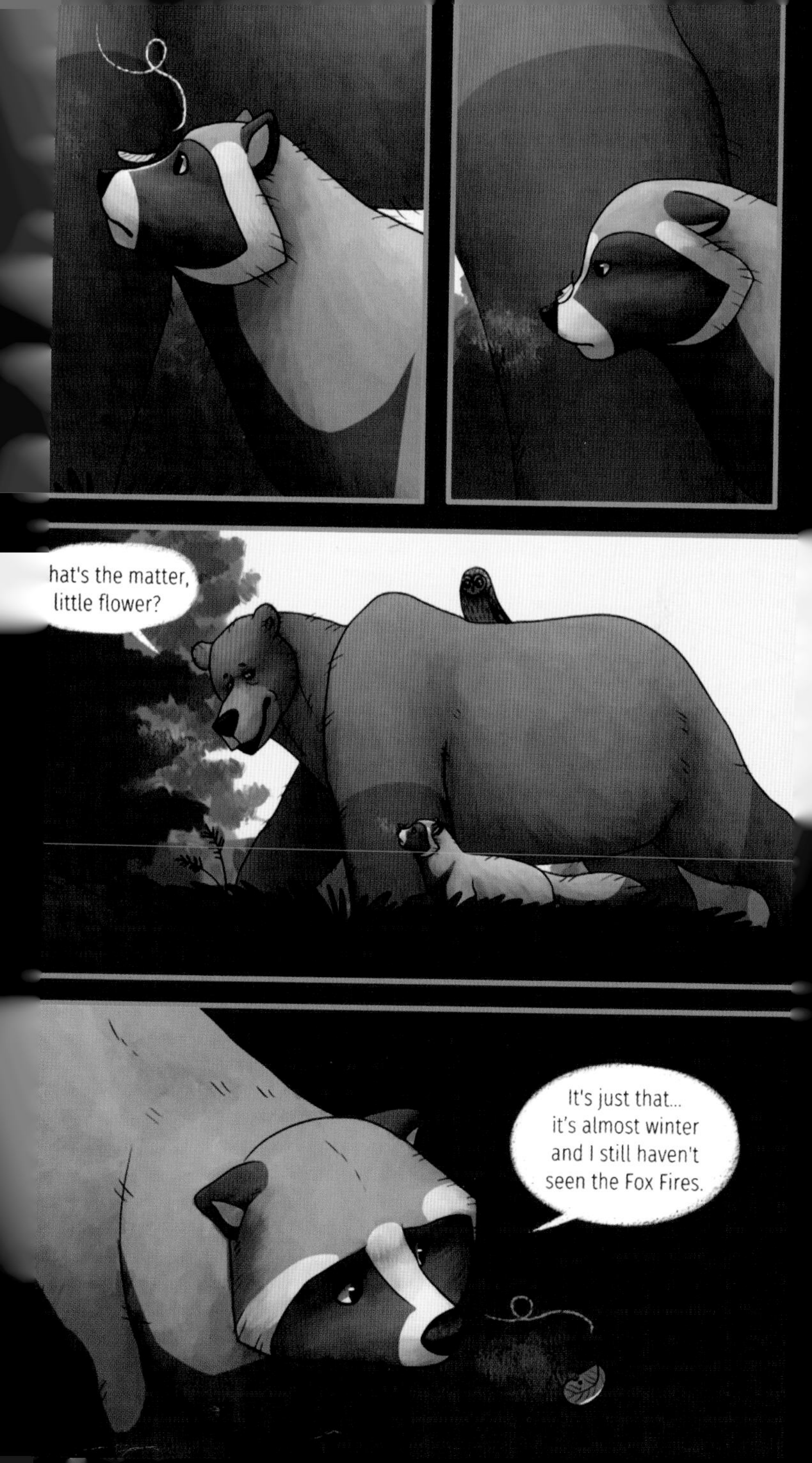
hat's the matter, little flower?
It's just that... it's almost winter and I still haven't seen the Fox Fires.

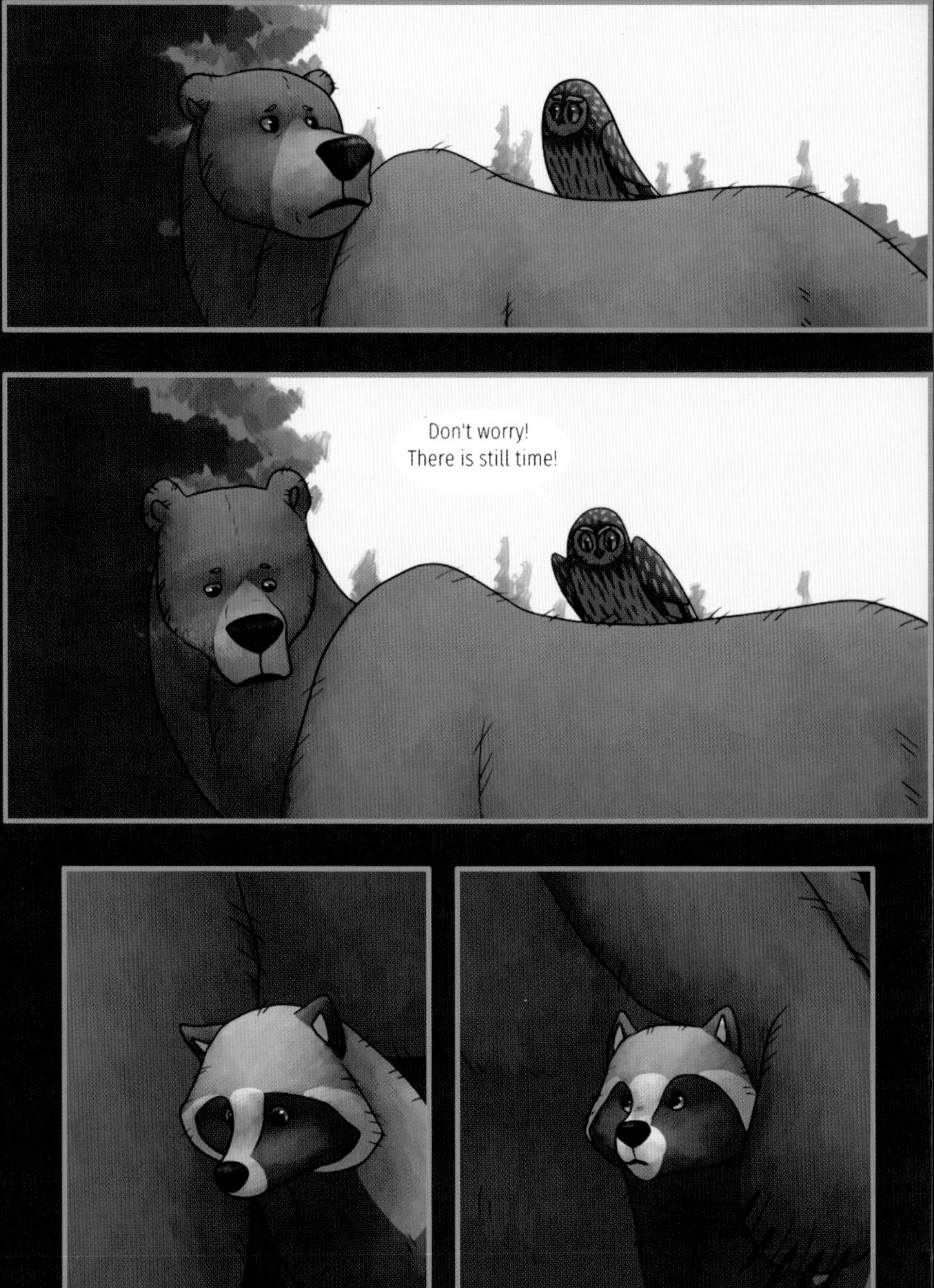
Don't worry!
There is still time!

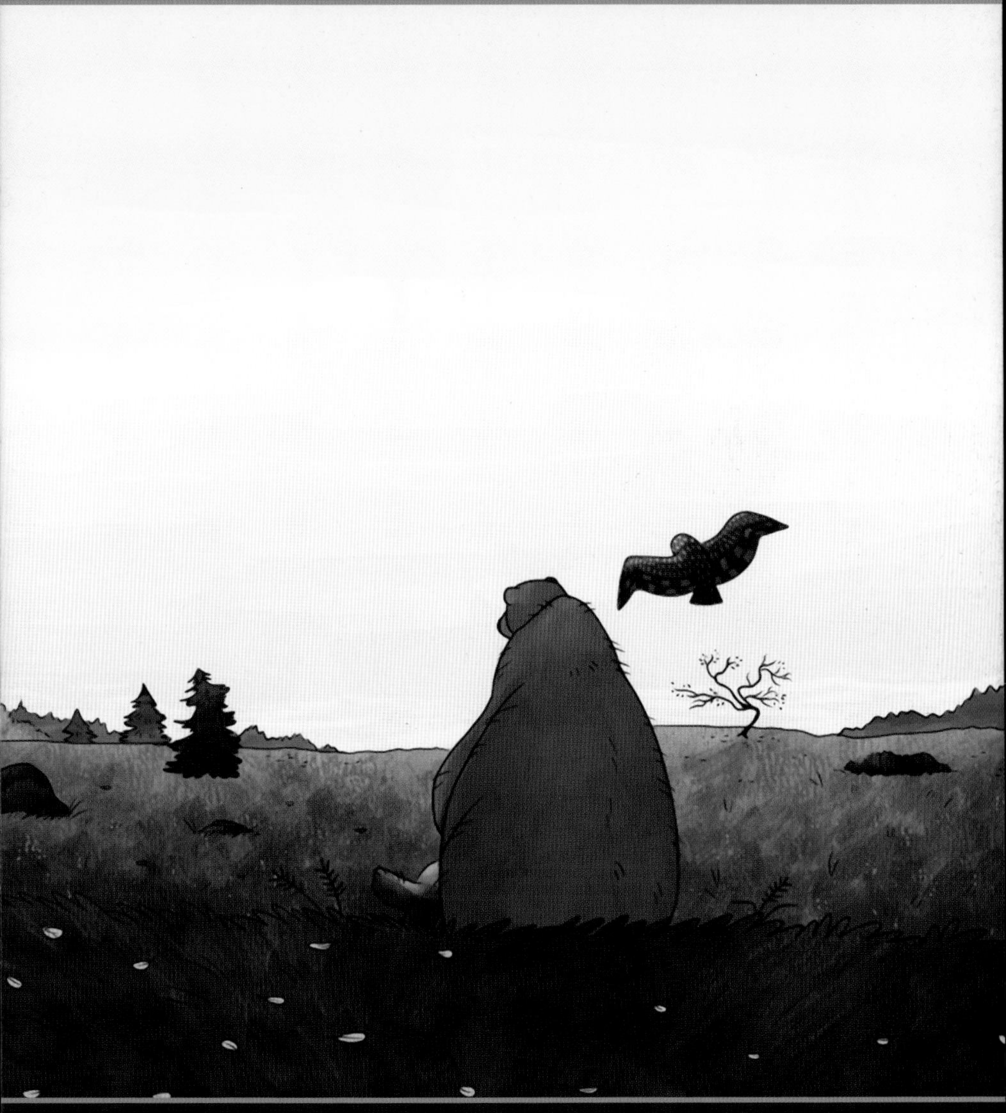

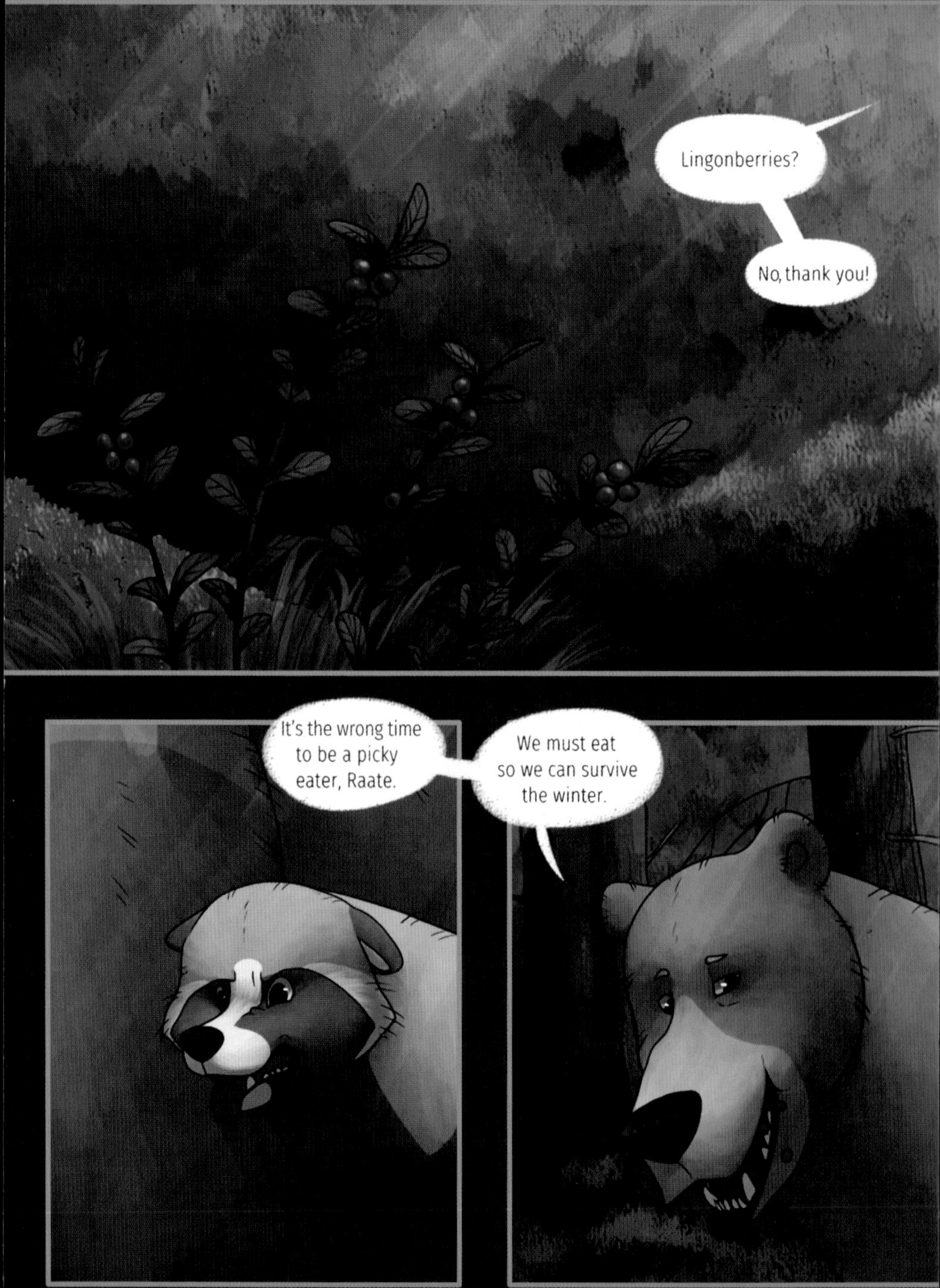

Lingonberries?
No, thank you!
It's the wrong time to be a picky eater, Raate.
We must eat so we can survive the winter.

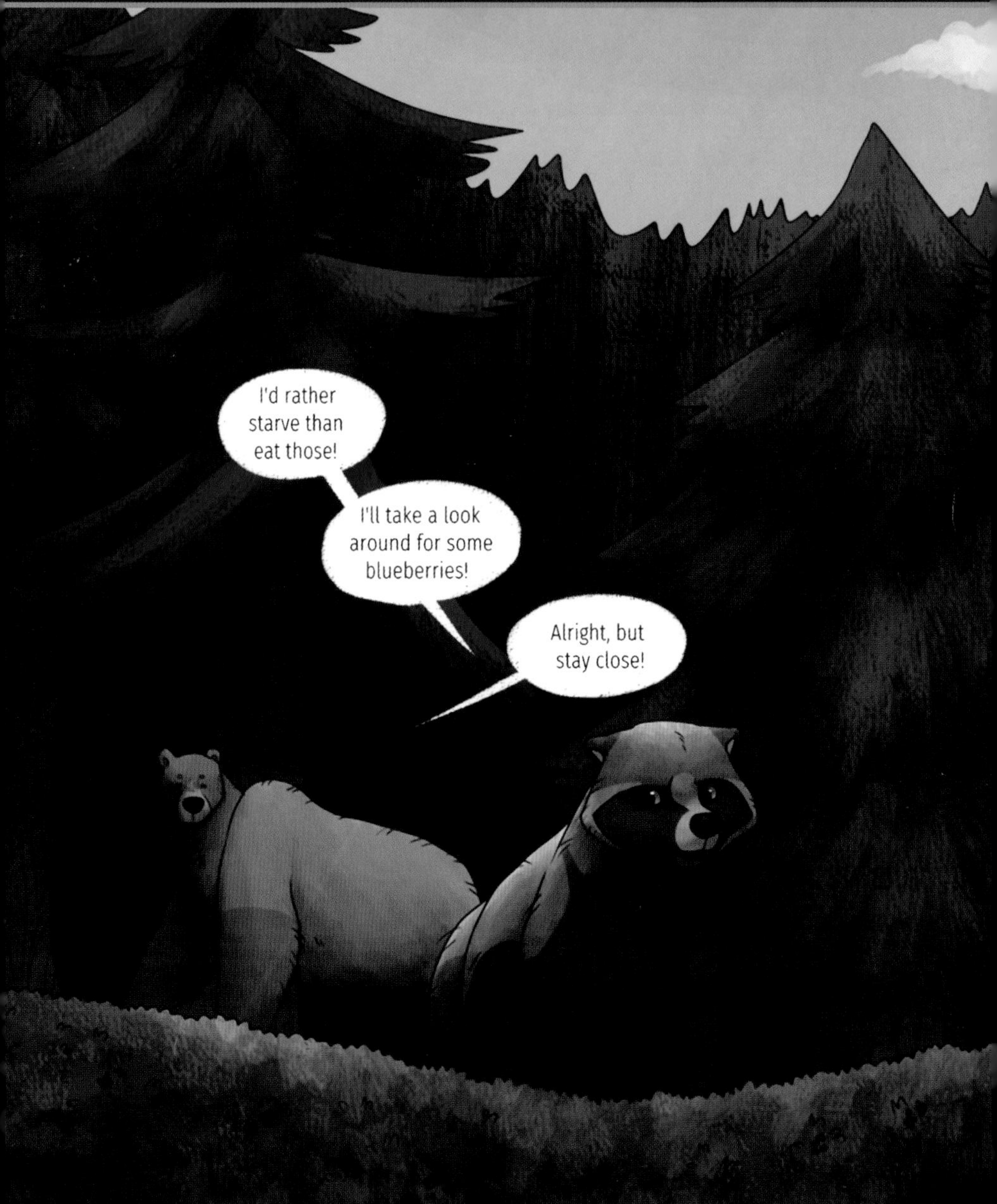
I'd rather starve than eat those!
I'll take a look around for some blueberries!
Alright, but stay close!

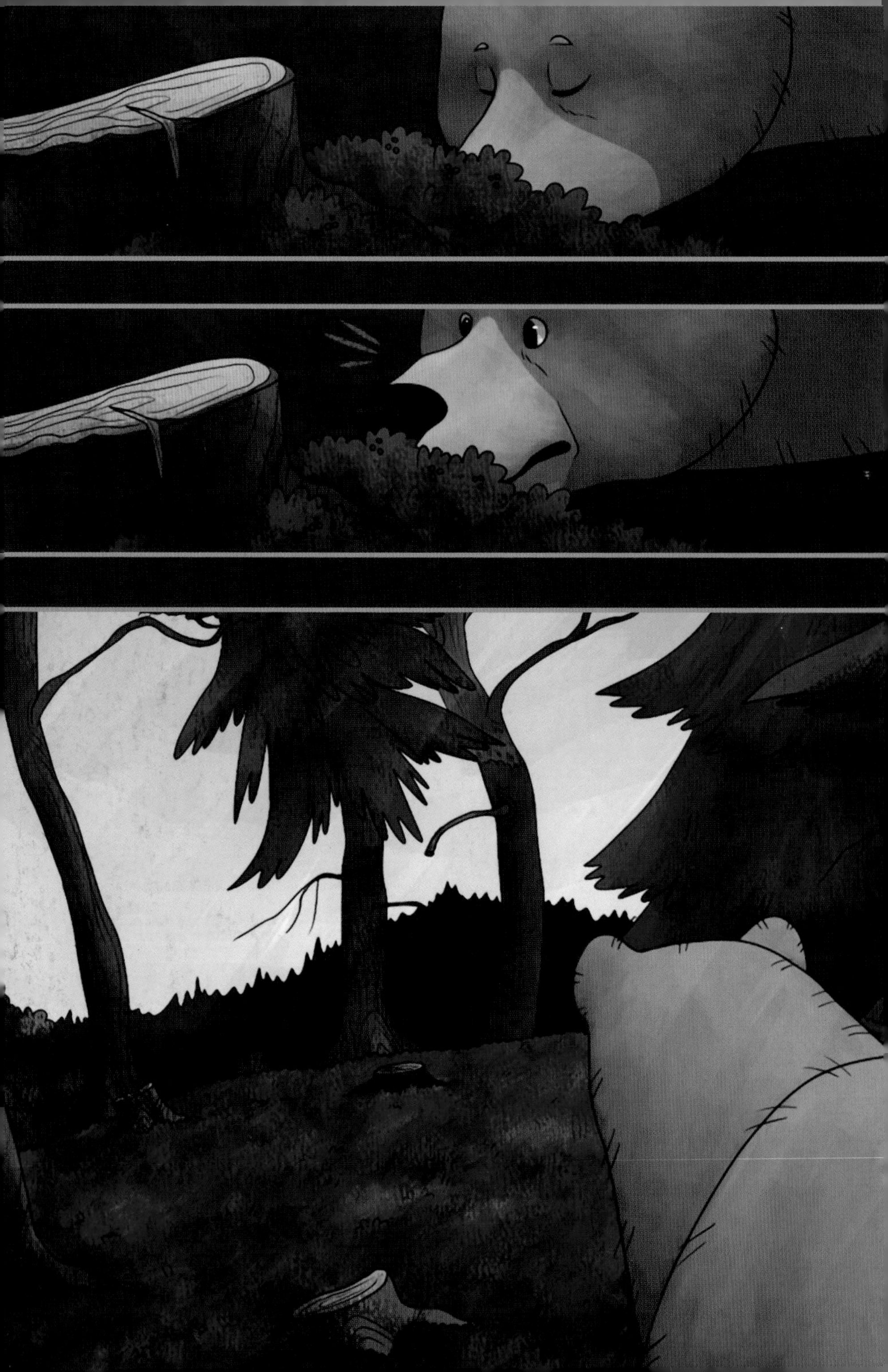

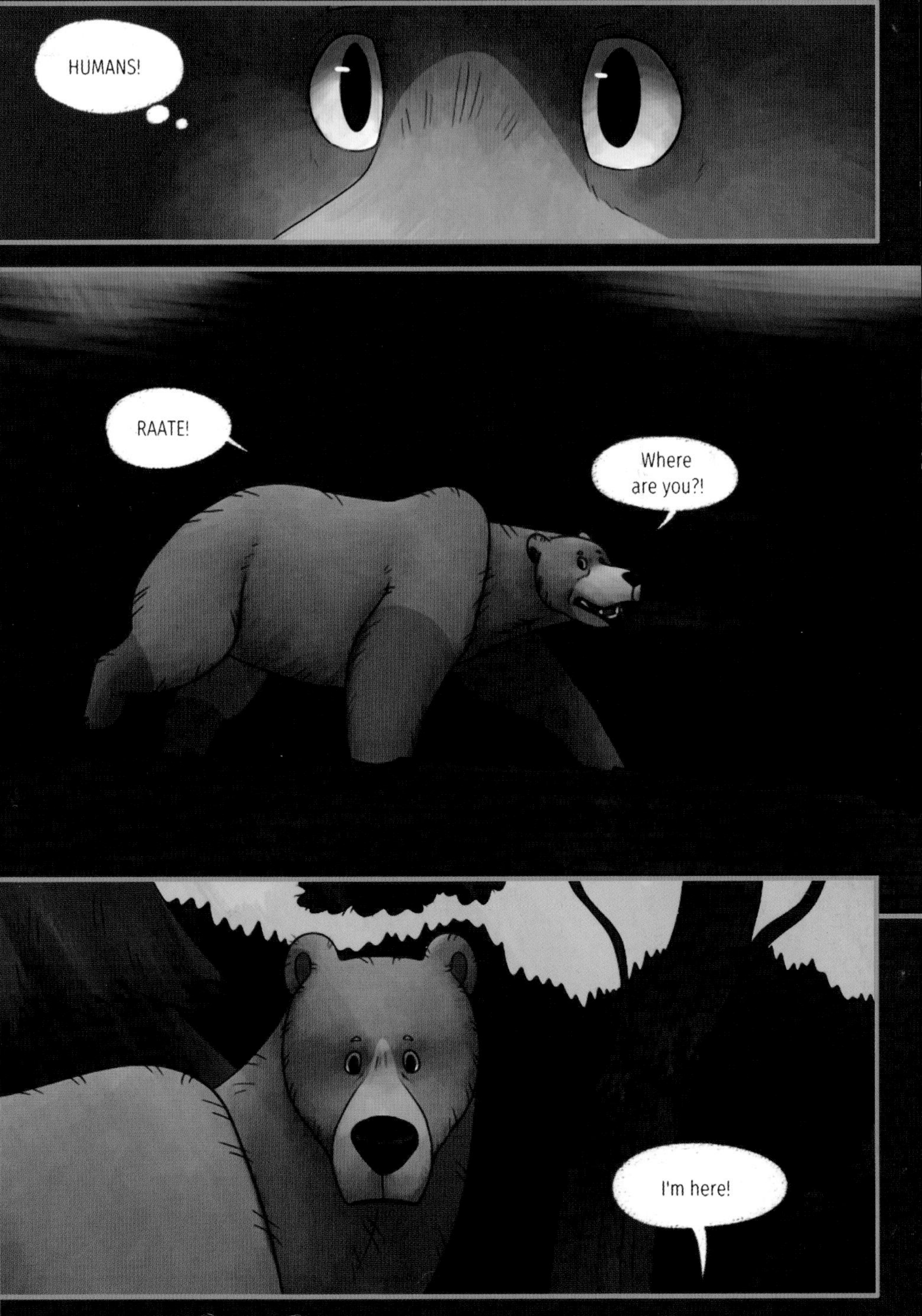
HUMANS!
RAATE!
Where are you?!
I'm here!

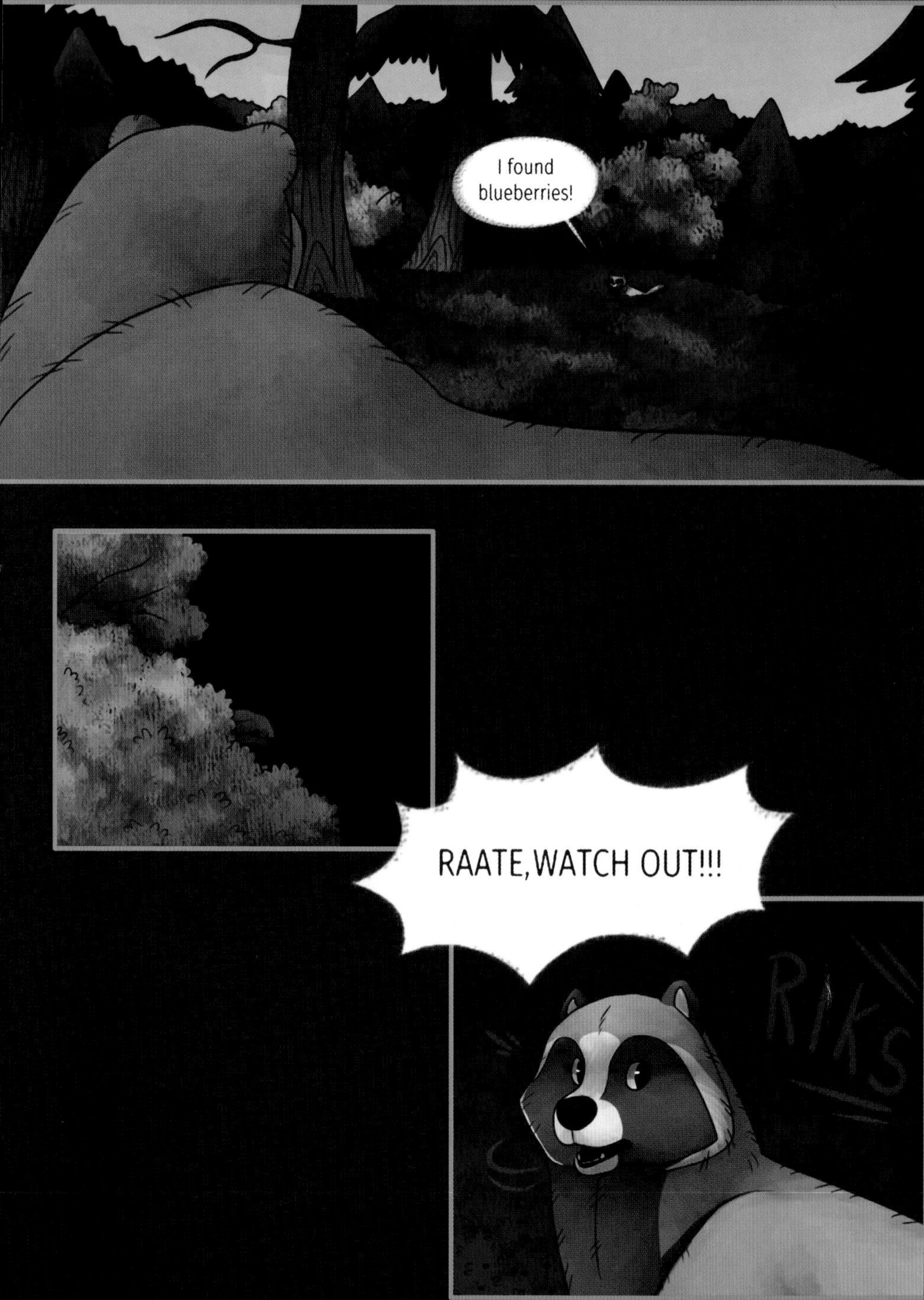
I found blueberries!
RAATE, WATCH OUT!!!
RIKS

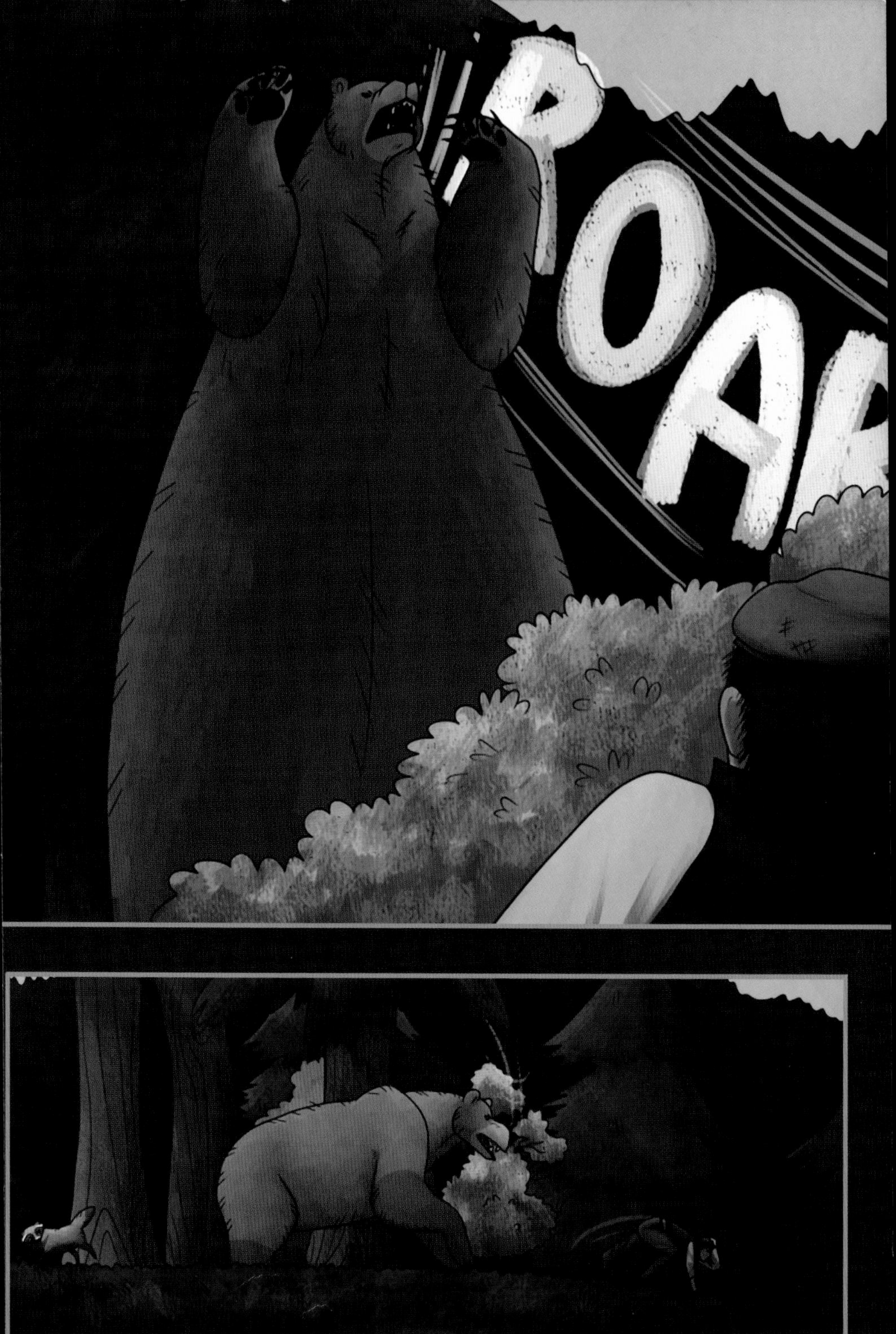
ROA

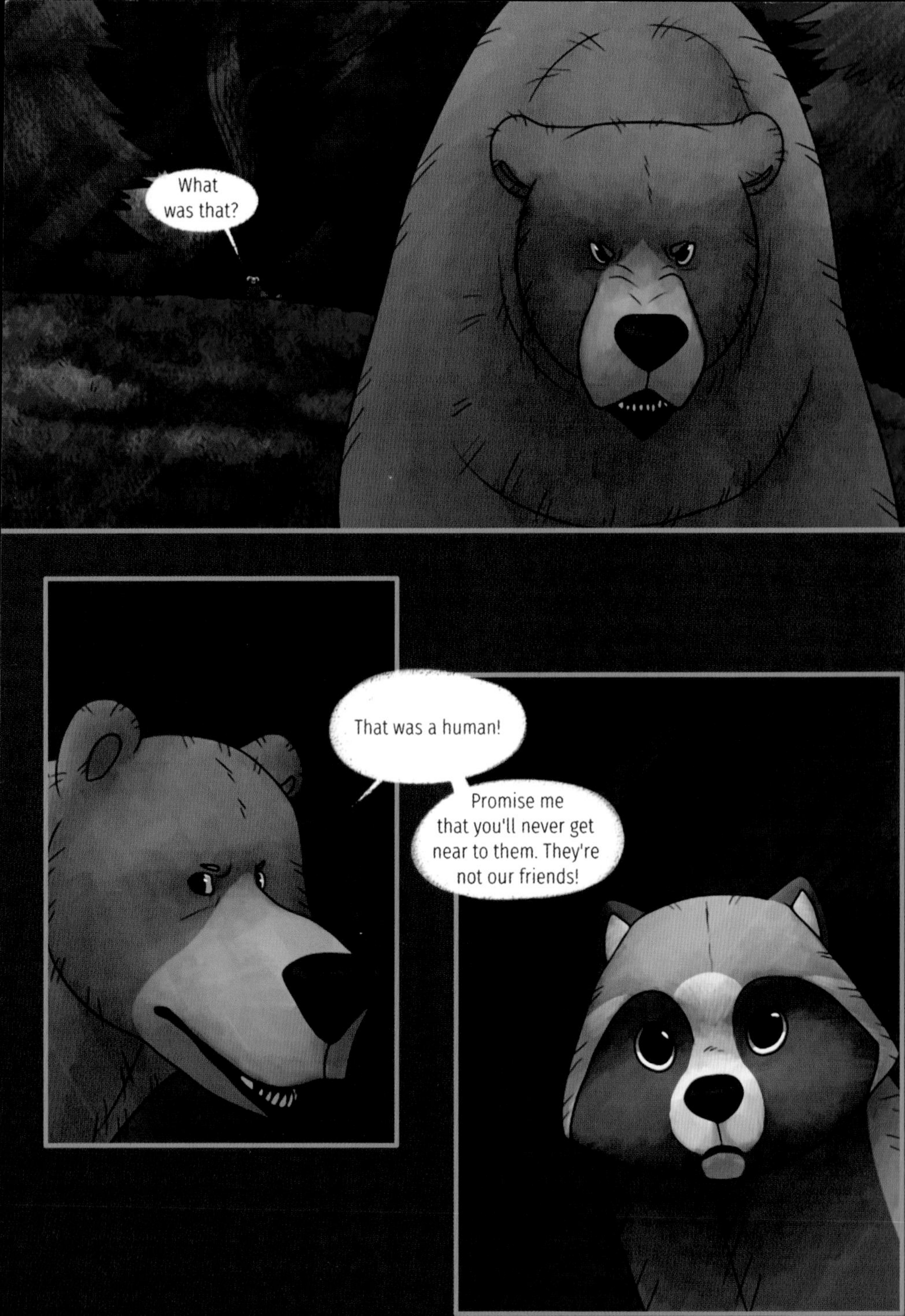
What was that?
That was a human!
Promise me that you'll never get near to them. They're not our friends!

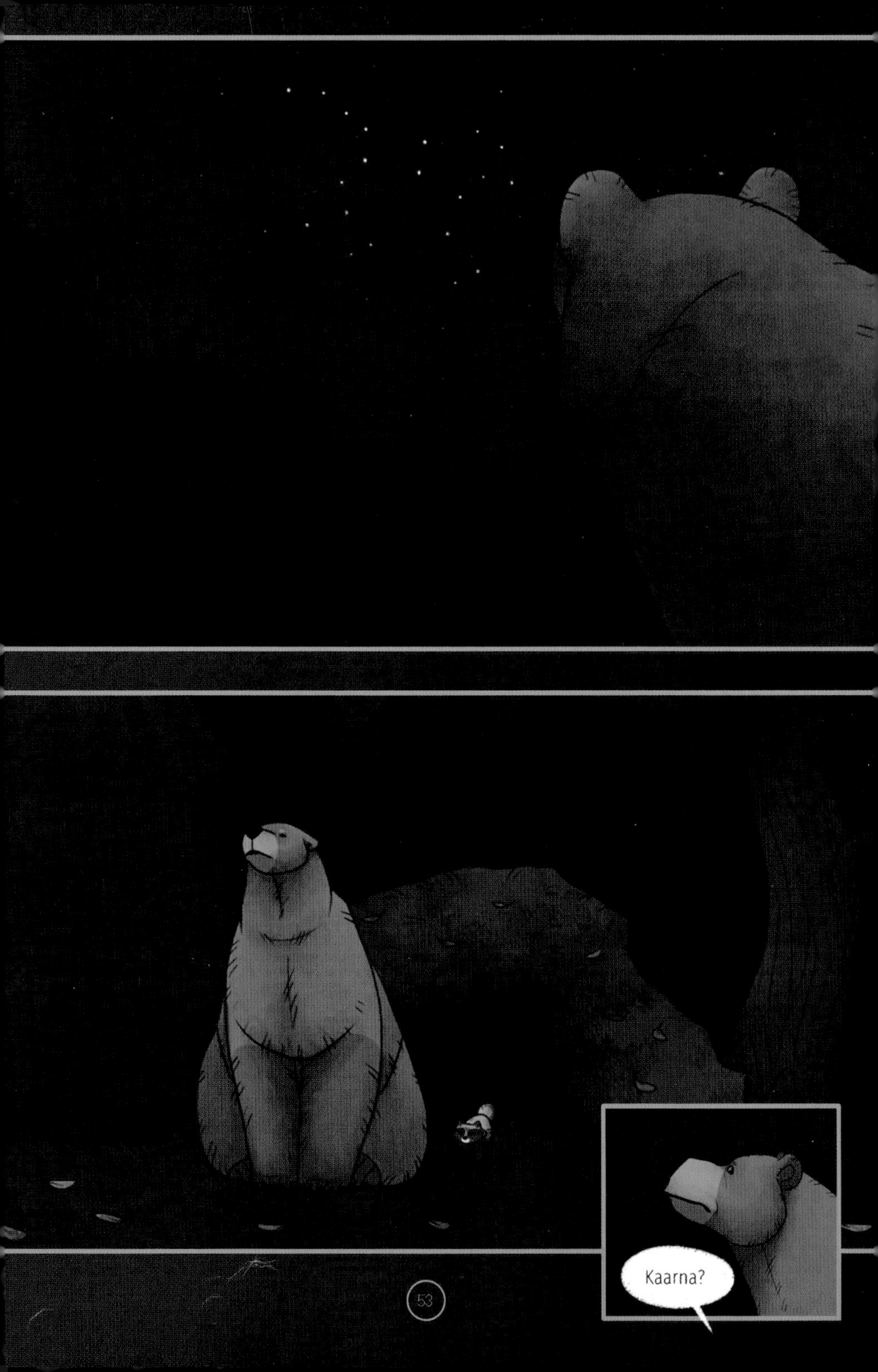
Kaarna?

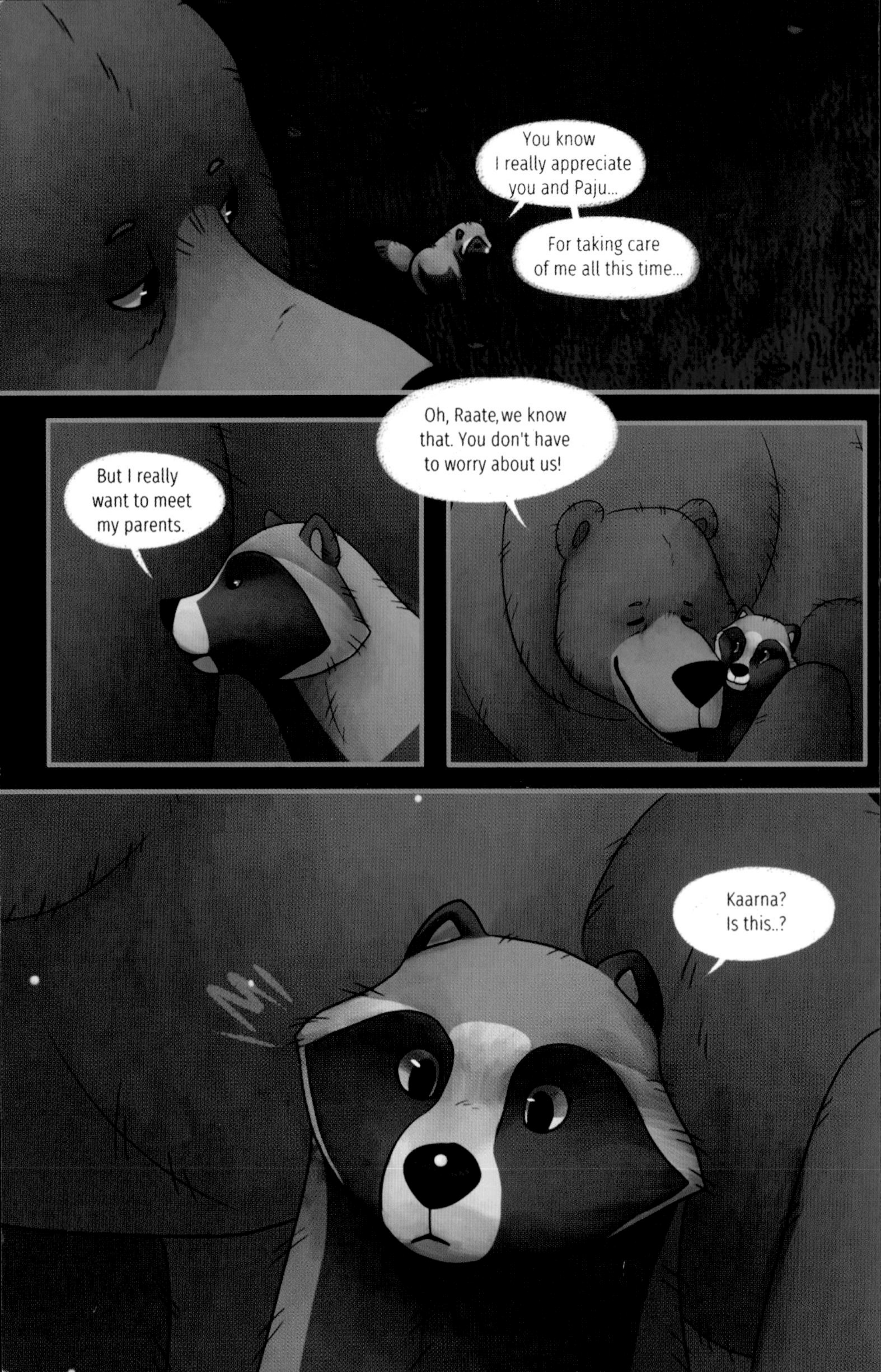
You know I really appreciate you and Paju...
For taking care of me all this time...
But I really want to meet my parents.
Oh, Raate, we know that. You don't have to worry about us!
Kaarna? Is this..?

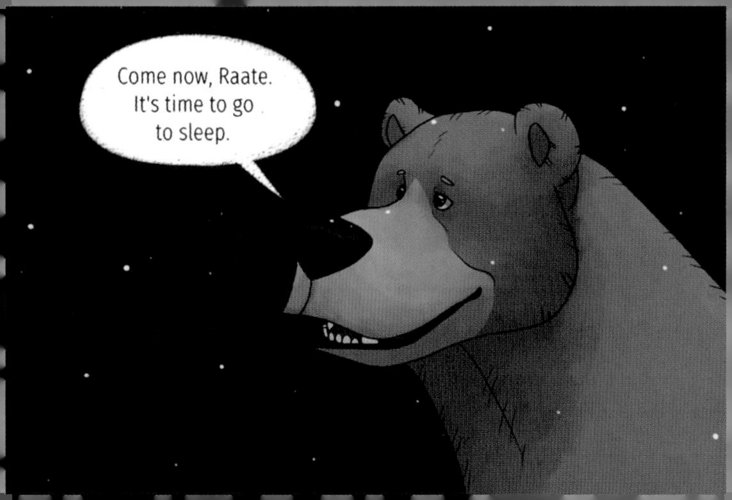
Come now, Raate. It's time to go to sleep.

Chapter 5

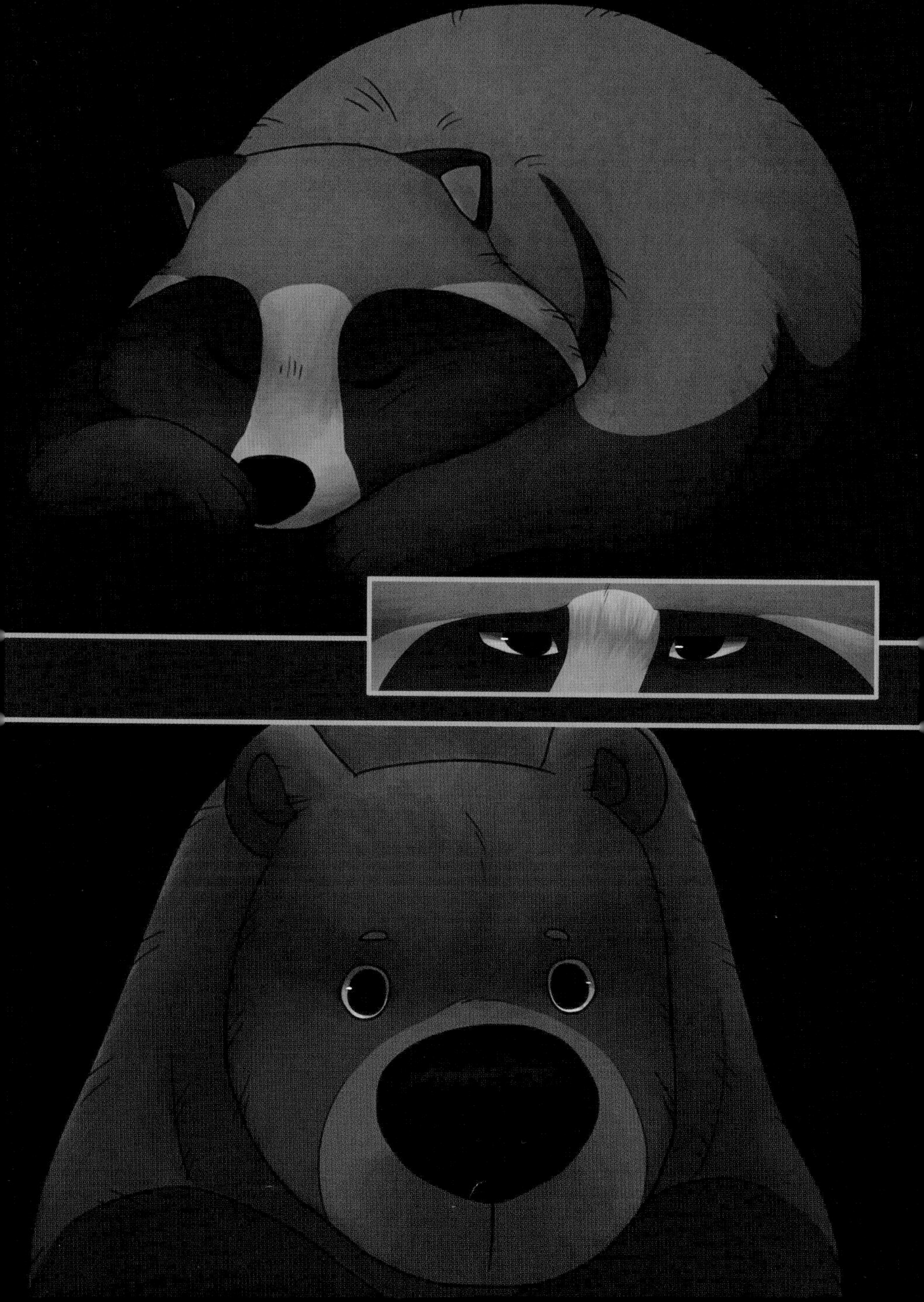

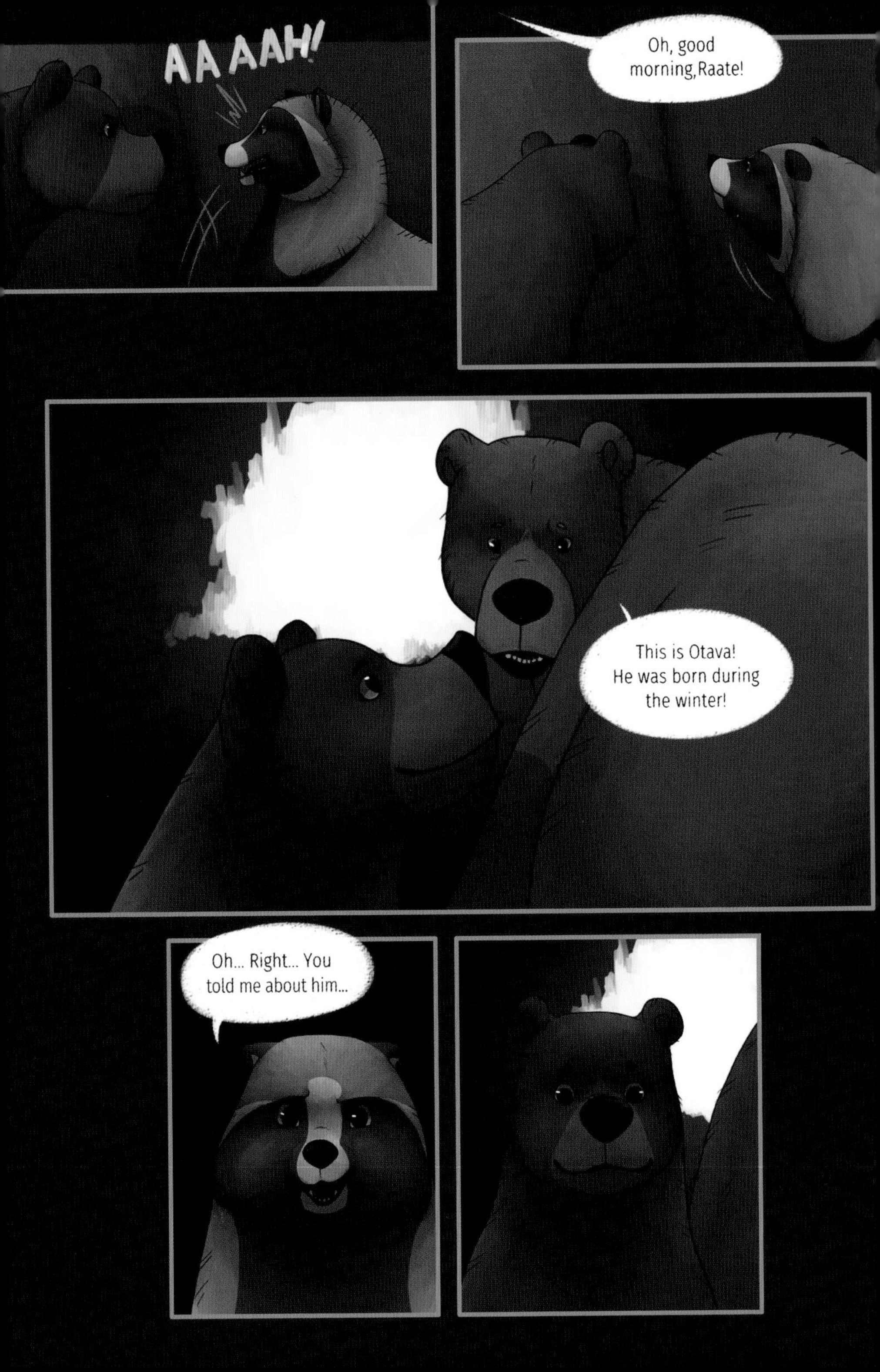
AAAAH!
Oh, good morning,Raate!
This is Otava! He was born during the winter!
Oh... Right... You told me about him...

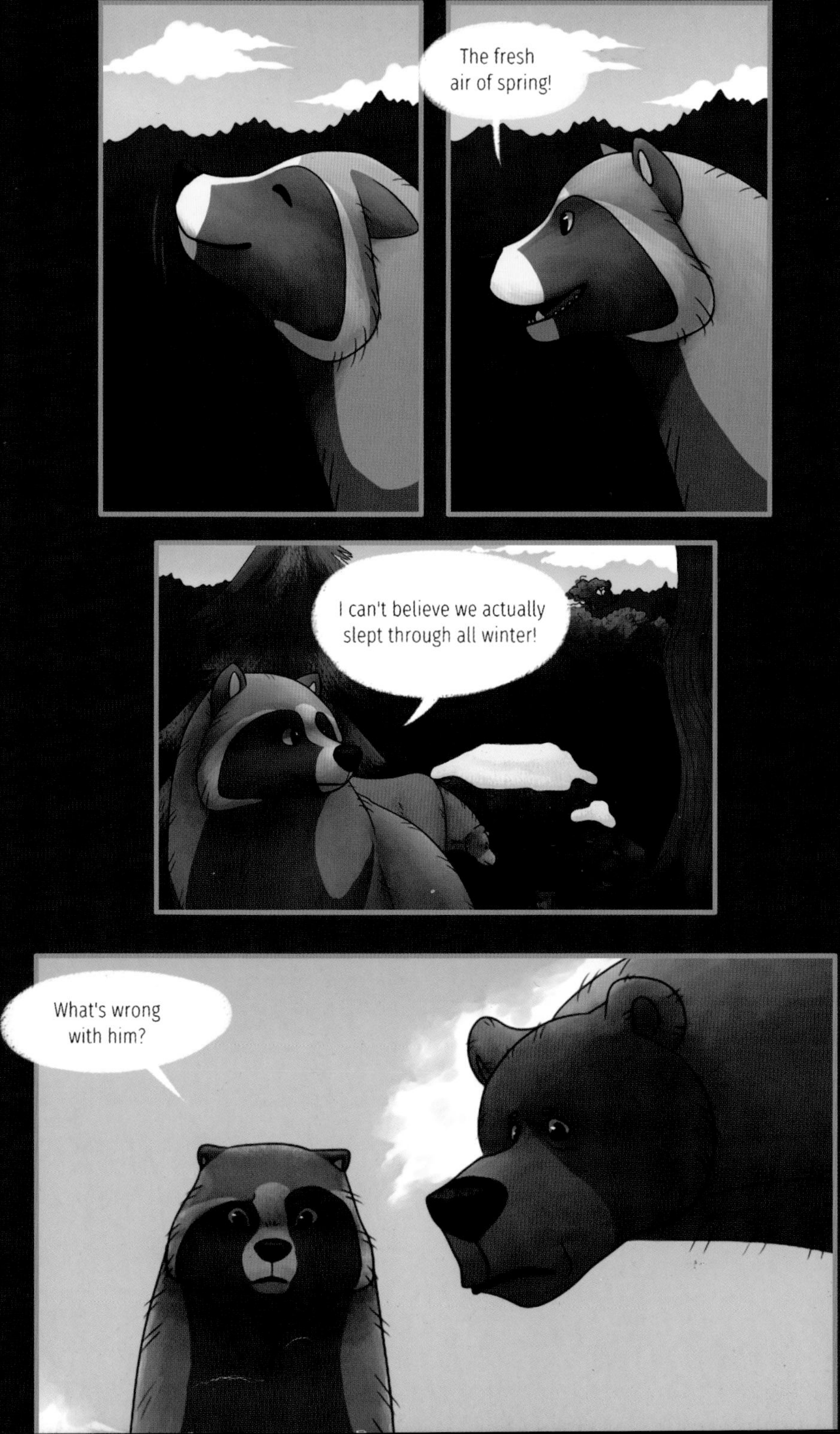
The fresh air of spring!
I can't believe we actually slept through all winter!
What's wrong with him?

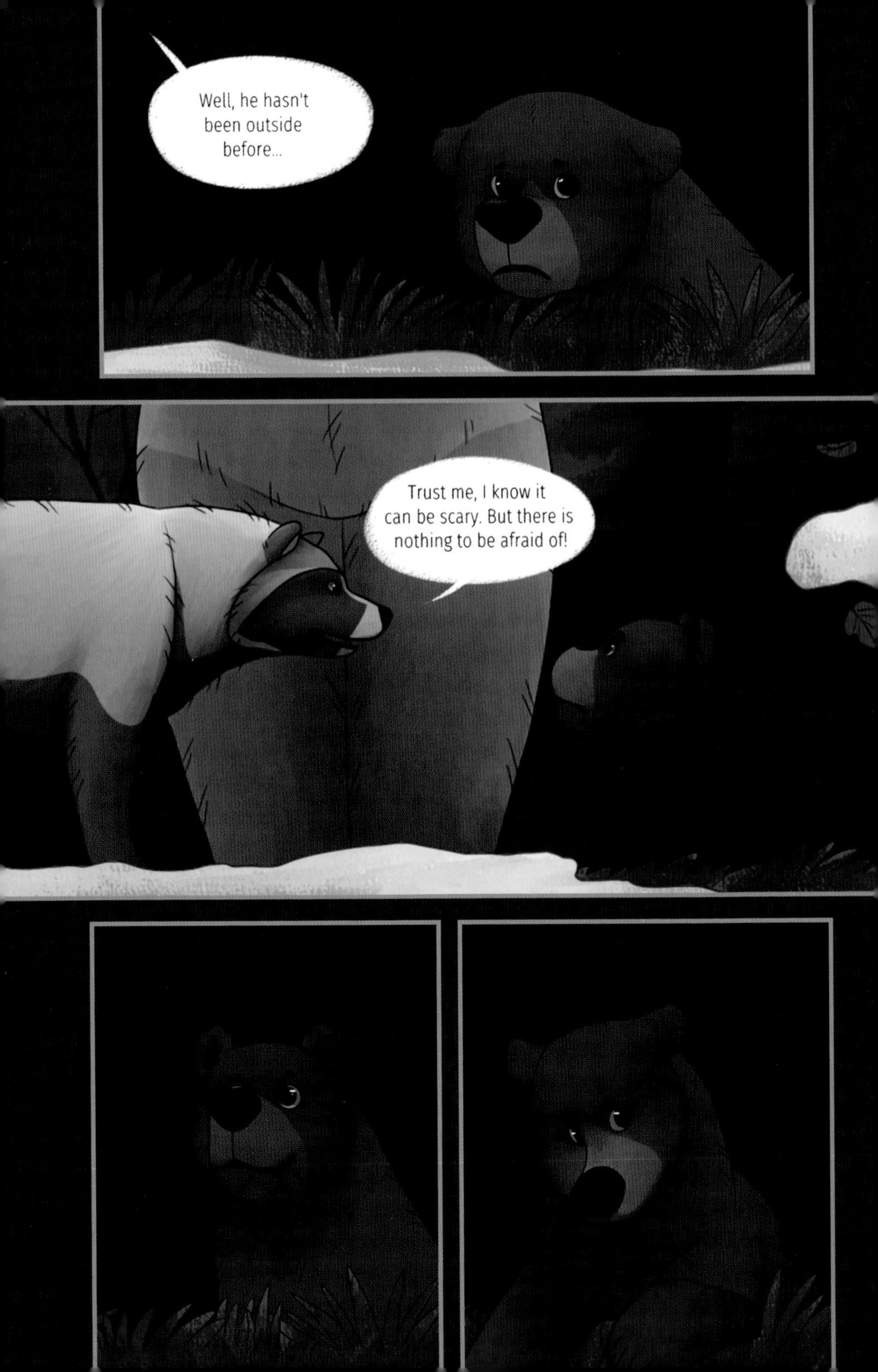
Well, he hasn't been outside before...
Trust me, I know it can be scary. But there is nothing to be afraid of!

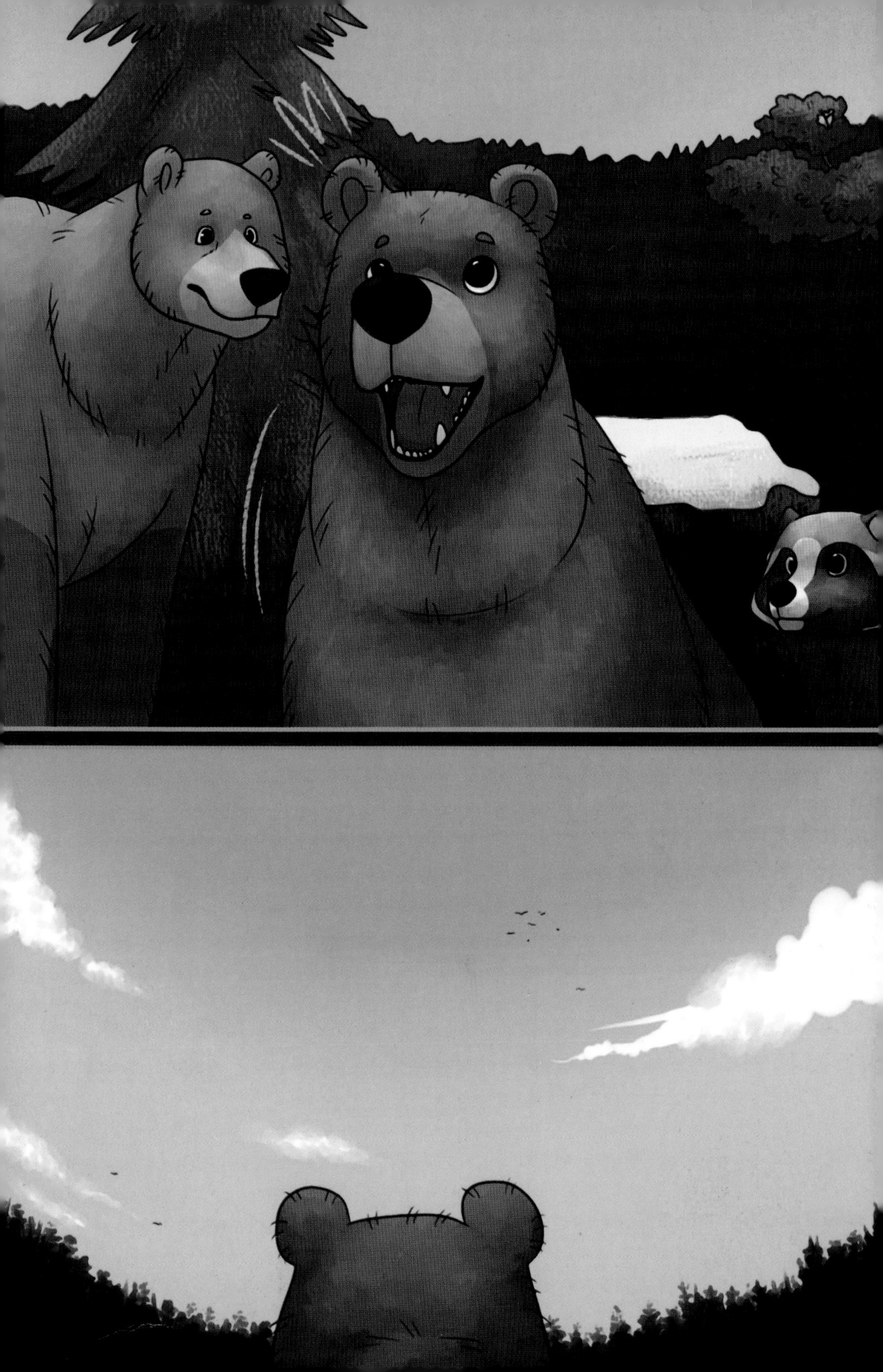

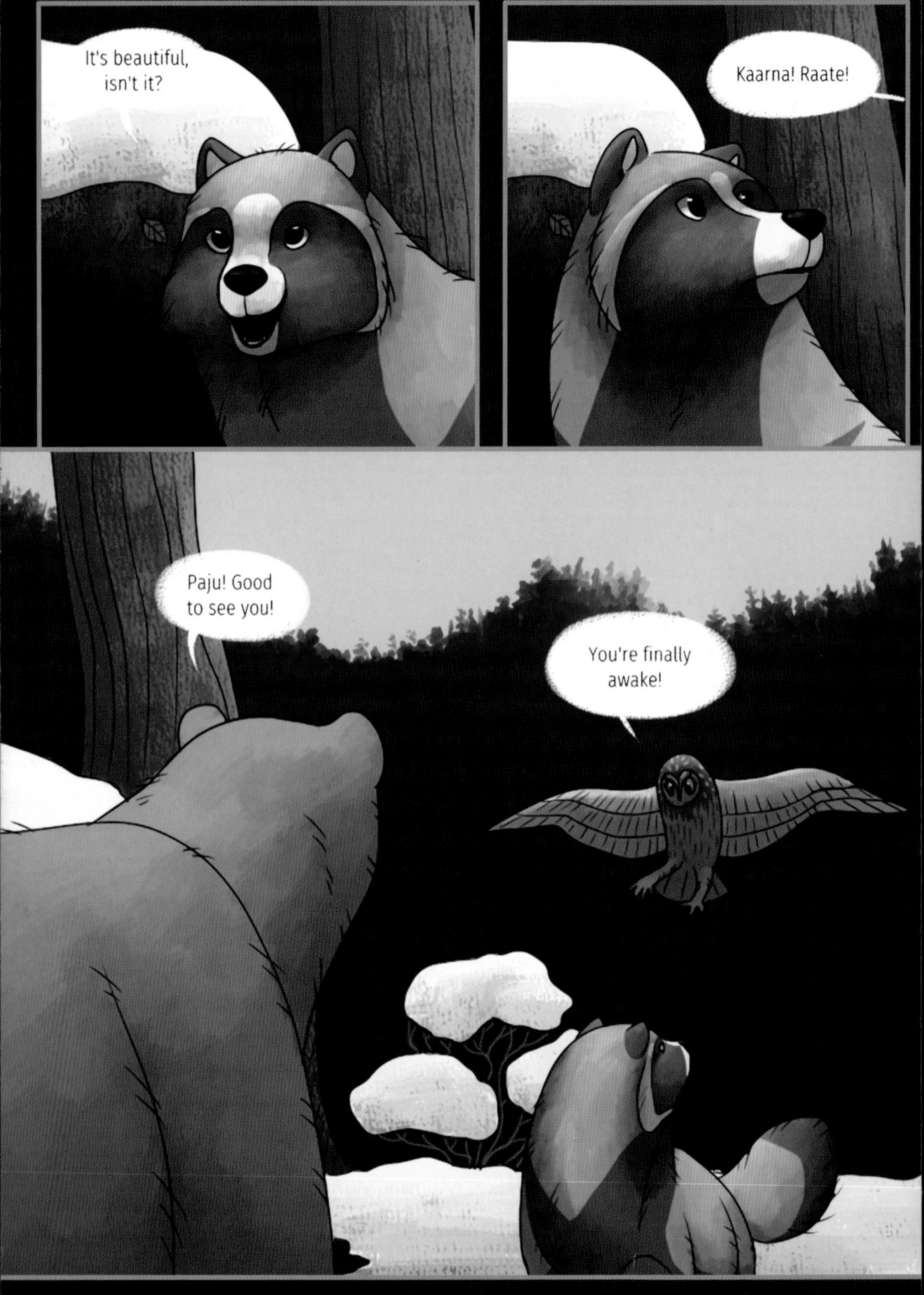
It's beautiful, isn't it?
Kaarna! Raate!
Paju! Good to see you!
You're finally awake!

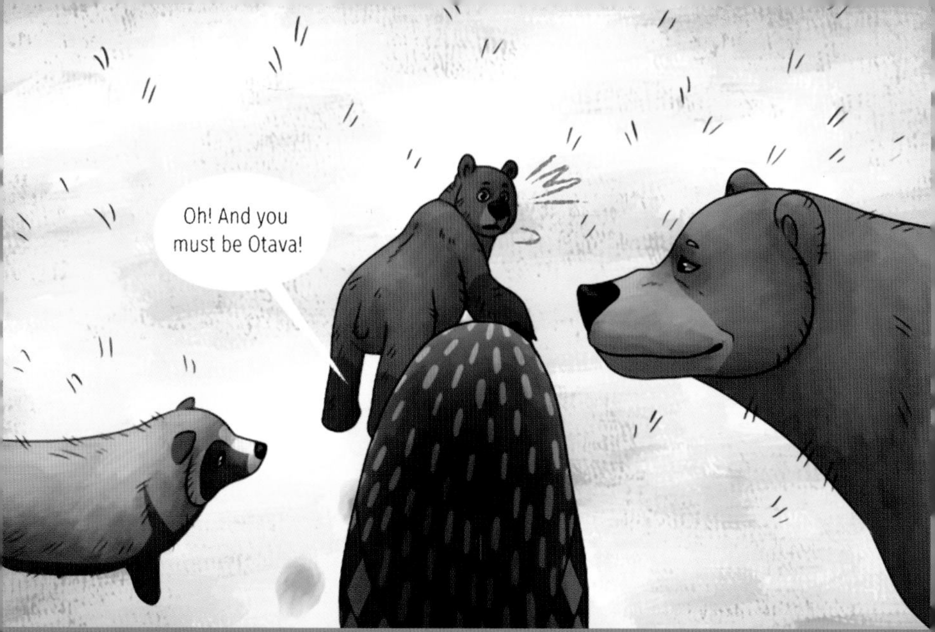
Oh! And you
must be Otava!

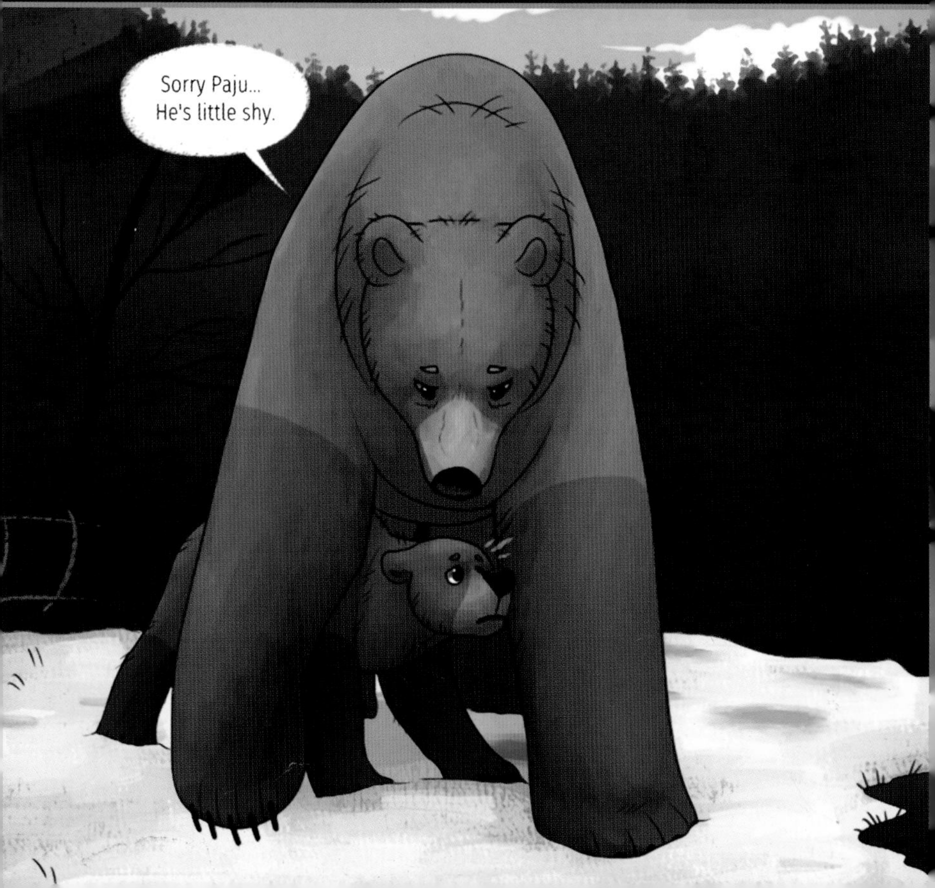
Sorry Paju...
He's little shy.

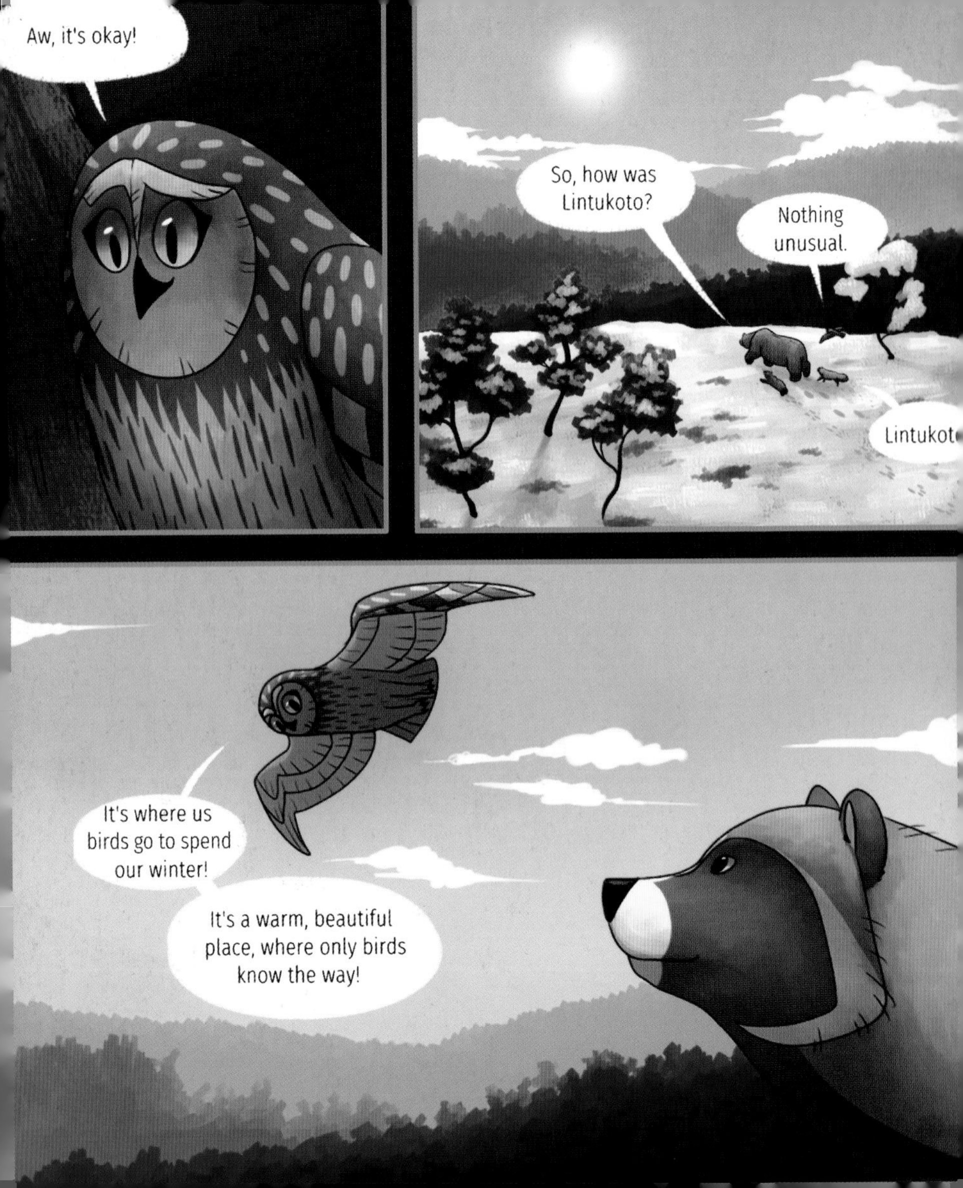
Aw, it's okay!
So, how was Lintukoto?
Nothing unusual.
Lintukot
It's where us birds go to spend our winter!
It's a warm, beautiful place, where only birds know the way!

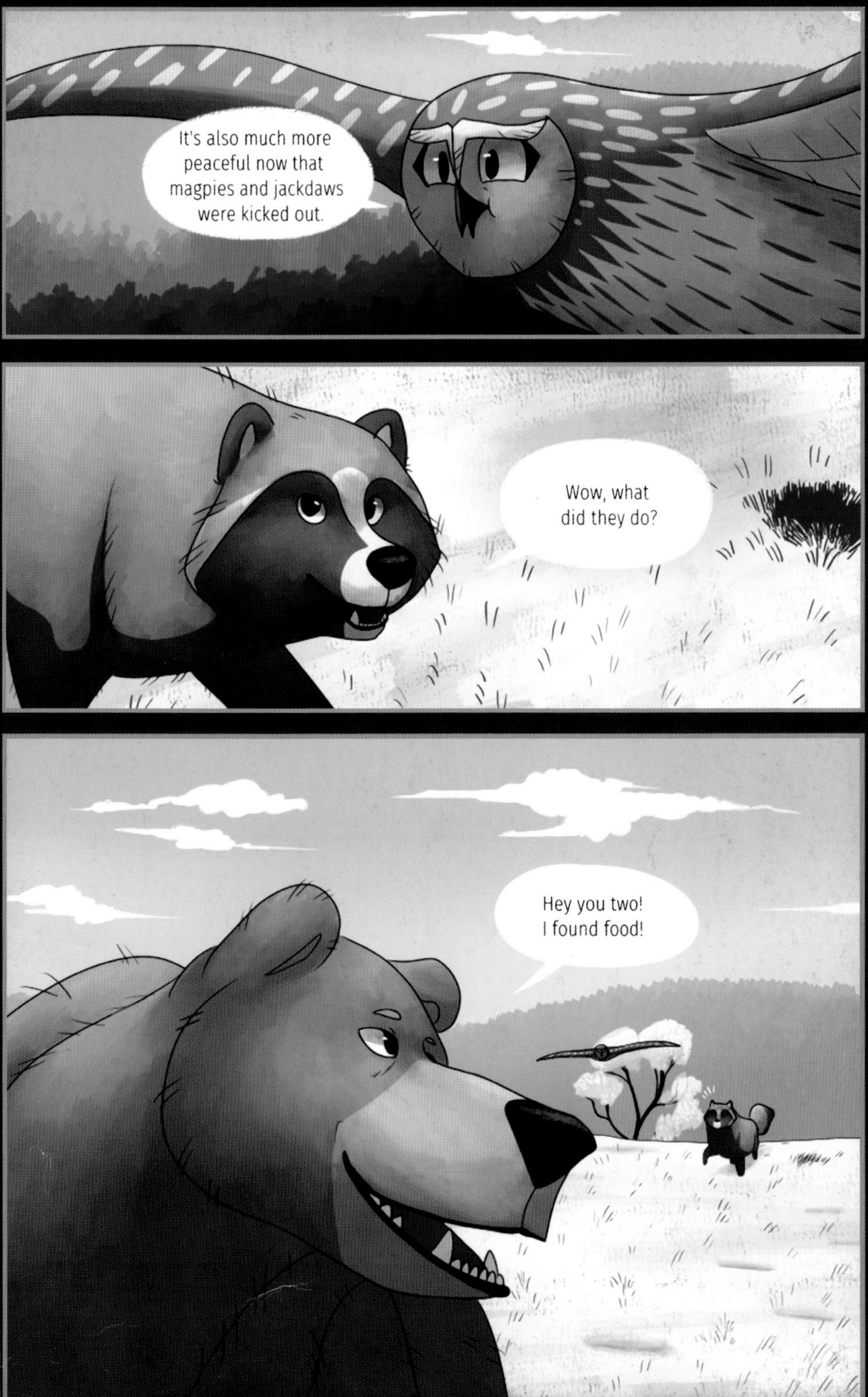
It's also much more peaceful now that magpies and jackdaws were kicked out.
Wow, what did they do?
Hey you two! I found food!

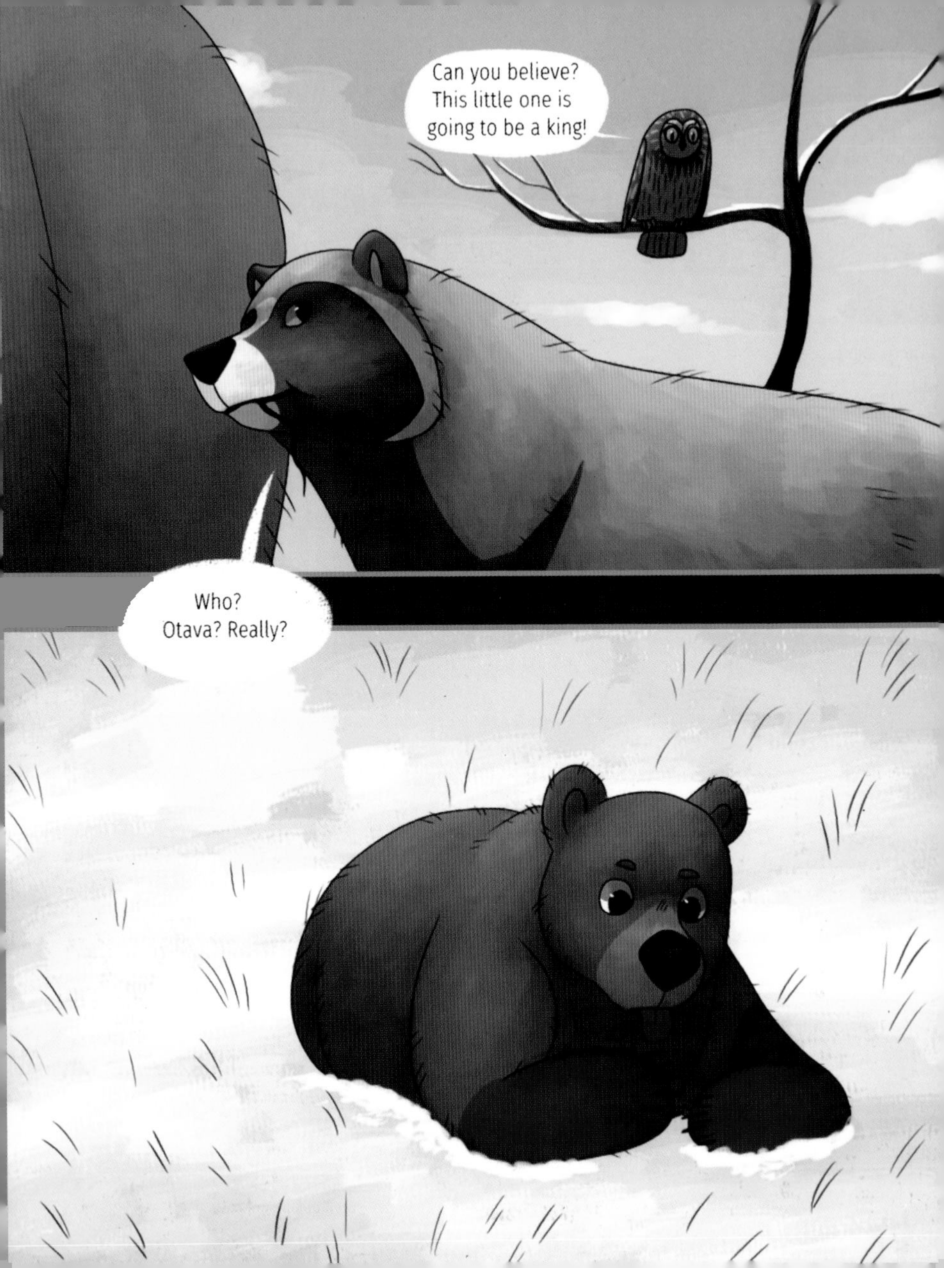
Can you believe? This little one is going to be a king!
Who? Otava? Really?

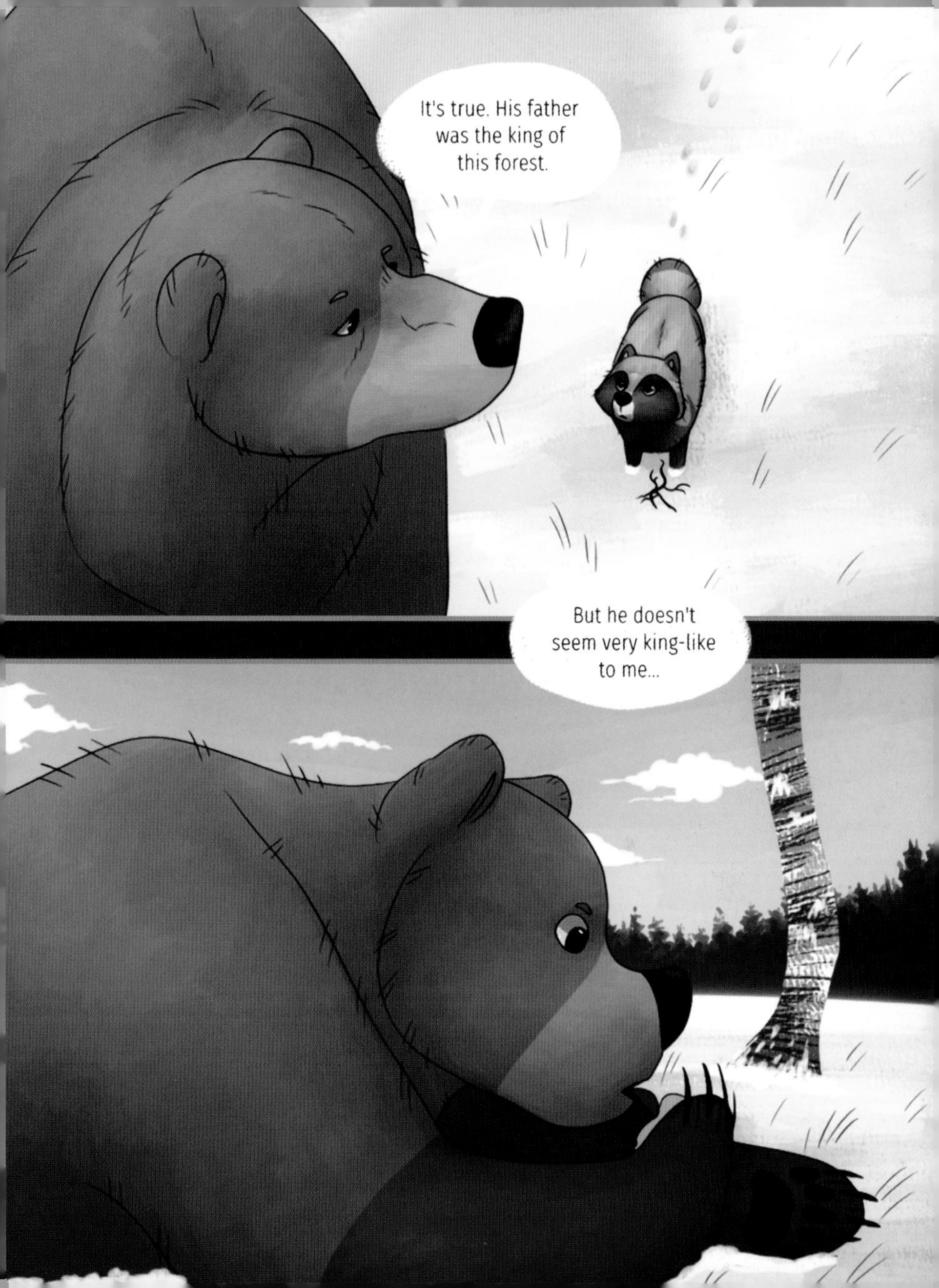
It's true. His father was the king of this forest.
But he doesn't seem very king-like to me...

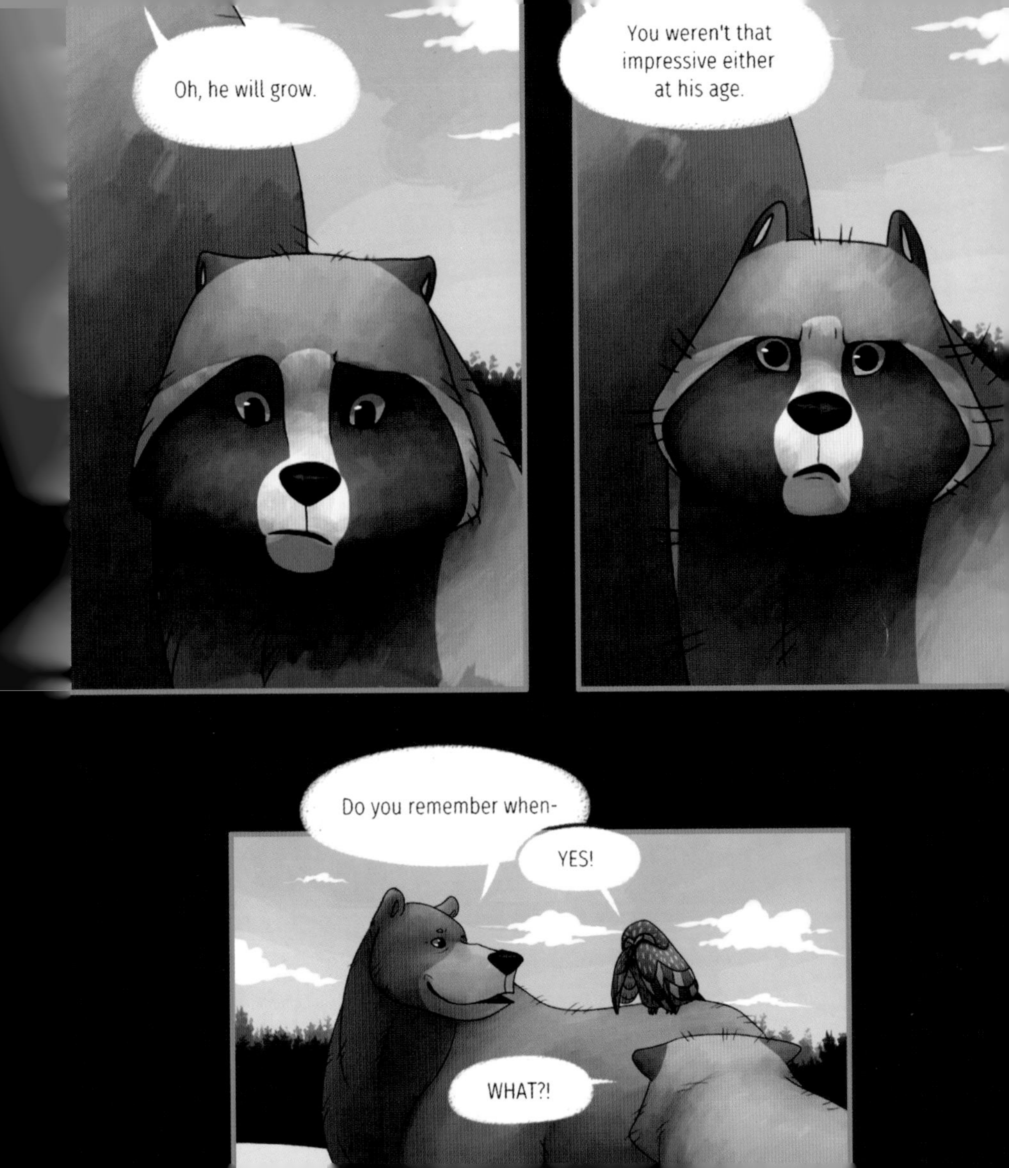
Oh, he will grow.
You weren't that impressive either at his age.
Do you remember when-
YES!
WHAT?!

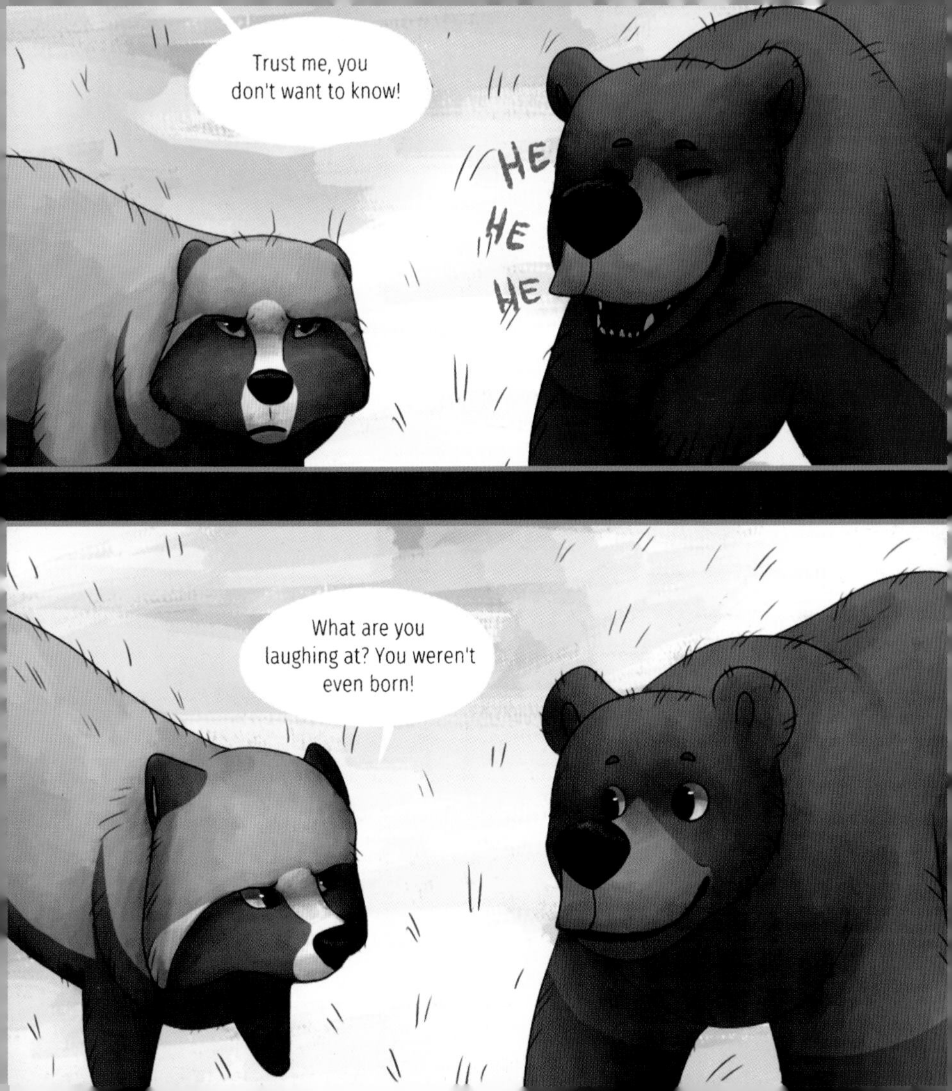
Trust me, you don't want to know!
HE HE HE
What are you laughing at? You weren't even born!

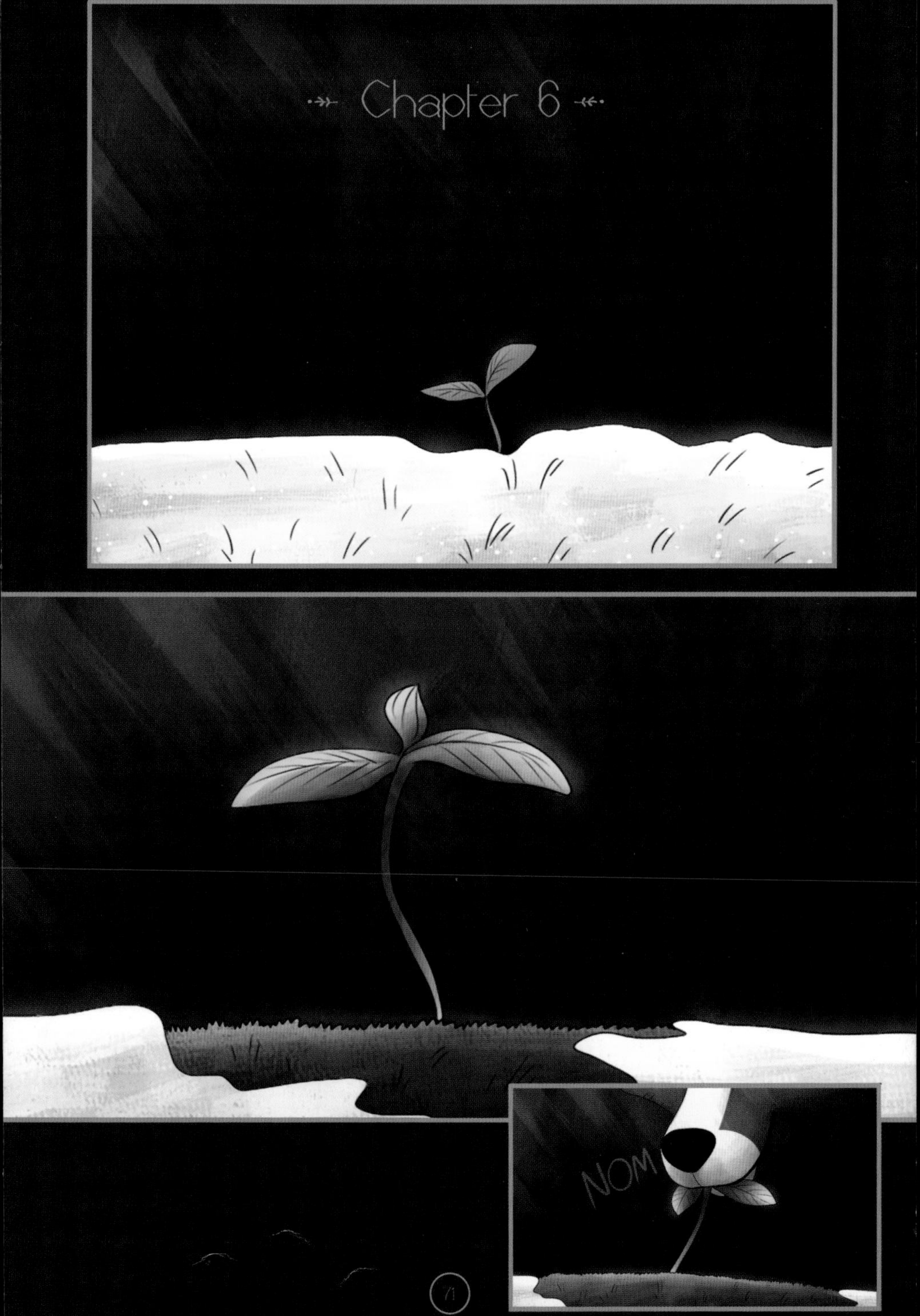
Chapter 6
NOM

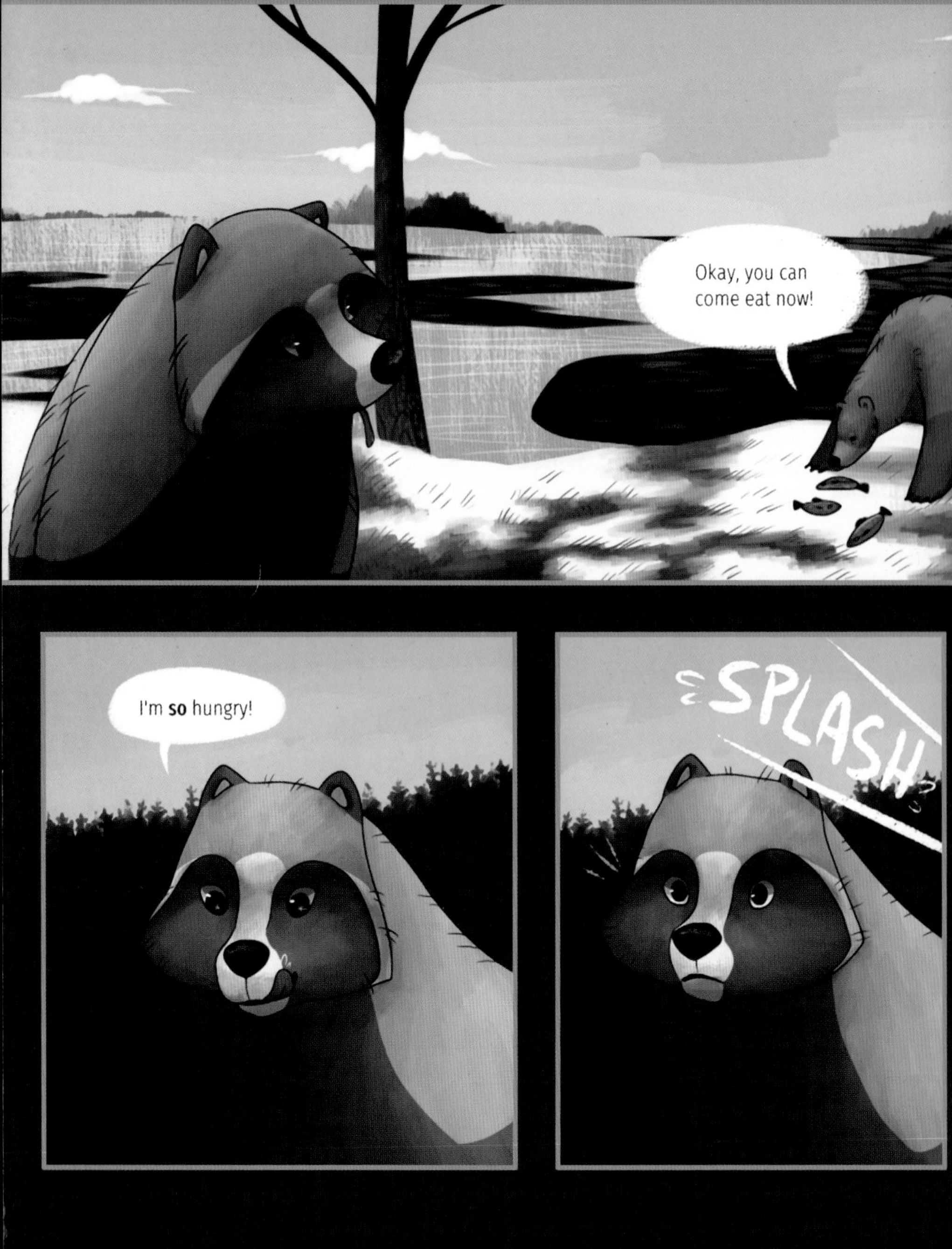
Okay, you can come eat now!
I'm **so** hungry!
SPLASH

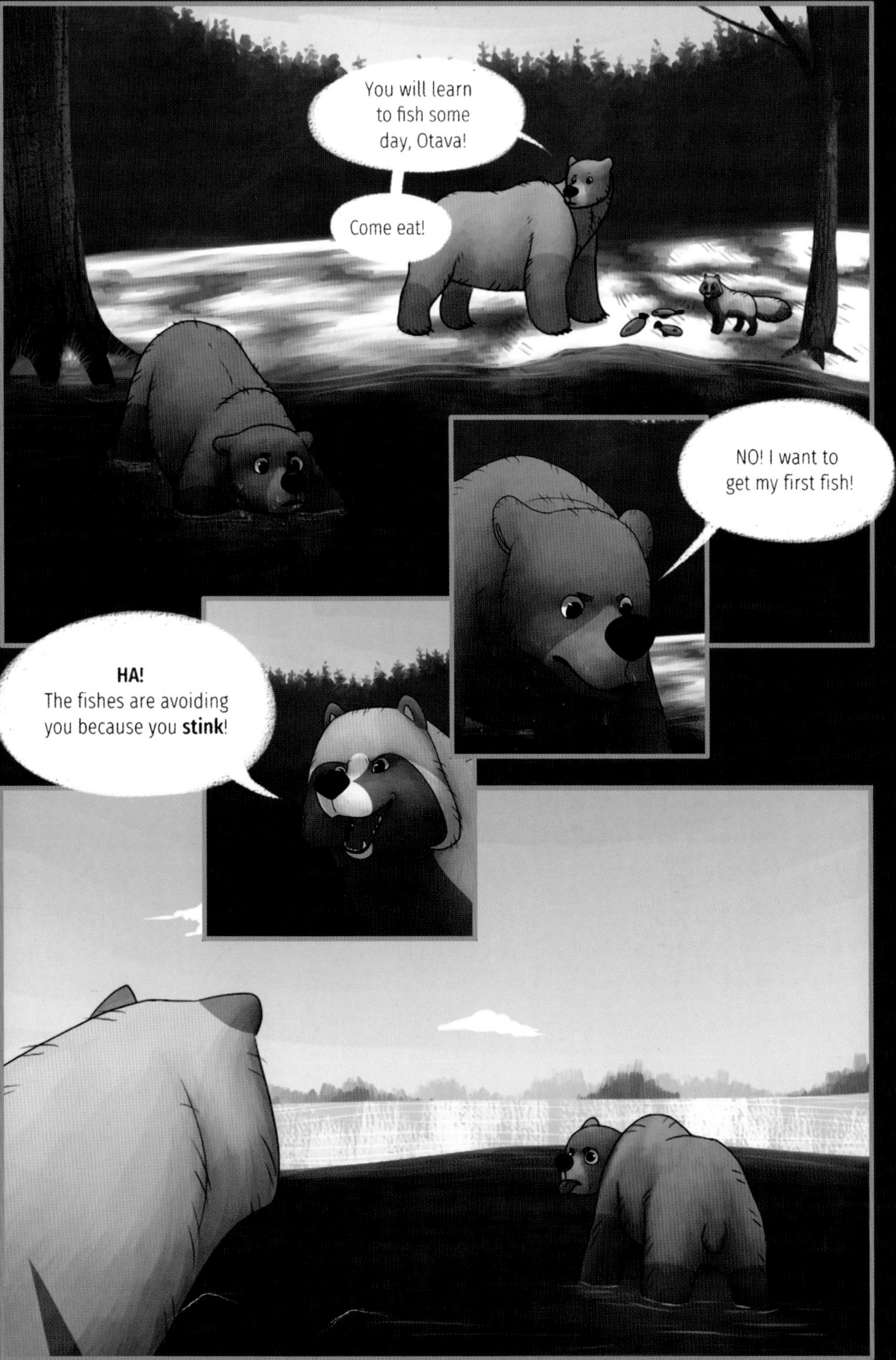
You will learn to fish some day, Otava!
Come eat!
NO! I want to get my first fish!
HA!
The fishes are avoiding you because you **stink**!

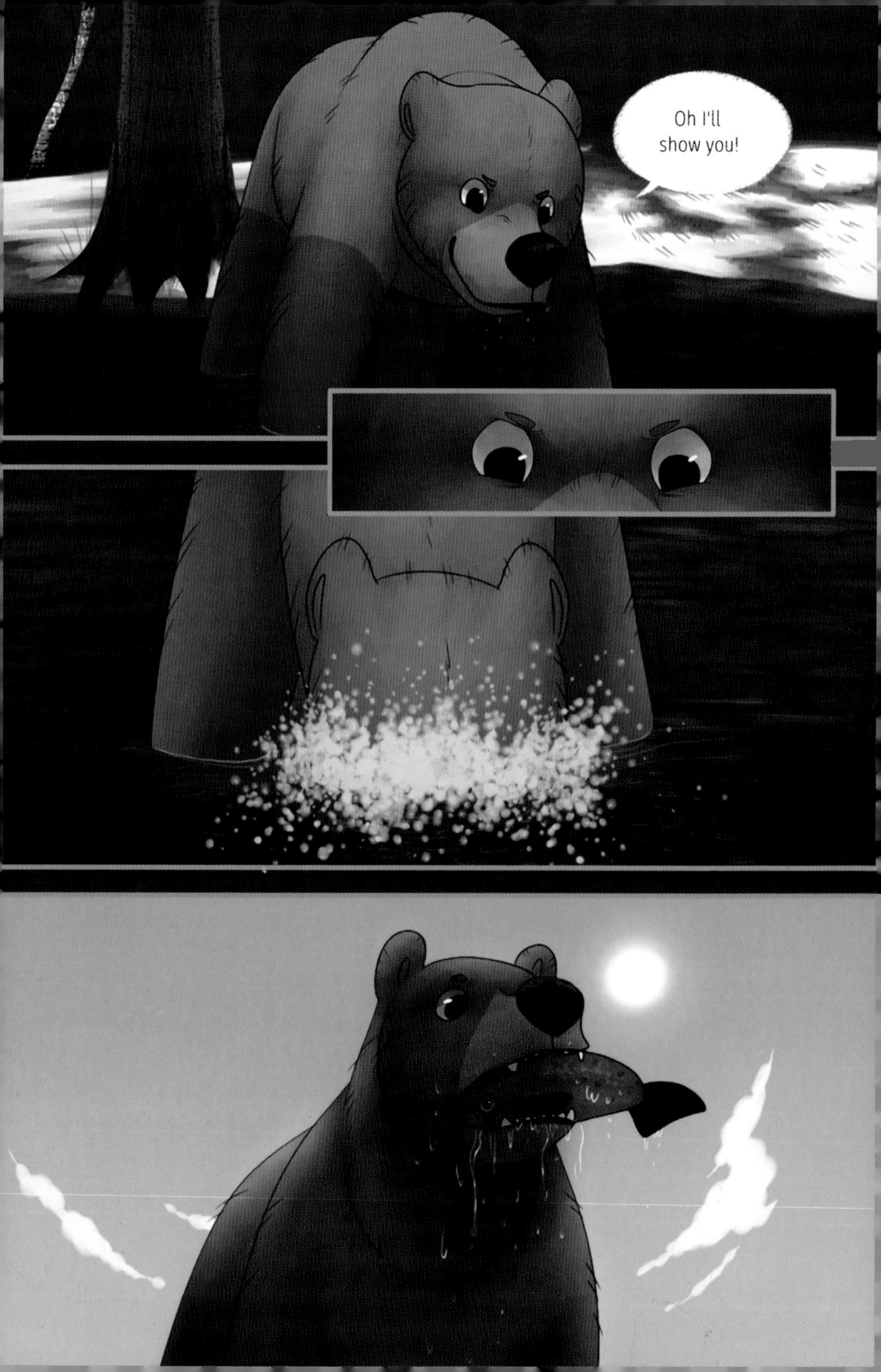
Oh I'll show you!

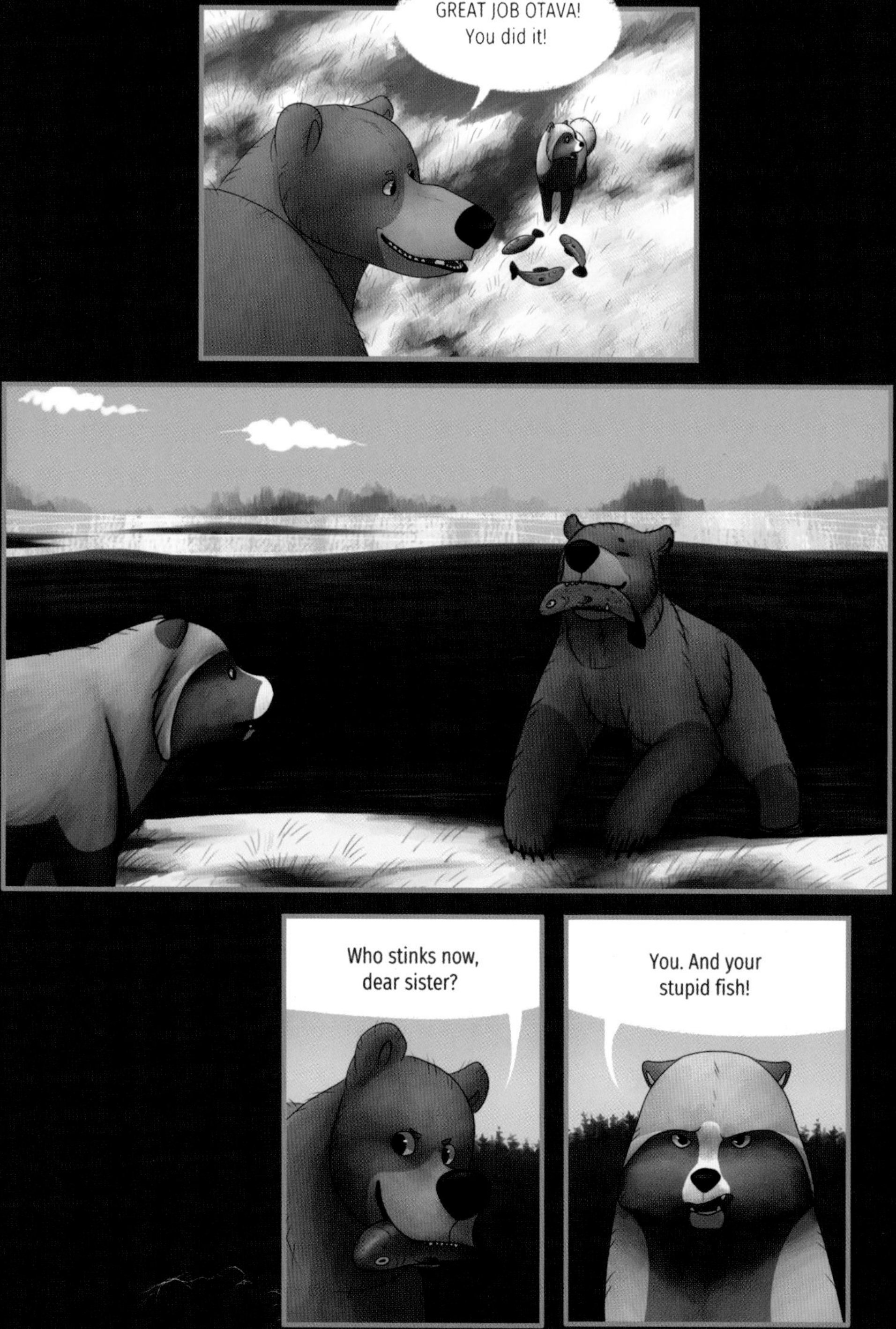
GREAT JOB OTAVA! You did it!
Who stinks now, dear sister?
You. And your stupid fish!

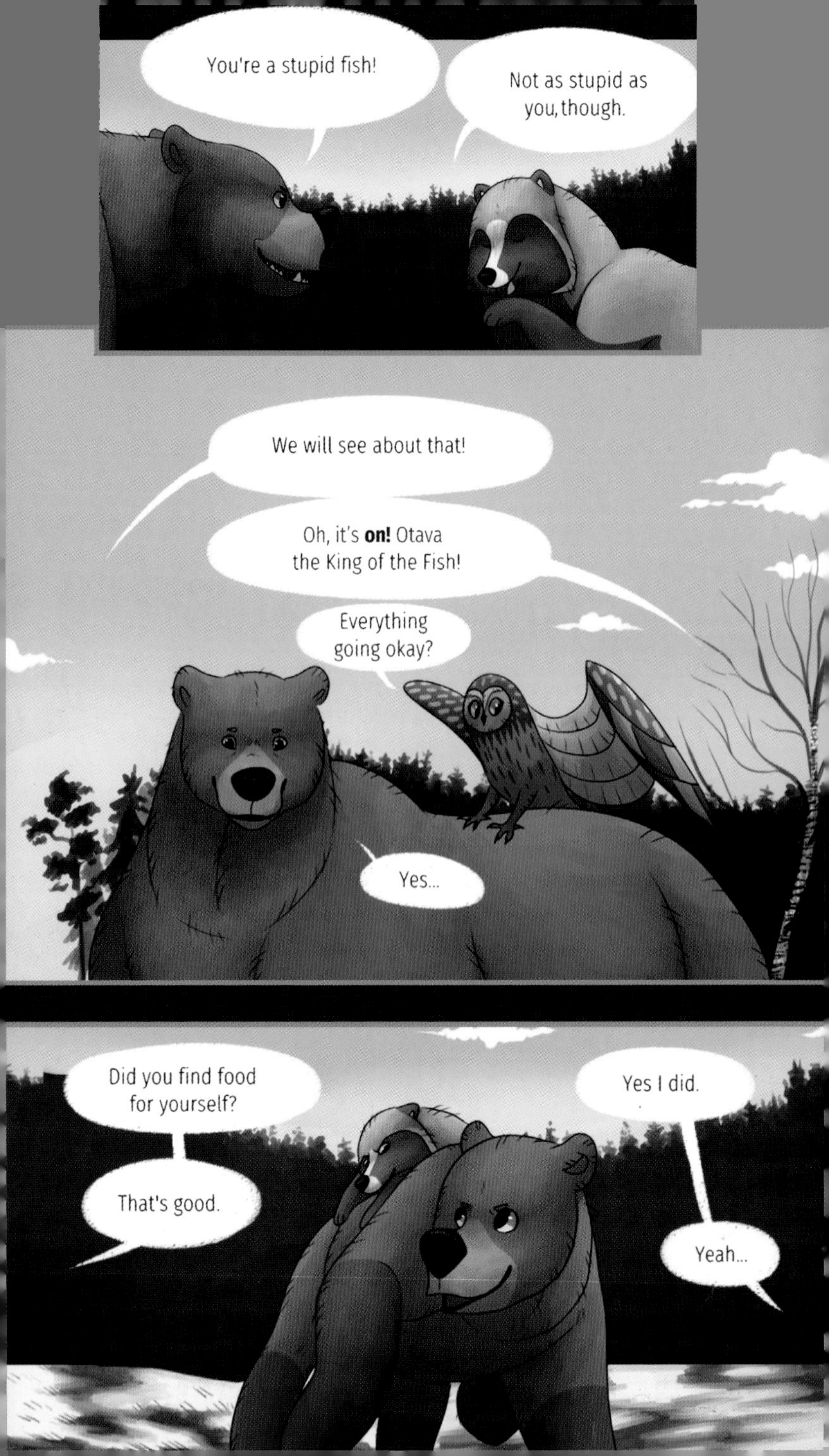
You're a stupid fish!
Not as stupid as you, though.
We will see about that!
Oh, it's **on!** Otava the King of the Fish!
Everything going okay?
Yes...
Did you find food for yourself?
Yes I did.
That's good.
Yeah...

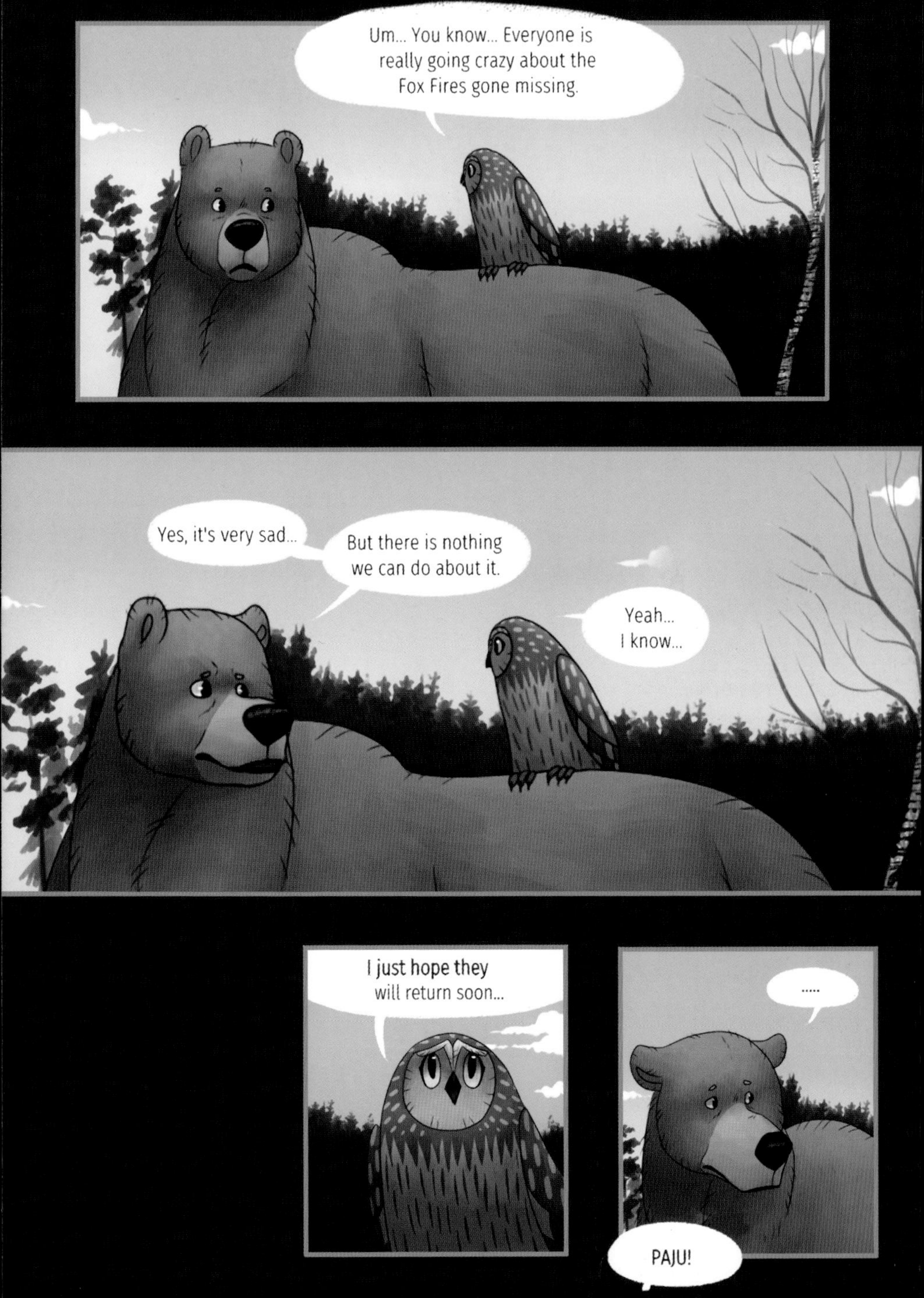
Um... You know... Everyone is really going crazy about the Fox Fires gone missing.
Yes, it's very sad...
But there is nothing we can do about it.
Yeah... I know...
I just hope they will return soon...
.....
PAJU!

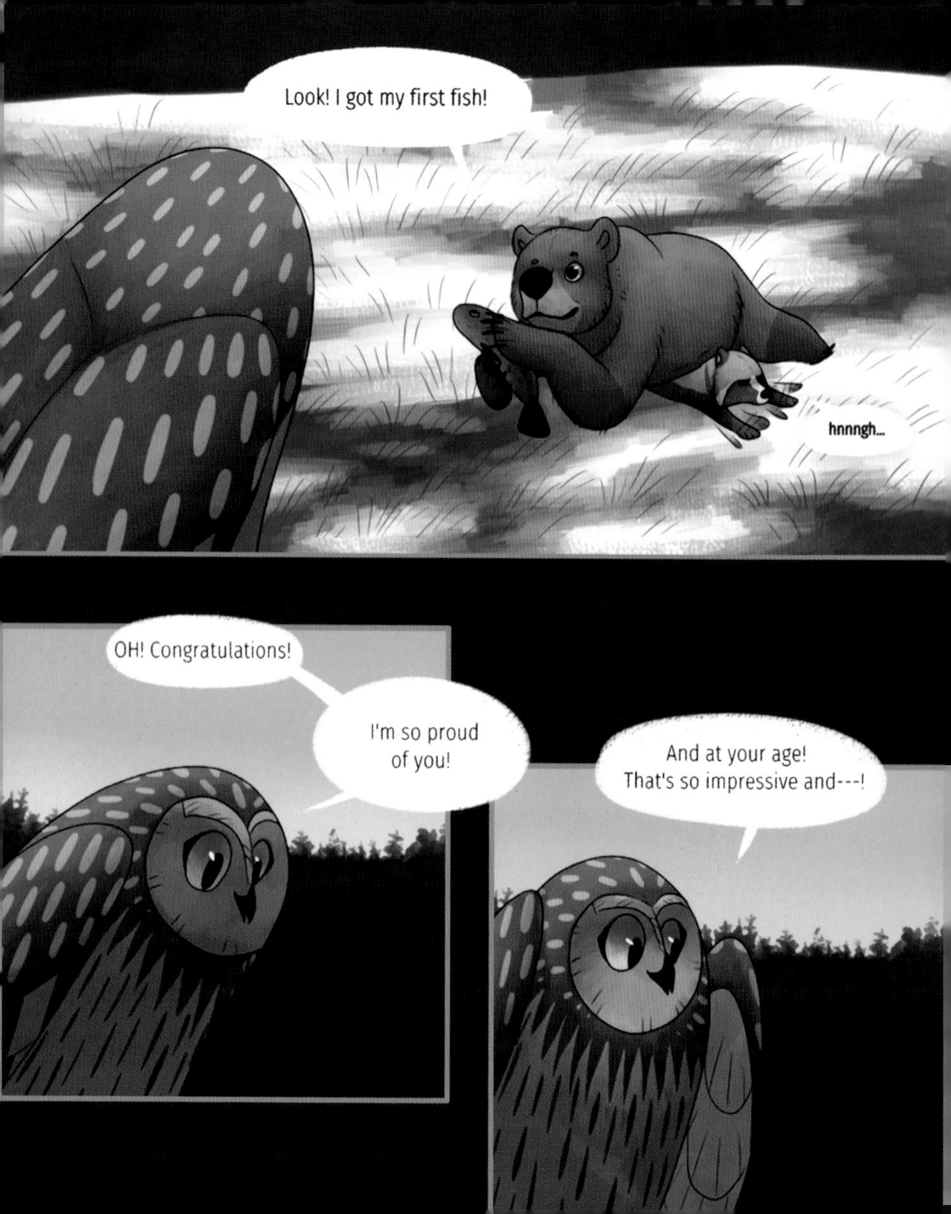
Look! I got my first fish!
hnnngh...
OH! Congratulations!
I'm so proud of you!
And at your age! That's so impressive and---!

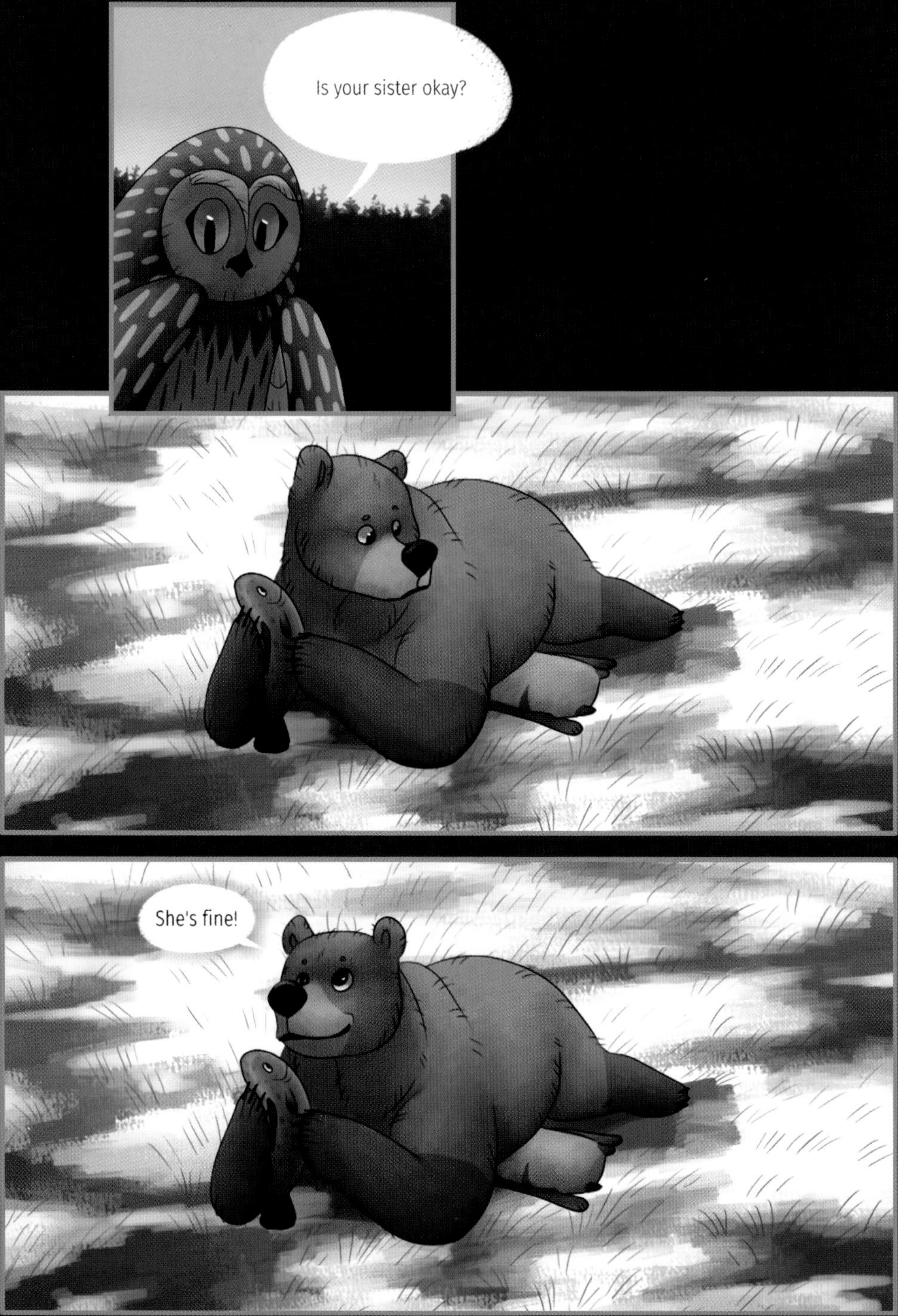
Is your sister okay?
She's fine!

Chapter 7

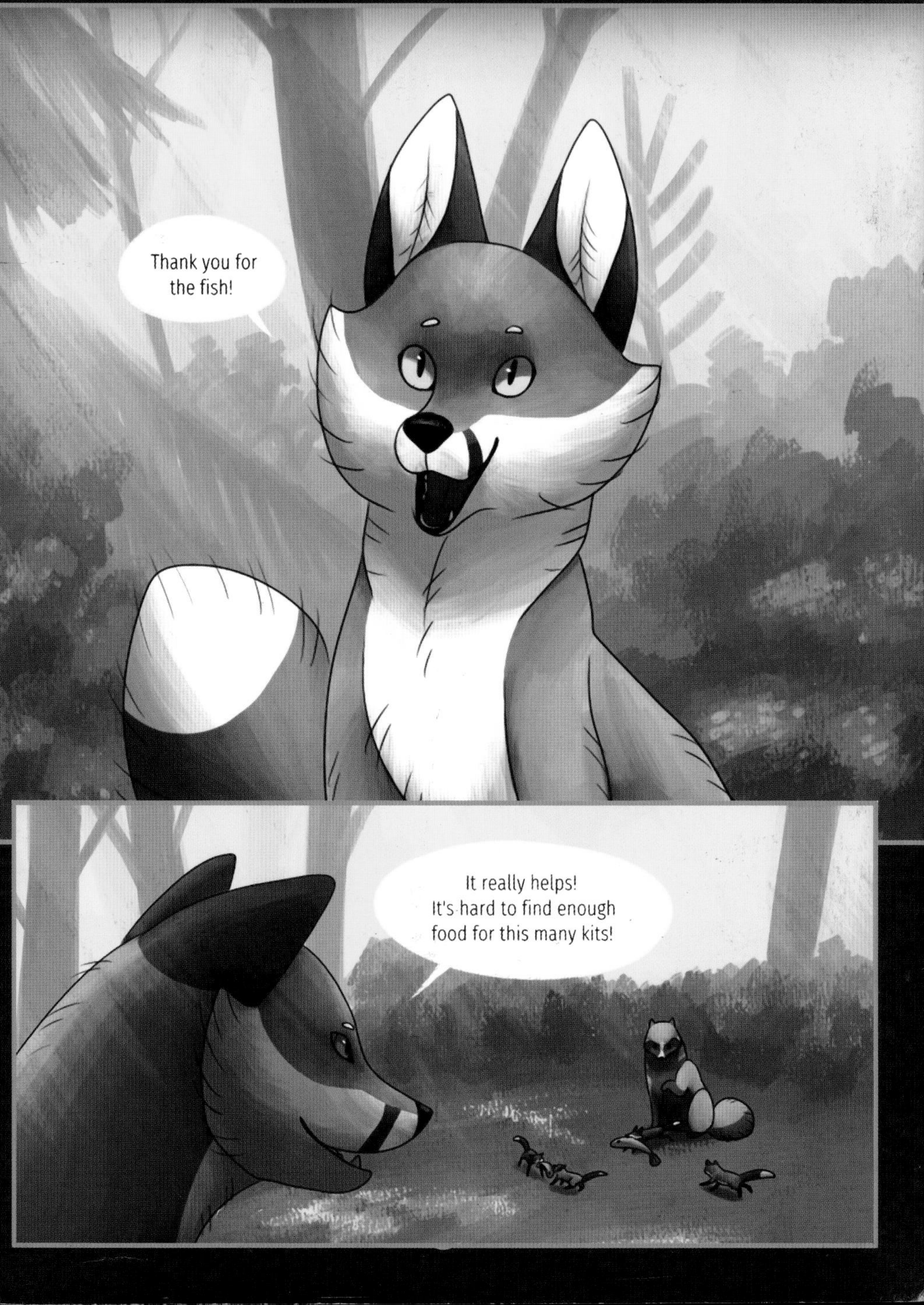
Thank you for the fish!
It really helps! It's hard to find enough food for this many kits!

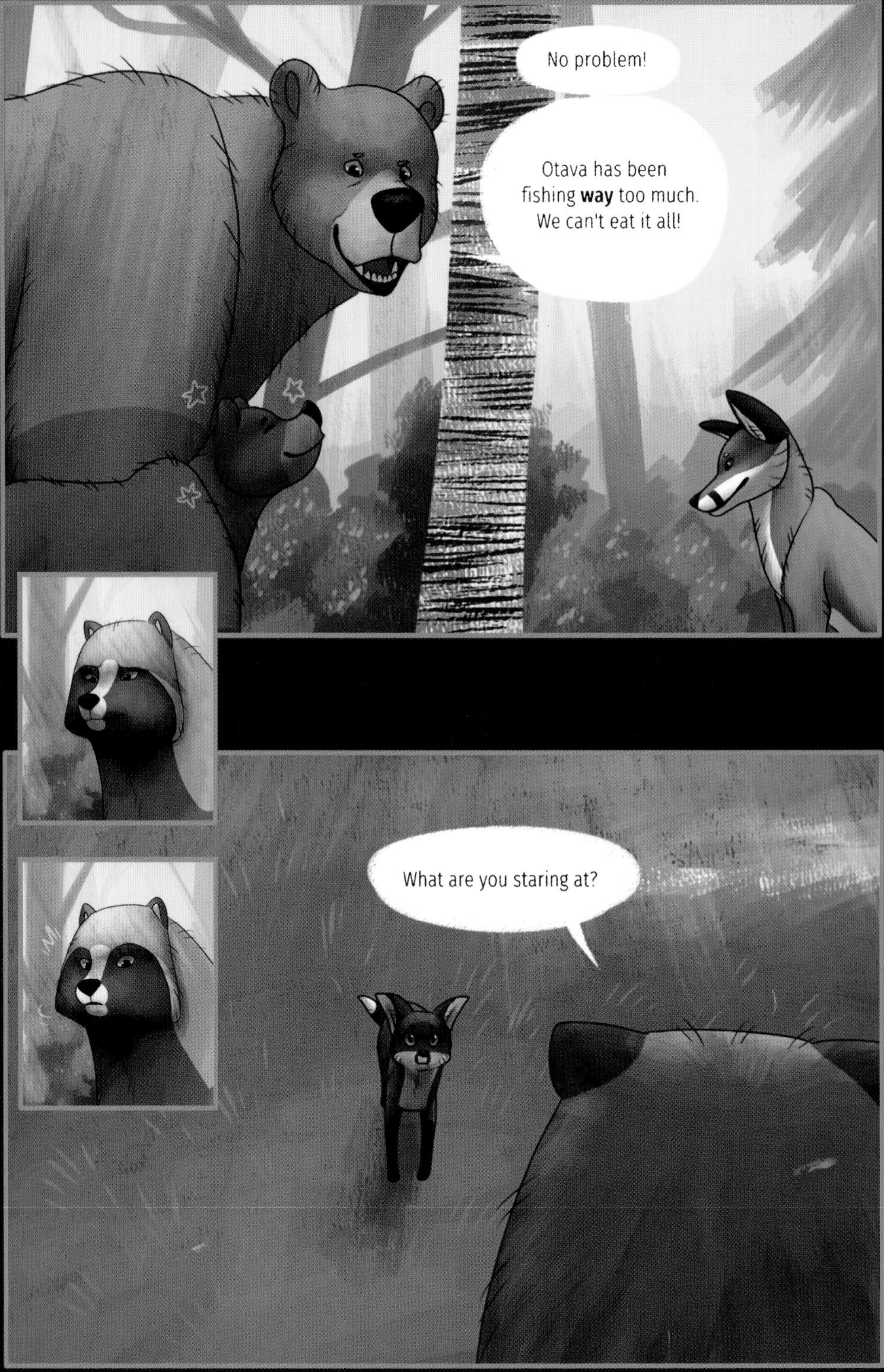
No problem!
Otava has been fishing **way** too much. We can't eat it all!
What are you staring at?

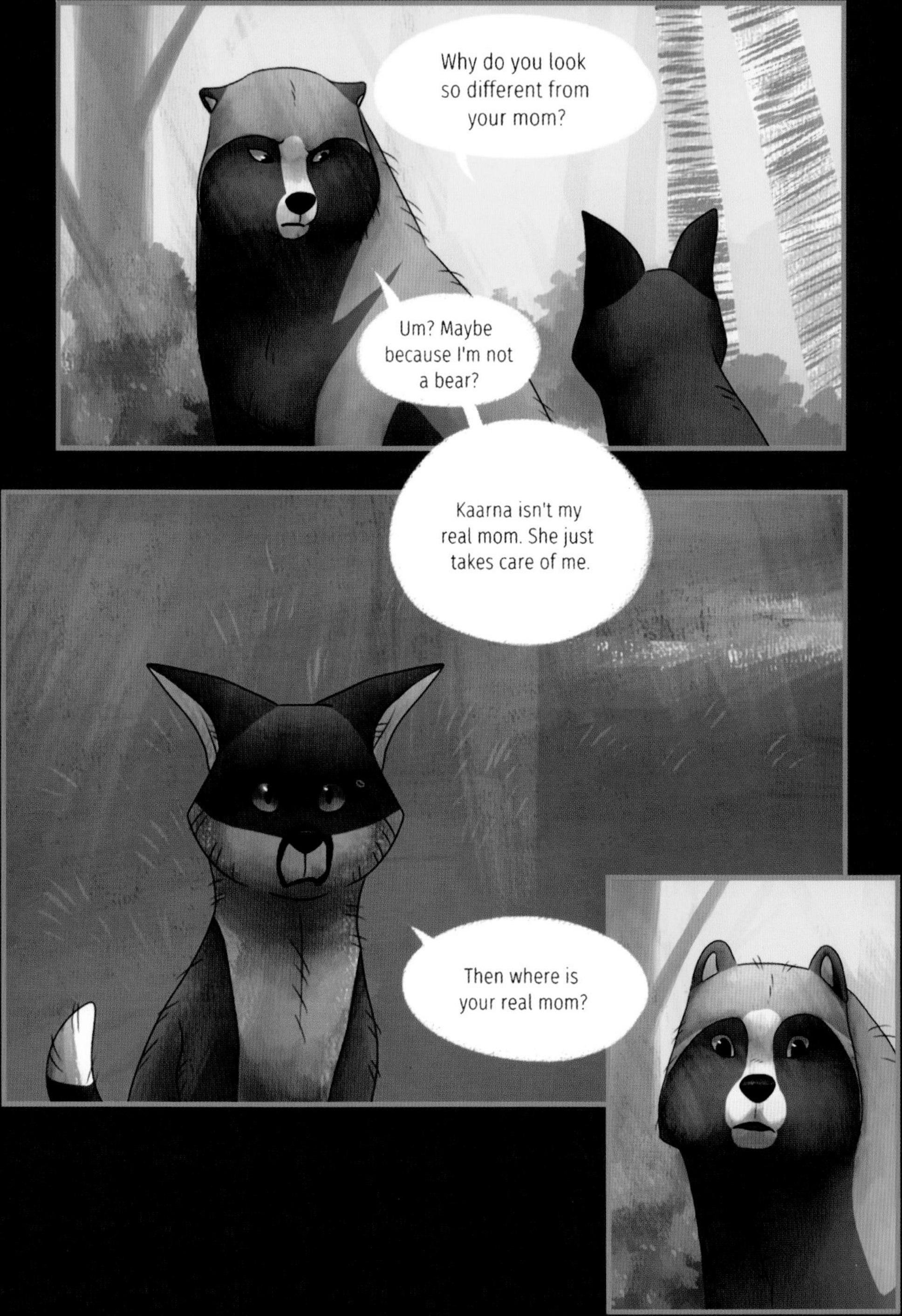
Why do you look so different from your mom?
Um? Maybe because I'm not a bear?
Kaarna isn't my real mom. She just takes care of me.
Then where is your real mom?

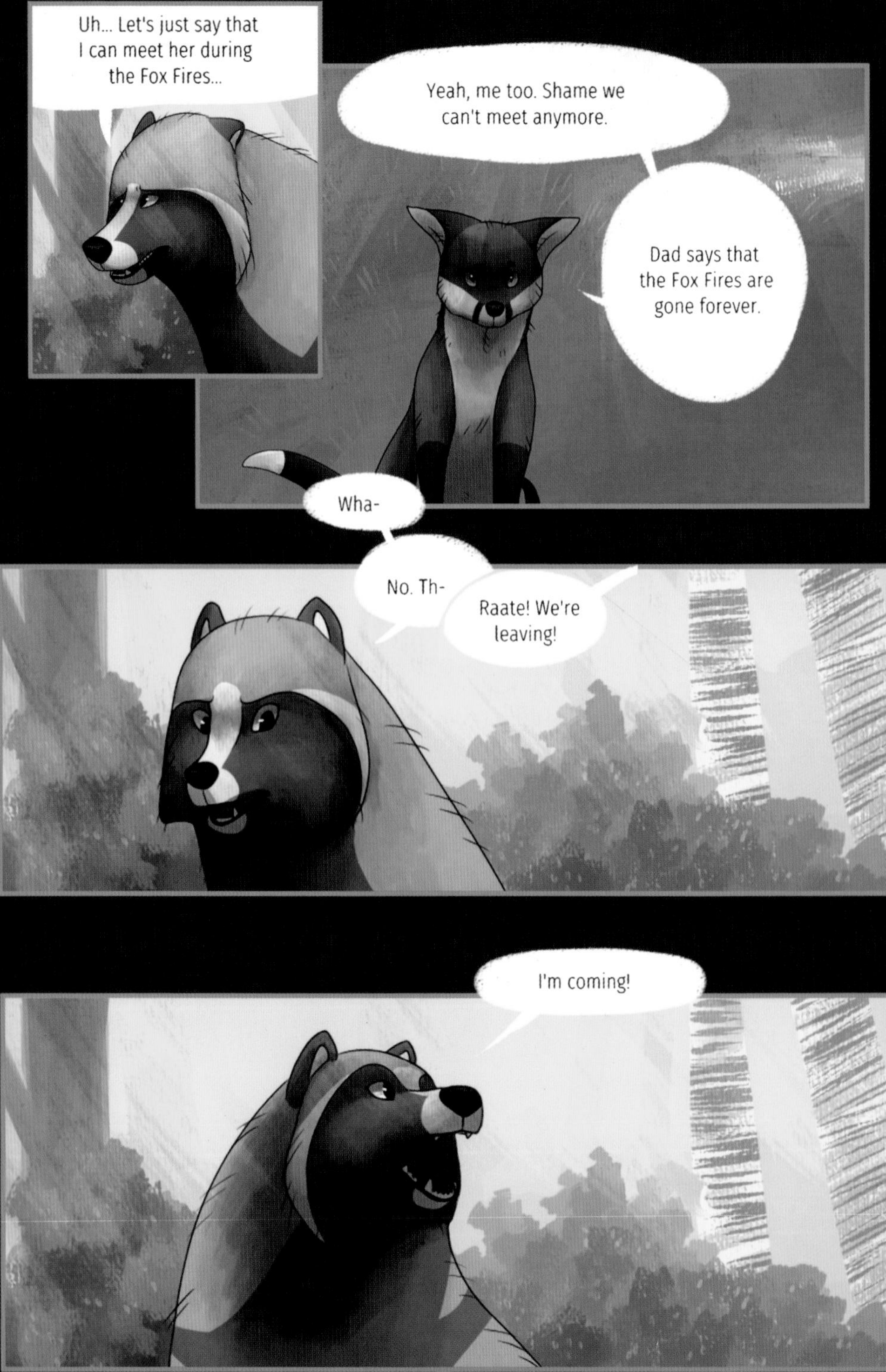
Uh... Let's just say that I can meet her during the Fox Fires...
Yeah, me too. Shame we can't meet anymore.
Dad says that the Fox Fires are gone forever.
Wha-
No. Th-
Raate! We're leaving!
I'm coming!

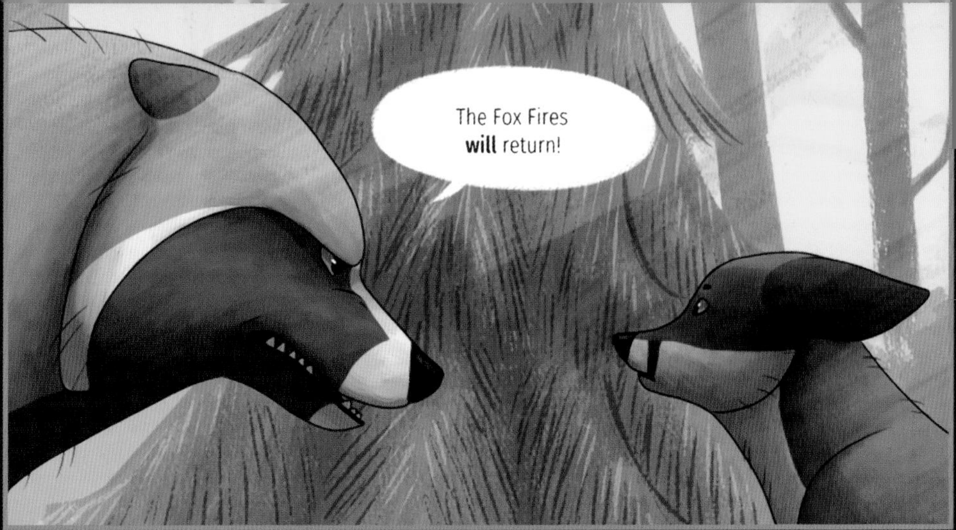
The Fox Fires
will return!

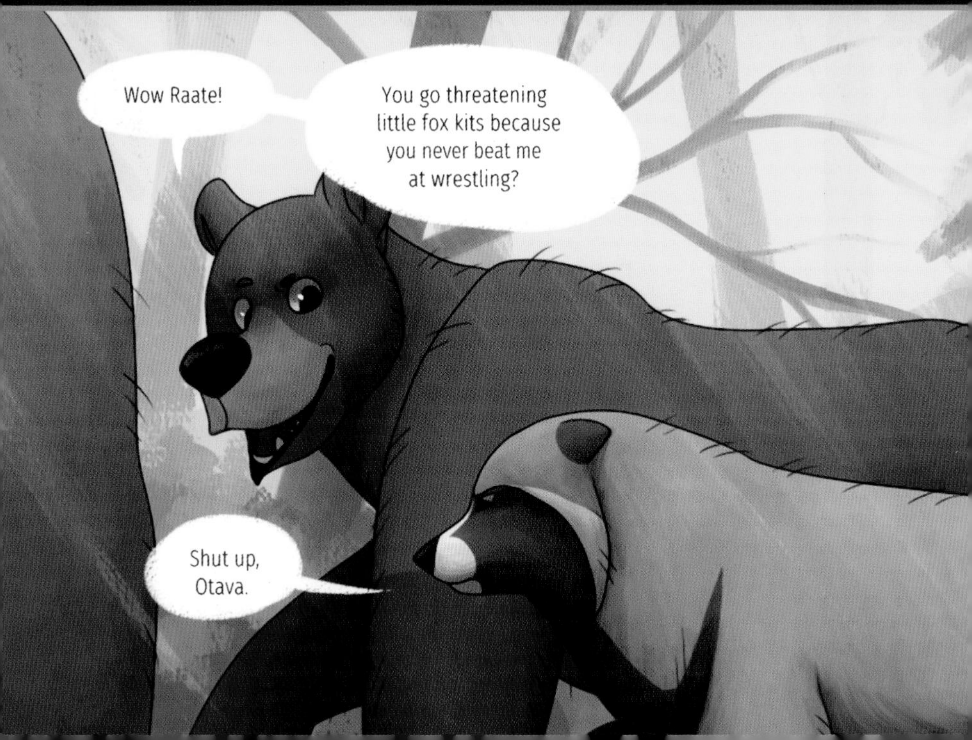
Wow Raate!
You go threatening little fox kits because you never beat me at wrestling?
Shut up, Otava.

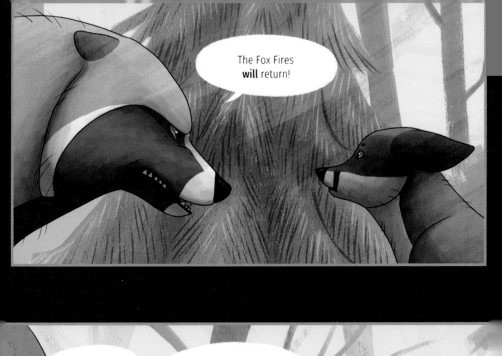

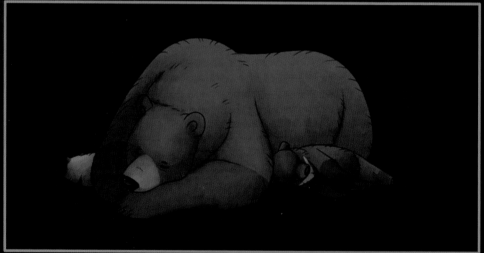

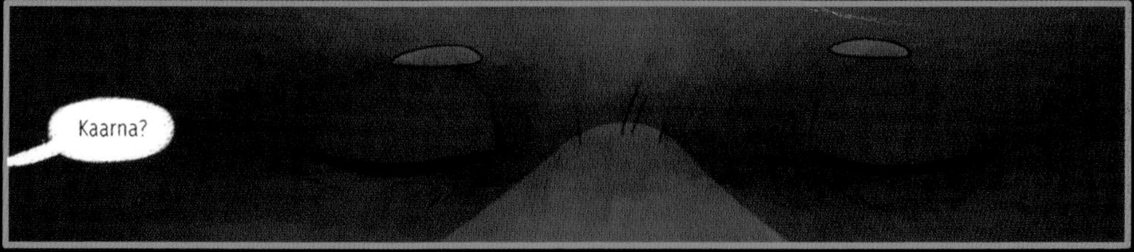
Kaarna?

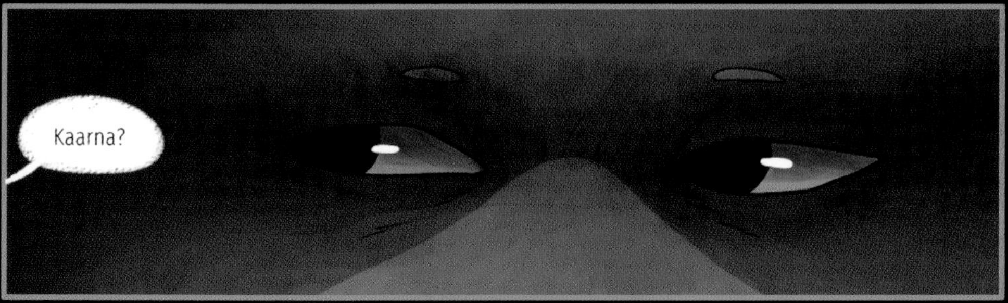
Kaarna?

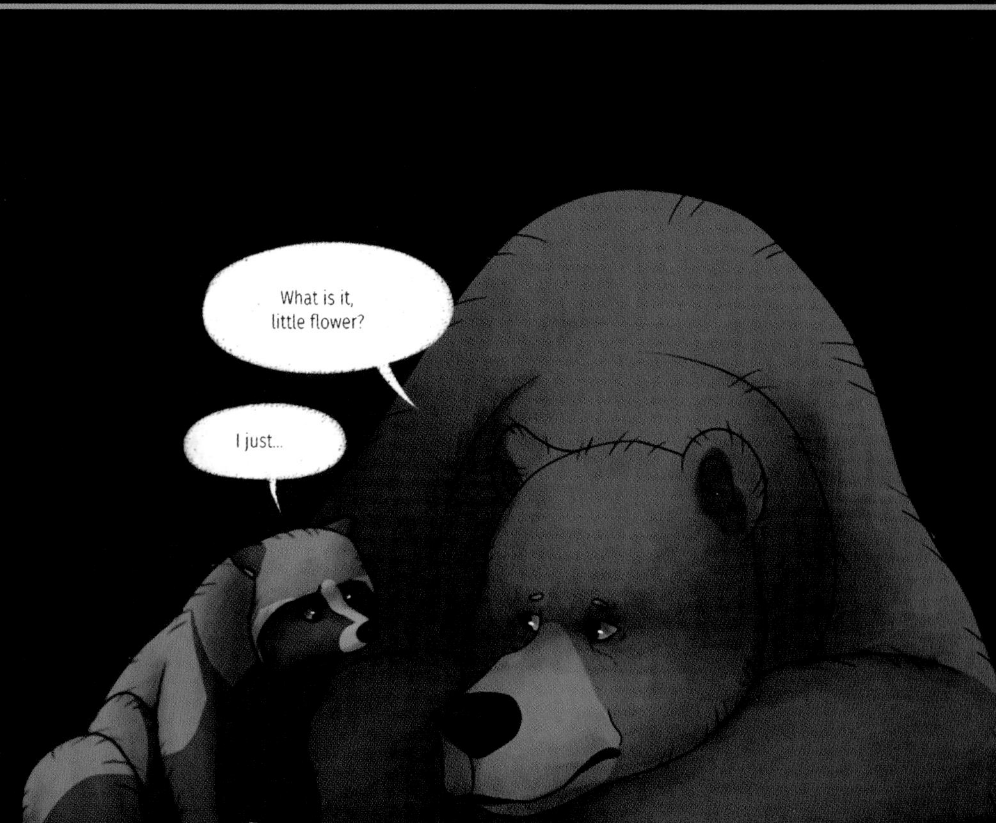
What is it,
little flower?
I just...

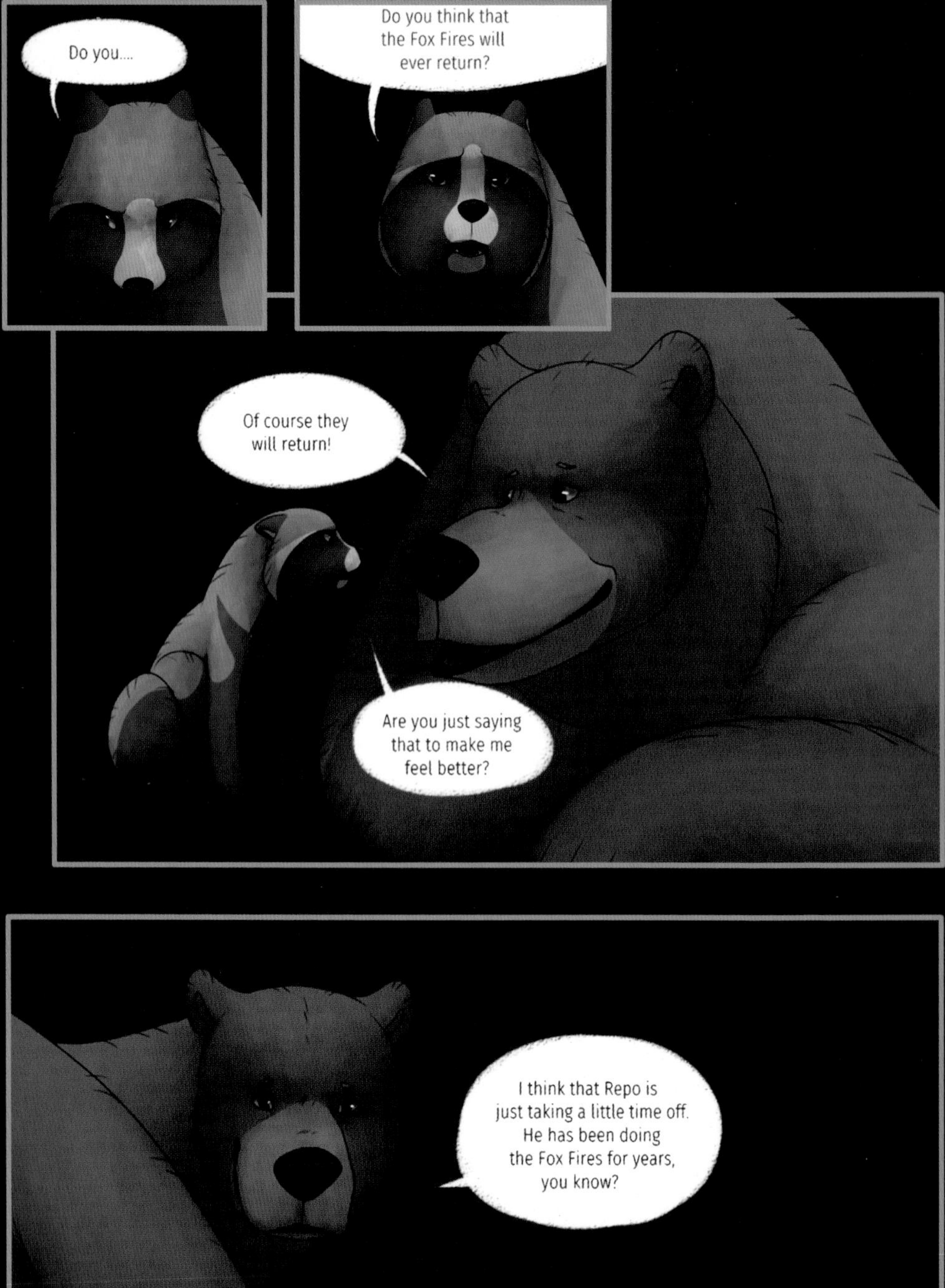
Do you....
Do you think that the Fox Fires will ever return?
Of course they will return!
Are you just saying that to make me feel better?
I think that Repo is just taking a little time off. He has been doing the Fox Fires for years, you know?

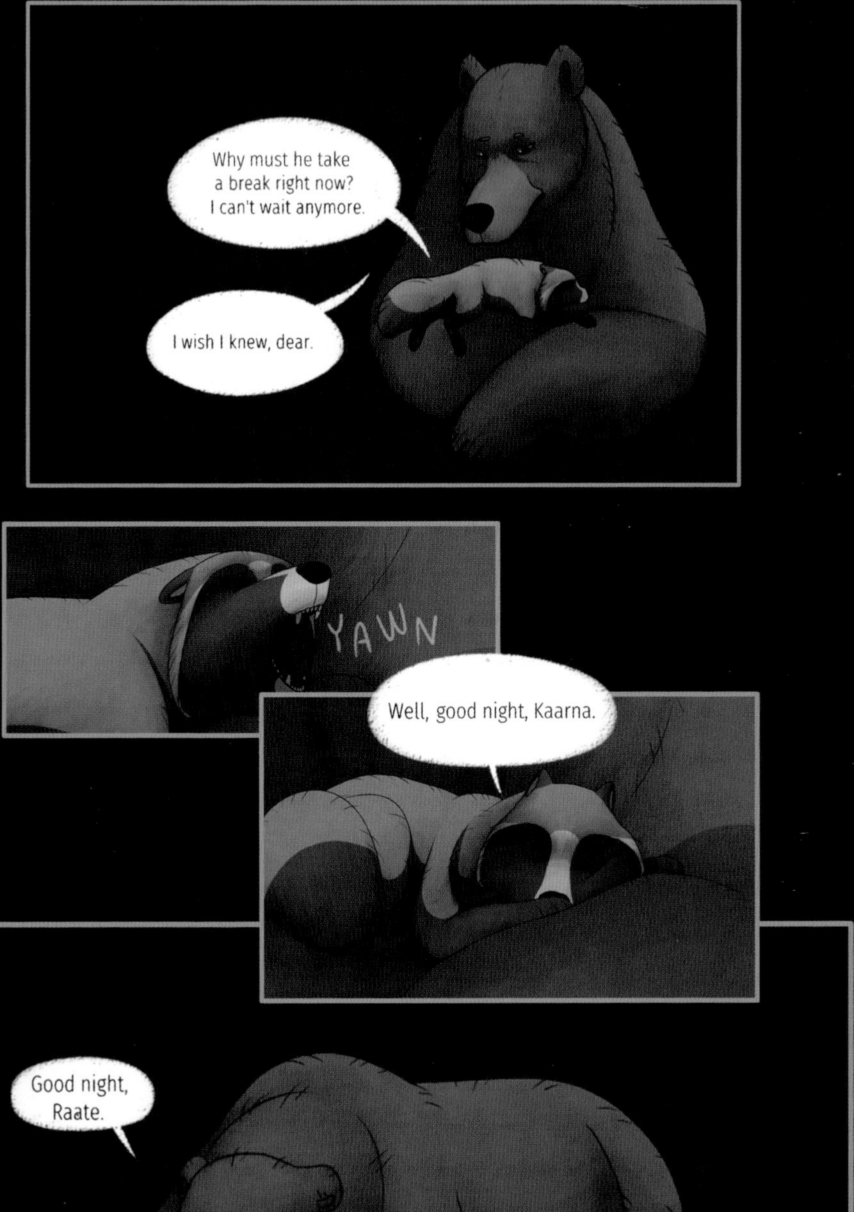
Why must he take a break right now? I can't wait anymore.
I wish I knew, dear.
YAWN
Well, good night, Kaarna.
Good night, Raate.

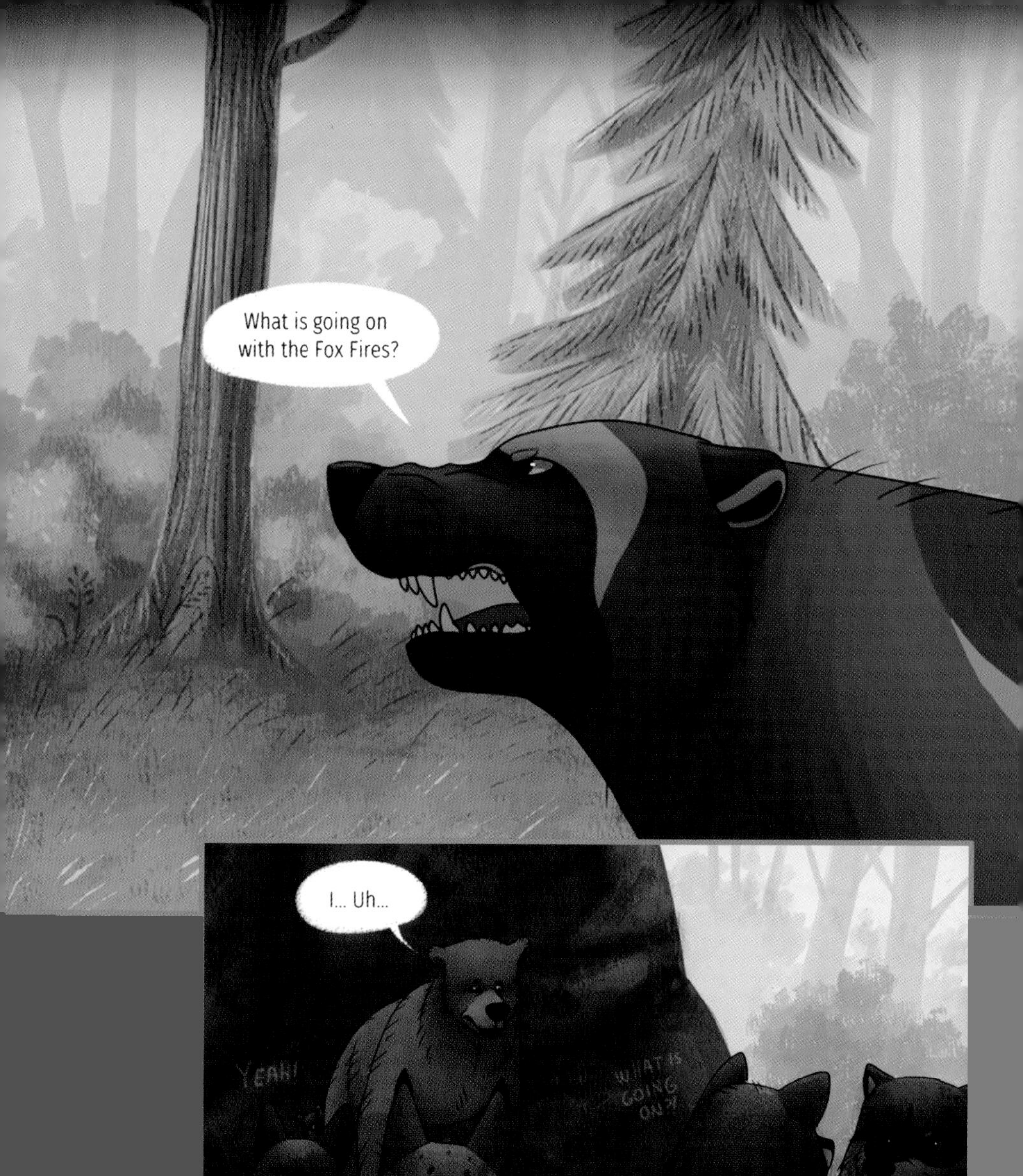
What is going on with the Fox Fires?
I... Uh...
YEAH!
WHAT IS GOING ON?!
THAT'S RIGHT!

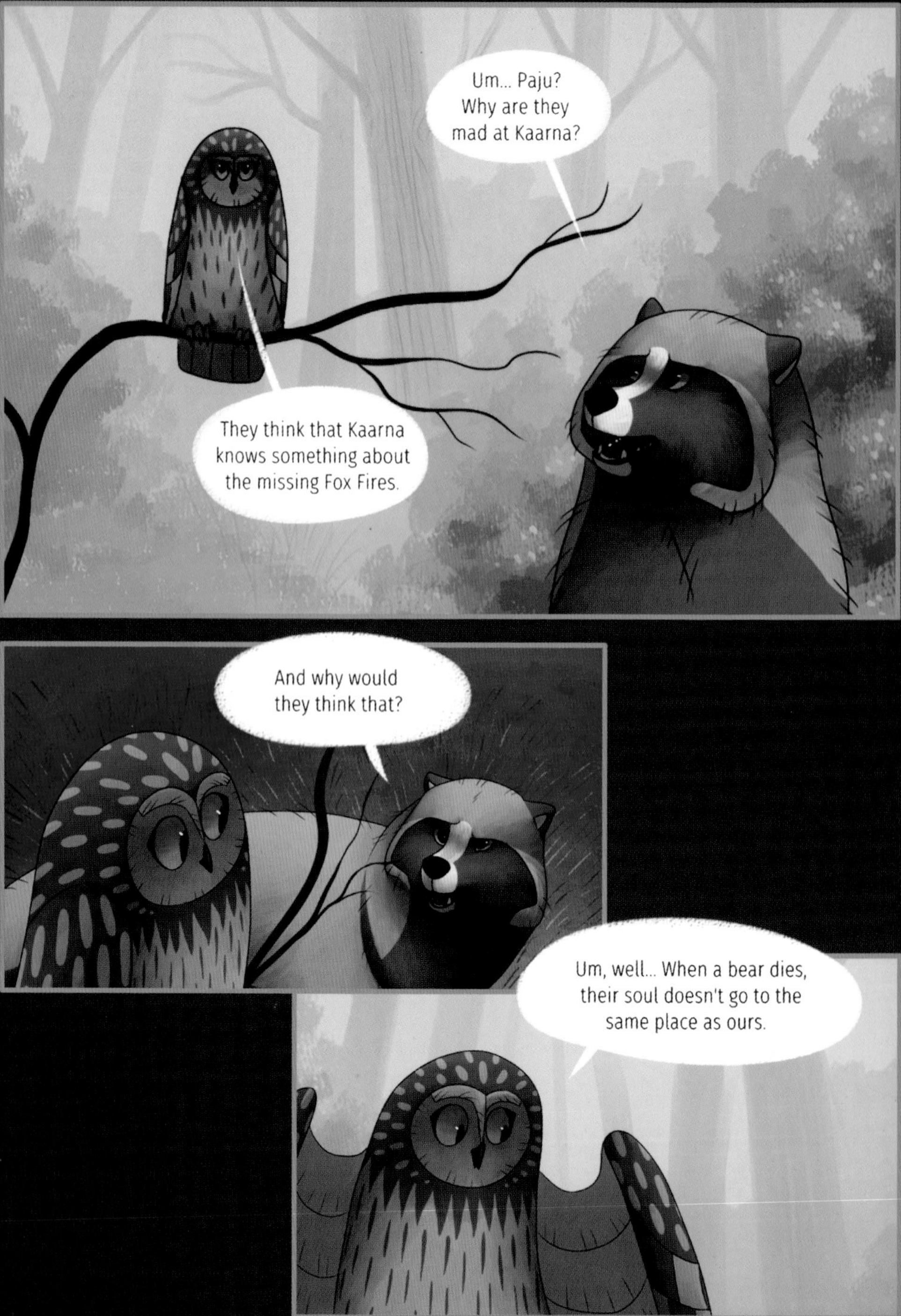
Um... Paju?
Why are they
mad at Kaarna?
They think that Kaarna
knows something about
the missing Fox Fires.
And why would
they think that?
Um, well... When a bear dies,
their soul doesn't go to the
same place as ours.

Since the first bear
was sent to the earth
by the gods themselves,

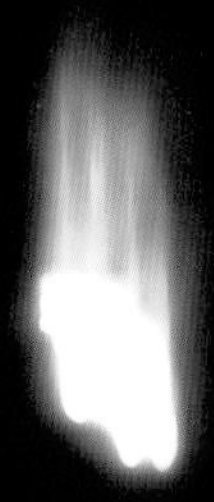

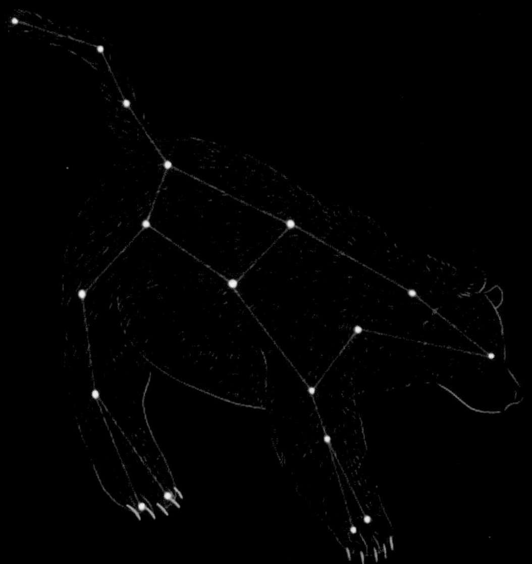

It's believed that
when they die, they
will return to the sky
and join the gods
once again.

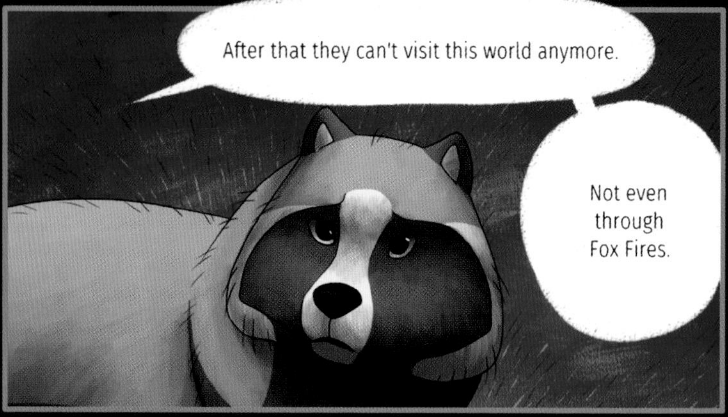
After that they can't visit this world anymore.
Not even through Fox Fires.

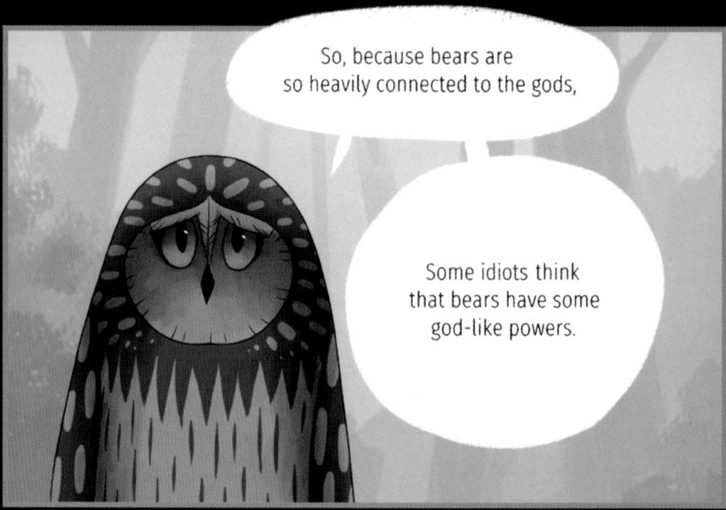
So, because bears are so heavily connected to the gods,
Some idiots think that bears have some god-like powers.

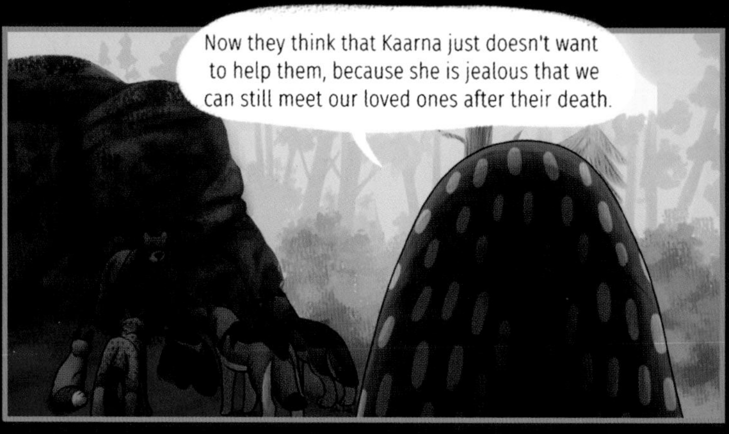
Now they think that Kaarna just doesn't want to help them, because she is jealous that we can still meet our loved ones after their death.

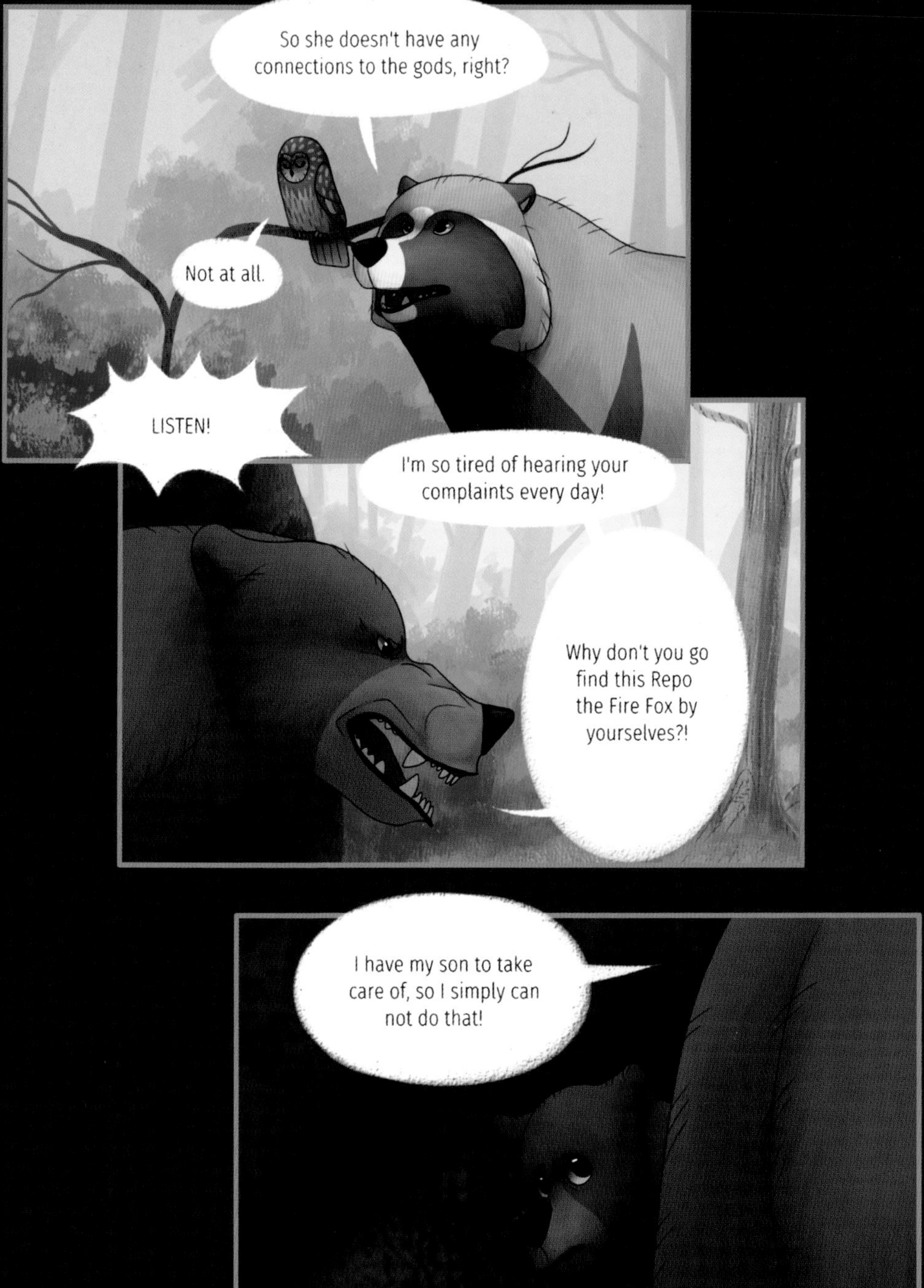
So she doesn't have any connections to the gods, right?
Not at all.
LISTEN!
I'm so tired of hearing your complaints every day!
Why don't you go find this Repo the Fire Fox by yourselves?!
I have my son to take care of, so I simply can not do that!

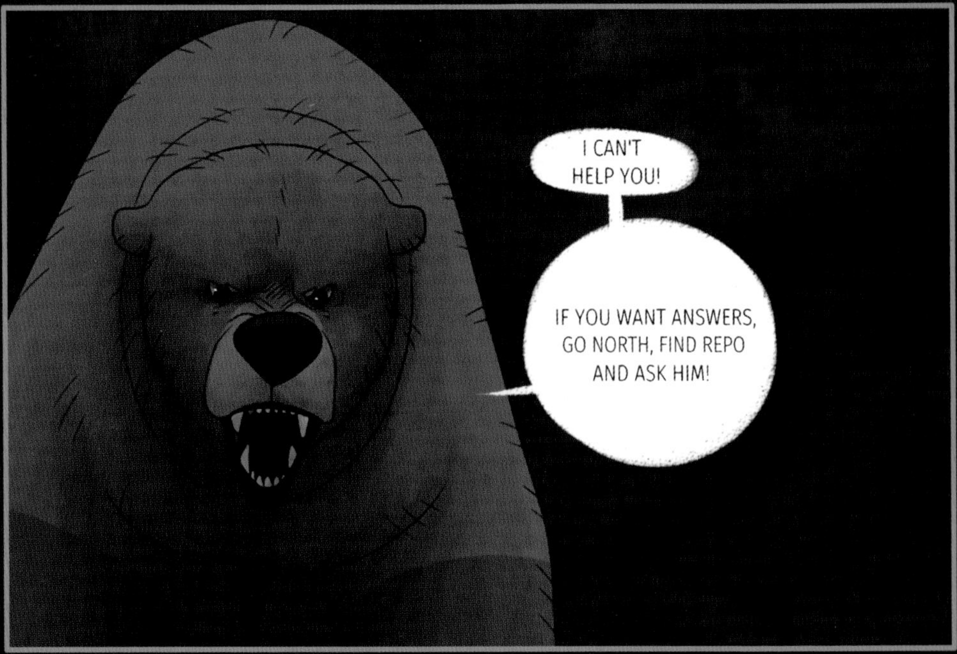
I CAN'T HELP YOU!
IF YOU WANT ANSWERS, GO NORTH, FIND REPO AND ASK HIM!

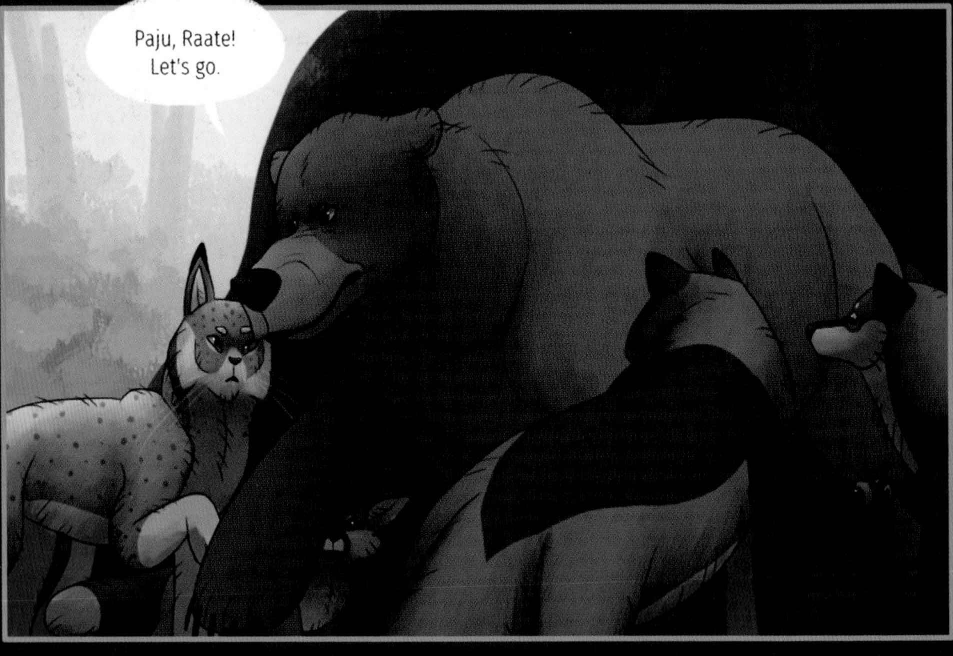
Paju, Raate! Let's go.

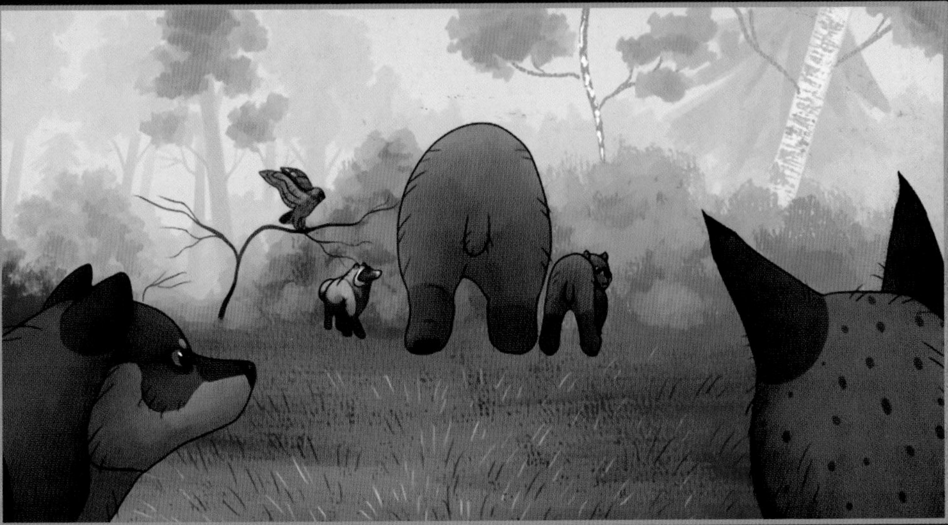

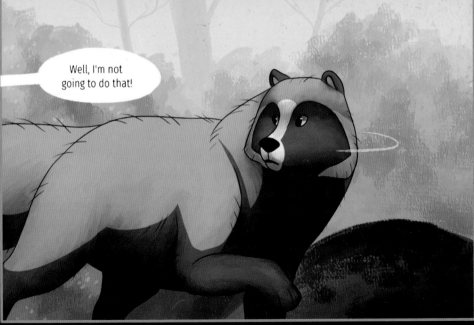

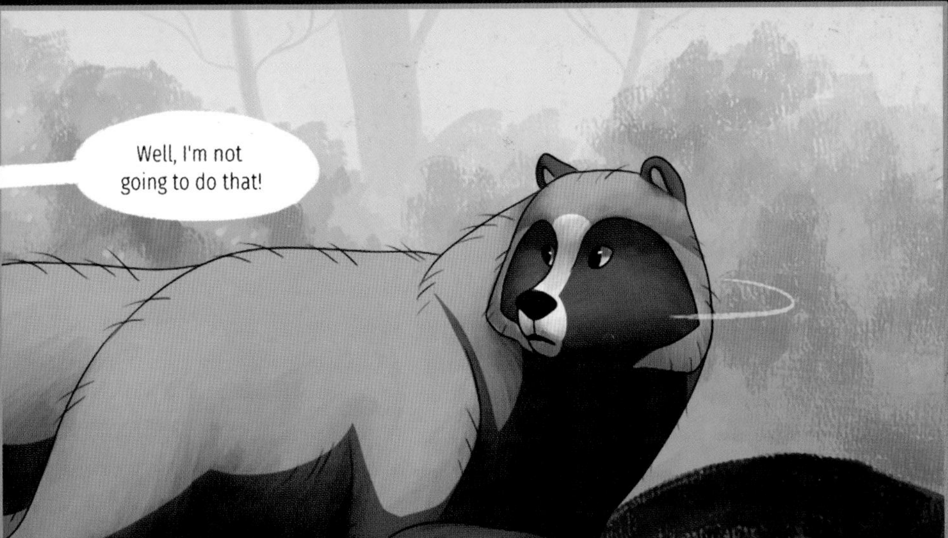
Well, I'm not going to do that!

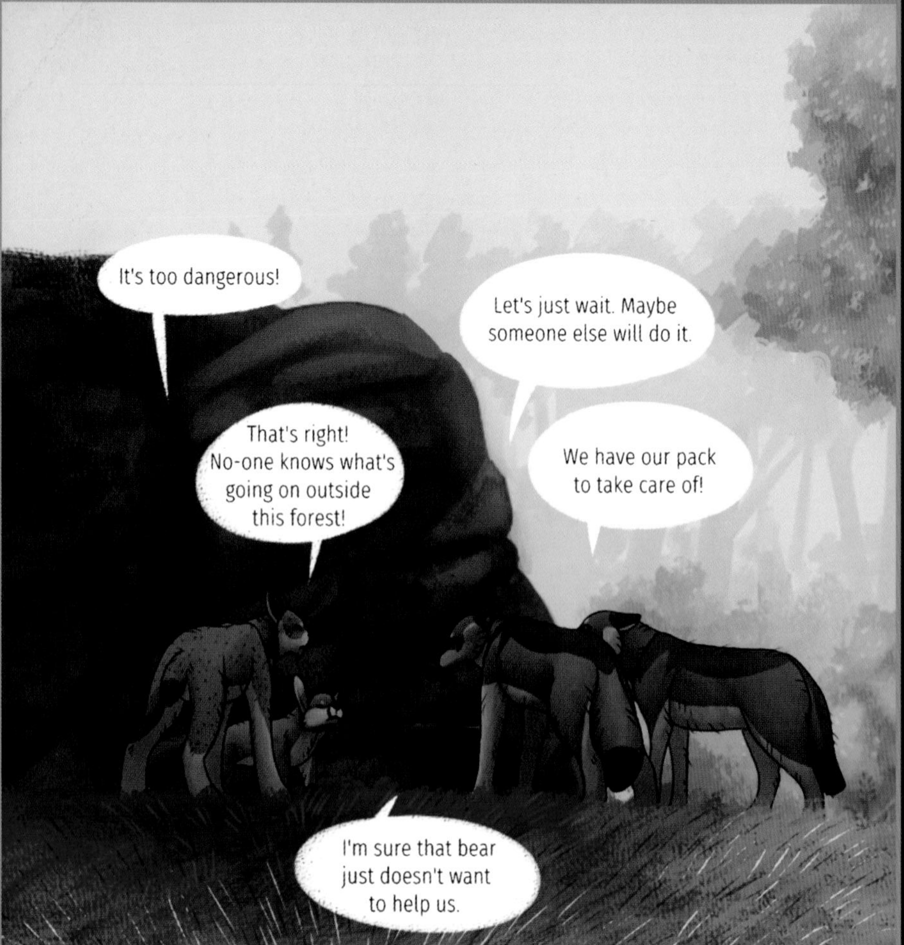
It's too dangerous!
Let's just wait. Maybe someone else will do it.
That's right! No-one knows what's going on outside this forest!
We have our pack to take care of!
I'm sure that bear just doesn't want to help us.

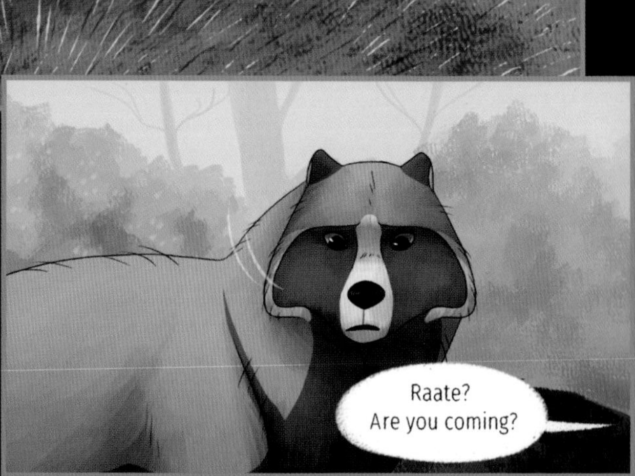
Raate? Are you coming?

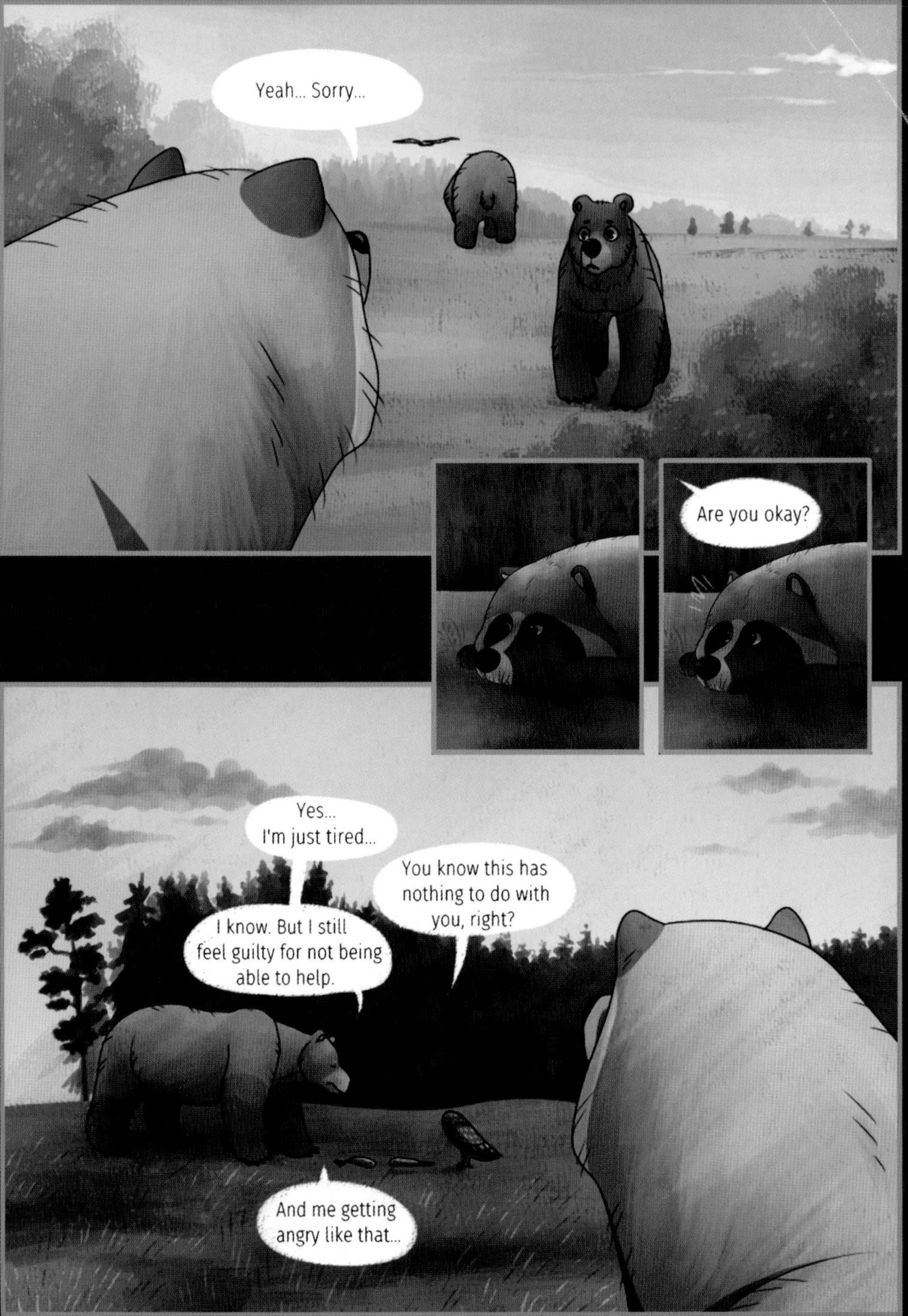
Yeah... Sorry...
Are you okay?
Yes...
I'm just tired...
You know this has nothing to do with you, right?
I know. But I still feel guilty for not being able to help.
And me getting angry like that...

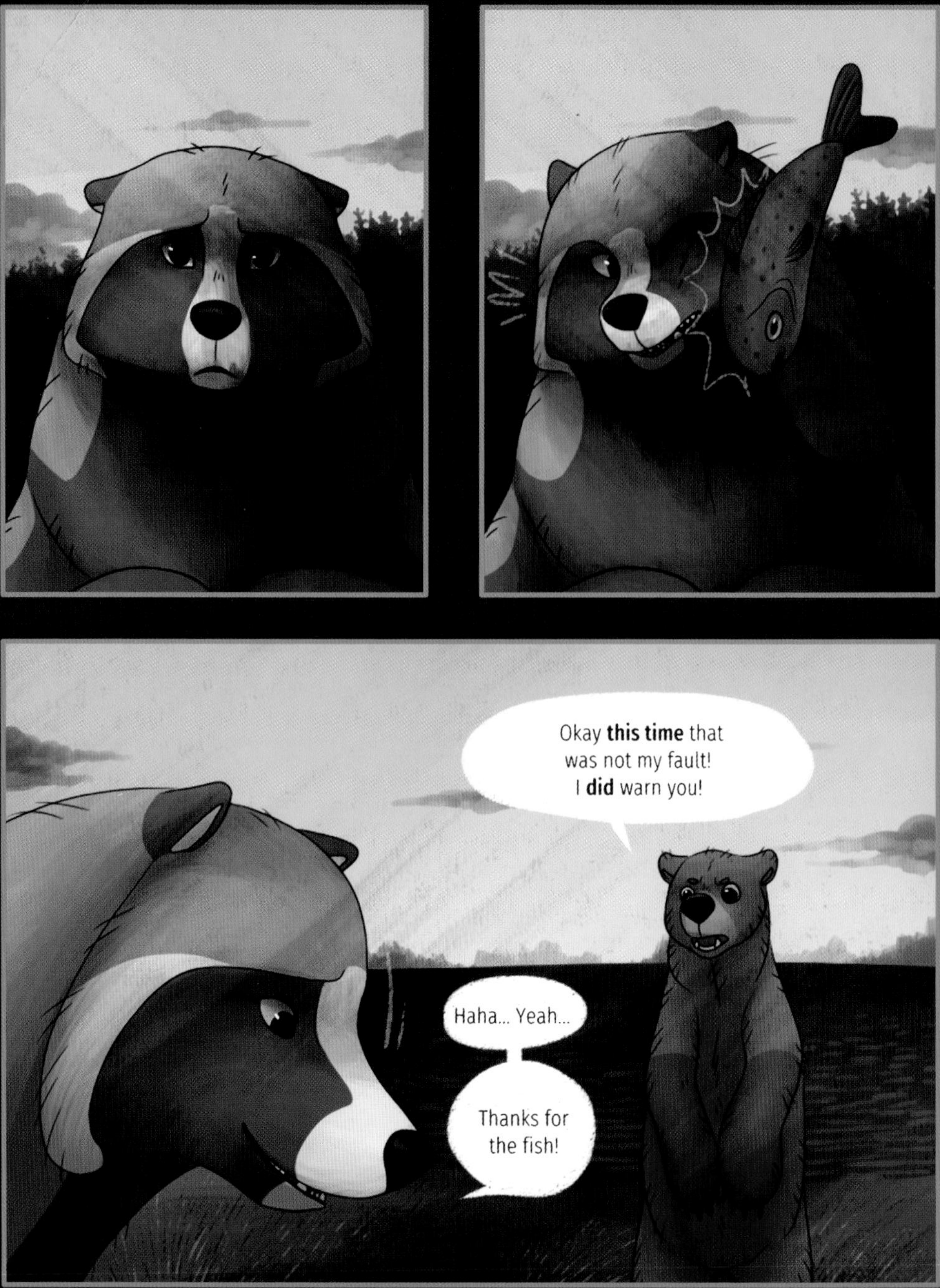

Okay **this time** that was not my fault! I **did** warn you!
Haha... Yeah...
Thanks for the fish!

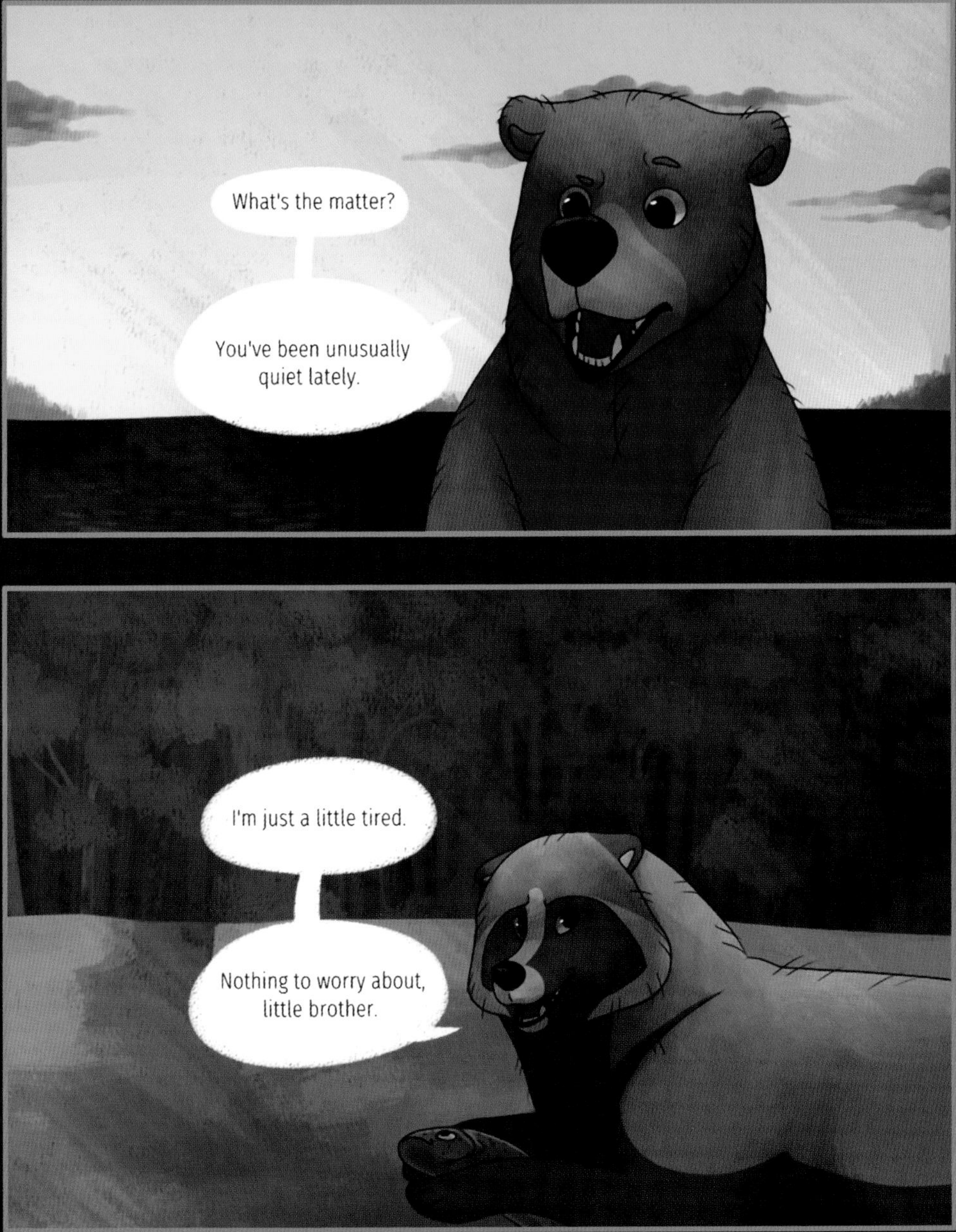
What's the matter?
You've been unusually quiet lately.
I'm just a little tired.
Nothing to worry about, little brother.

Chapter 9

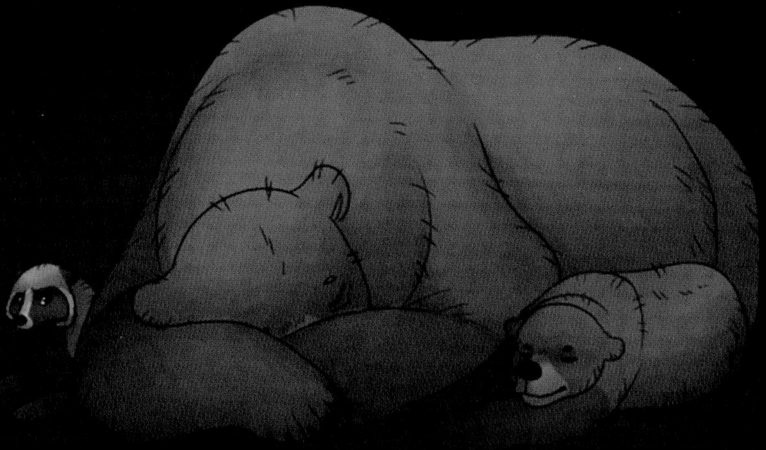

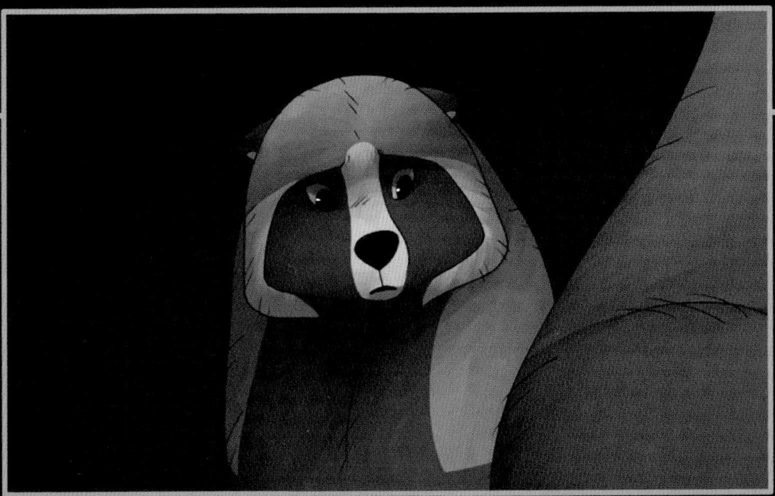

Are you leaving?

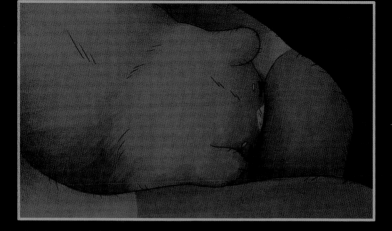

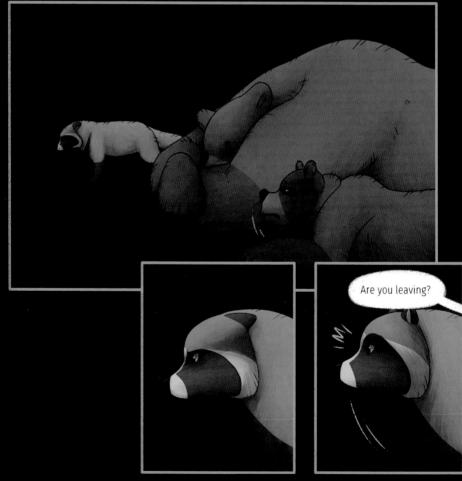

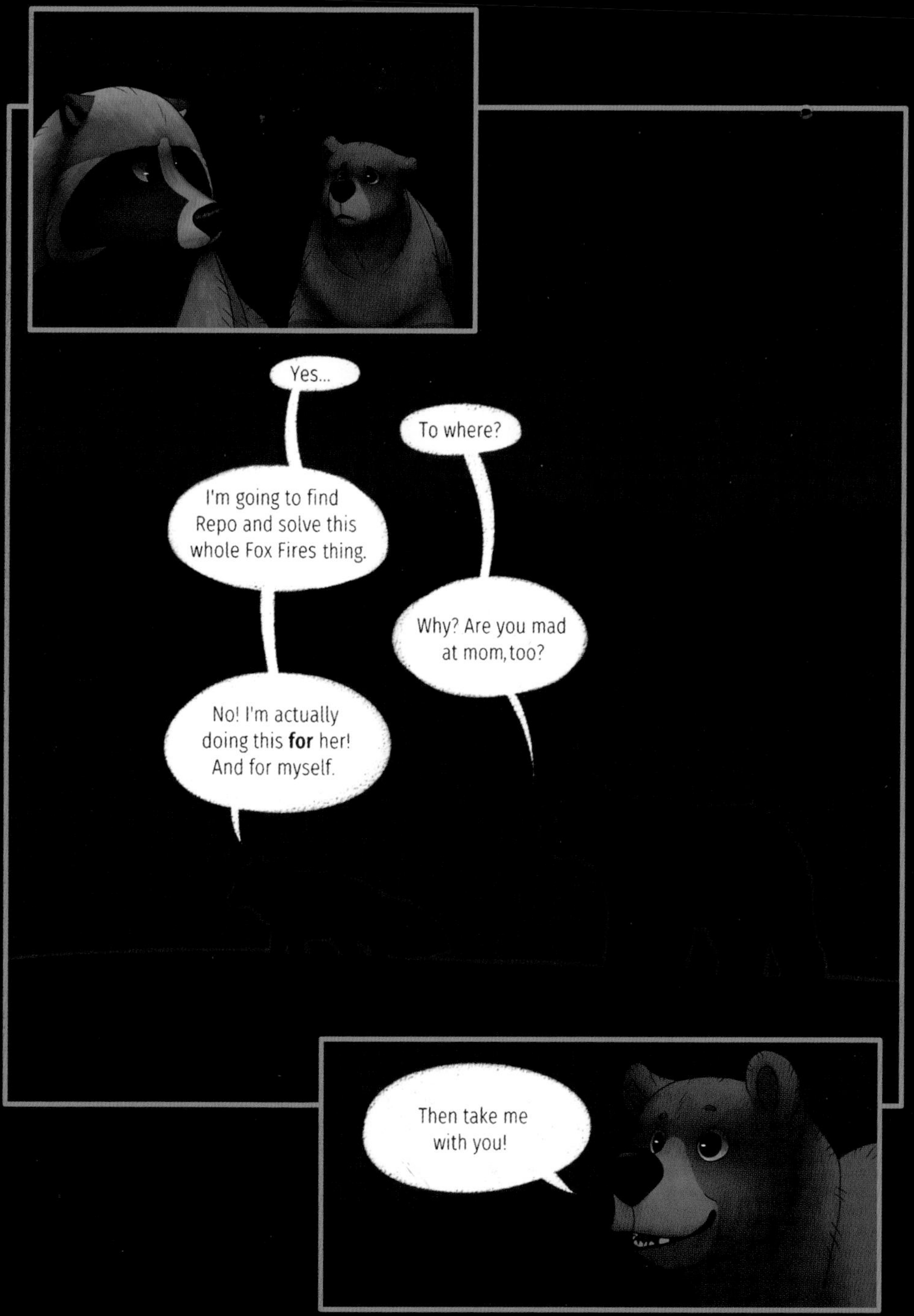
Yes...
To where?
I'm going to find Repo and solve this whole Fox Fires thing.
Why? Are you mad at mom, too?
No! I'm actually doing this **for** her! And for myself.
Then take me with you!

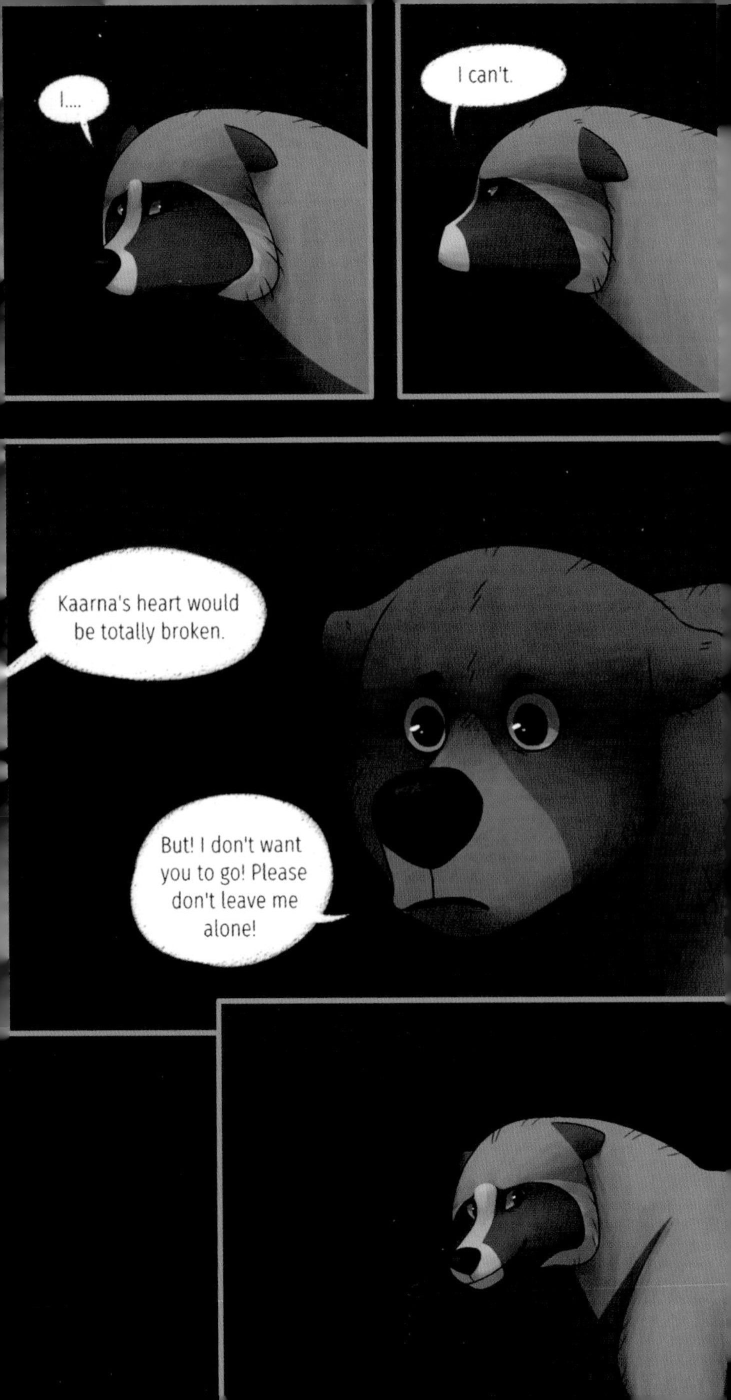
I....
I can't.
Kaarna's heart would be totally broken.
But! I don't want you to go! Please don't leave me alone!

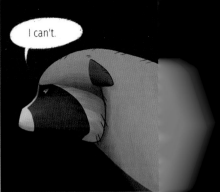

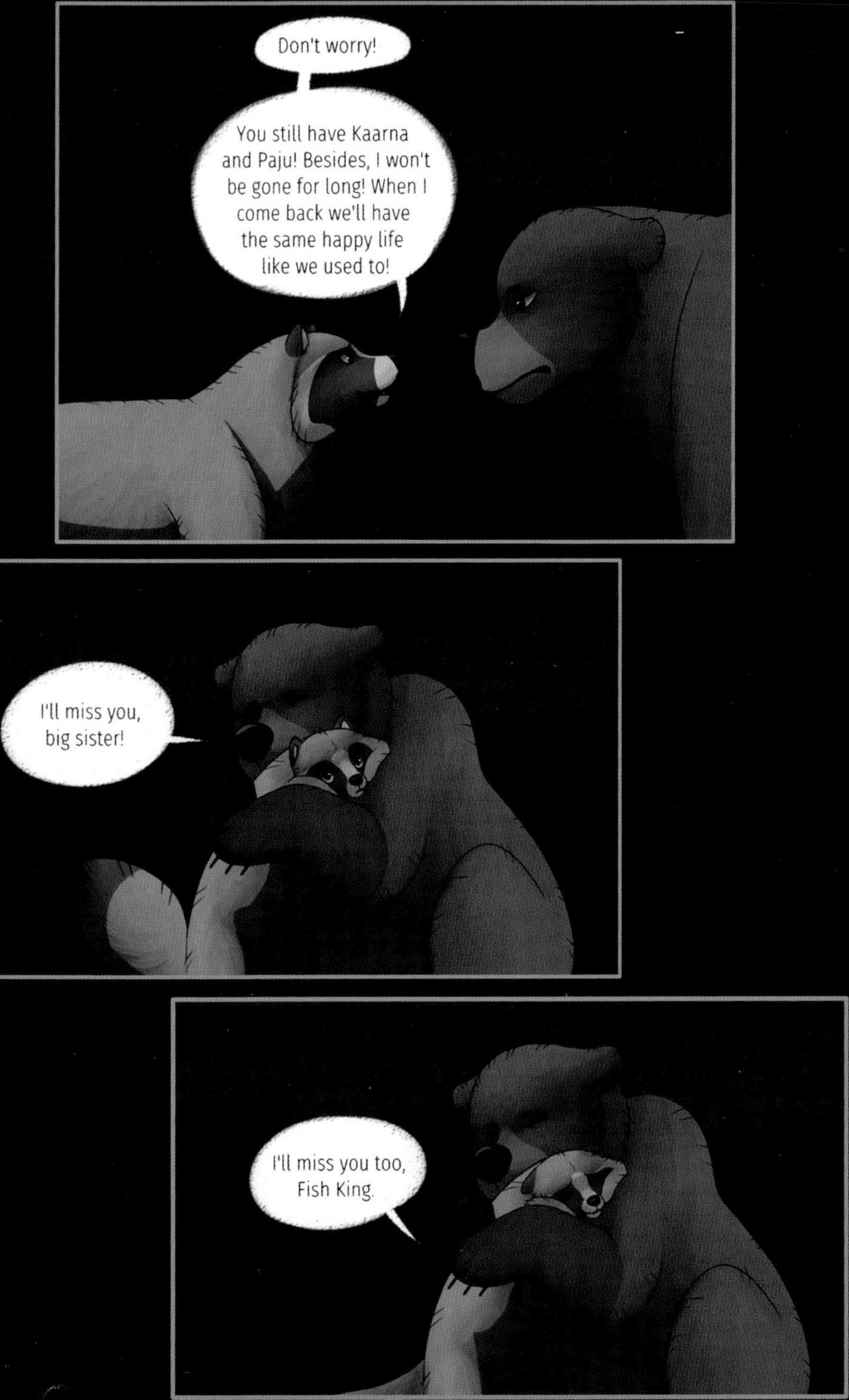
Don't worry!
You still have Kaarna and Paju! Besides, I won't be gone for long! When I come back we'll have the same happy life like we used to!
I'll miss you, big sister!
I'll miss you too, Fish King.

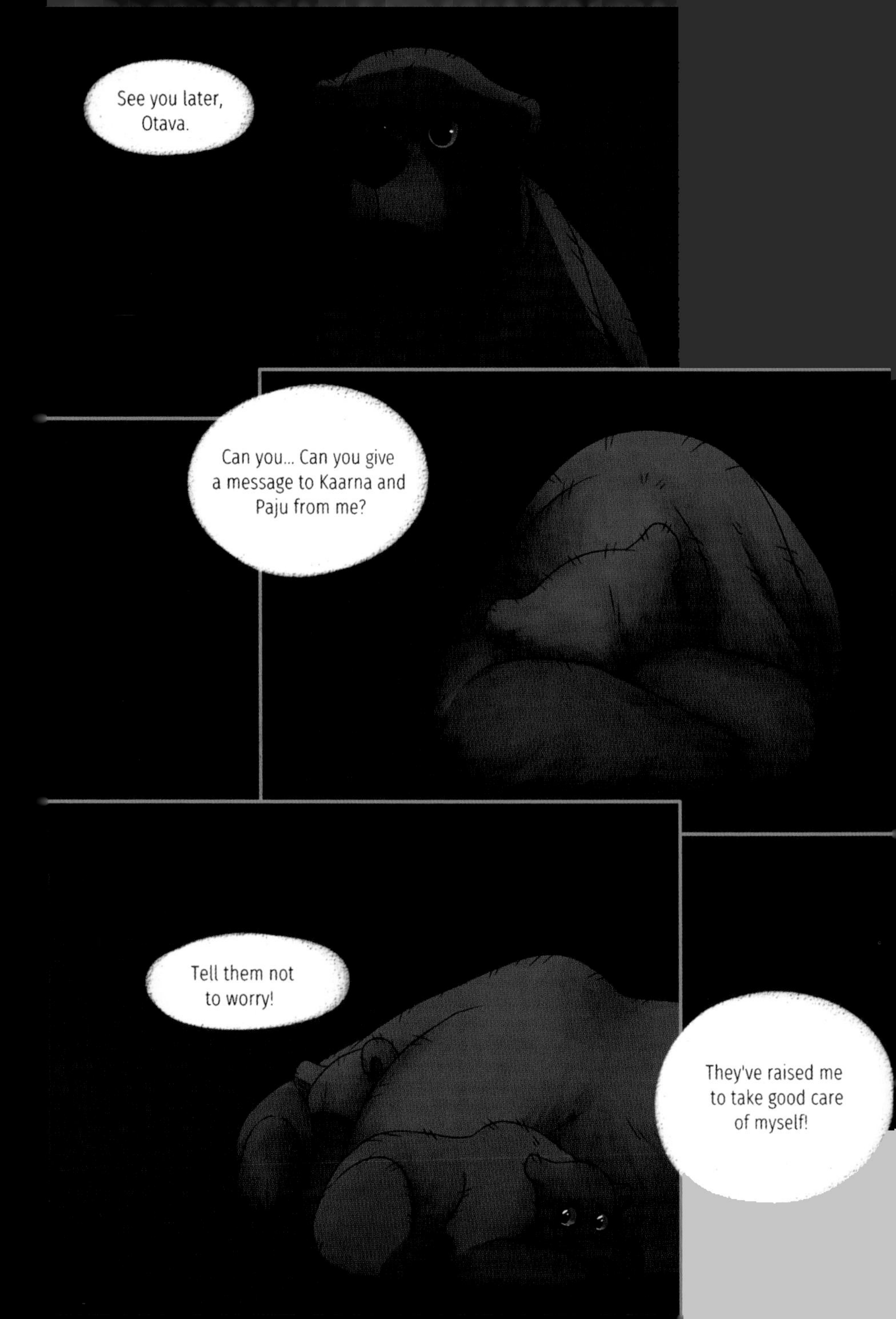
See you later, Otava.
Can you... Can you give a message to Kaarna and Paju from me?
Tell them not to worry!
They've raised me to take good care of myself!

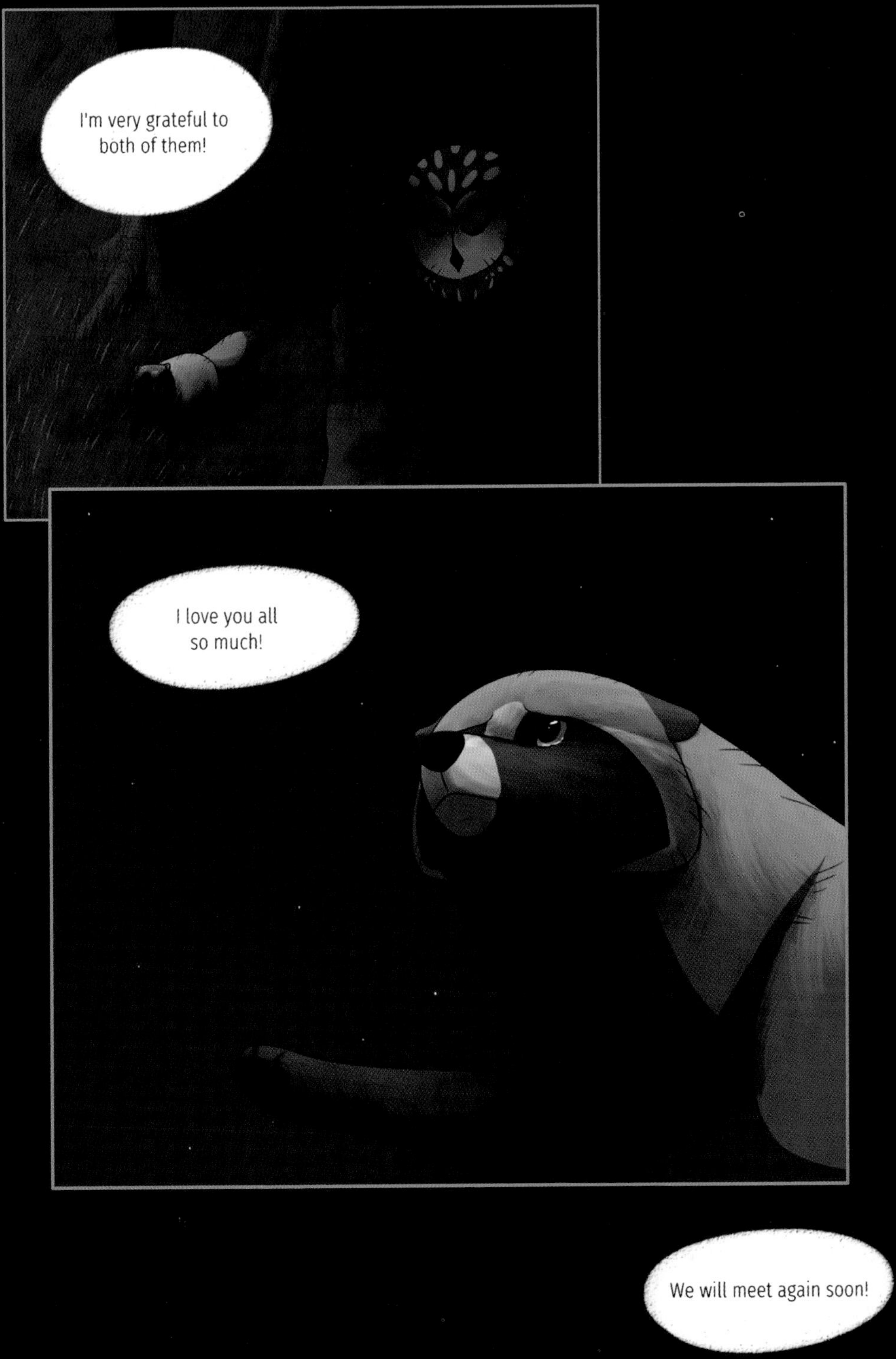
I'm very grateful to both of them!
I love you all so much!
We will meet again soon!

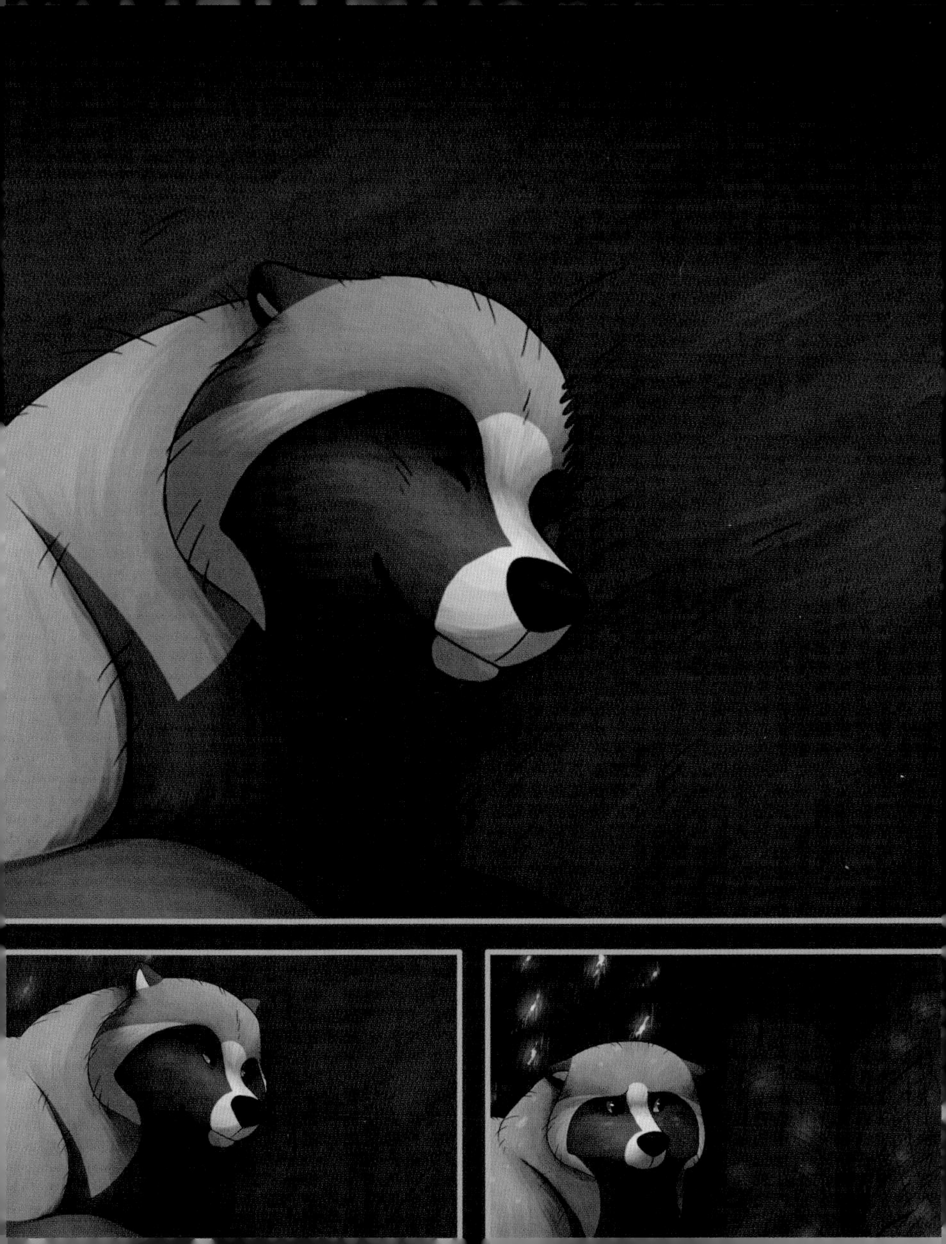

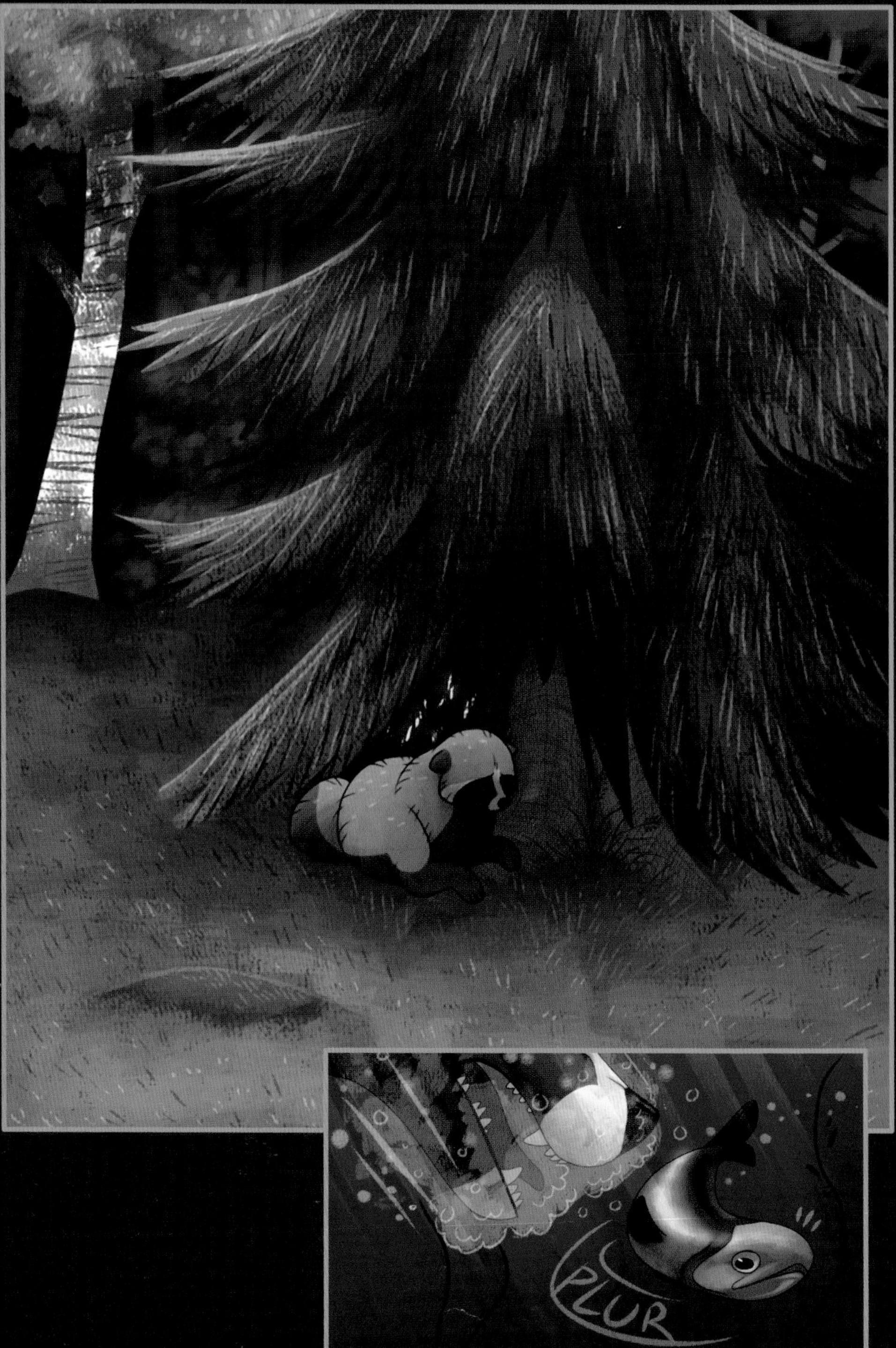
PLUR

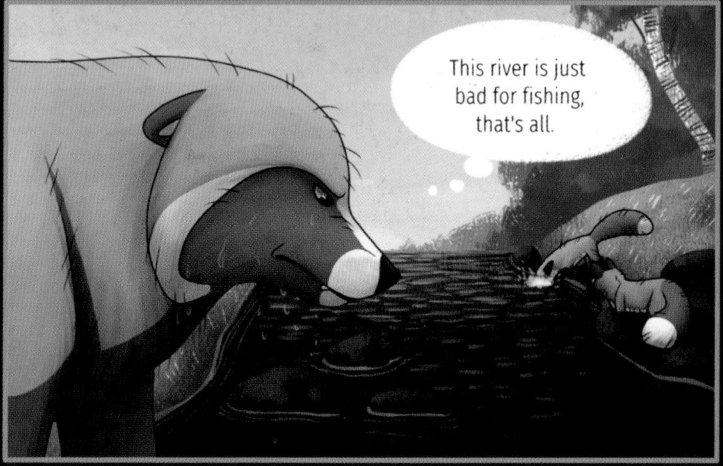
This river is just bad for fishing, that's all.

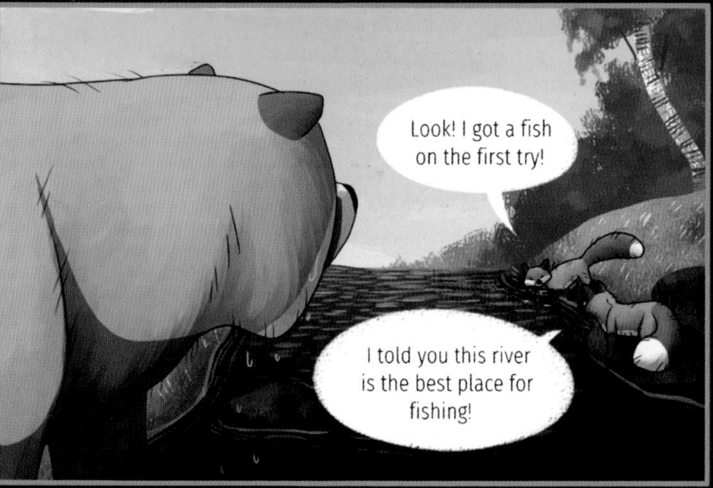
Look! I got a fish on the first try!
I told you this river is the best place for fishing!

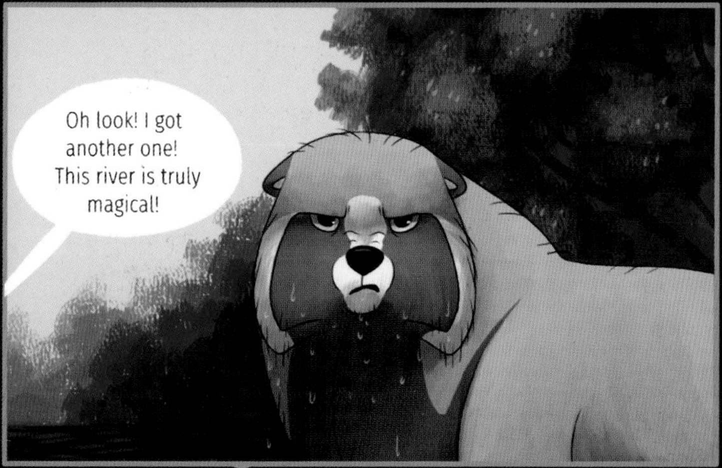
Oh look! I got another one! This river is truly magical!

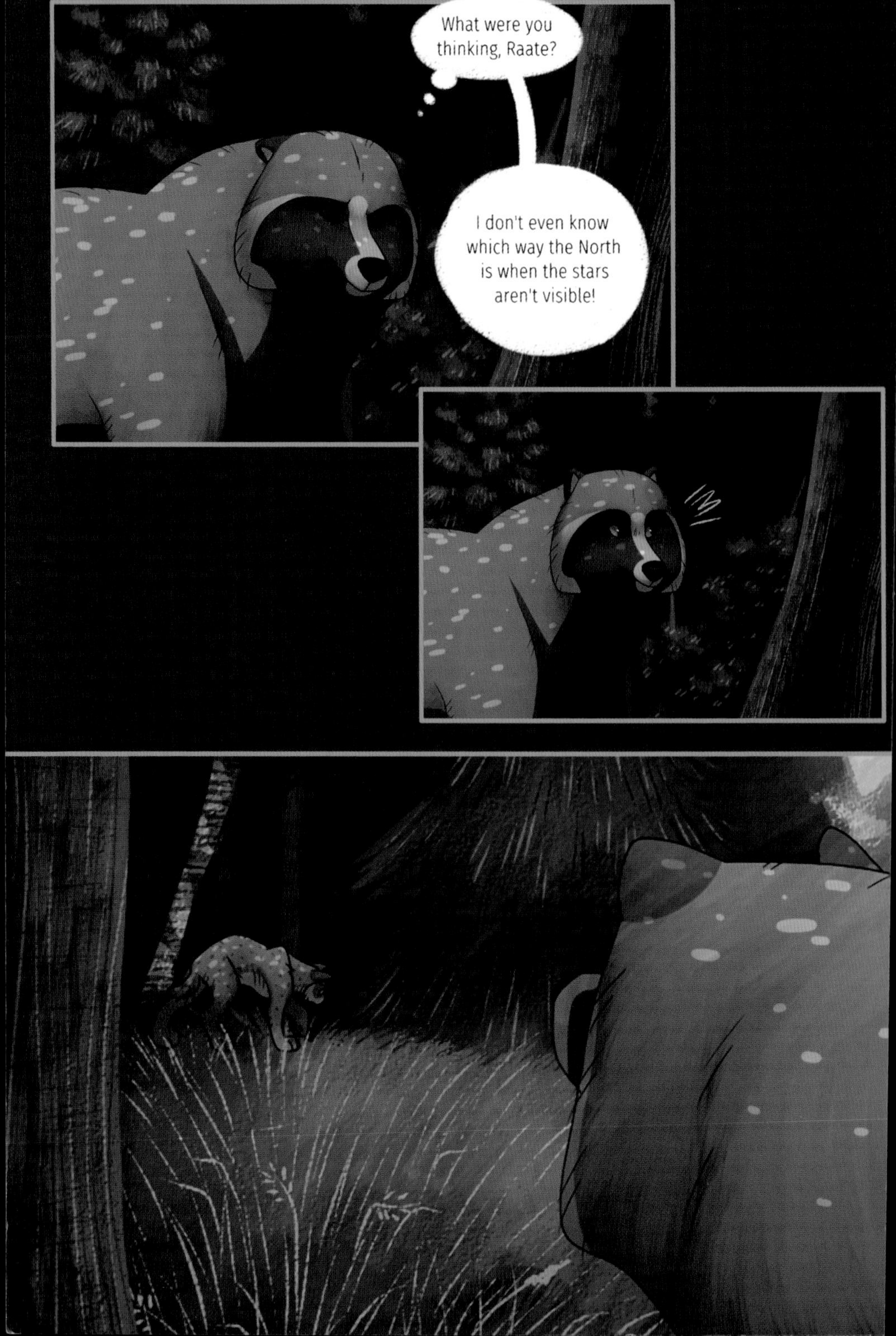
What were you thinking, Raate?
I don't even know which way the North is when the stars aren't visible!

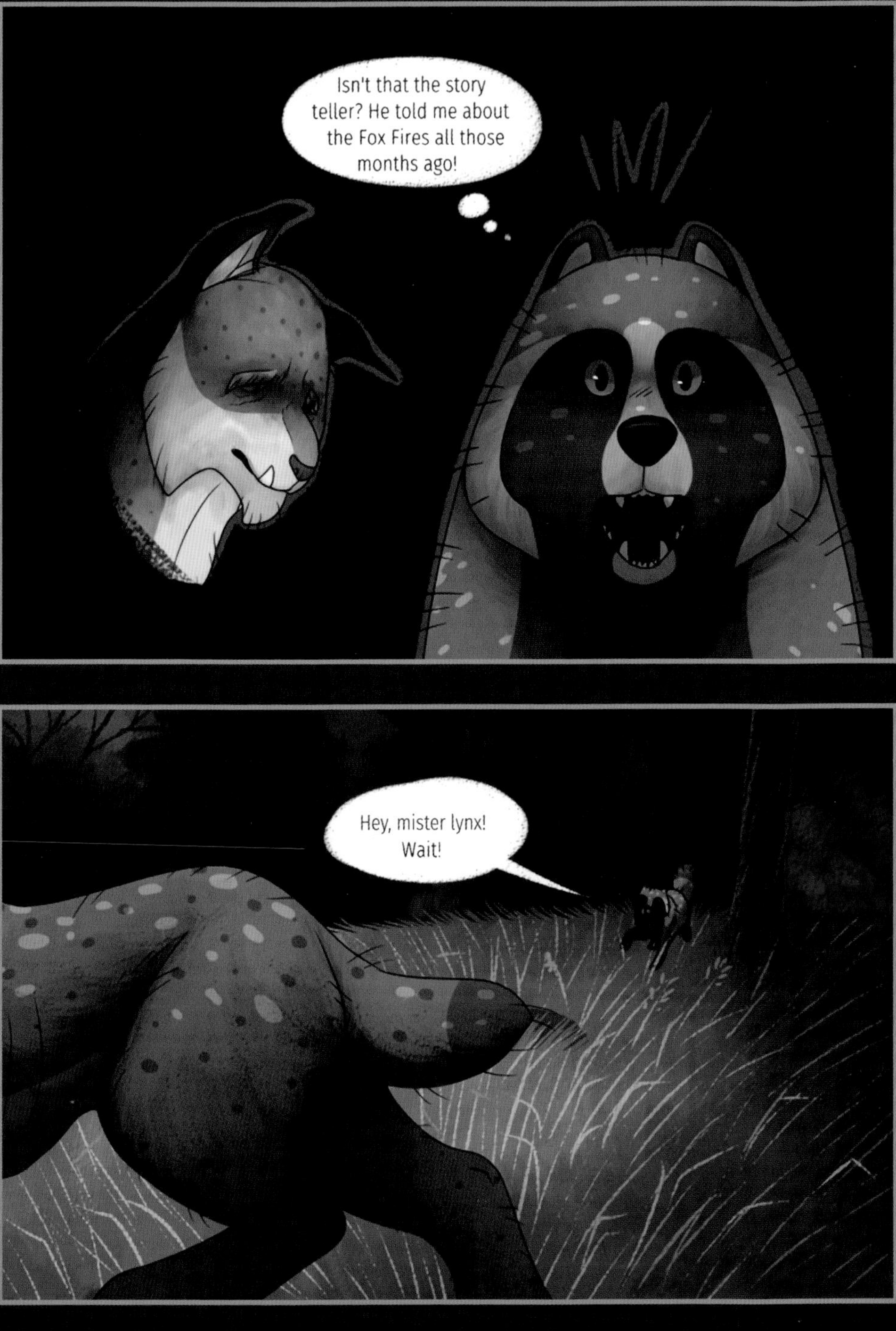
Isn't that the story teller? He told me about the Fox Fires all those months ago!
Hey, mister lynx! Wait!

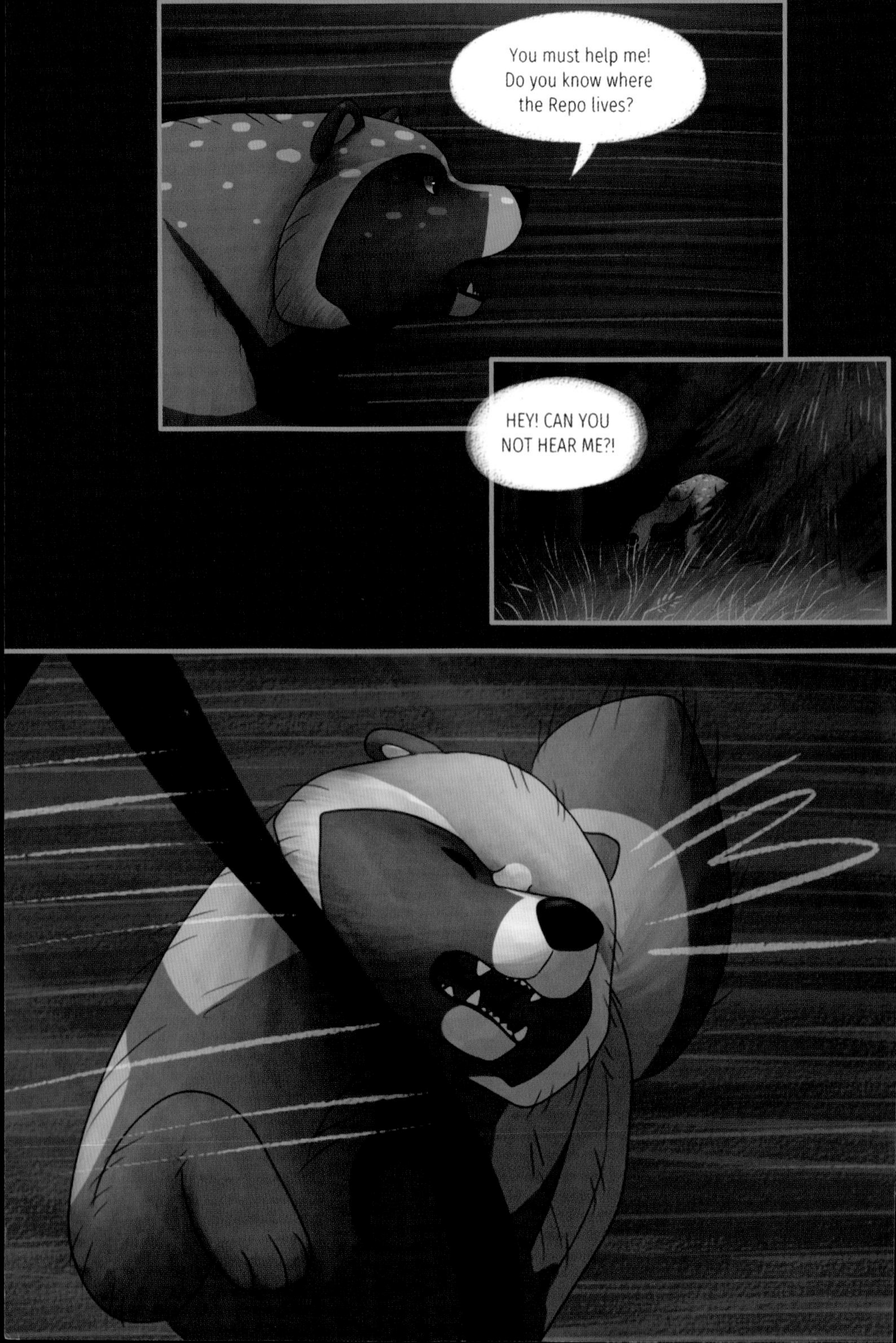
You must help me! Do you know where the Repo lives?
HEY! CAN YOU NOT HEAR ME?!

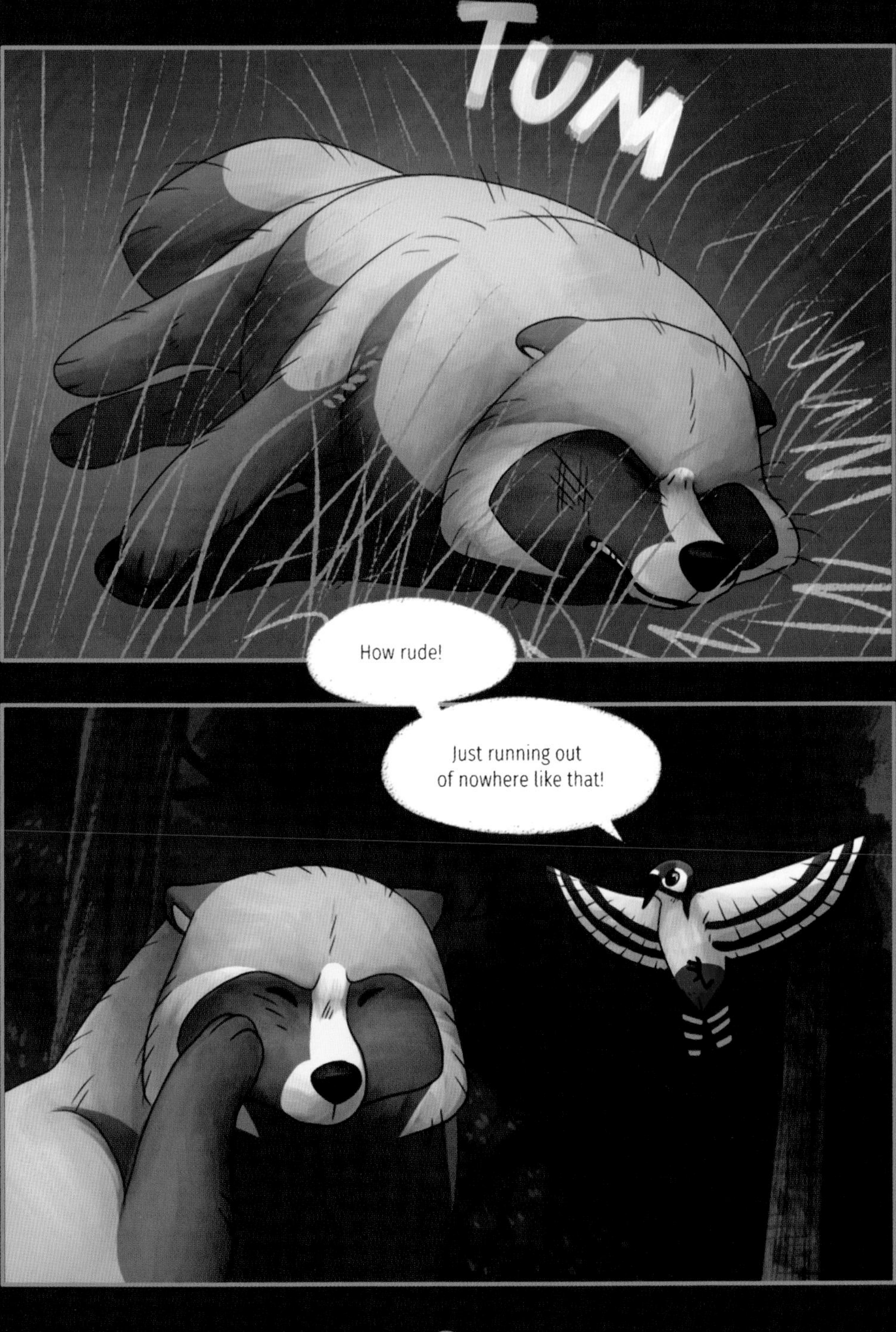
TUM
How rude!
Just running out
of nowhere like that!

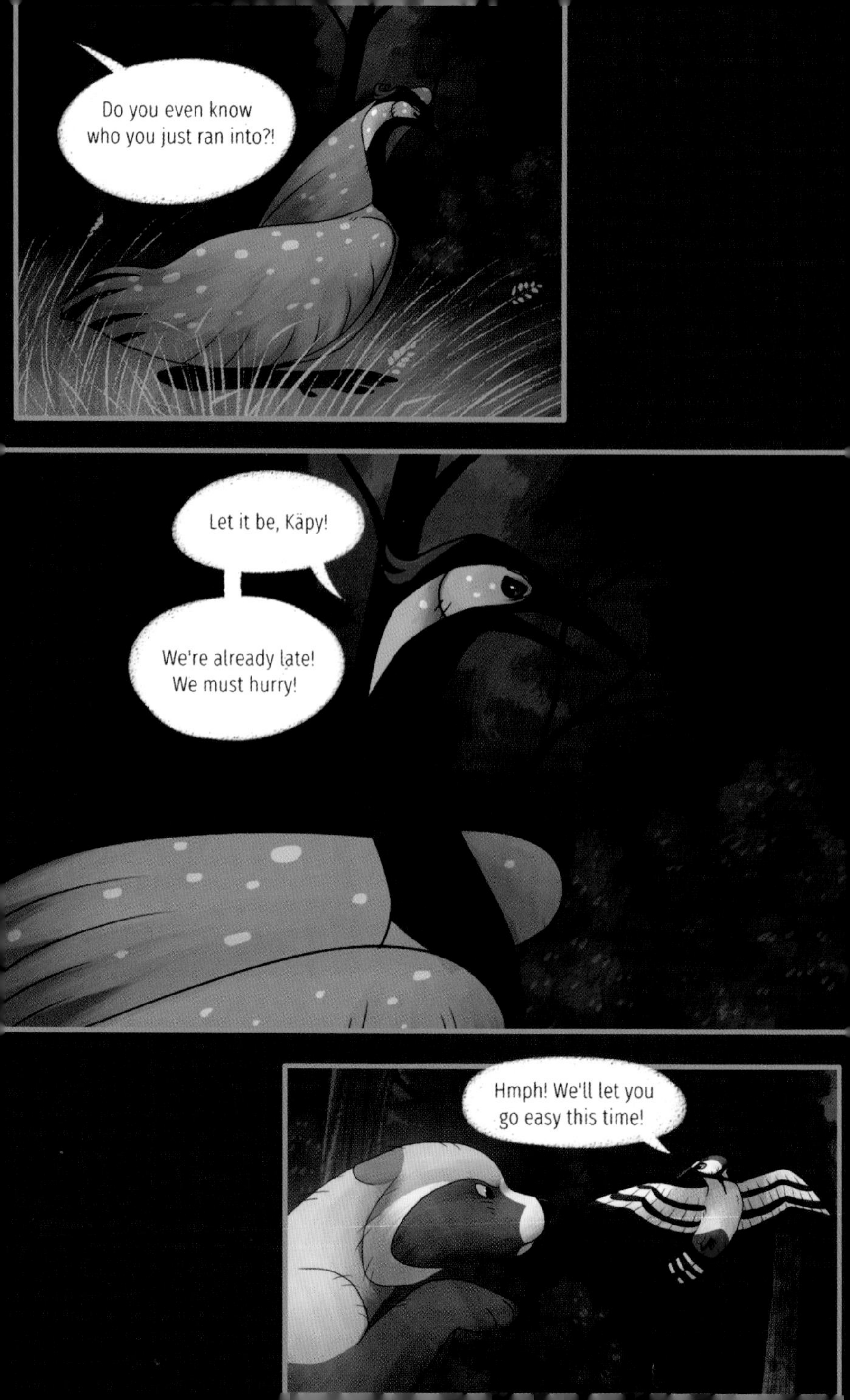
Do you even know who you just ran into?!
Let it be, Käpy!
We're already late! We must hurry!
Hmph! We'll let you go easy this time!

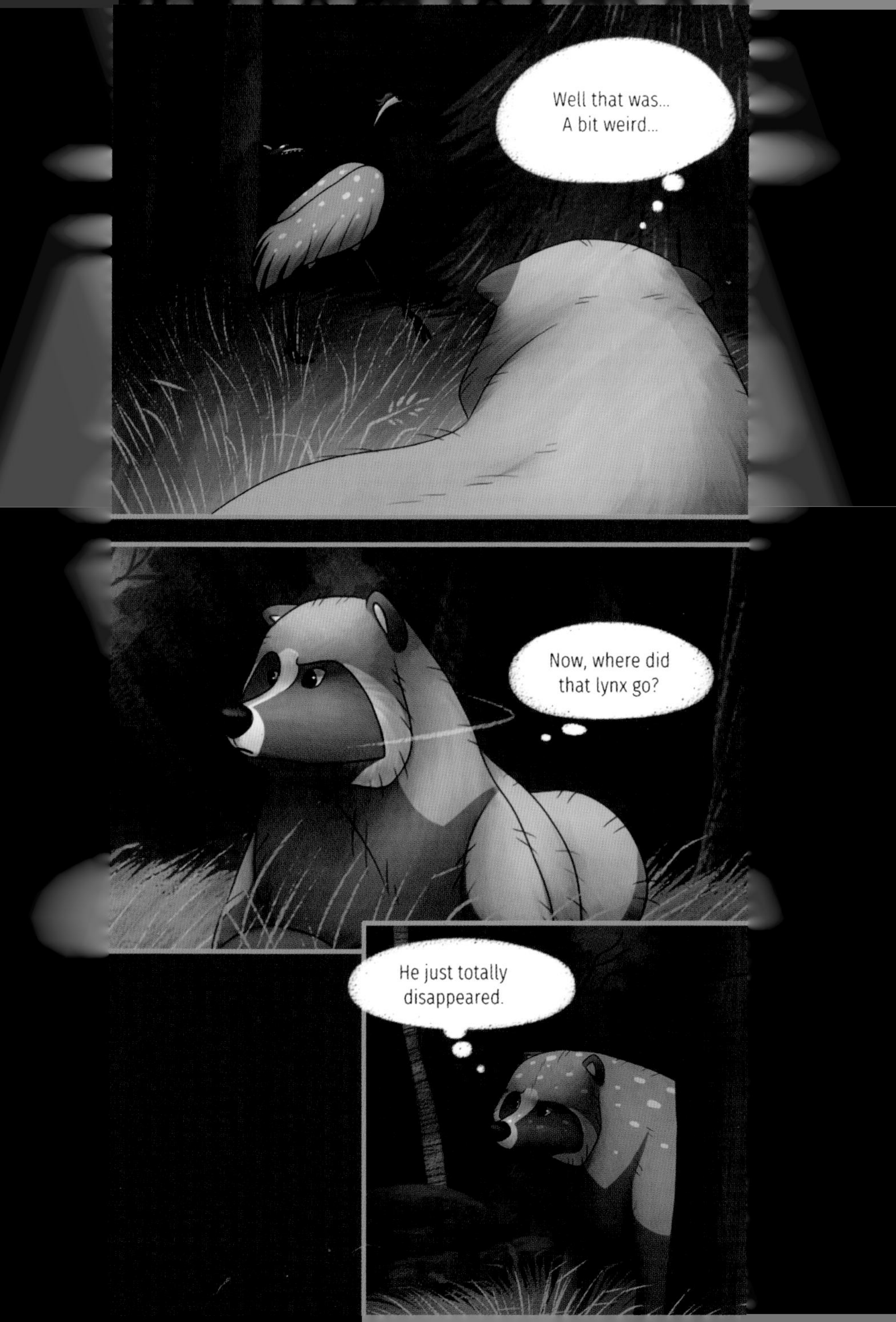
Well that was...
A bit weird...
Now, where did that lynx go?
He just totally disappeared.

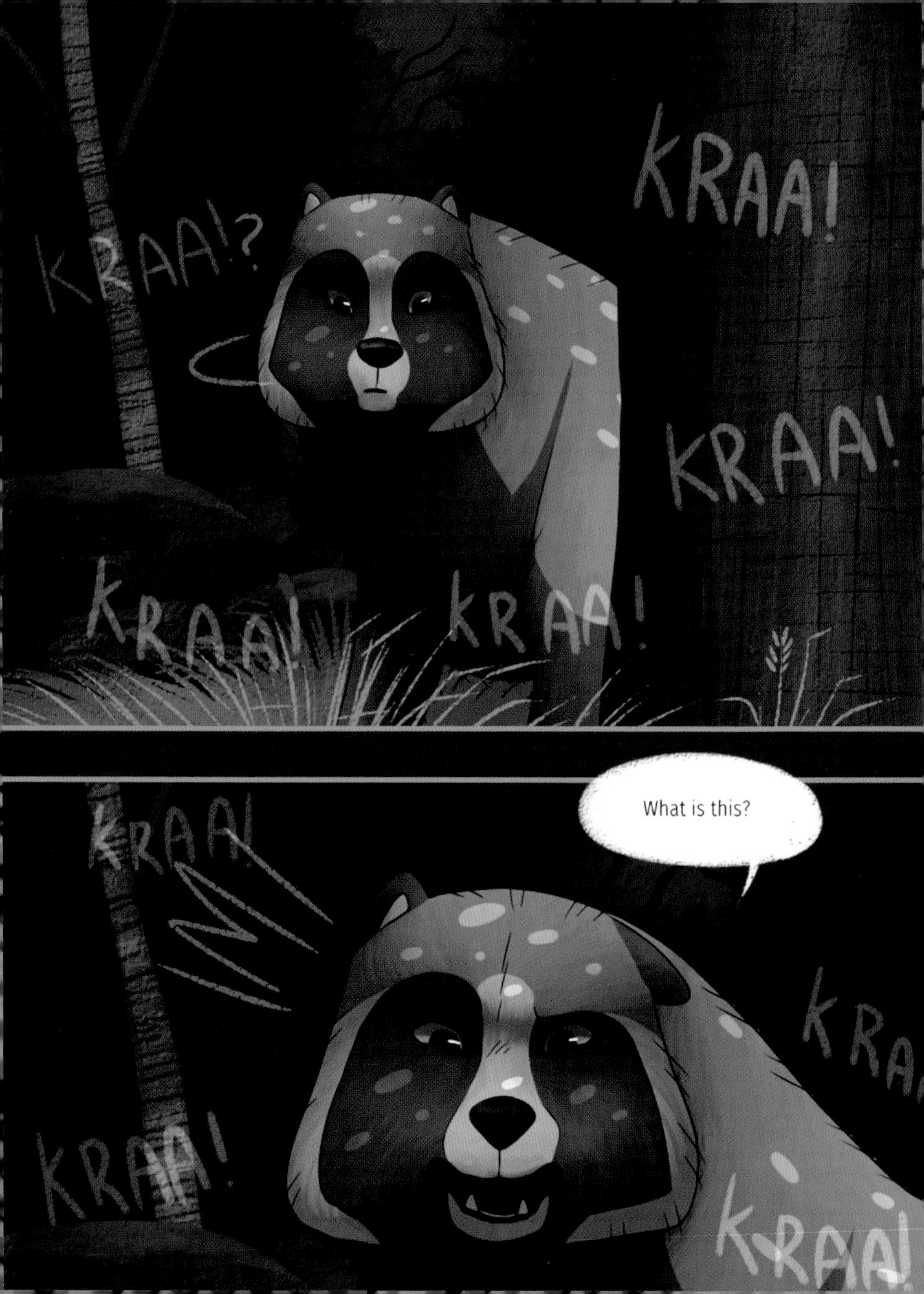
KRAA!?
KRAA!
KRAA!
KRAA!
KRAA!
KRAA!
What is this?
KRAA!
KRAA!

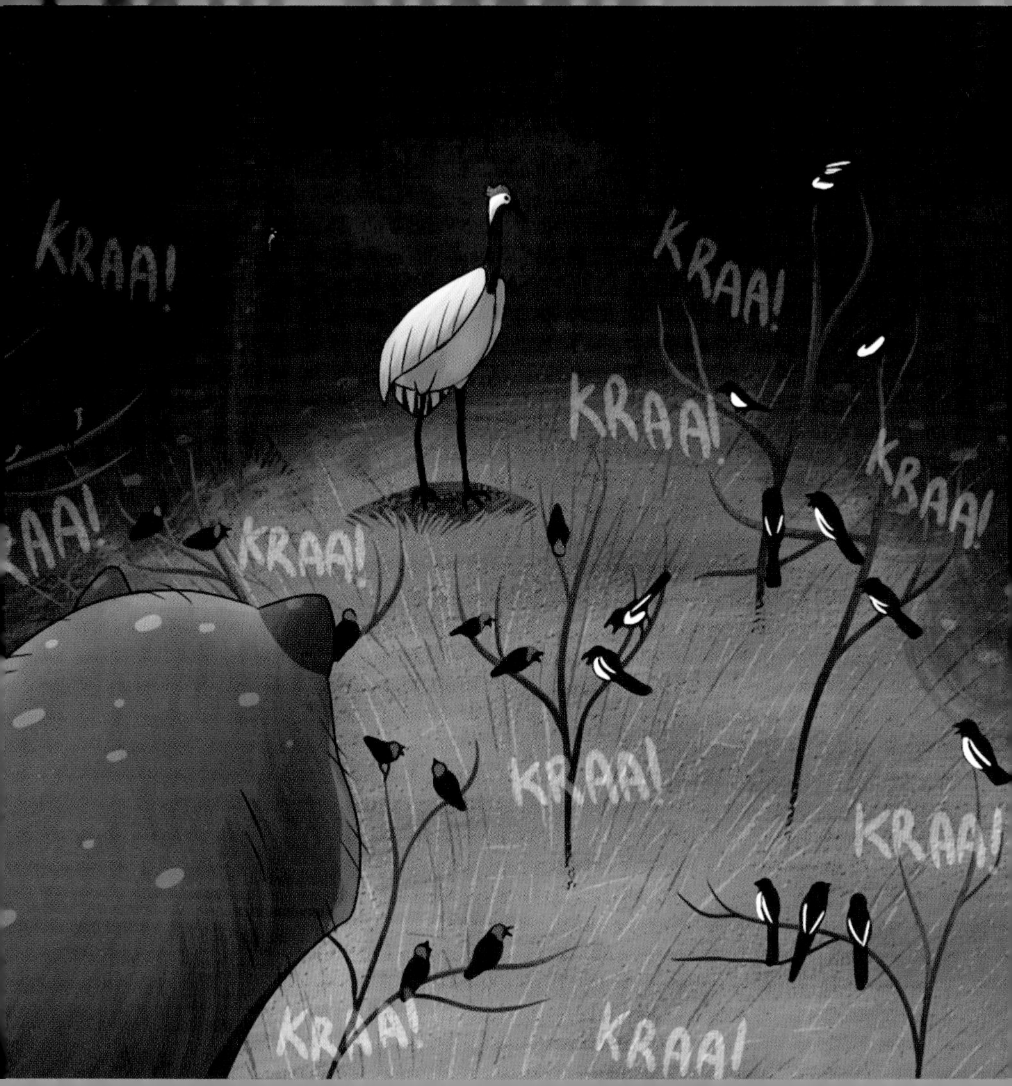
KRAA!
KRAA!
KRAA!
KRAA!
RAA!
KRAA!
KRAA!
KRAA!
KRAA!
KRAA!

Chapter 11

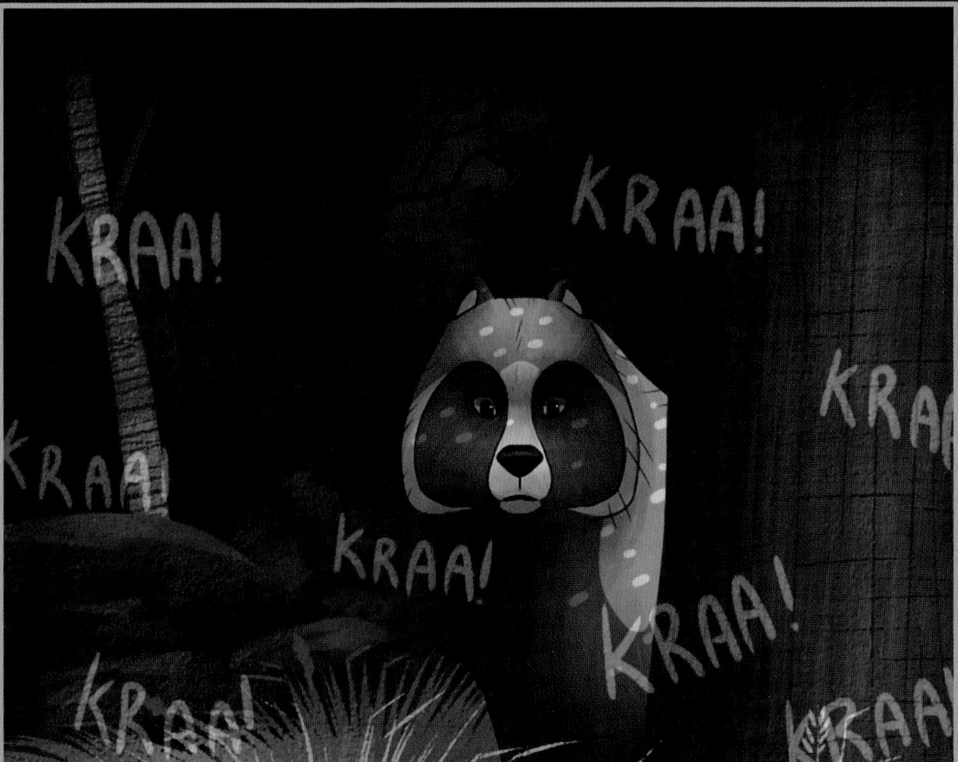
KRAA!
KRAA!
KRAA!
KRAA!
KRAA!
KRAA!
KRAA!
KRAA!
KRAA!
KRAA!
KRAA!
KRAA!
KRAA!
KRAA!
TAK TAK TAK TAK

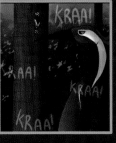

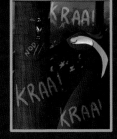

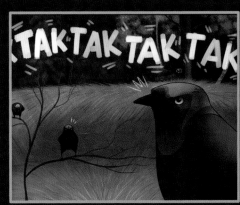

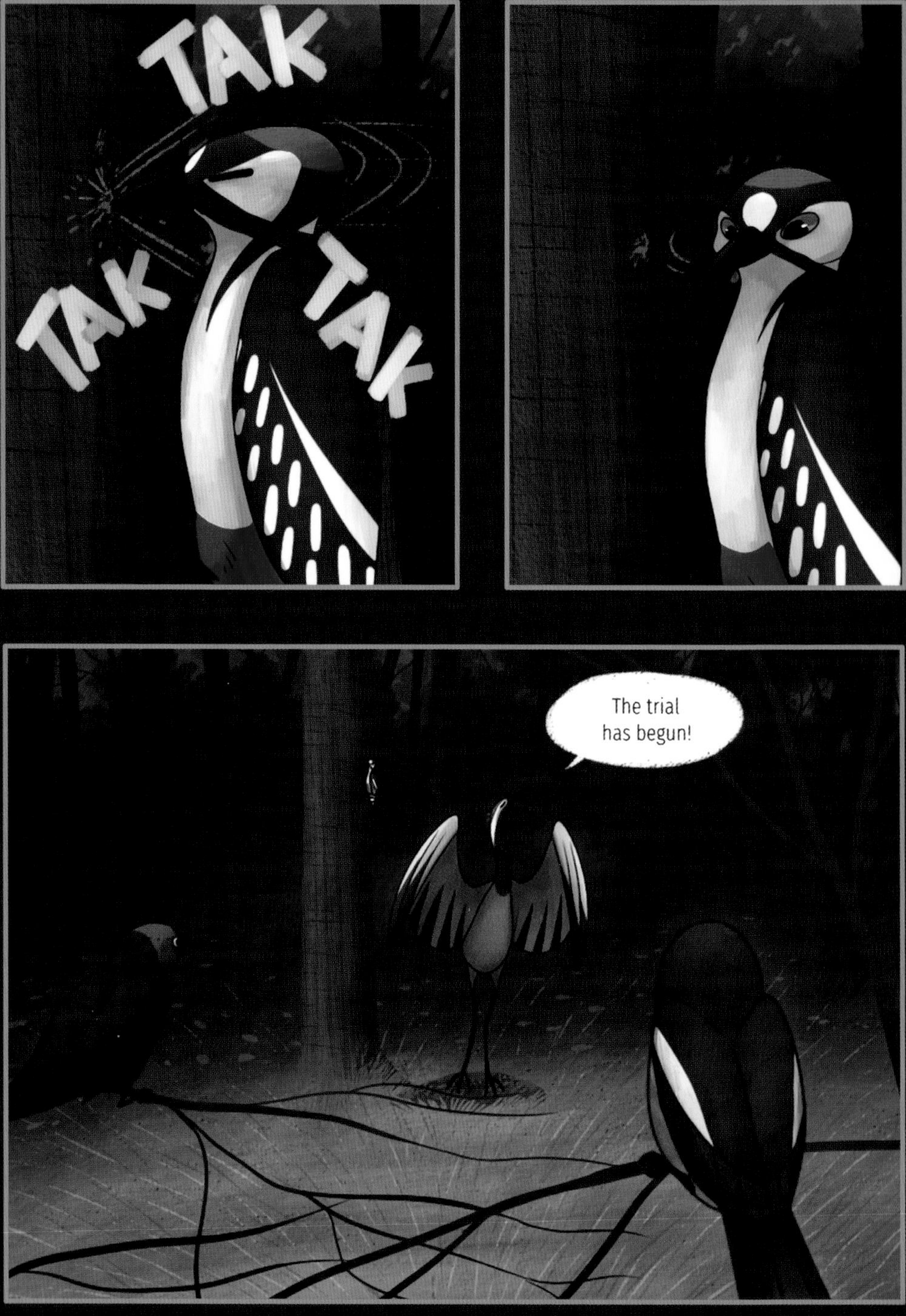
TAK
TAK
TAK
The trial has begun!

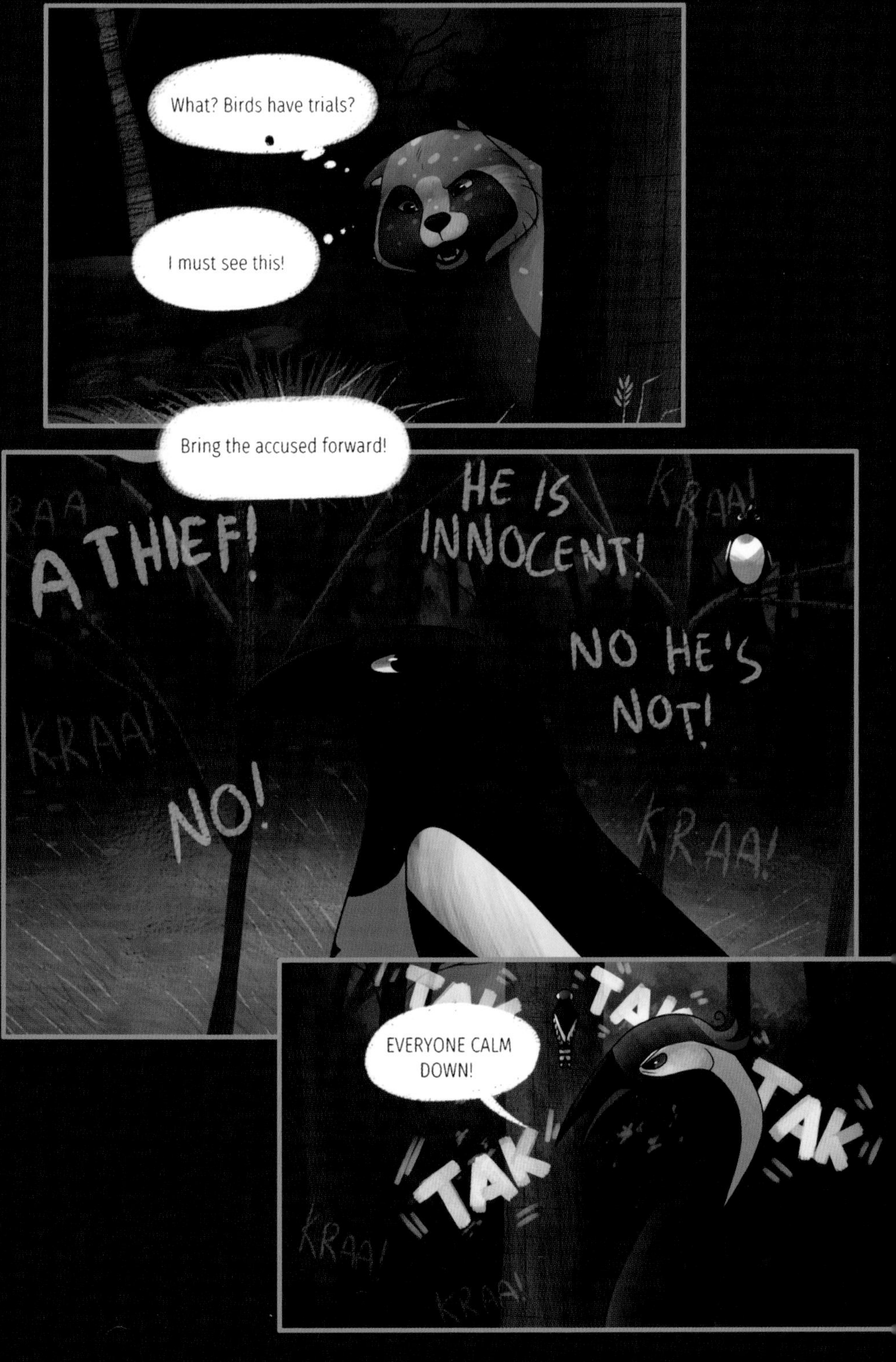
What? Birds have trials?
I must see this!
Bring the accused forward!
KRAA
A THIEF!
HE IS INNOCENT!
KRAA!
NO HE'S NOT!
KRAA!
NO!
KRAA!
TAK
TAK
EVERYONE CALM DOWN!
TAK
TAK
KRAA!
KRAA!

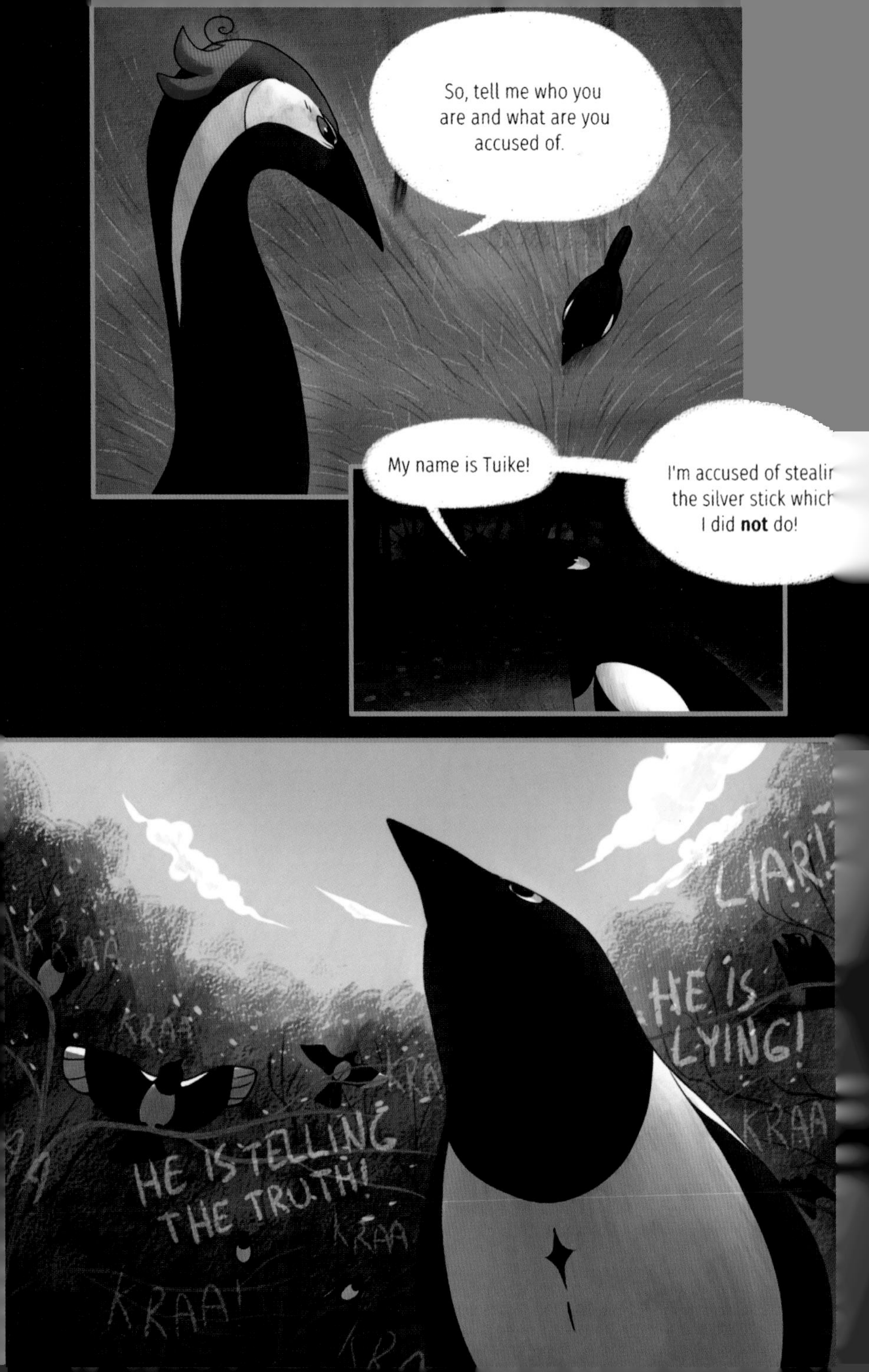

So, tell me who you are and what are you accused of.
My name is Tuike!
I'm accused of steali
the silver stick whic
I did **not** do!
LIAR!
HE IS LYING!
KRAA
HE IS TELLING THE TRUTH!
KRAA
KRAA!

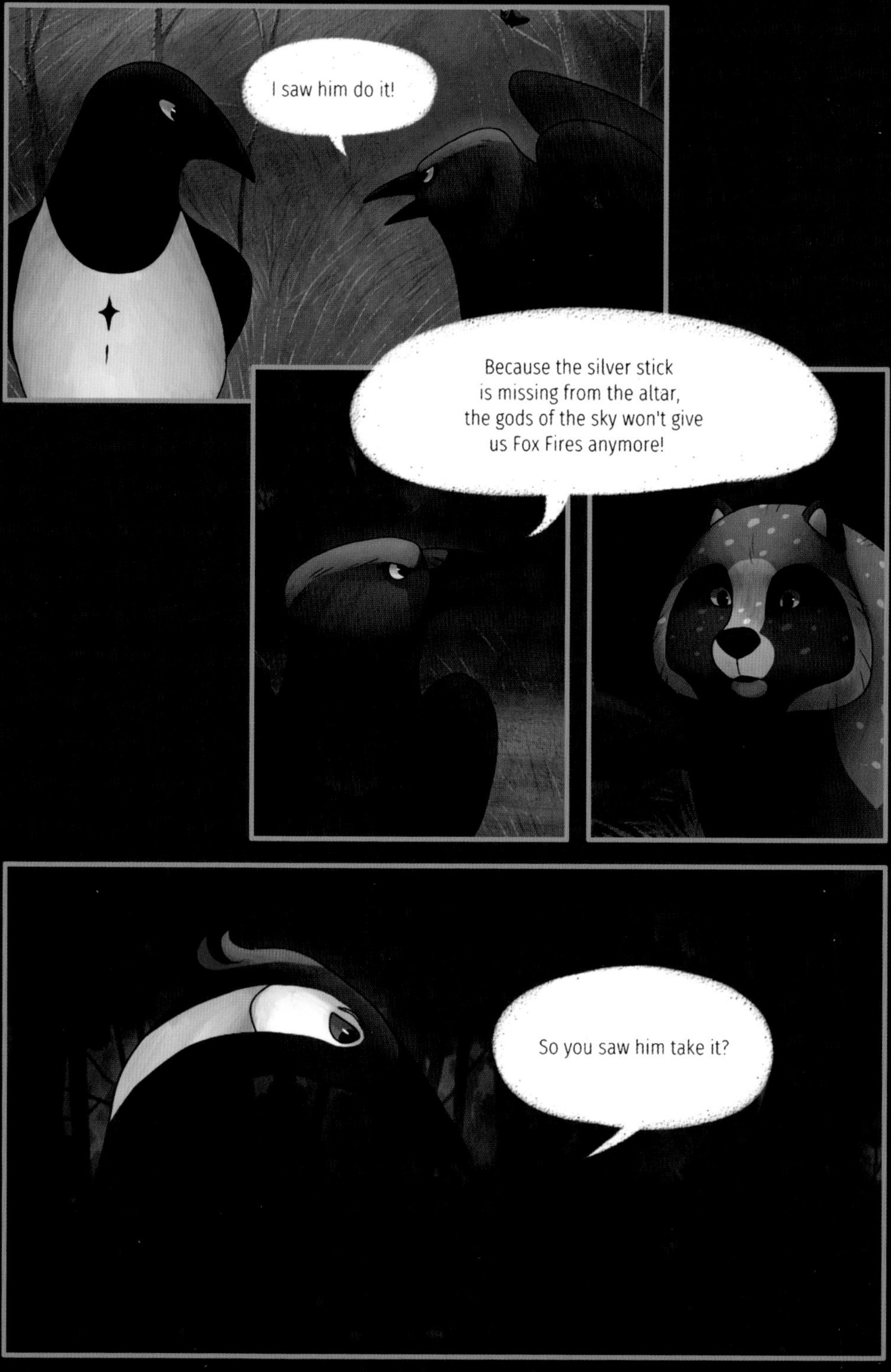
I saw him do it!
Because the silver stick is missing from the altar, the gods of the sky won't give us Fox Fires anymore!
So you saw him take it?

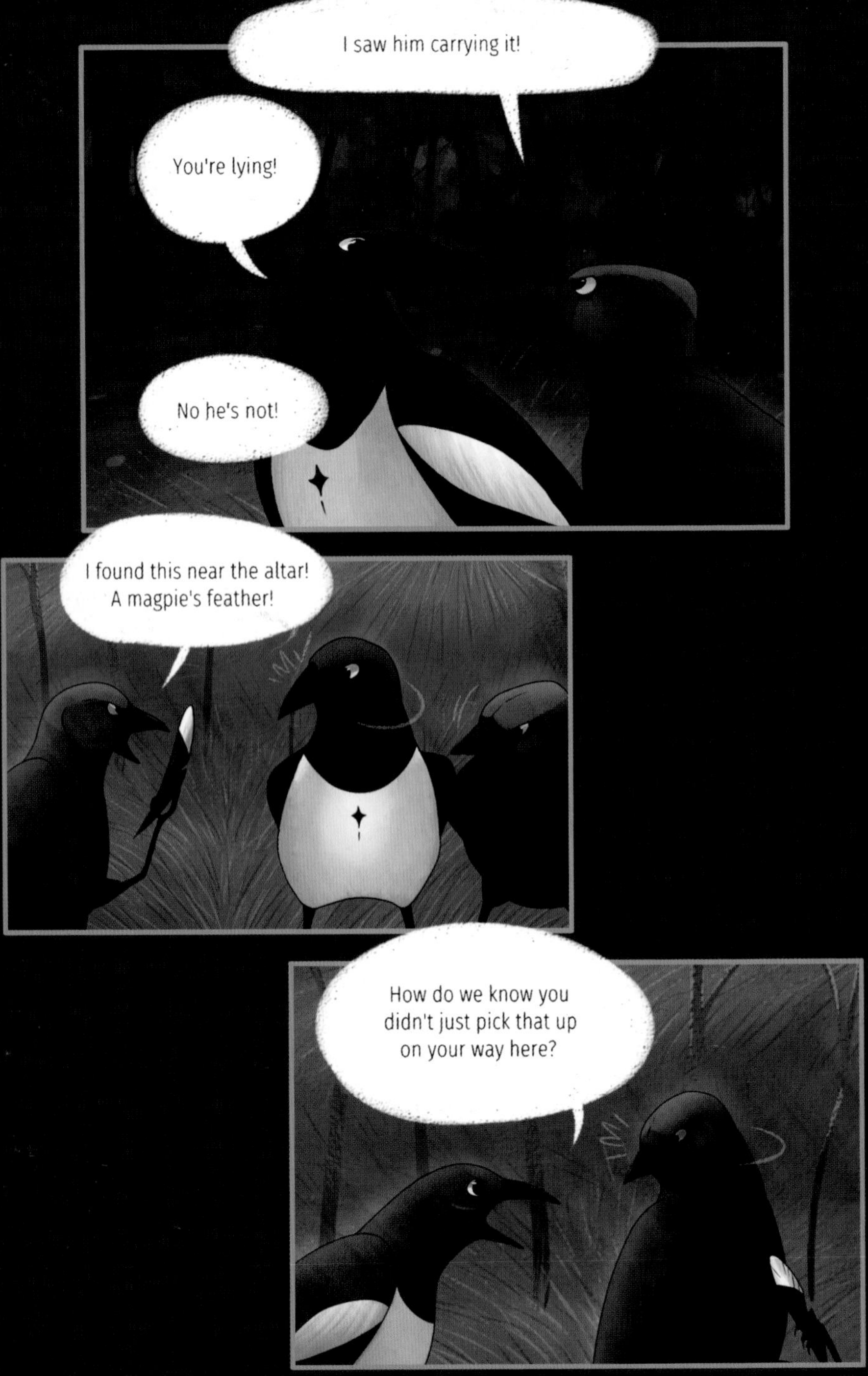

I saw him carrying it!
You're lying!
No he's not!
I found this near the altar! A magpie's feather!
How do we know you didn't just pick that up on your way here?

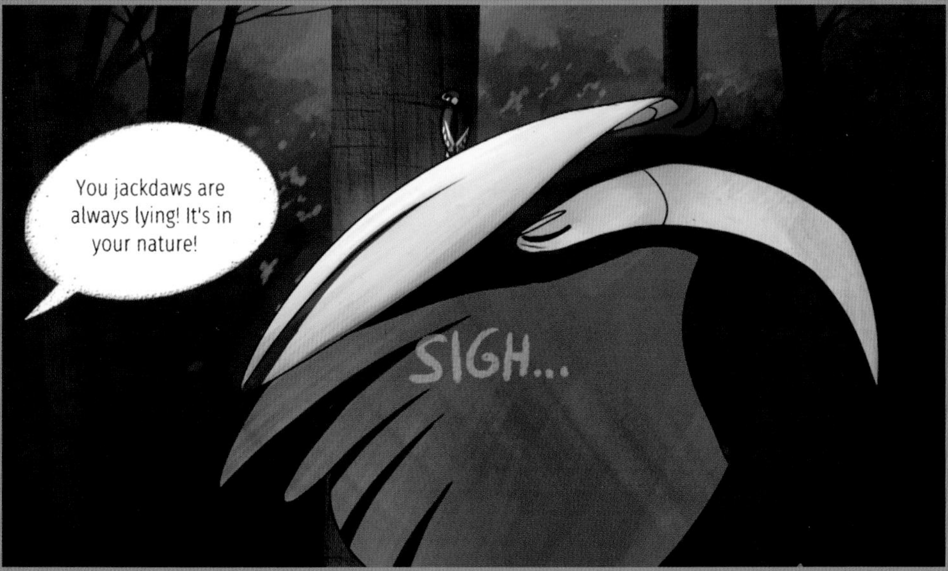
You jackdaws are always lying! It's in your nature!
SIGH...

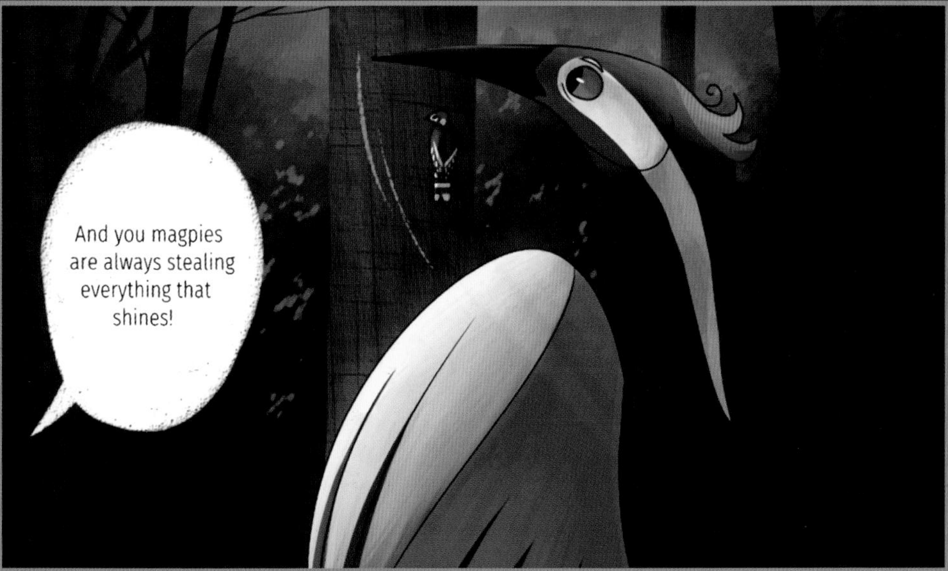
And you magpies are always stealing everything that shines!

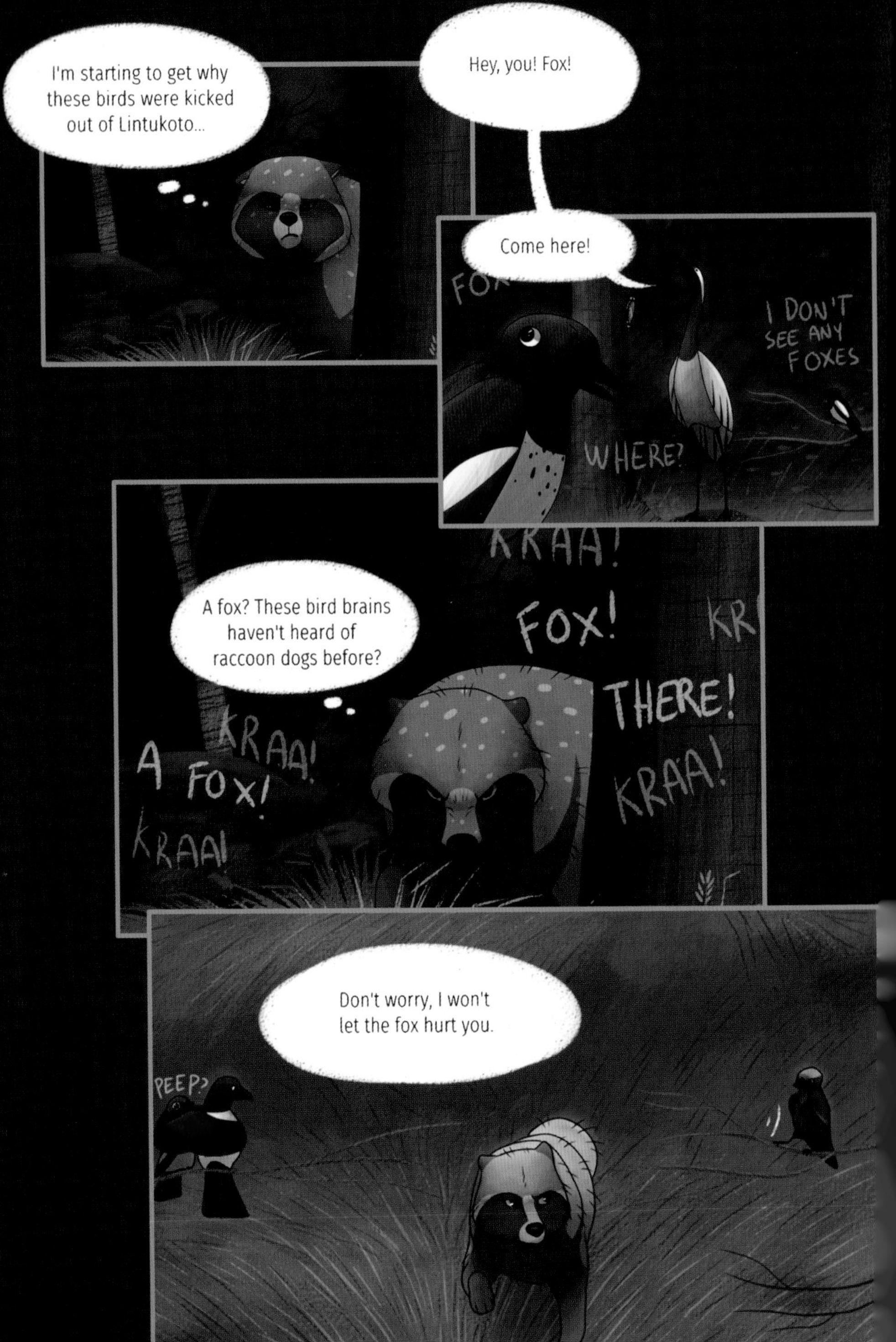
I'm starting to get why these birds were kicked out of Lintukoto...
Hey, you! Fox!
Come here!
FOX
I DON'T SEE ANY FOXES
WHERE?
KRAA!
A fox? These bird brains haven't heard of raccoon dogs before?
FOX!
THERE!
KRAA!
A FOX!
KRAA!
KRAA!
Don't worry, I won't let the fox hurt you.
PEEP?

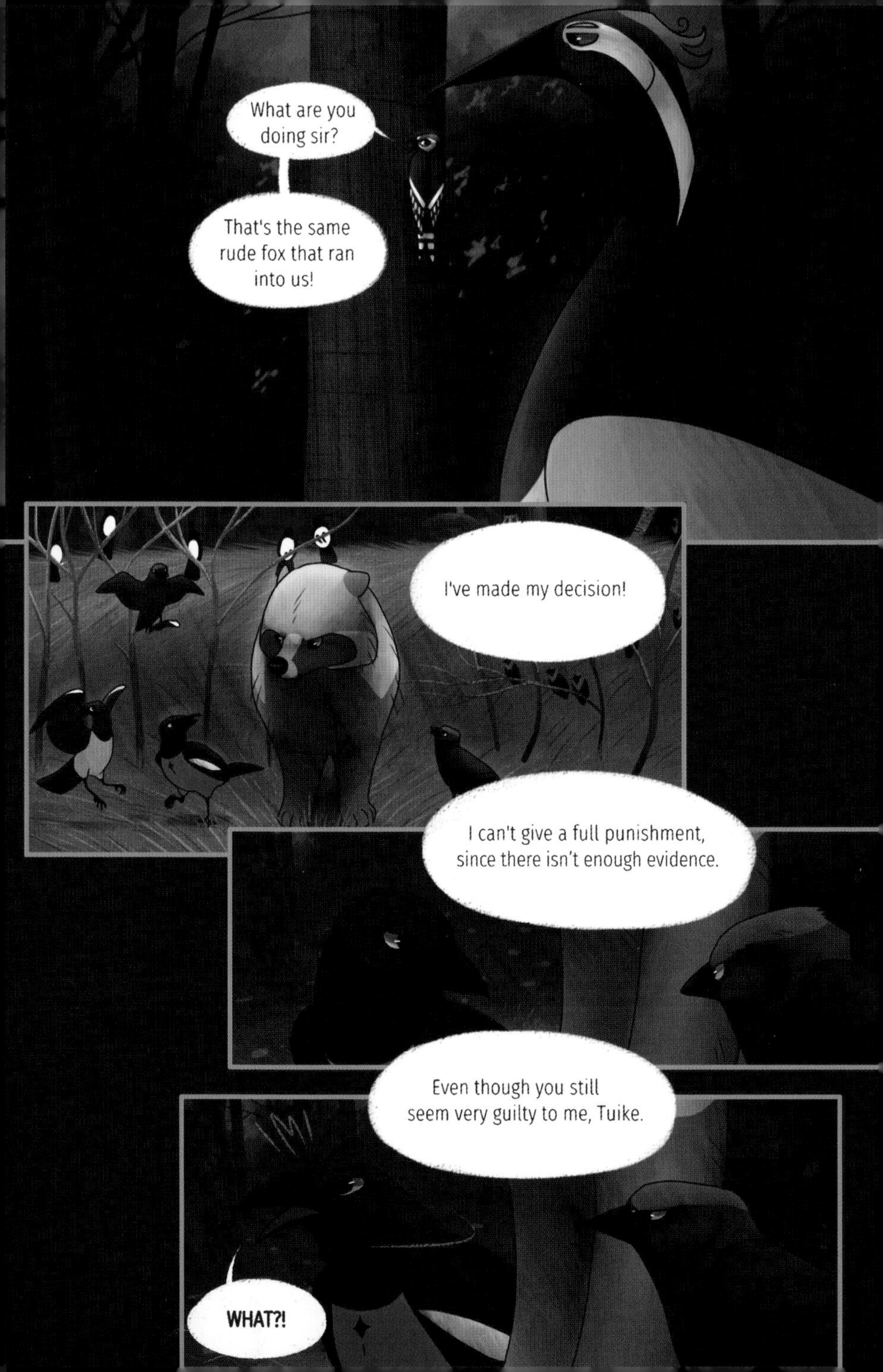
What are you doing sir?
That's the same rude fox that ran into us!
I've made my decision!
I can't give a full punishment, since there isn't enough evidence.
Even though you still seem very guilty to me, Tuike.
WHAT?!

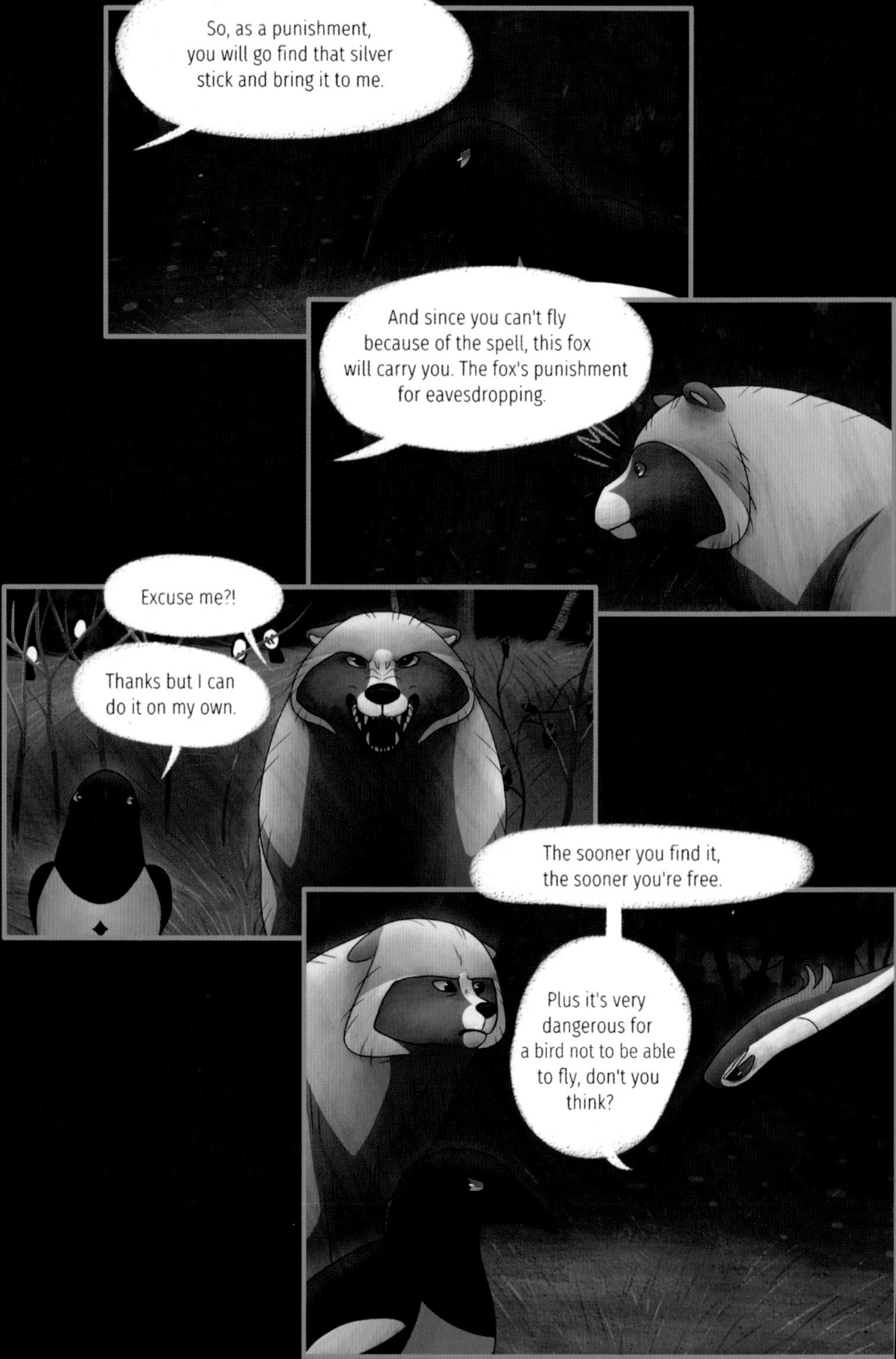
So, as a punishment, you will go find that silver stick and bring it to me.
And since you can't fly because of the spell, this fox will carry you. The fox's punishment for eavesdropping.
Excuse me?!
Thanks but I can do it on my own.
The sooner you find it, the sooner you're free.
Plus it's very dangerous for a bird not to be able to fly, don't you think?

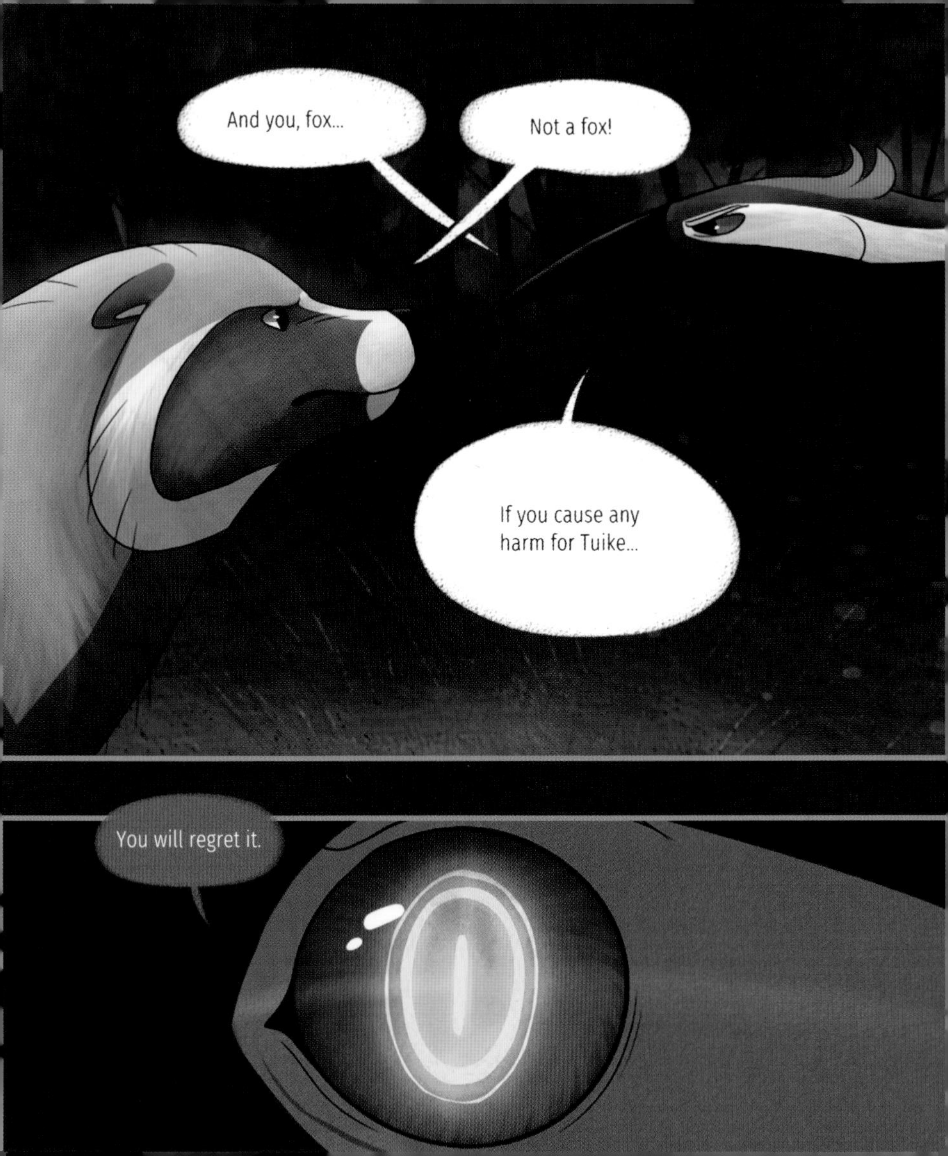
And you, fox...
Not a fox!
If you cause any harm for Tuike...
You will regret it.

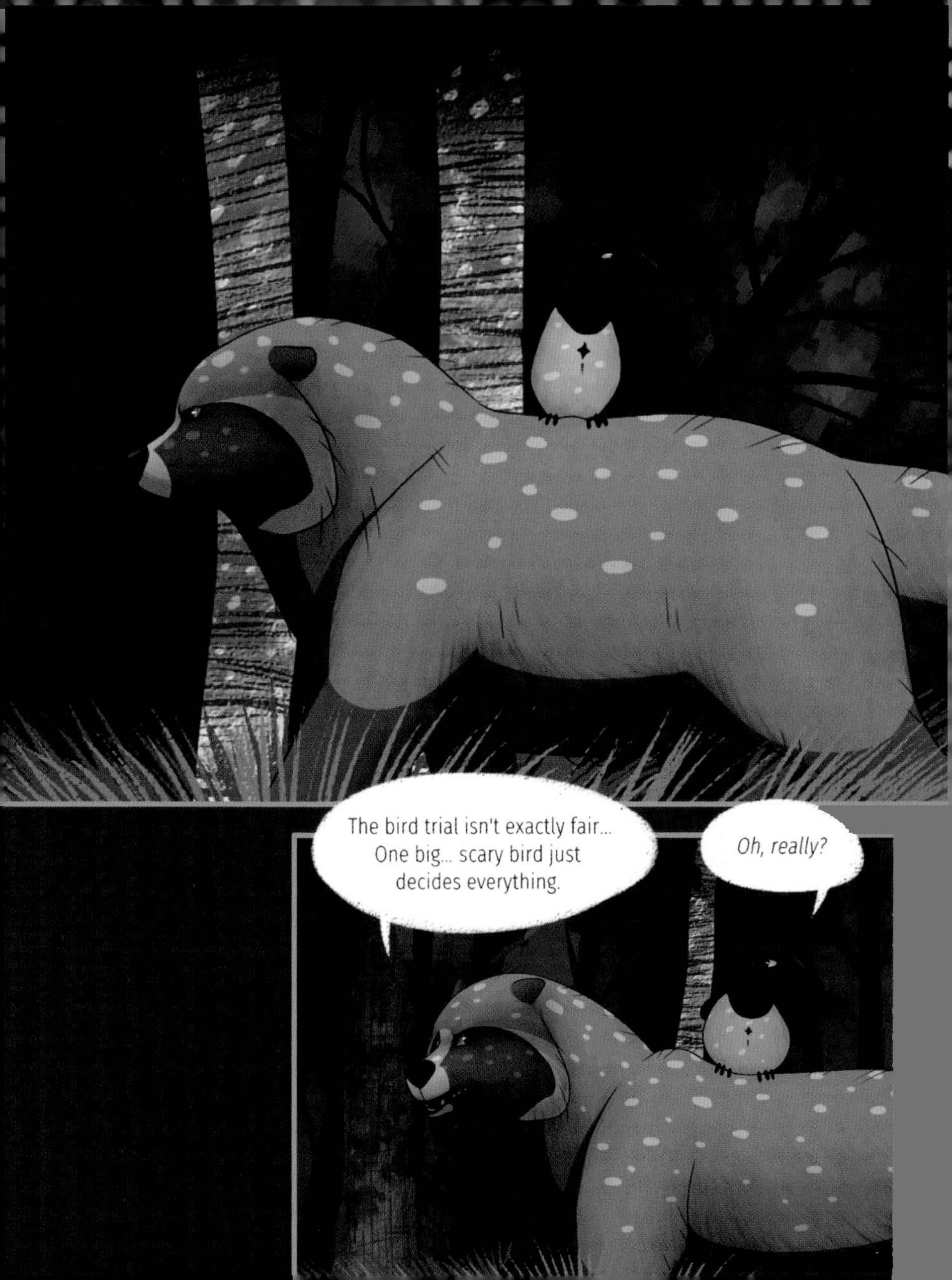
The bird trial isn't exactly fair... One big... scary bird just decides everything.
Oh, really?

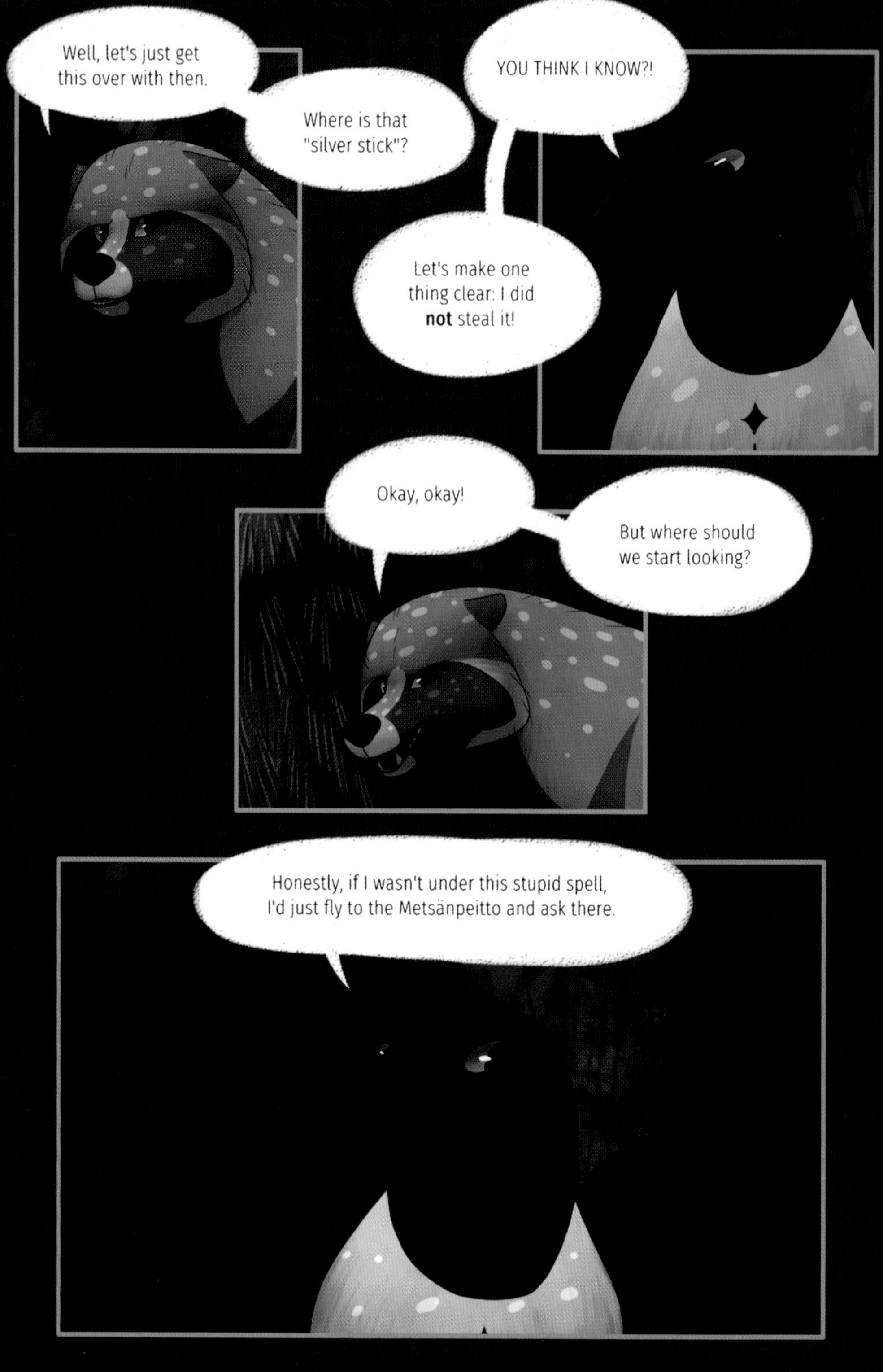
Well, let's just get this over with then.
Where is that "silver stick"?
YOU THINK I KNOW?!
Let's make one thing clear: I did **not** steal it!
Okay, okay!
But where should we start looking?
Honestly, if I wasn't under this stupid spell, I'd just fly to the Metsänpeitto and ask there.

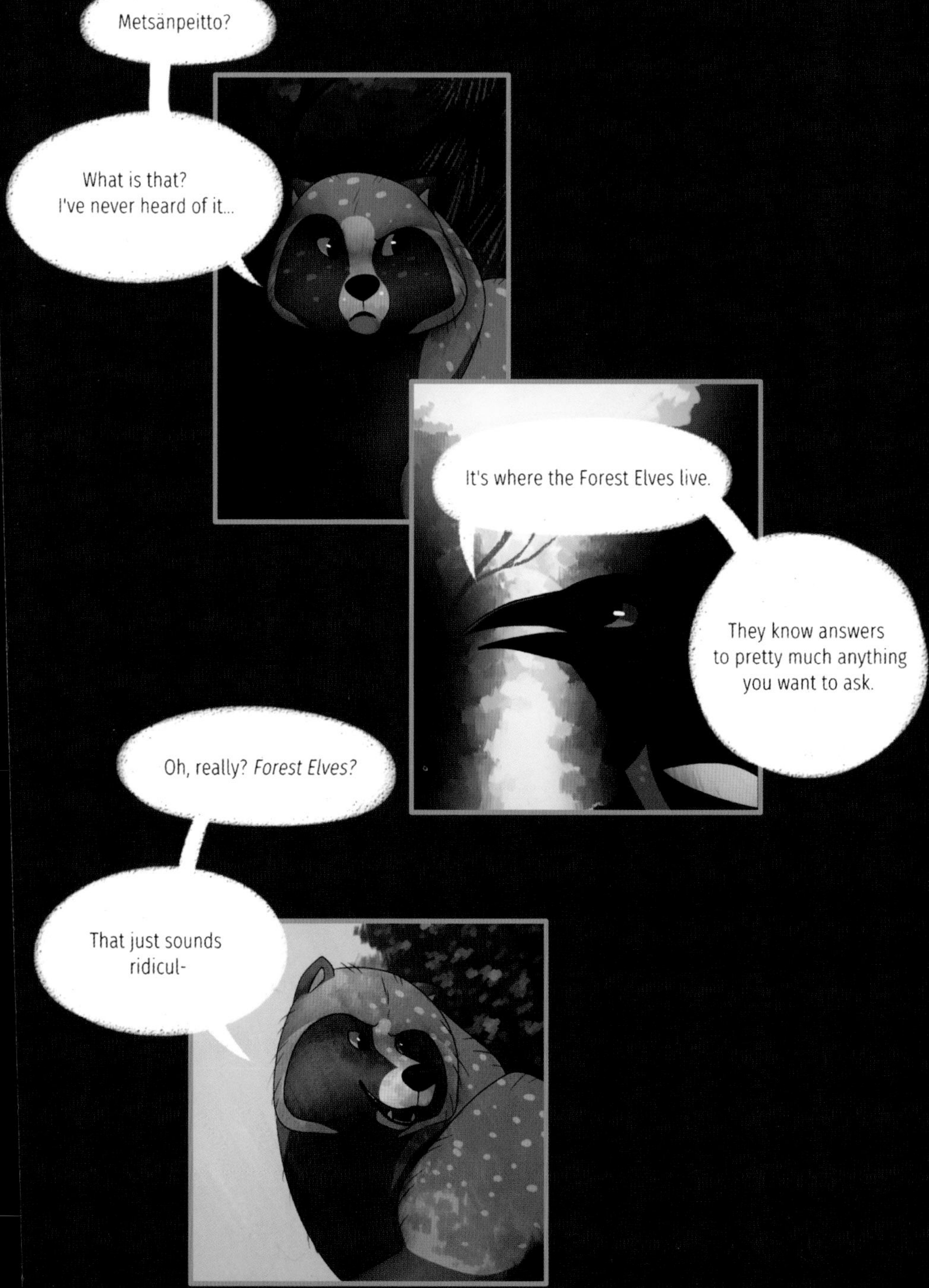
Metsänpeitto?
What is that? I've never heard of it...
It's where the Forest Elves live.
They know answers to pretty much anything you want to ask.
Oh, really? *Forest Elves?*
That just sounds ridicul-

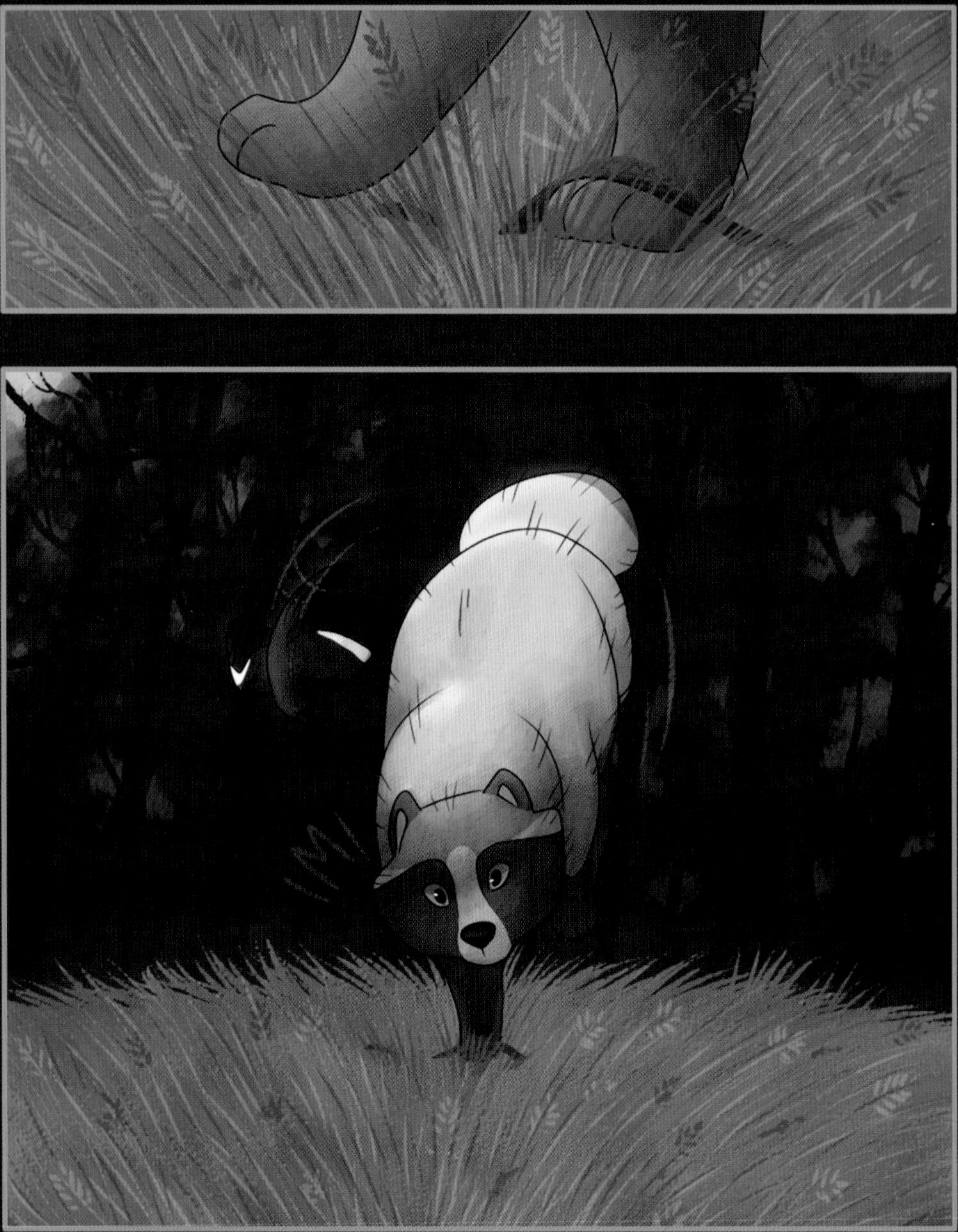

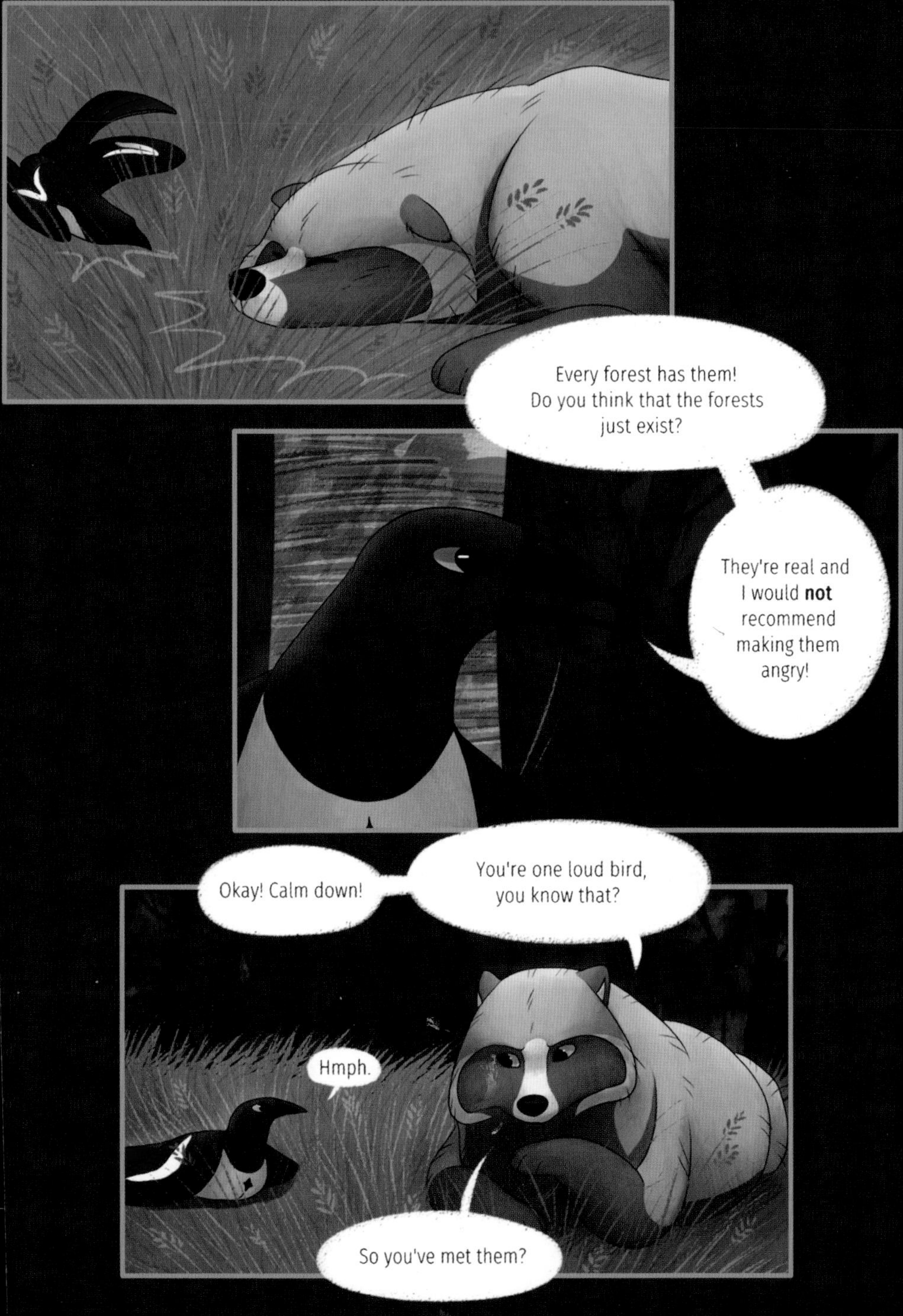
Every forest has them! Do you think that the forests just exist?
They're real and I would **not** recommend making them angry!
Okay! Calm down!
You're one loud bird, you know that?
Hmph.
So you've met them?

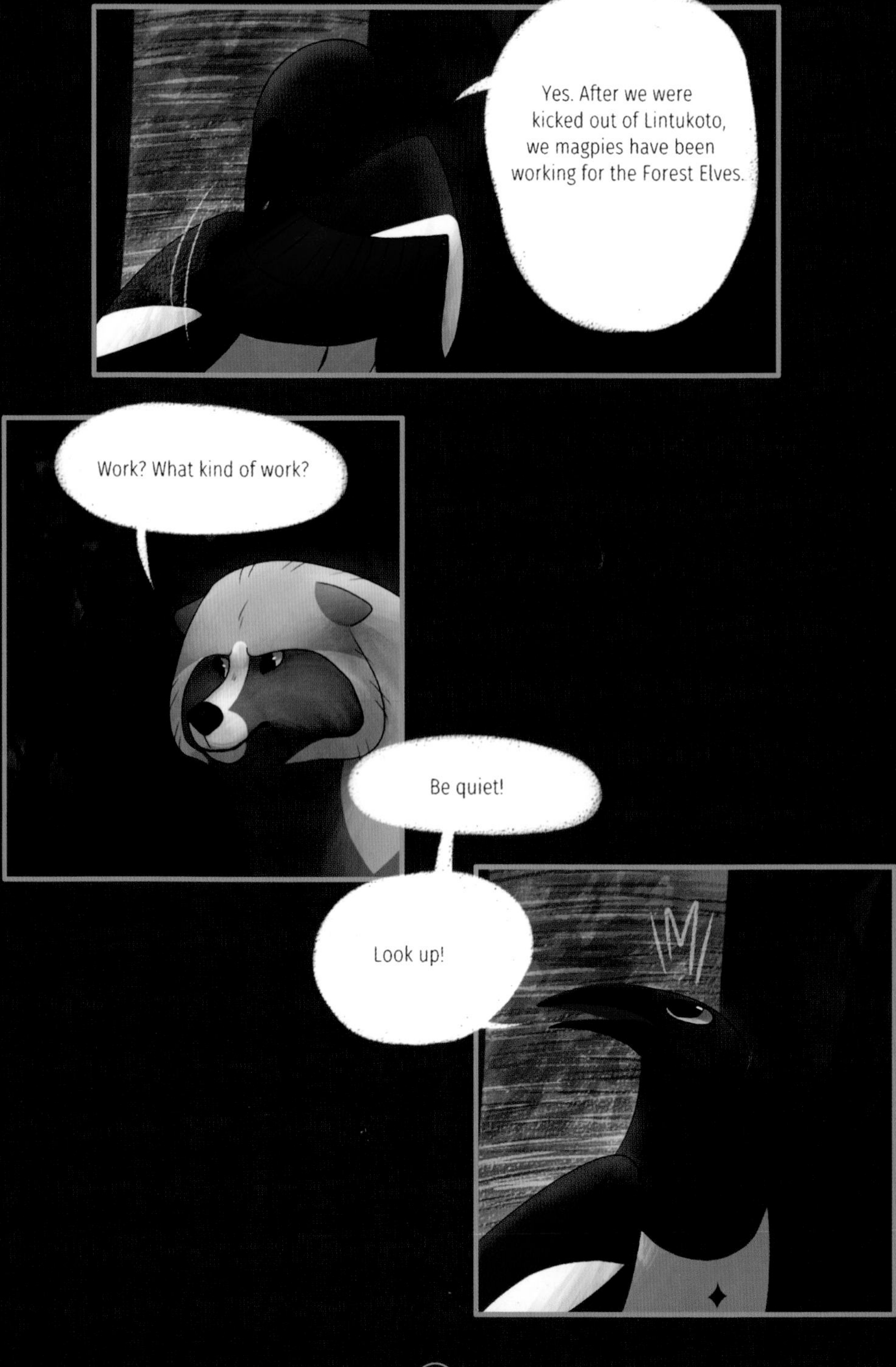
Yes. After we were kicked out of Lintukoto, we magpies have been working for the Forest Elves.
Work? What kind of work?
Be quiet!
Look up!

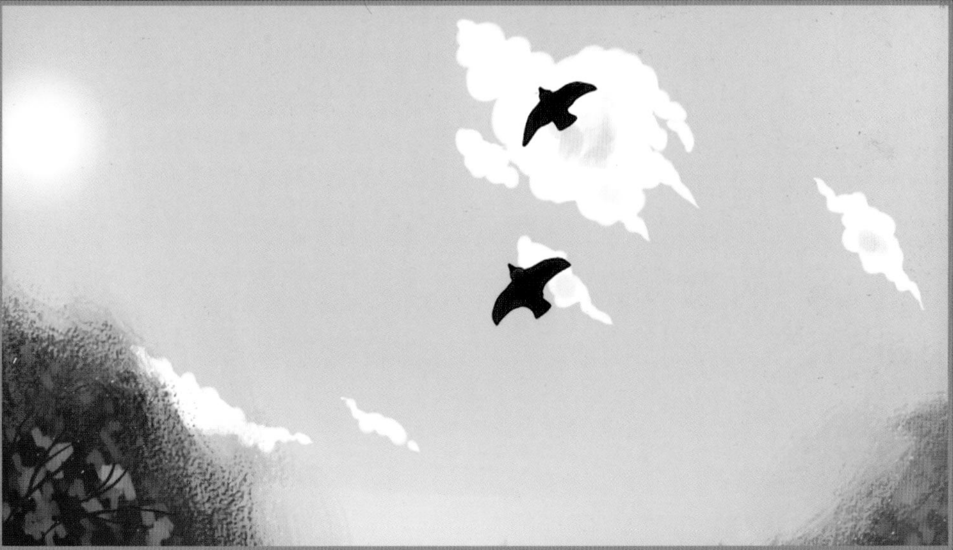

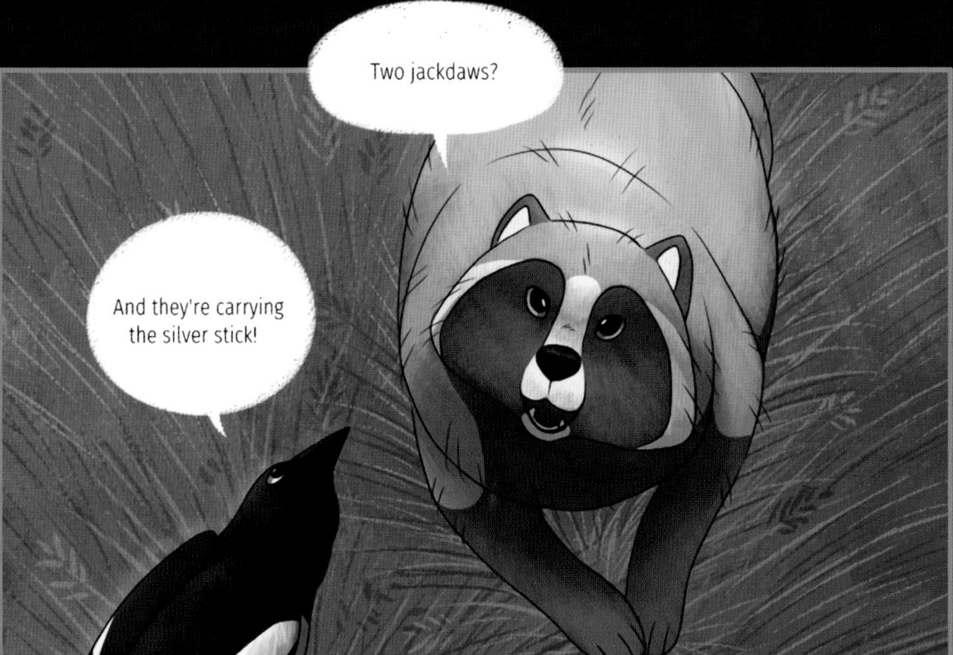
Two jackdaws?
And they're carrying the silver stick!

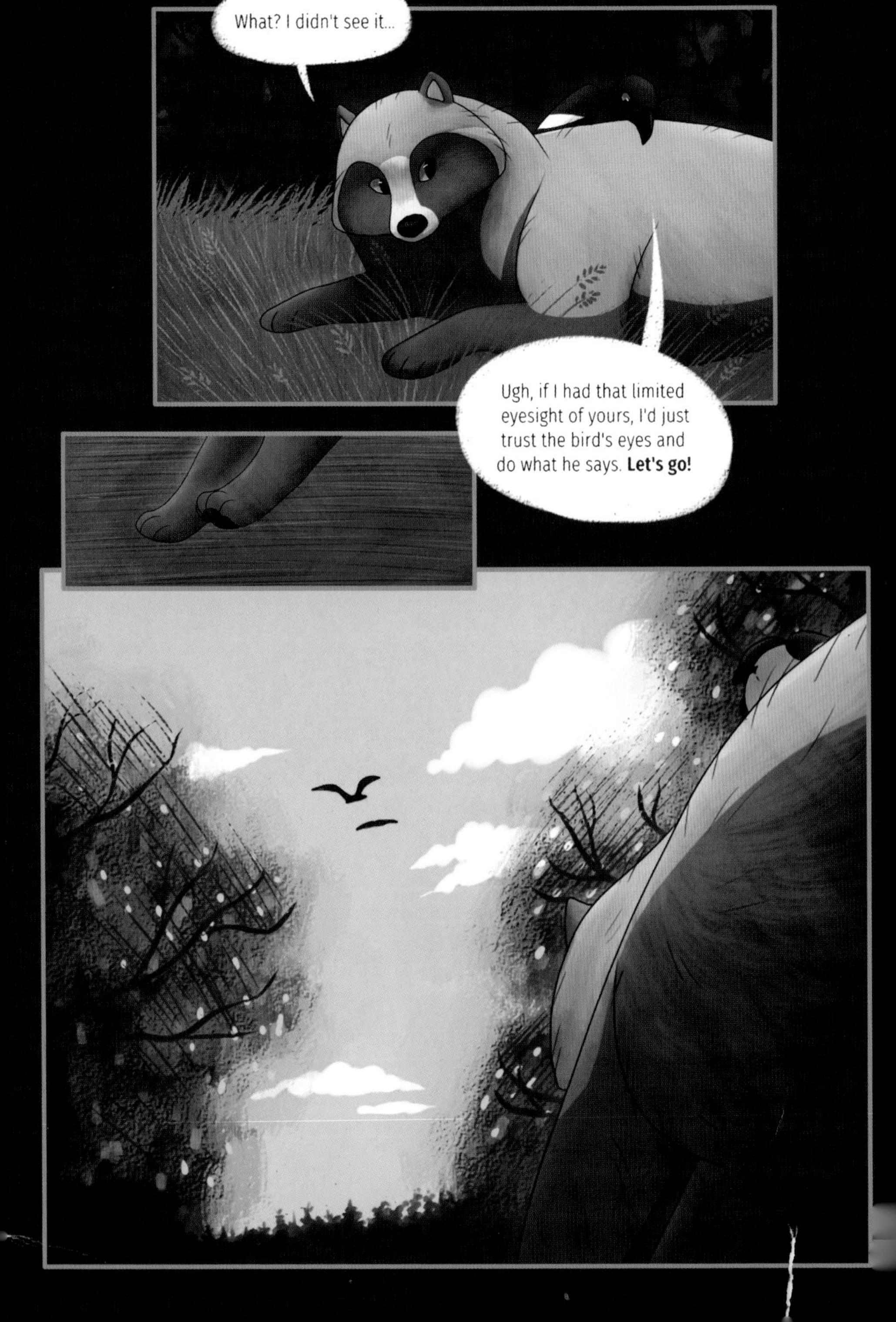
What? I didn't see it...
Ugh, if I had that limited eyesight of yours, I'd just trust the bird's eyes and do what he says. **Let's go!**

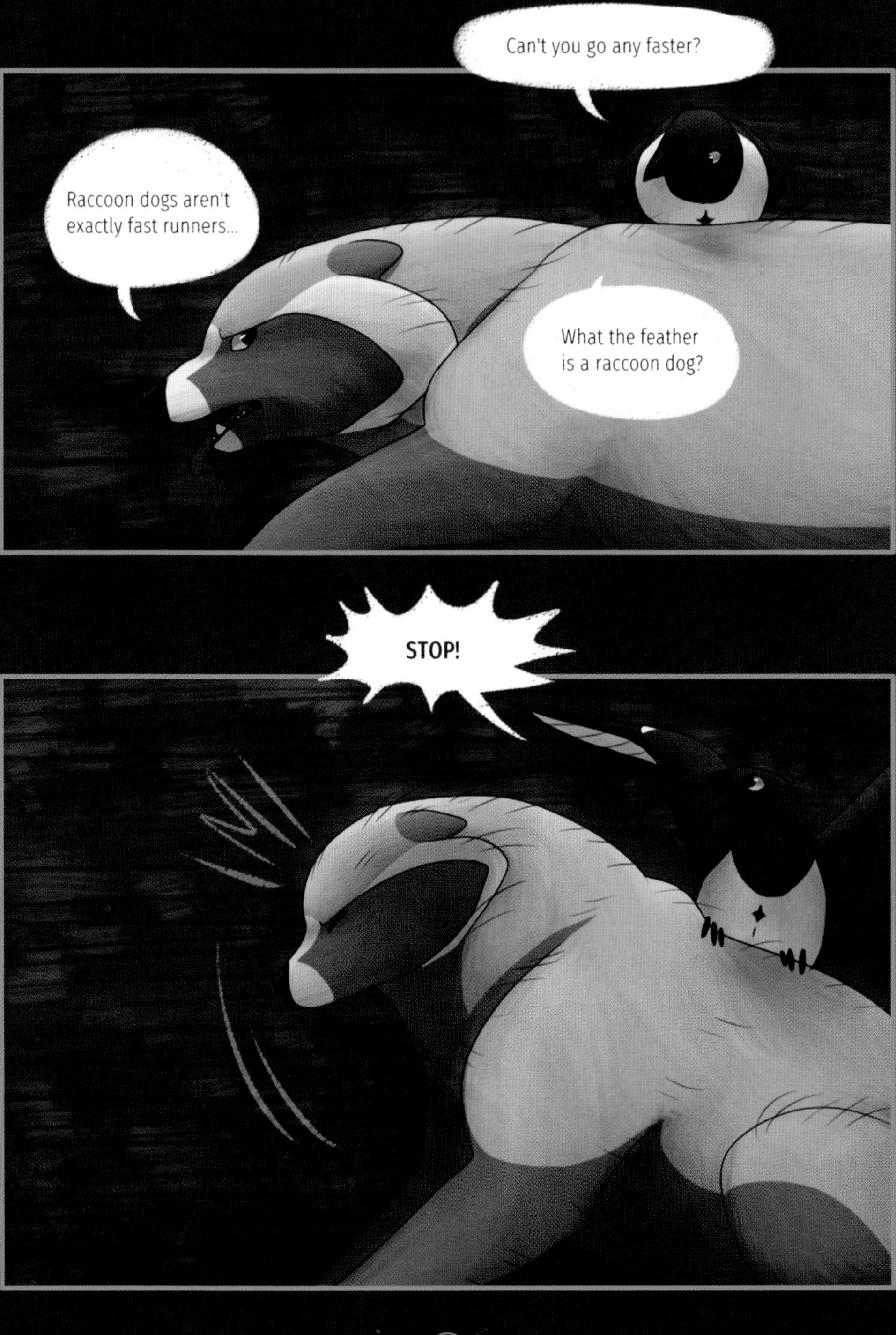

Can't you go any faster?
Raccoon dogs aren't exactly fast runners...
What the feather is a raccoon dog?
STOP!

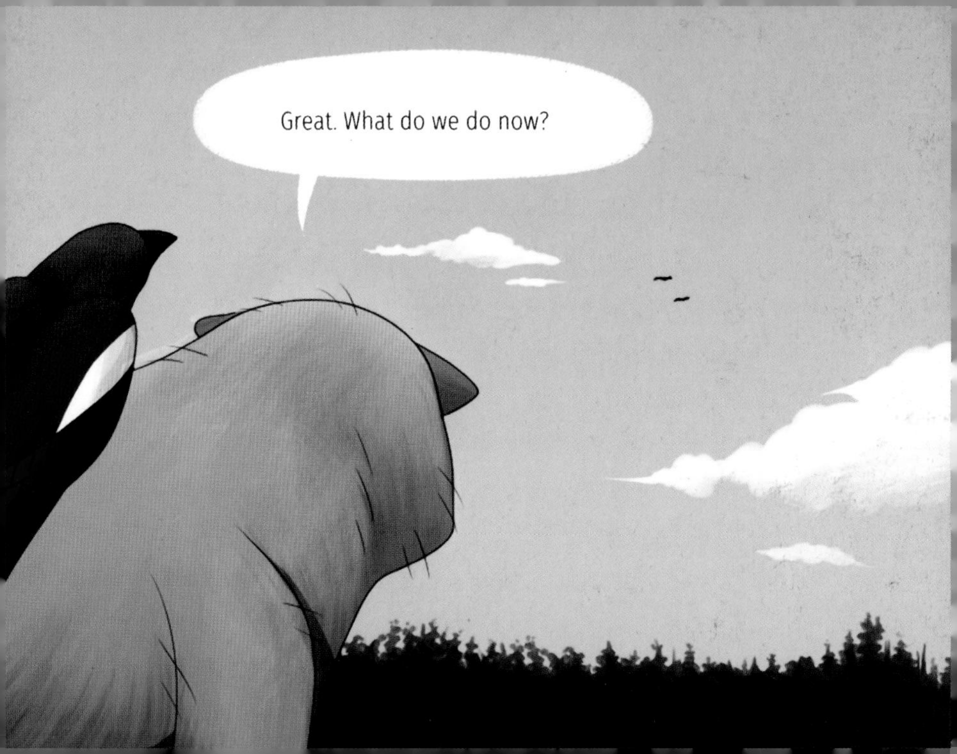
Great. What do we do now?

Chapter 13

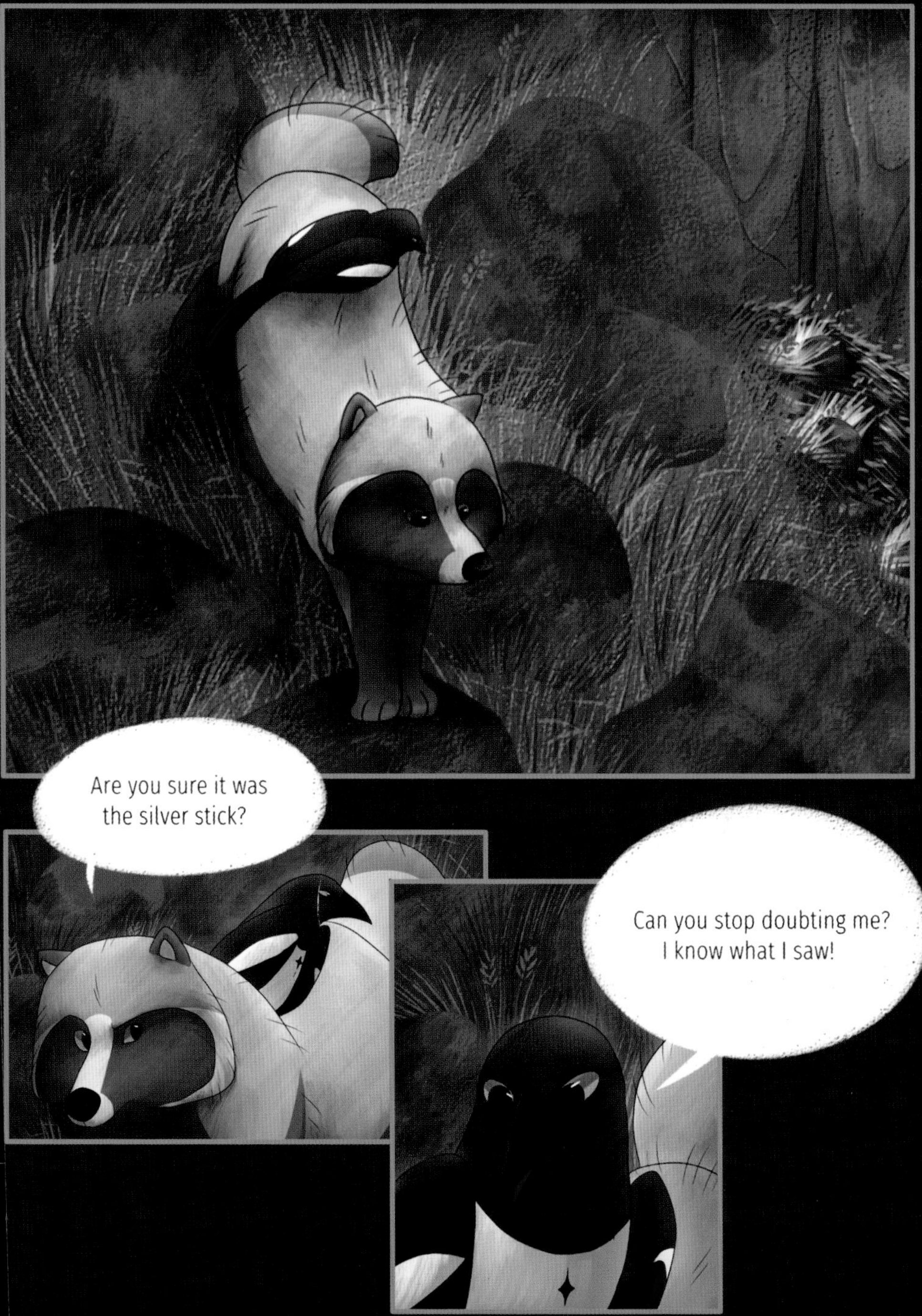
Are you sure it was the silver stick?
Can you stop doubting me? I know what I saw!

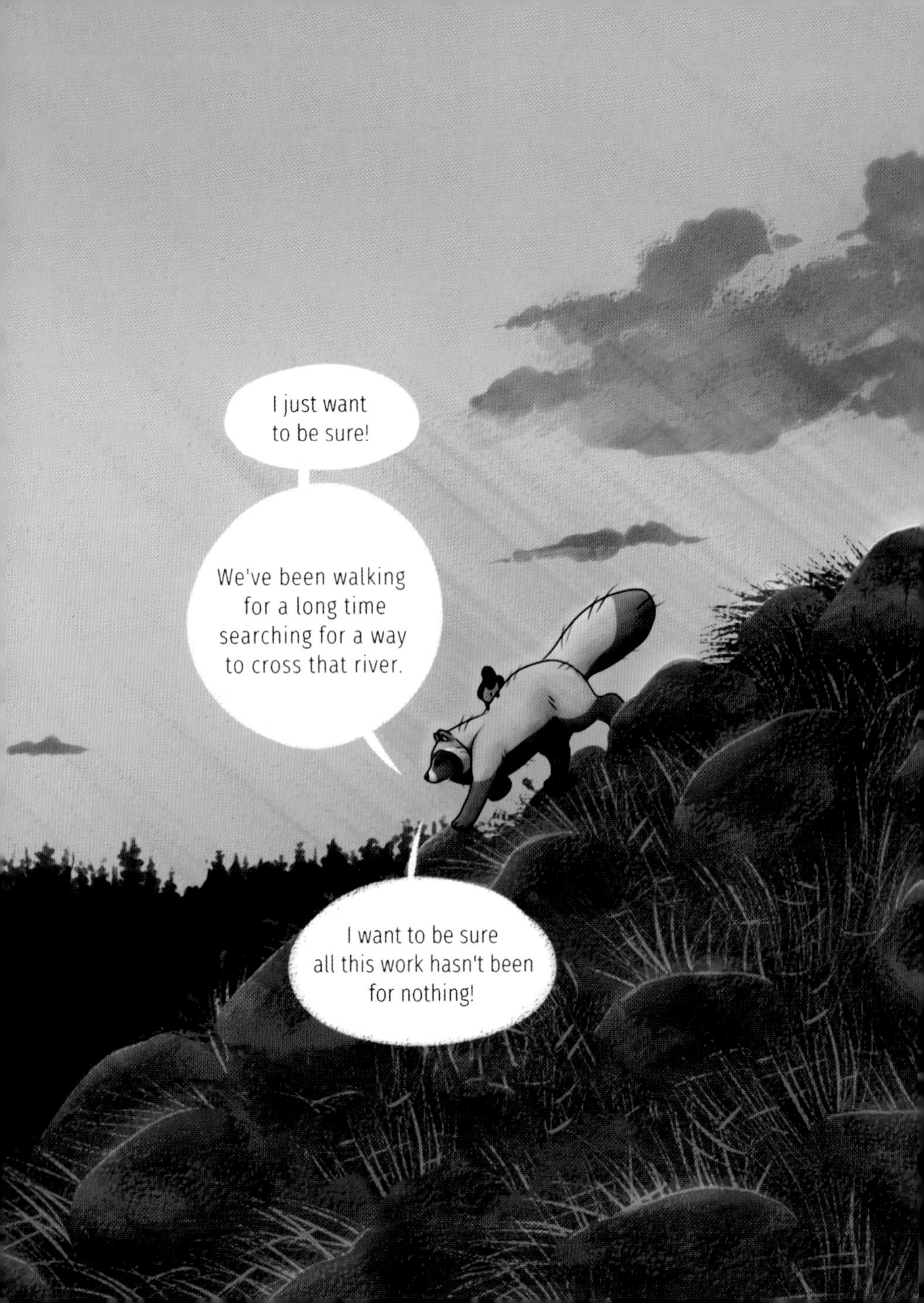
I just want to be sure!
We've been walking for a long time searching for a way to cross that river.
I want to be sure all this work hasn't been for nothing!

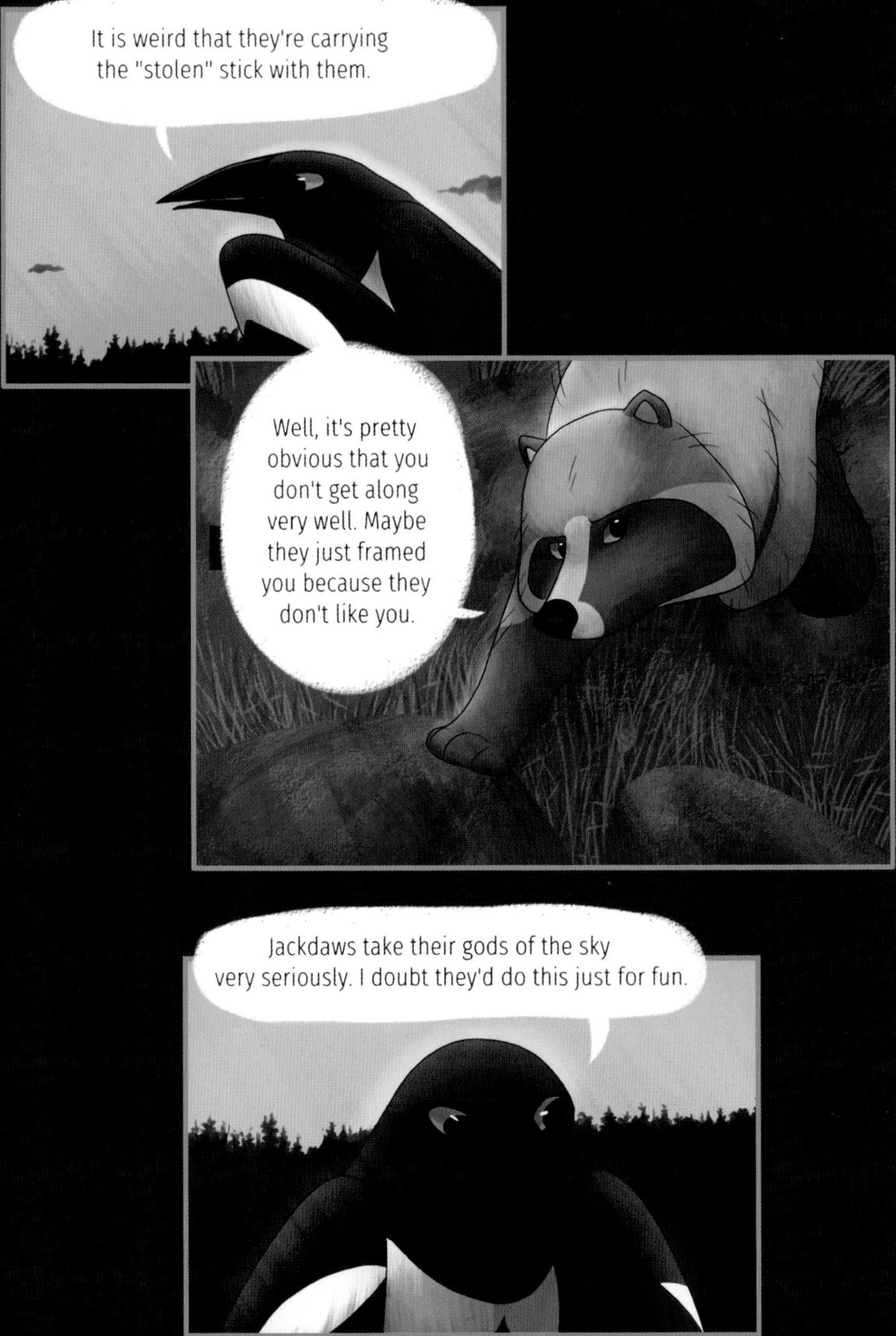
It is weird that they're carrying the "stolen" stick with them.
Well, it's pretty obvious that you don't get along very well. Maybe they just framed you because they don't like you.
Jackdaws take their gods of the sky very seriously. I doubt they'd do this just for fun.

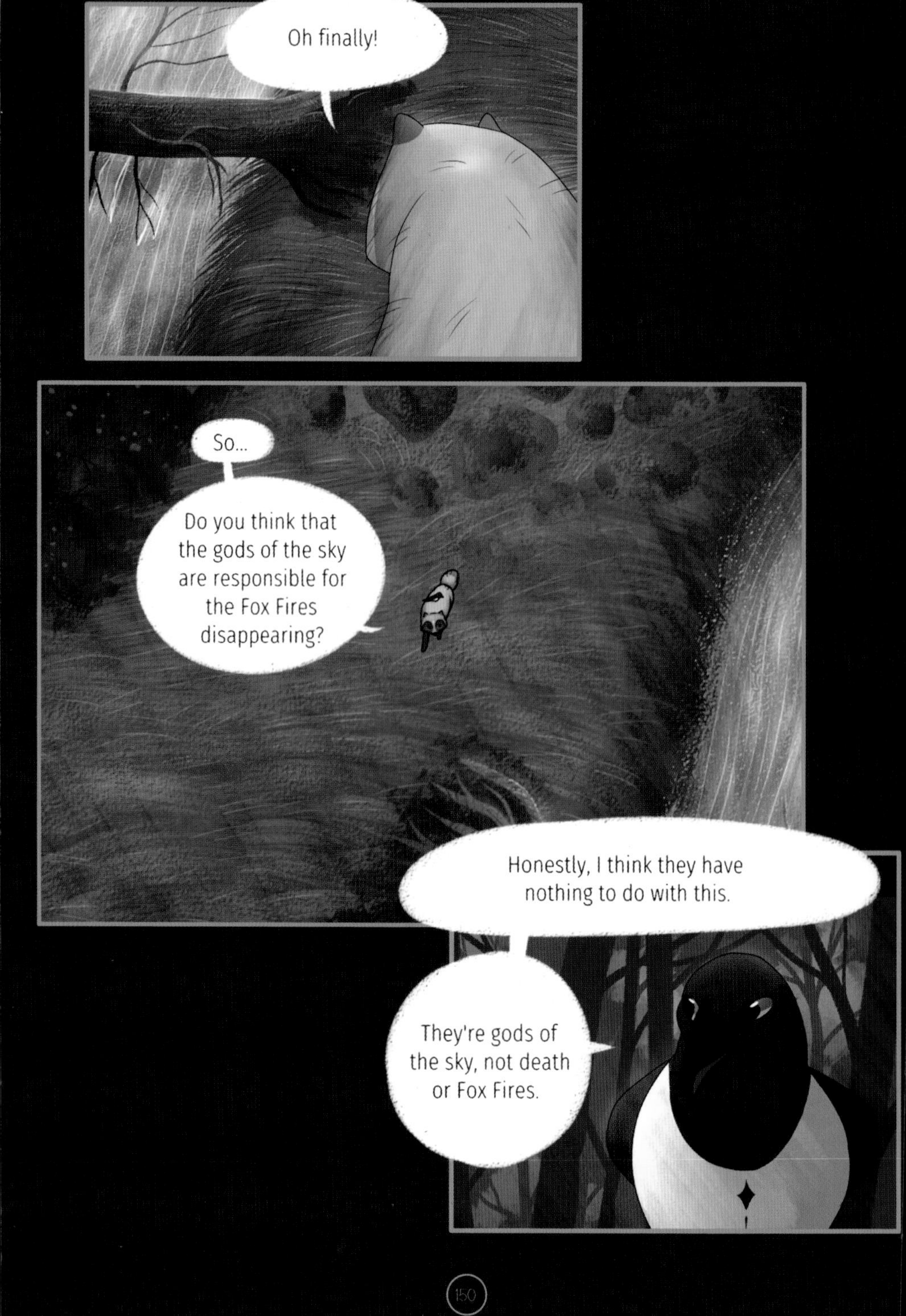
Oh finally!
So...
Do you think that the gods of the sky are responsible for the Fox Fires disappearing?
Honestly, I think they have nothing to do with this.
They're gods of the sky, not death or Fox Fires.

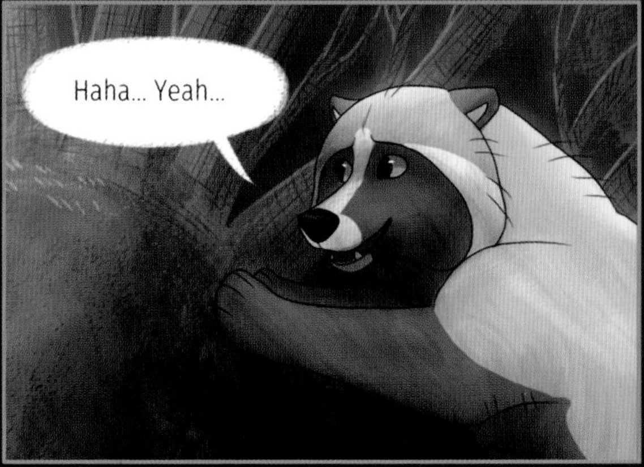
Haha... Yeah...

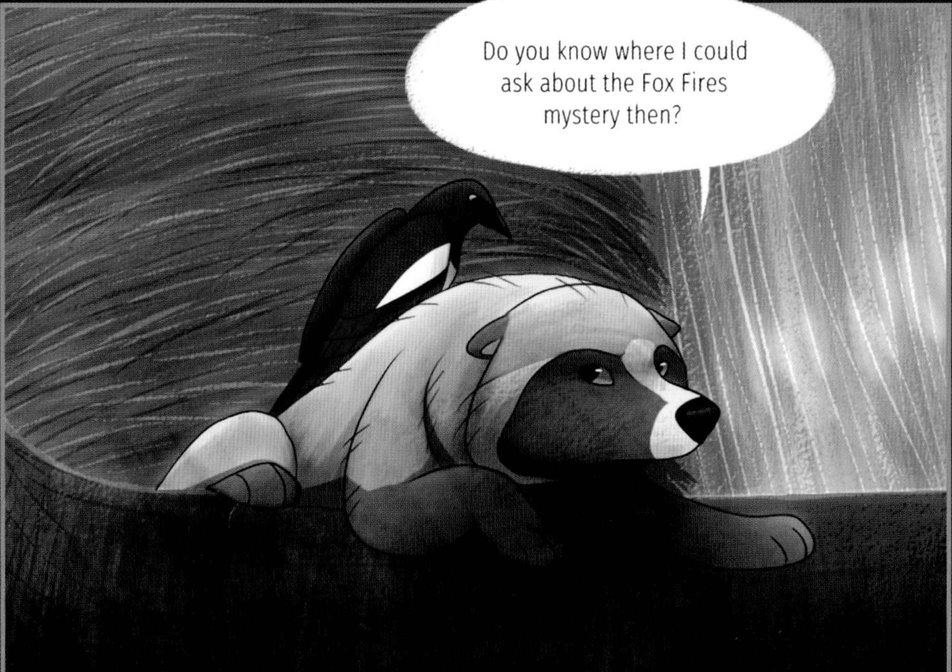
Do you know where I could ask about the Fox Fires mystery then?

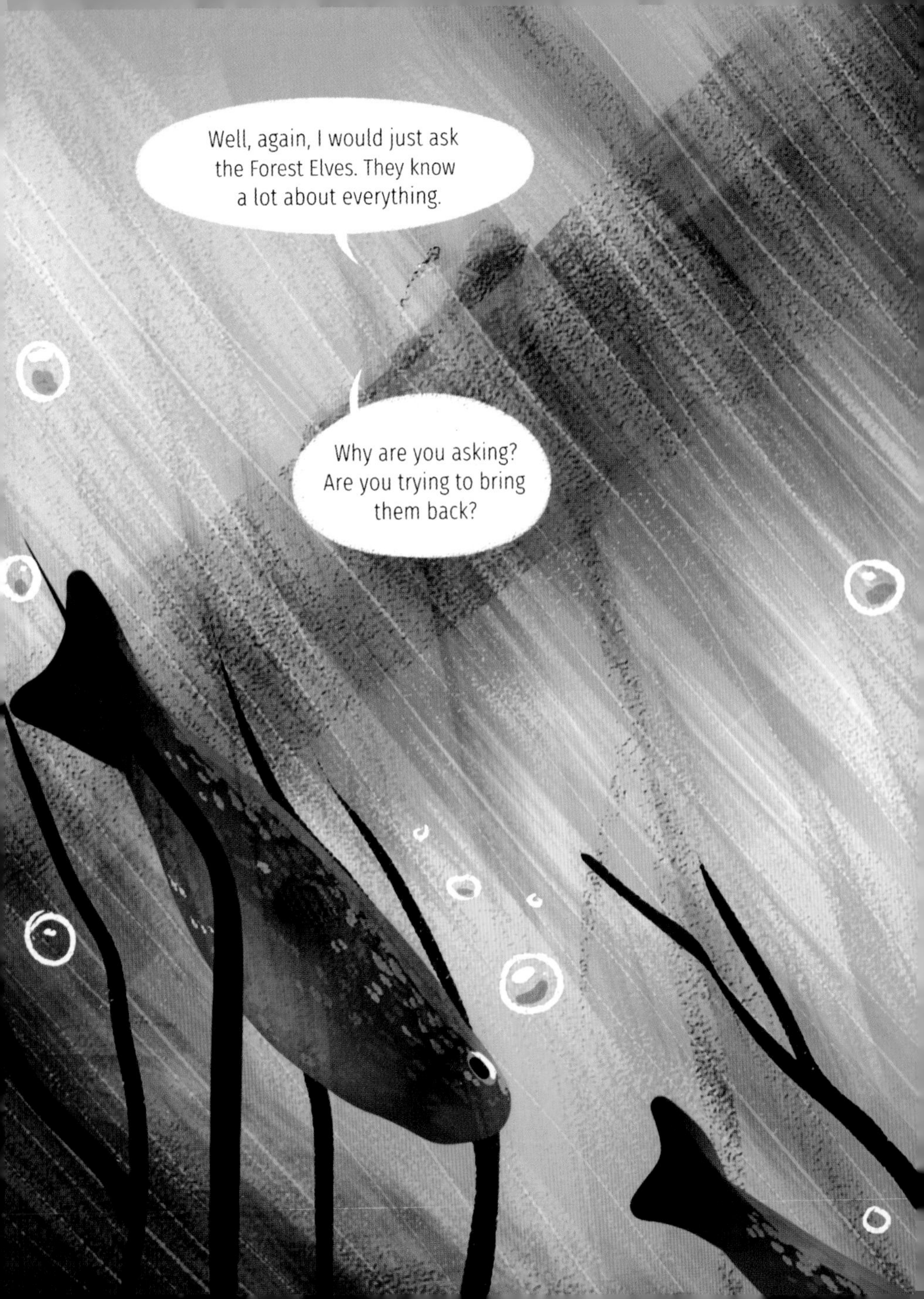
Well, again, I would just ask the Forest Elves. They know a lot about everything.
Why are you asking? Are you trying to bring them back?

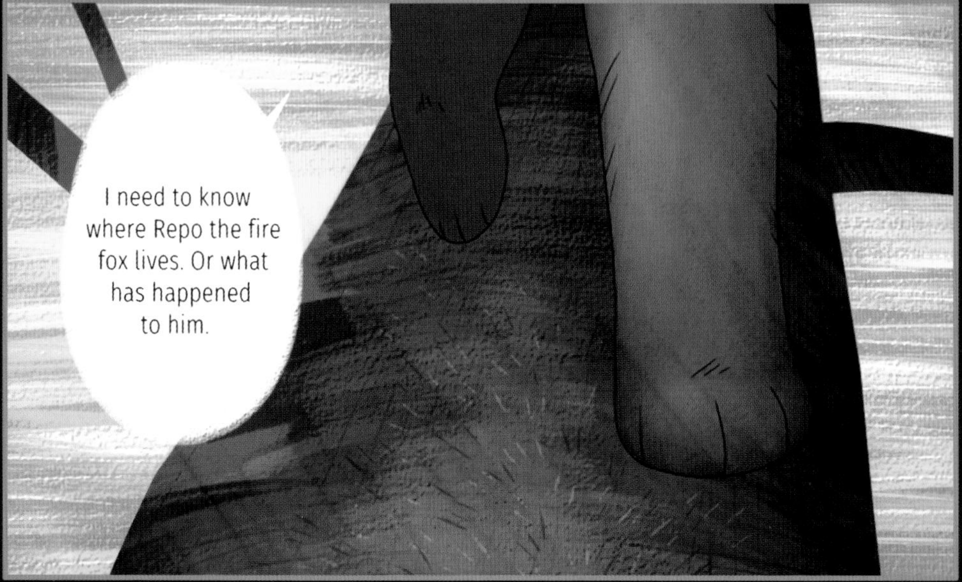
I need to know where Repo the fire fox lives. Or what has happened to him.

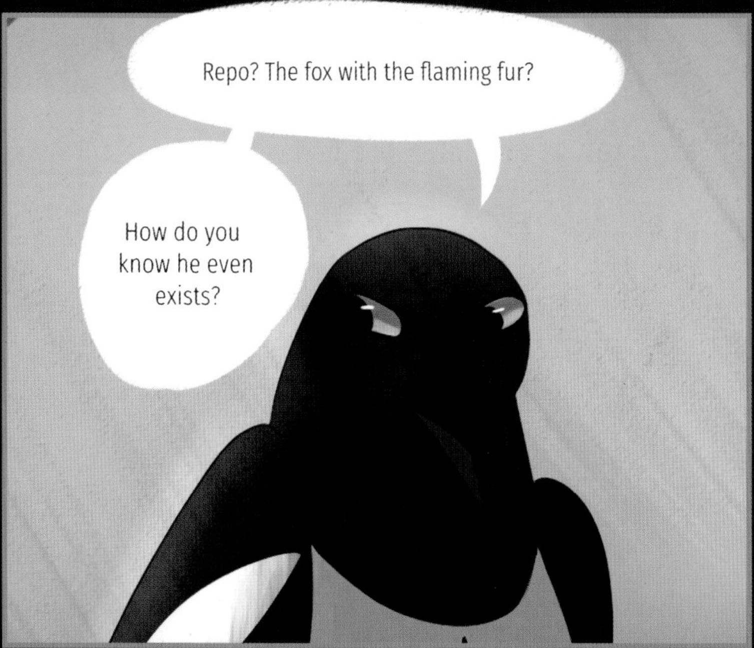
Repo? The fox with the flaming fur?
How do you know he even exists?

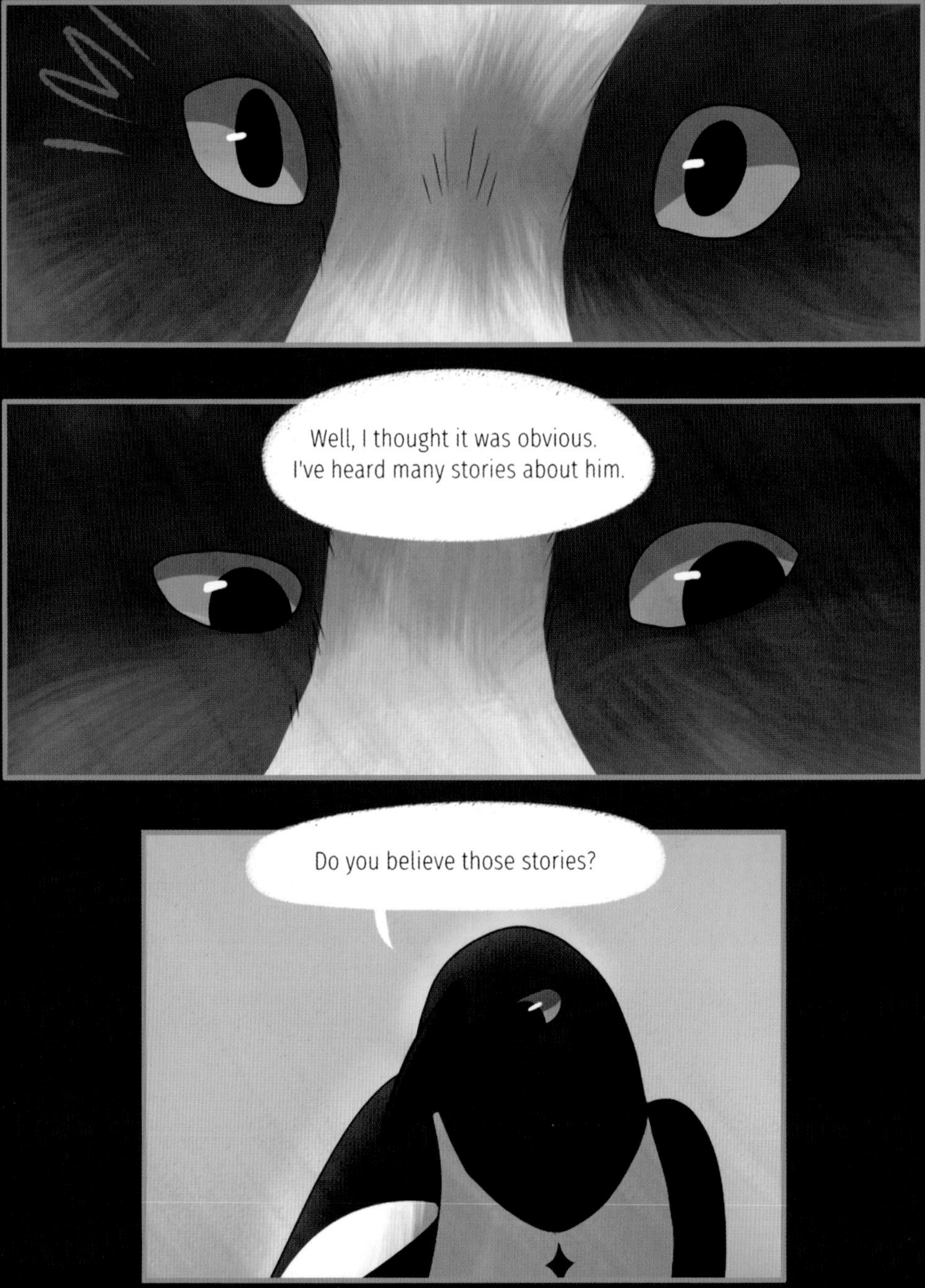
Well, I thought it was obvious.
I've heard many stories about him.
Do you believe those stories?

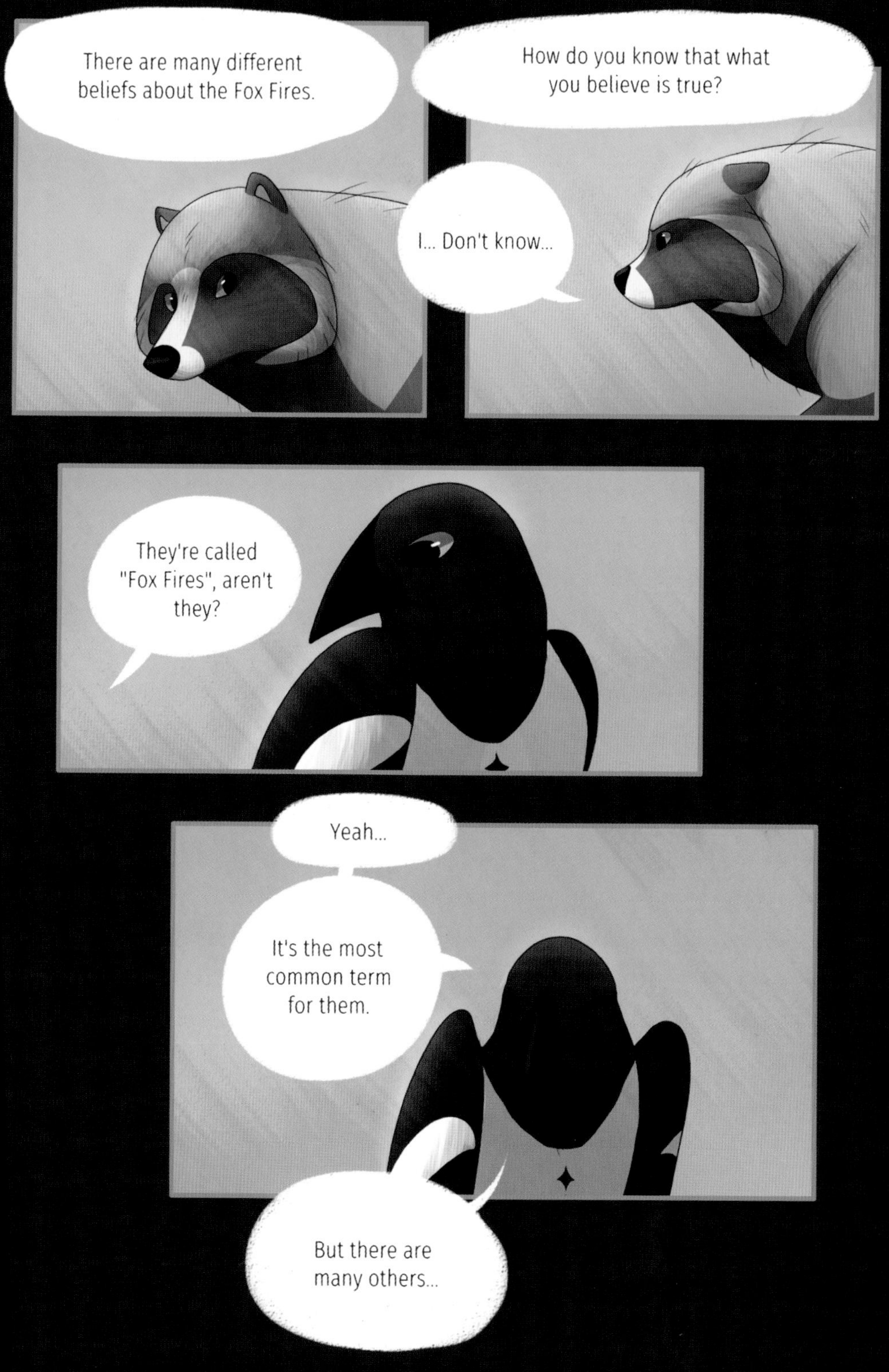

There are many different beliefs about the Fox Fires.
How do you know that what you believe is true?
I... Don't know...
They're called "Fox Fires", aren't they?
Yeah...
It's the most common term for them.
But there are many others...

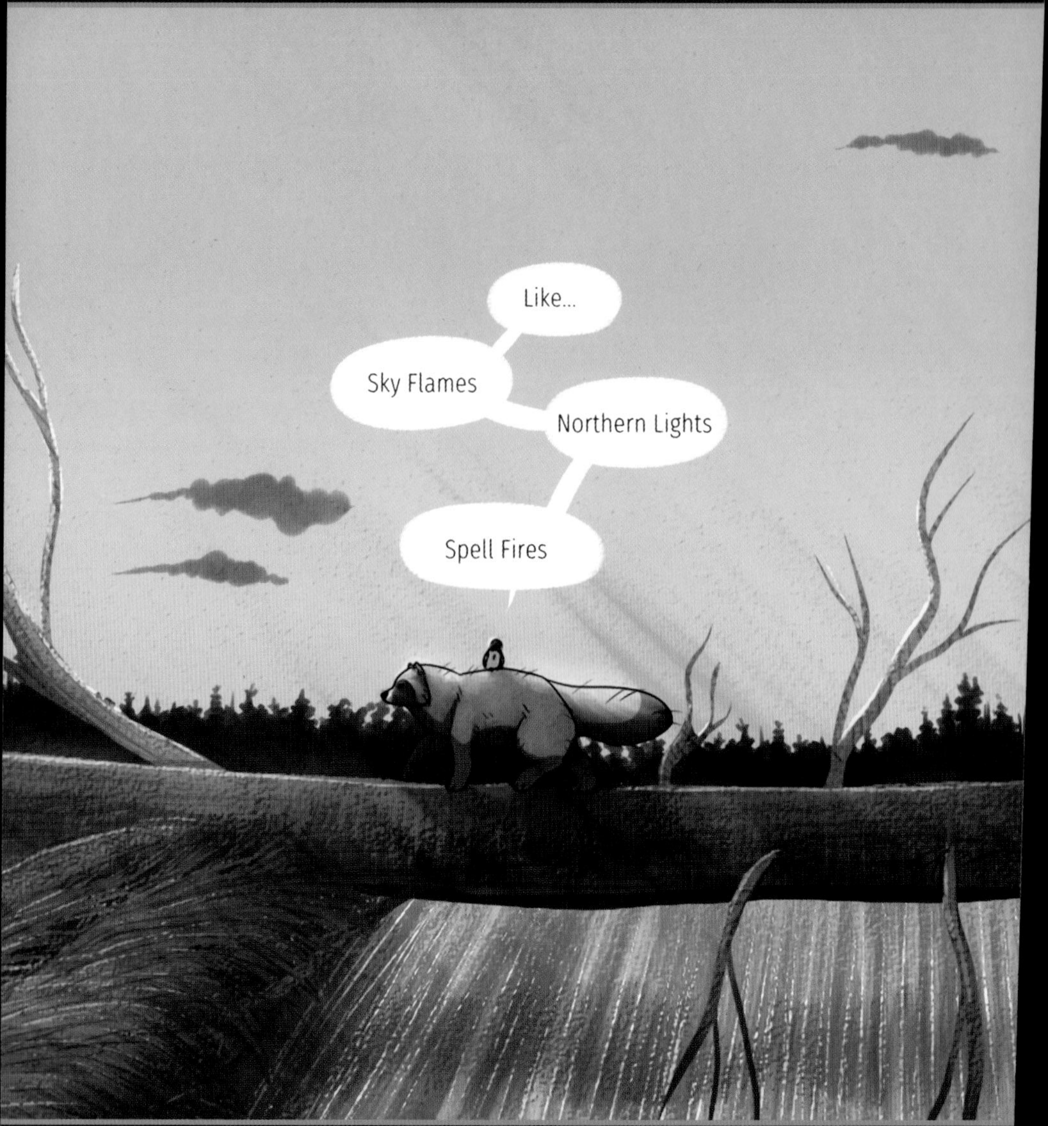
Like...
Sky Flames
Northern Lights
Spell Fires

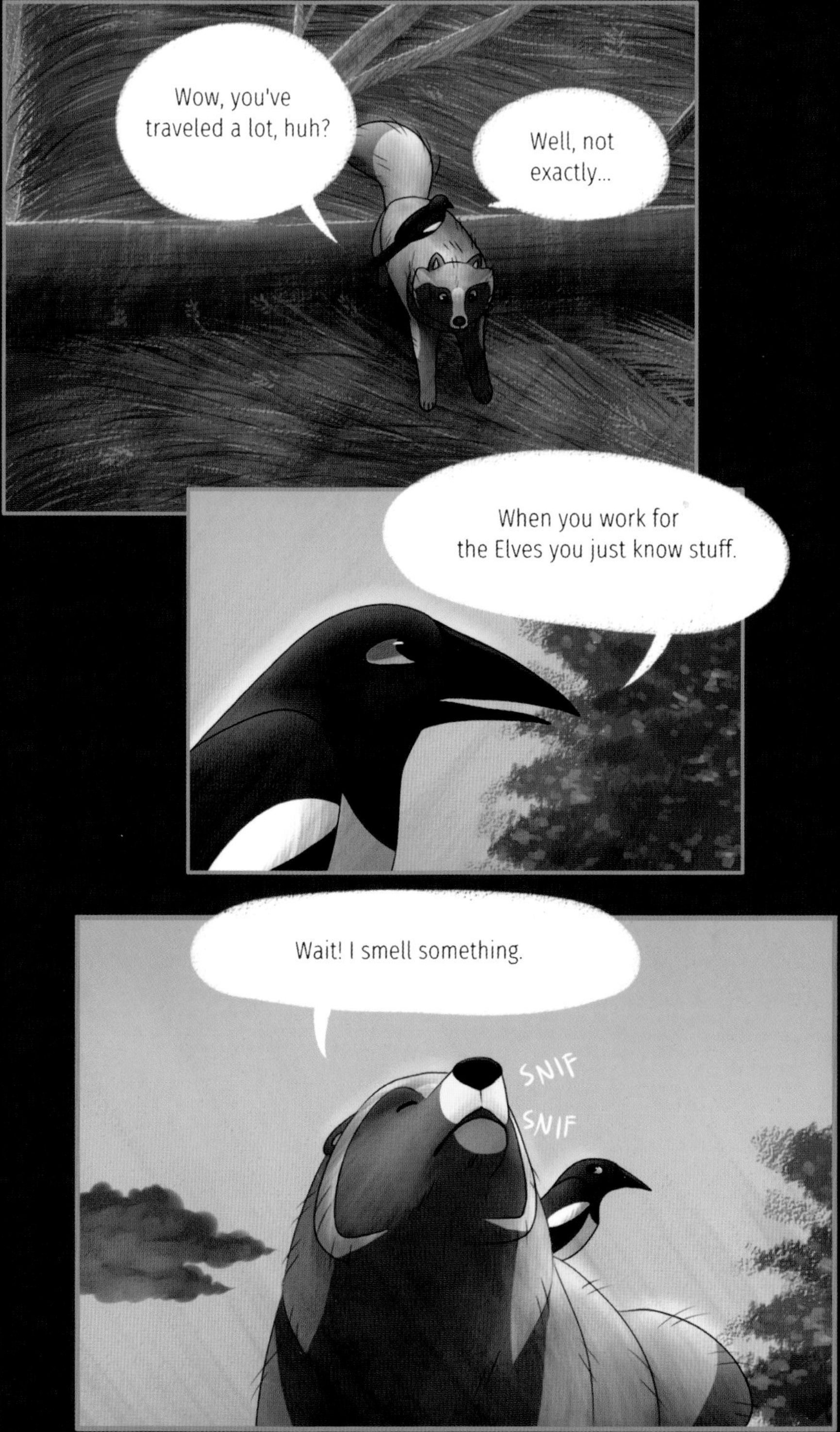
Wow, you've traveled a lot, huh?
Well, not exactly...
When you work for the Elves you just know stuff.
Wait! I smell something.
SNIF
SNIF

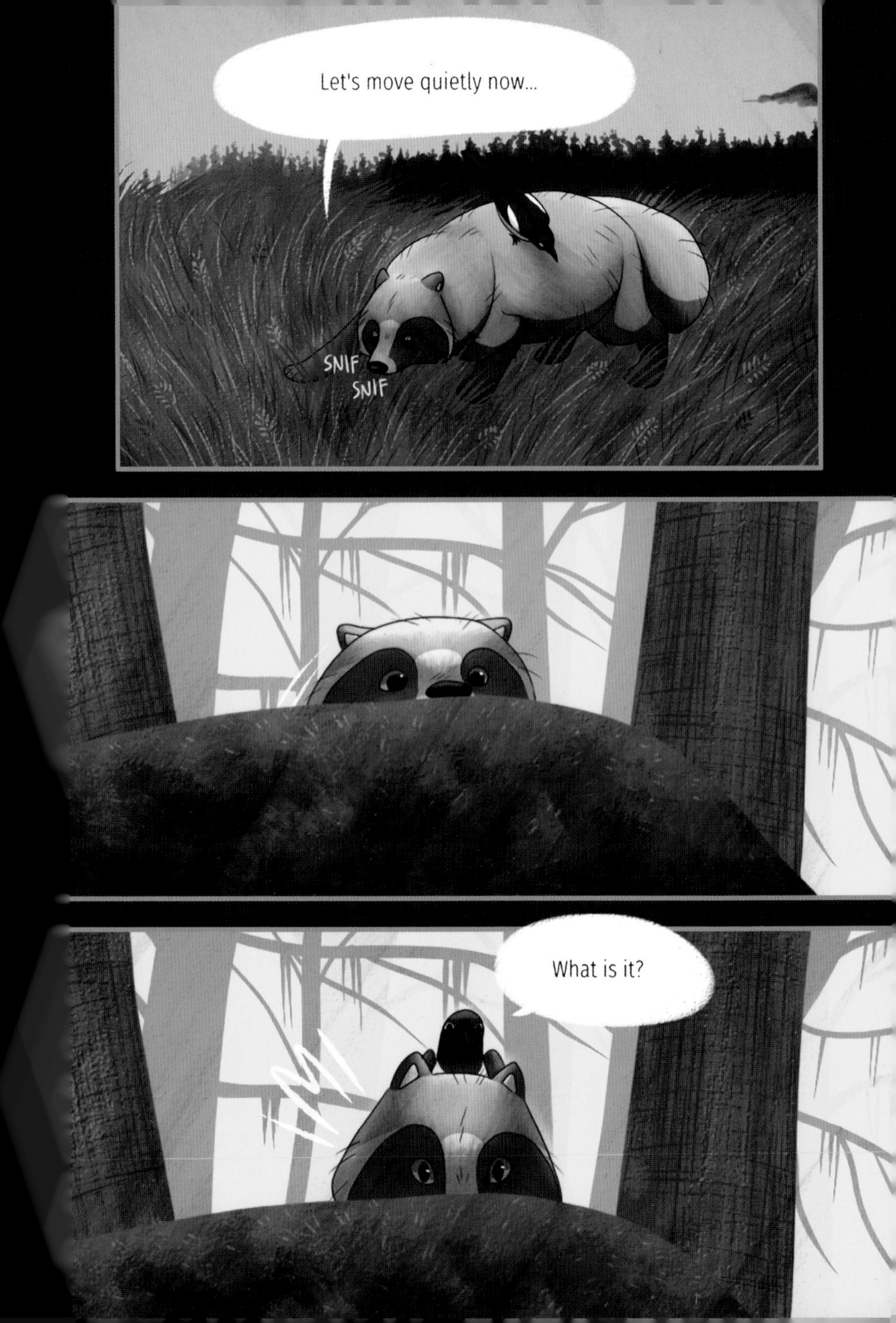

Let's move quietly now...
SNIF
SNIF
What is it?

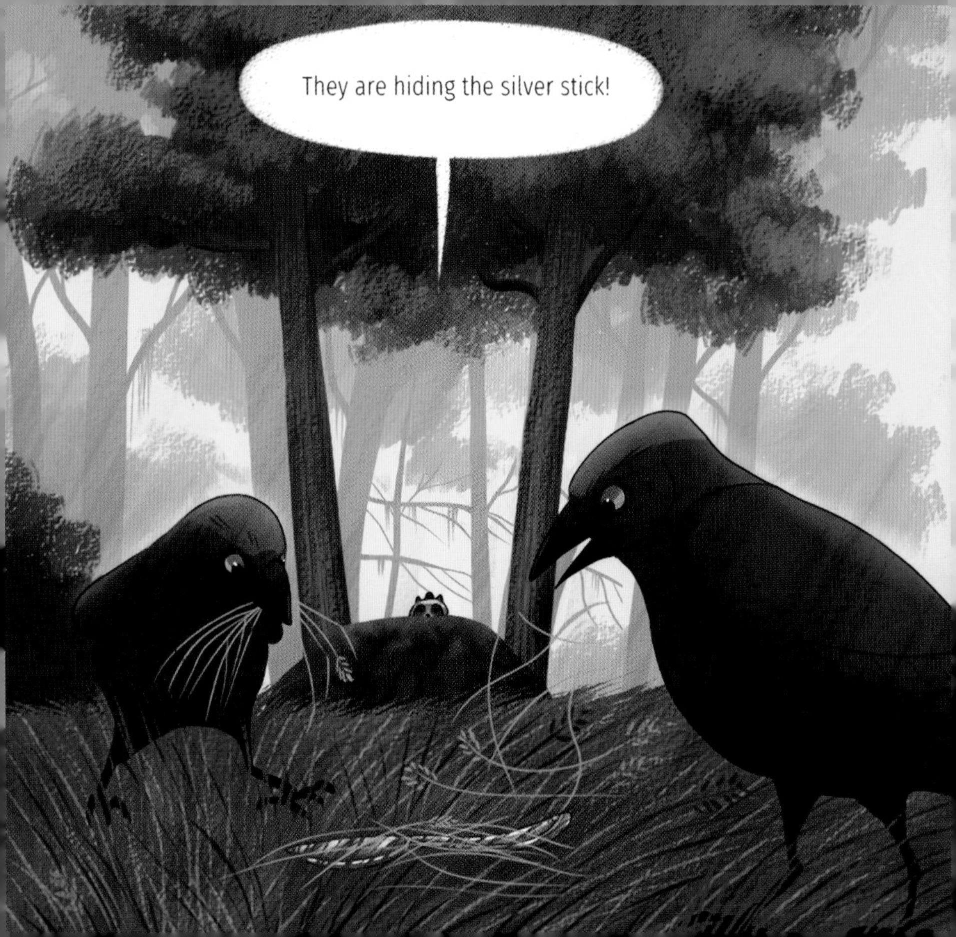
They are hiding the silver stick!

Chapter 14

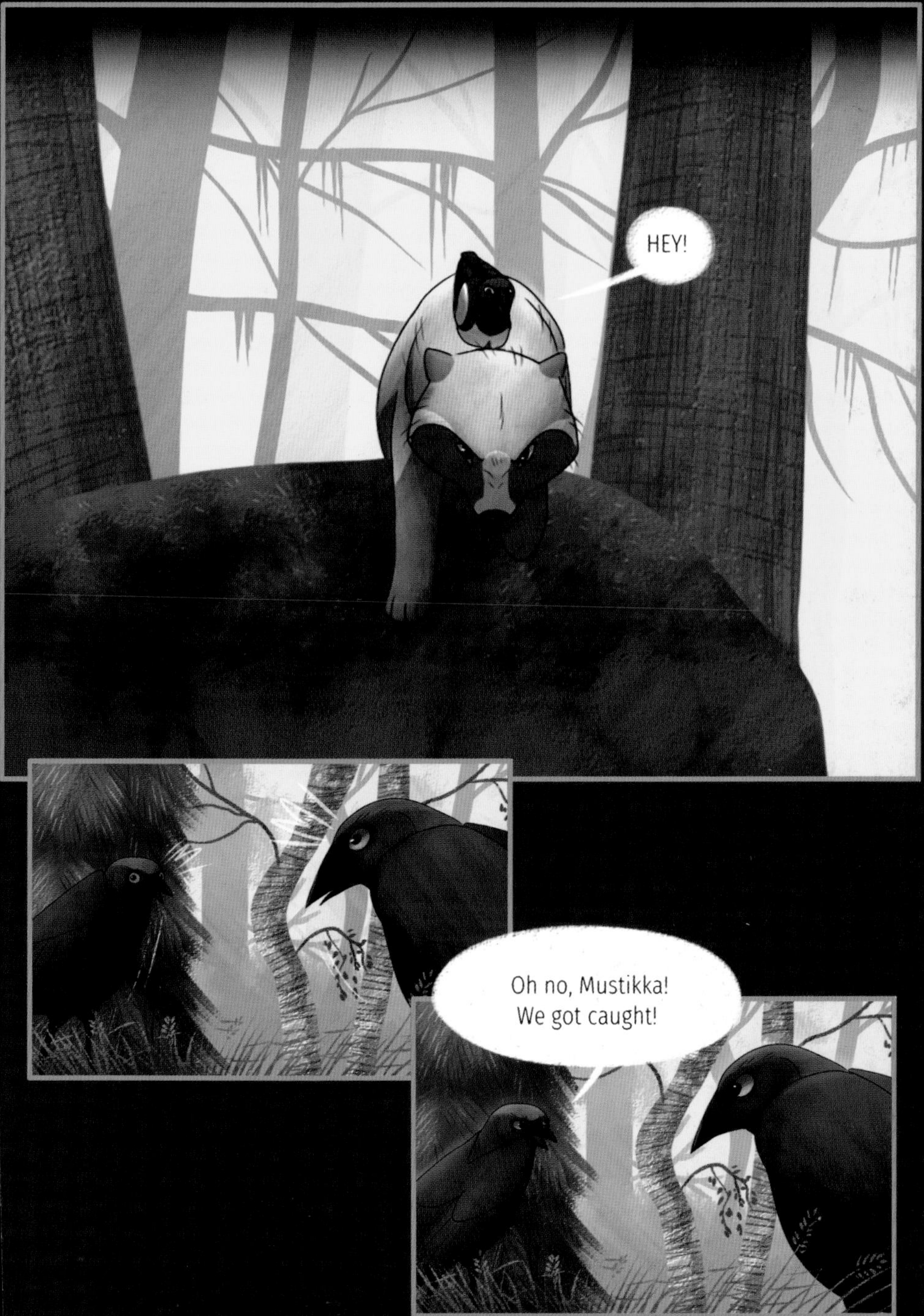

HEY!
Oh no, Mustikka! We got caught!

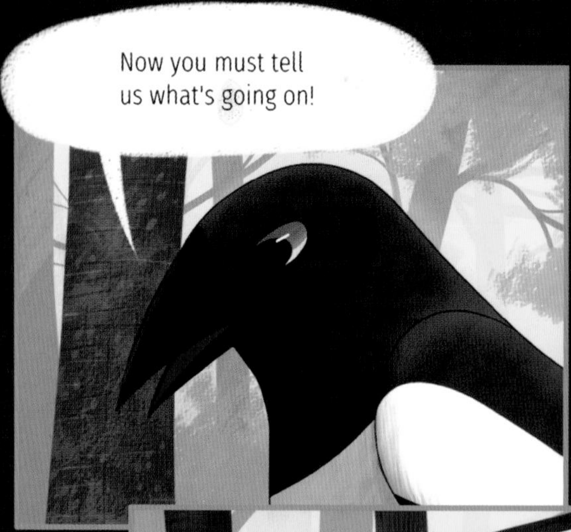
Now you must tell us what's going on!

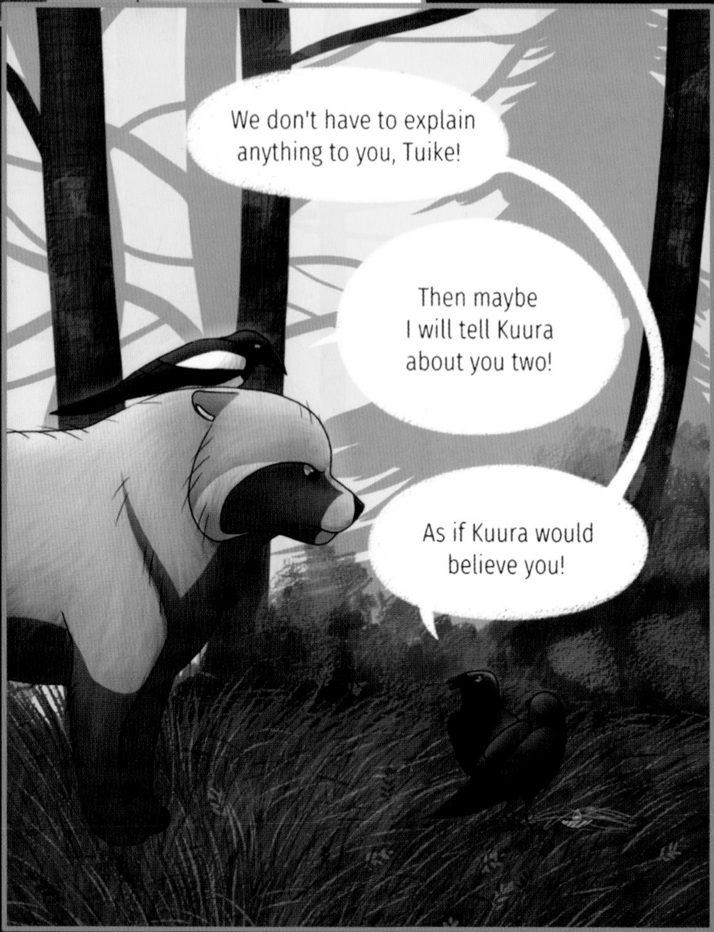
We don't have to explain anything to you, Tuike!
Then maybe I will tell Kuura about you two!
As if Kuura would believe you!

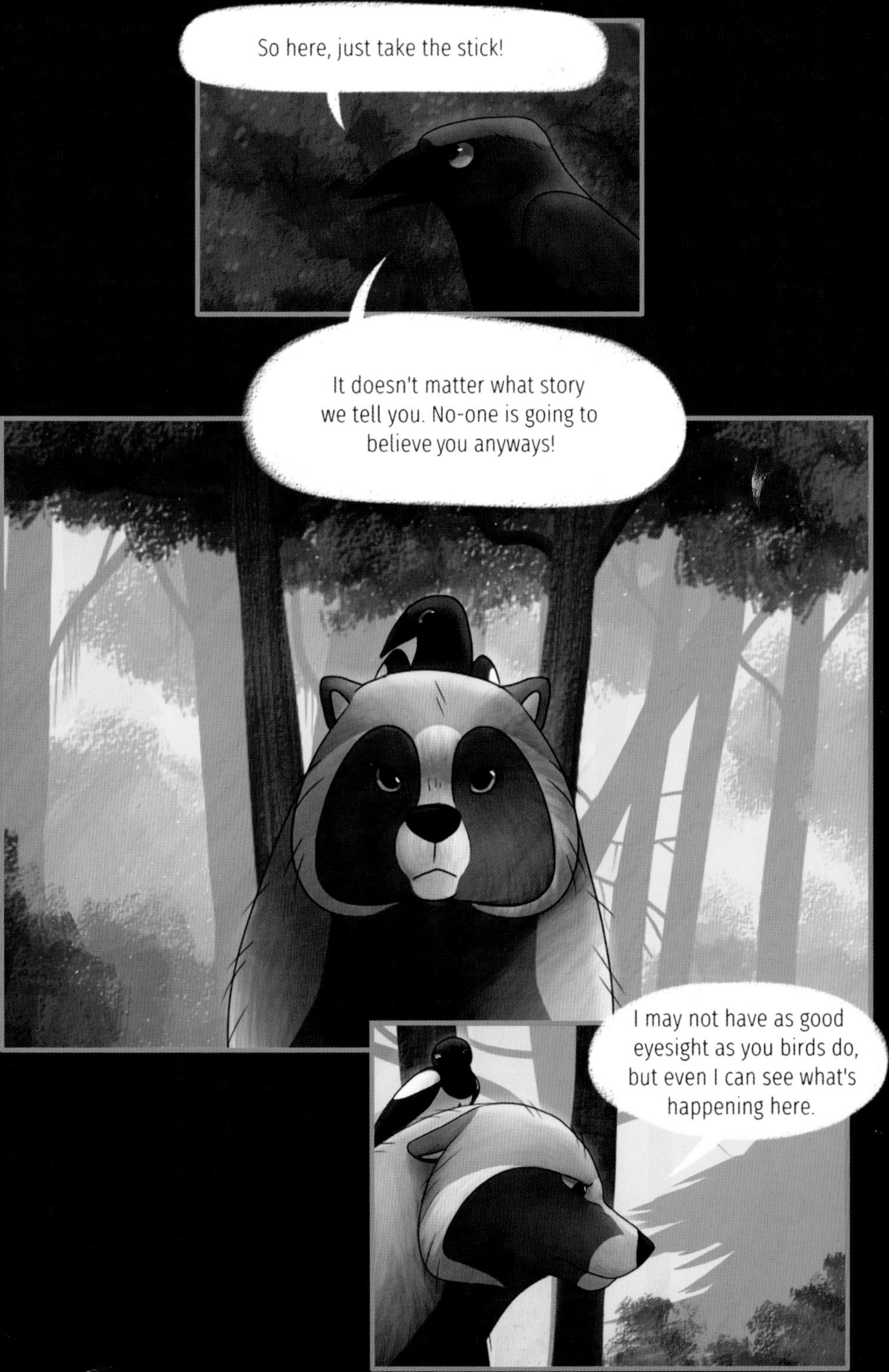
So here, just take the stick!
It doesn't matter what story we tell you. No-one is going to believe you anyways!
I may not have as good eyesight as you birds do, but even I can see what's happening here.

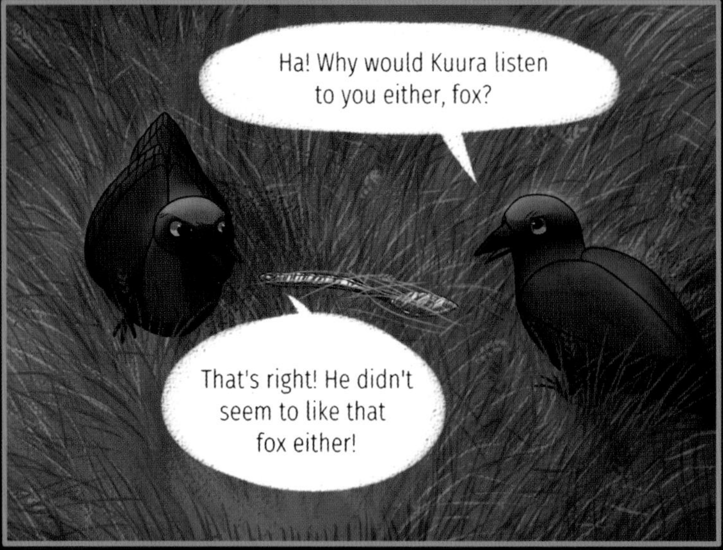
Ha! Why would Kuura listen to you either, fox?
That's right! He didn't seem to like that fox either!

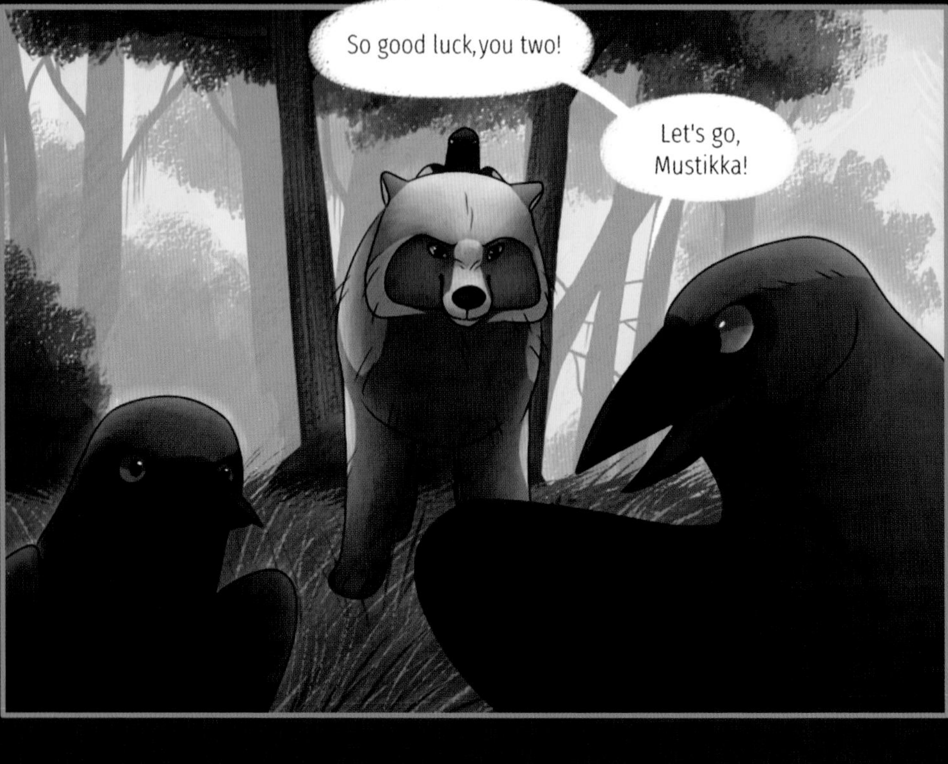
So good luck,you two!
Let's go, Mustikka!

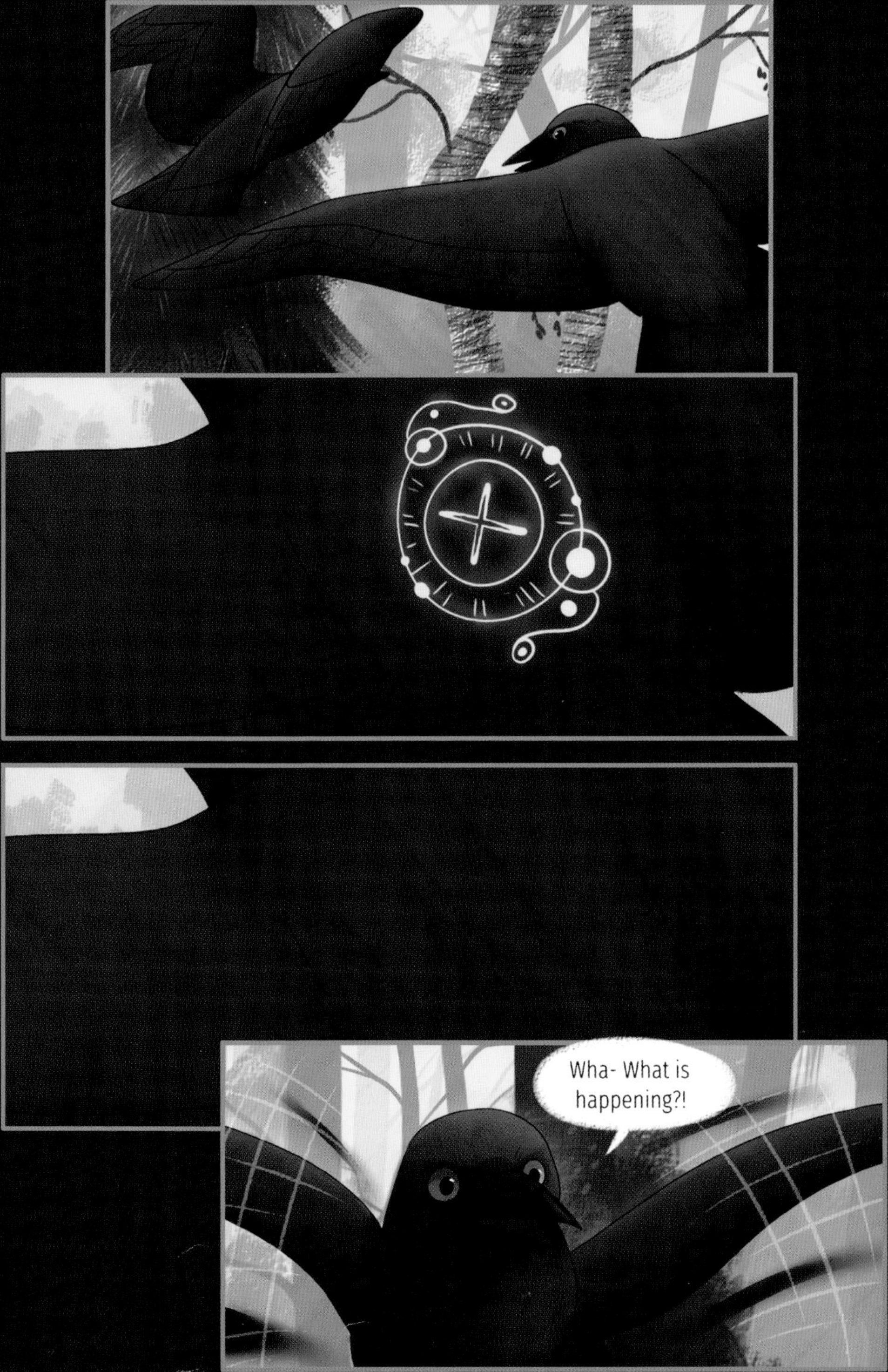
Wha- What is happening?!

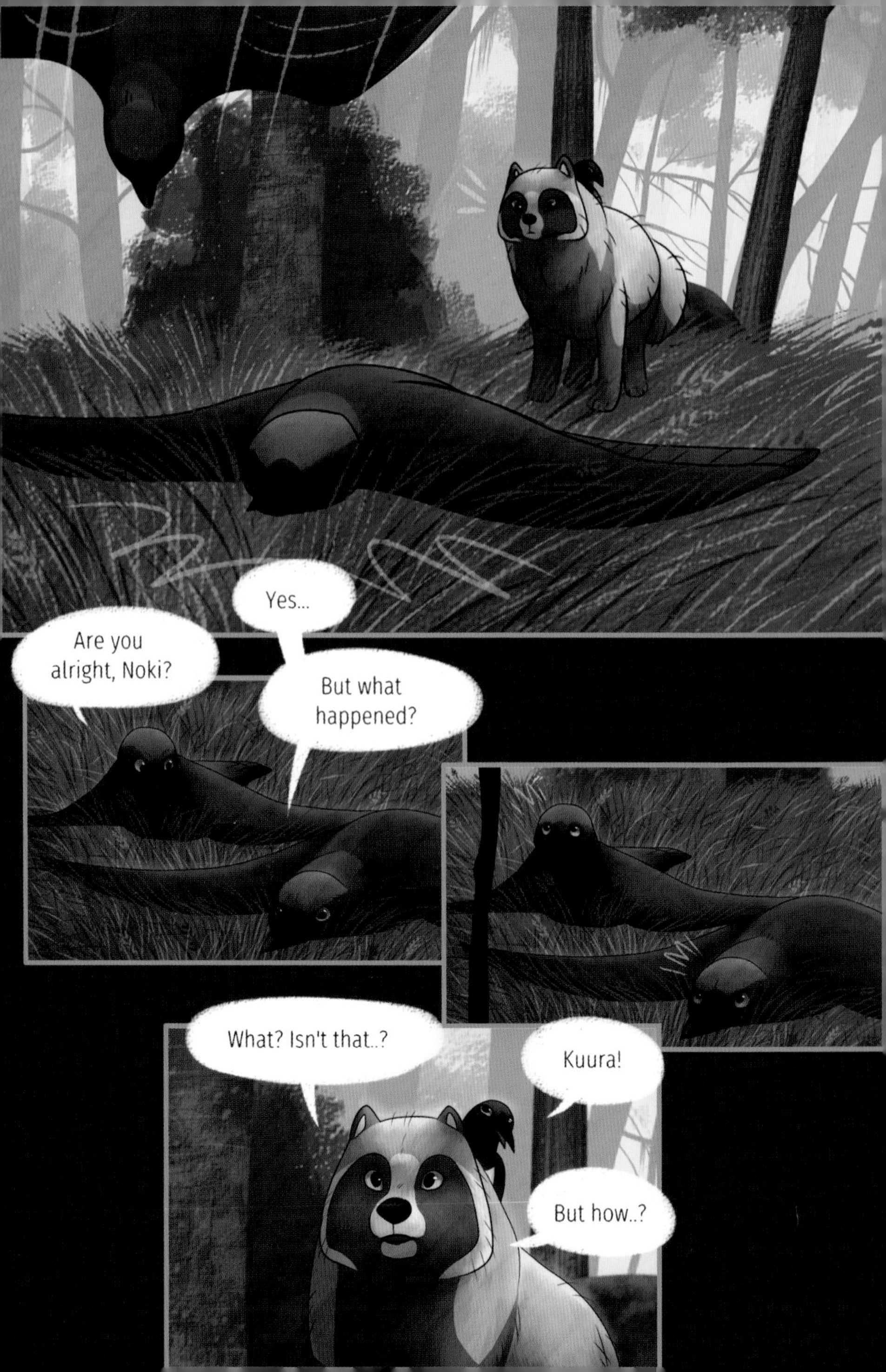

Are you alright, Noki?
Yes...
But what happened?
What? Isn't that..?
Kuura!
But how..?

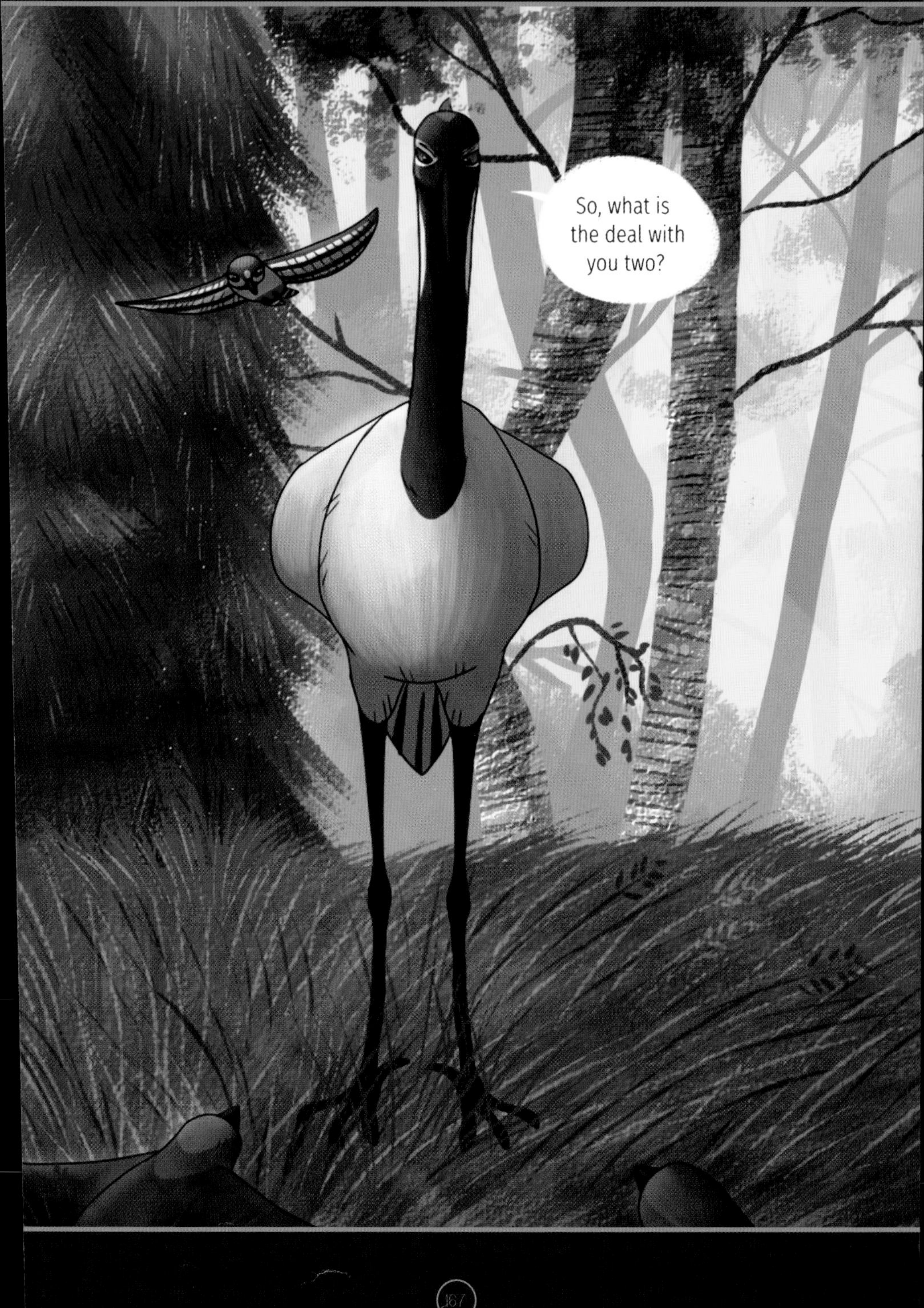
So, what is the deal with you two?

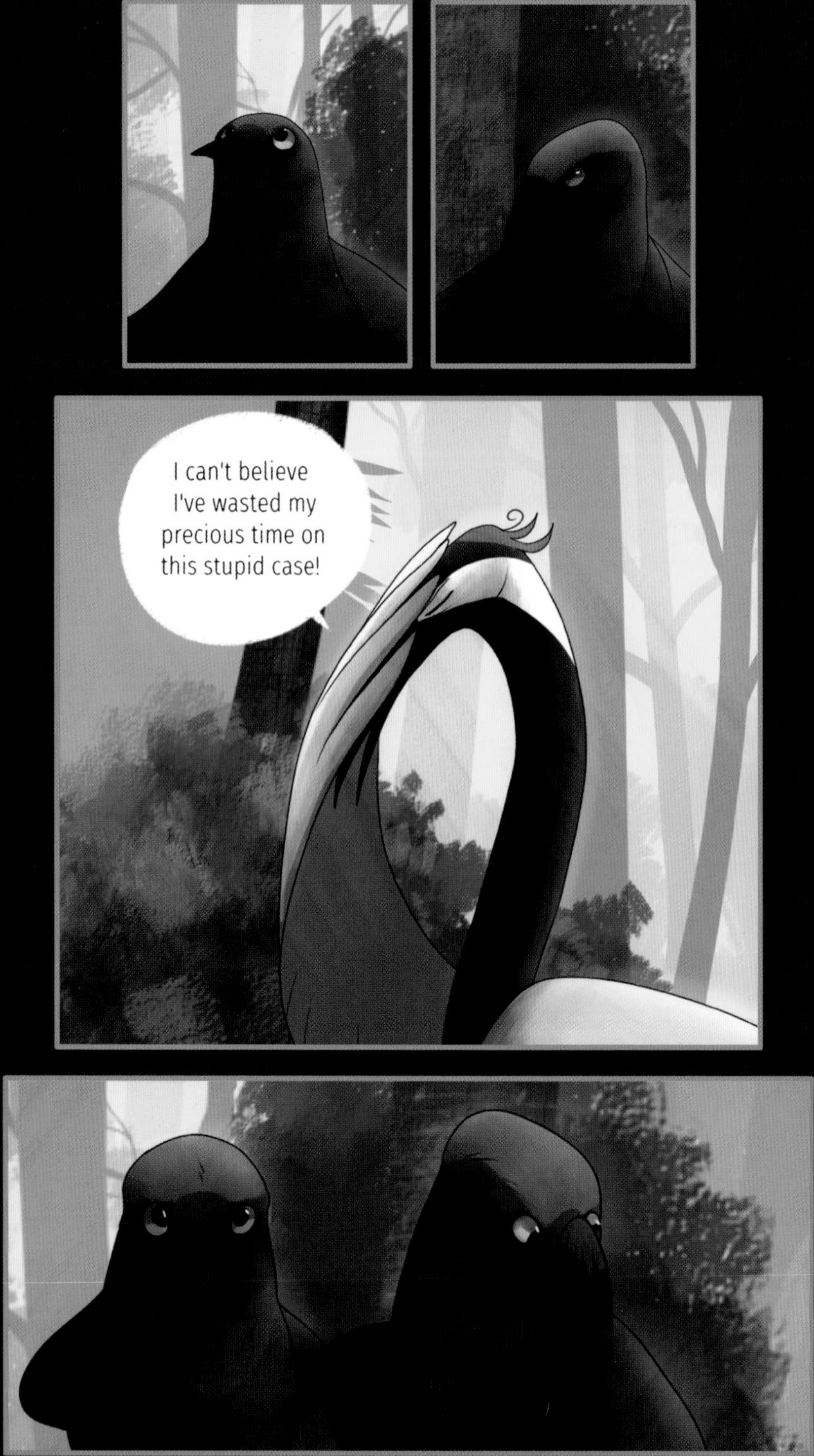
I can't believe I've wasted my precious time on this stupid case!

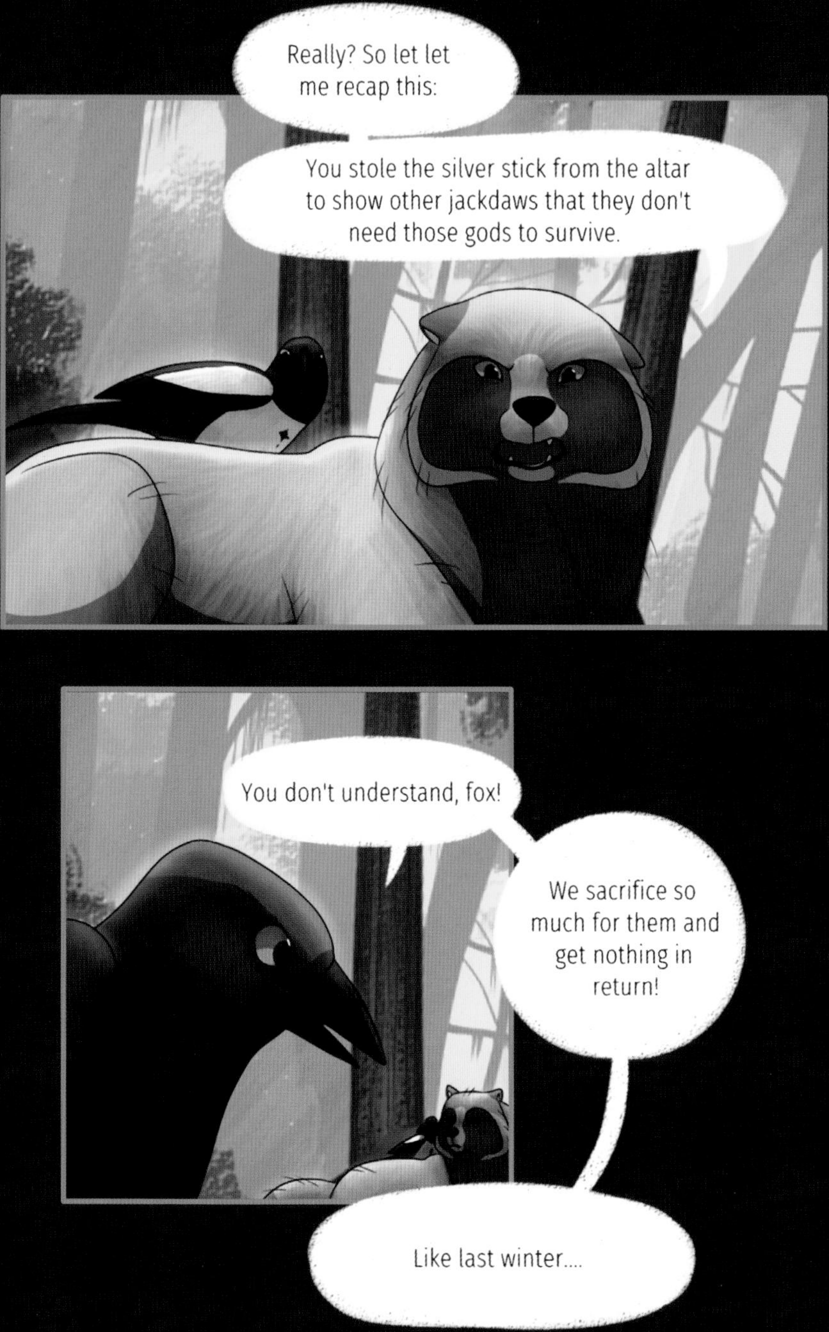
Really? So let let me recap this:
You stole the silver stick from the altar to show other jackdaws that they don't need those gods to survive.
You don't understand, fox!
We sacrifice so much for them and get nothing in return!
Like last winter....

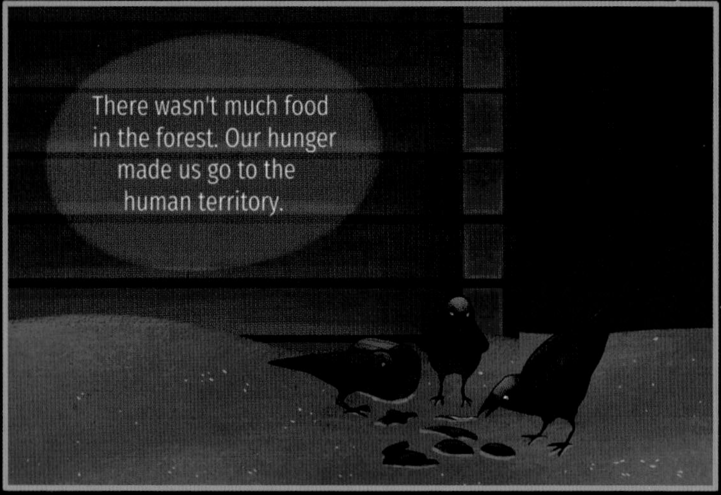
There wasn't much food in the forest. Our hunger made us go to the human territory.

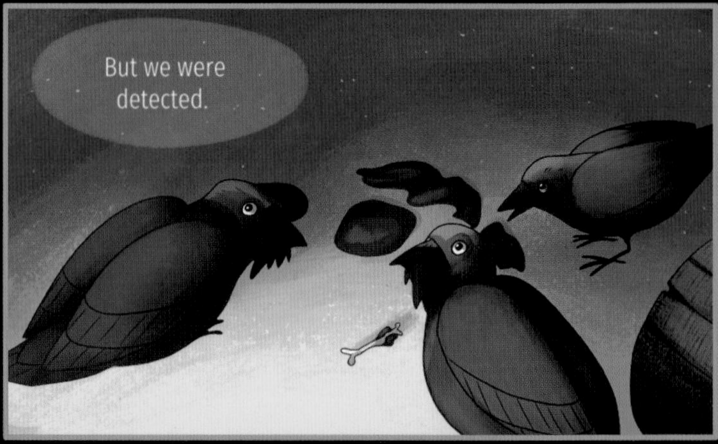
But we were detected.

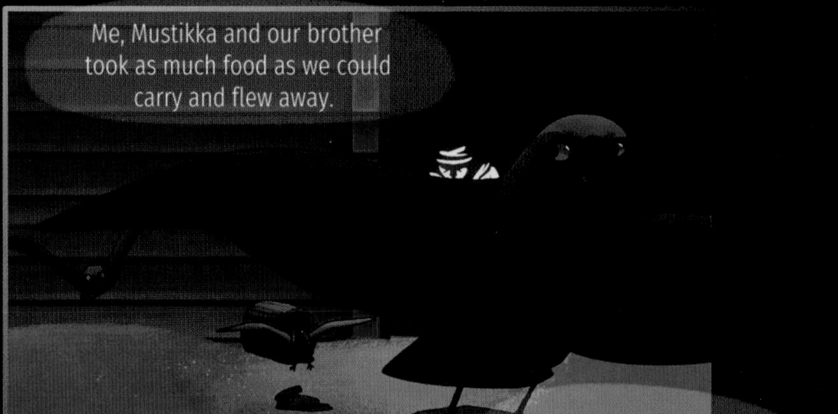
Me, Mustikka and our brother took as much food as we could carry and flew away.

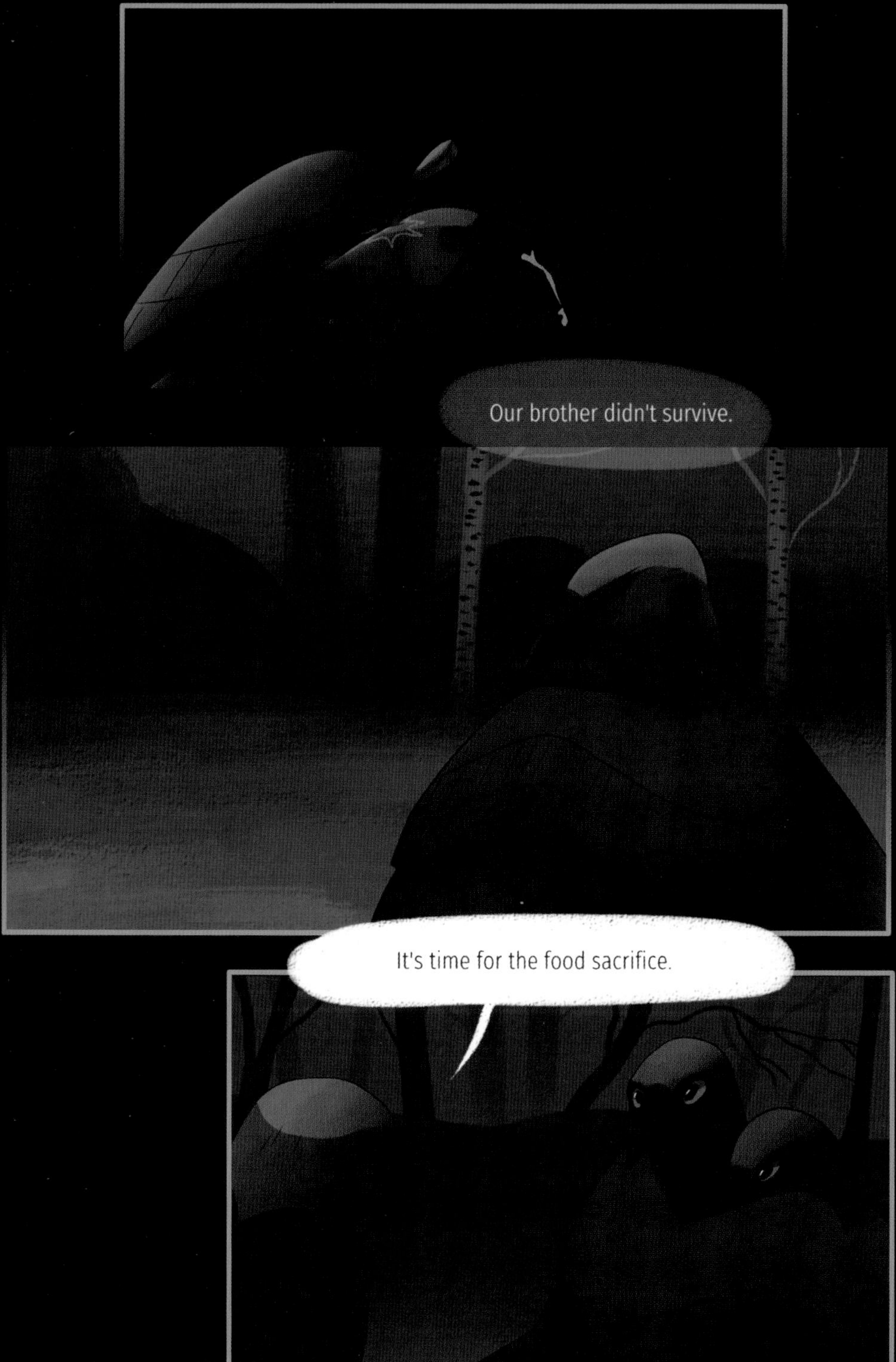
Our brother didn't survive.
It's time for the food sacrifice.

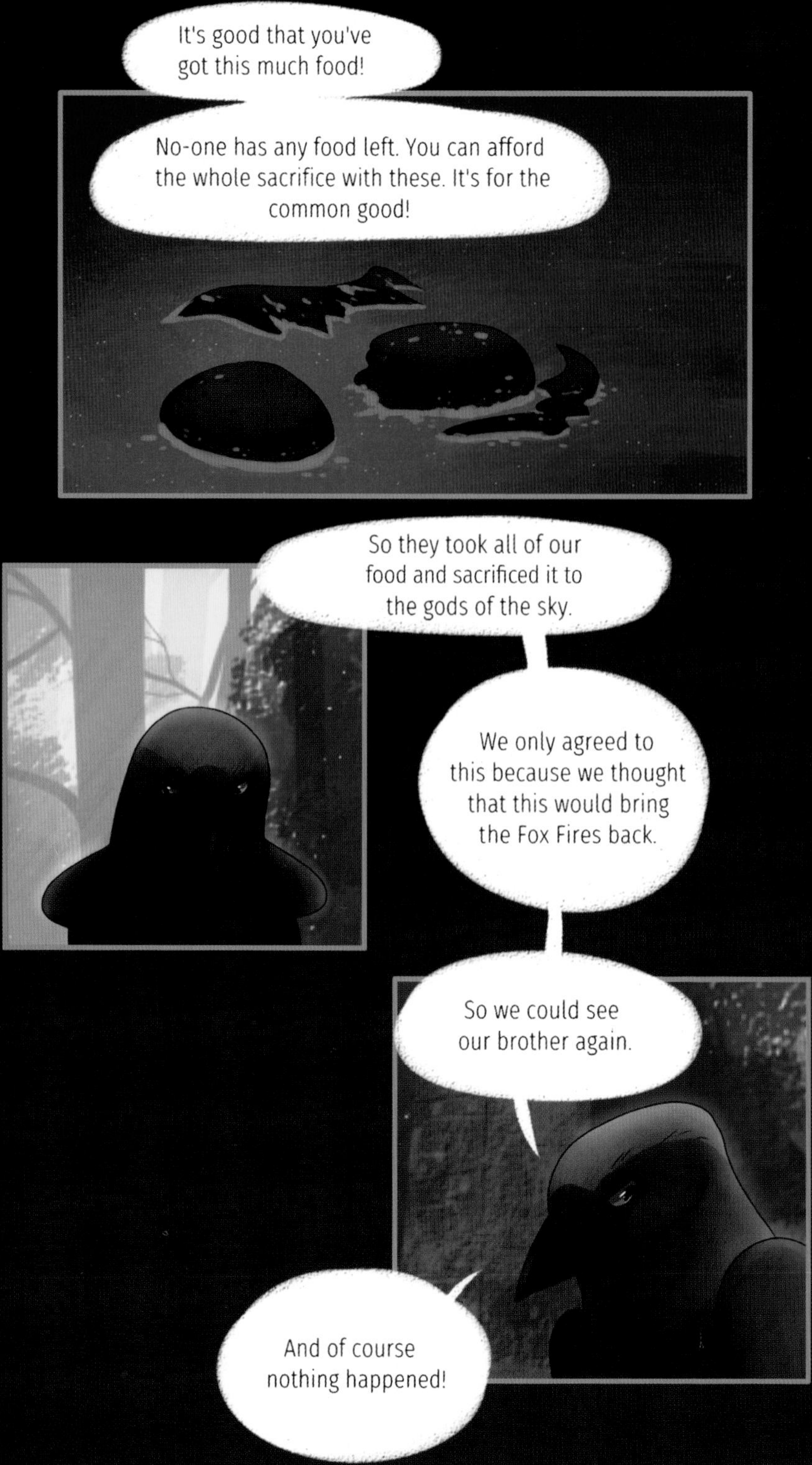
It's good that you've got this much food!
No-one has any food left. You can afford the whole sacrifice with these. It's for the common good!
So they took all of our food and sacrificed it to the gods of the sky.
We only agreed to this because we thought that this would bring the Fox Fires back.
So we could see our brother again.
And of course nothing happened!

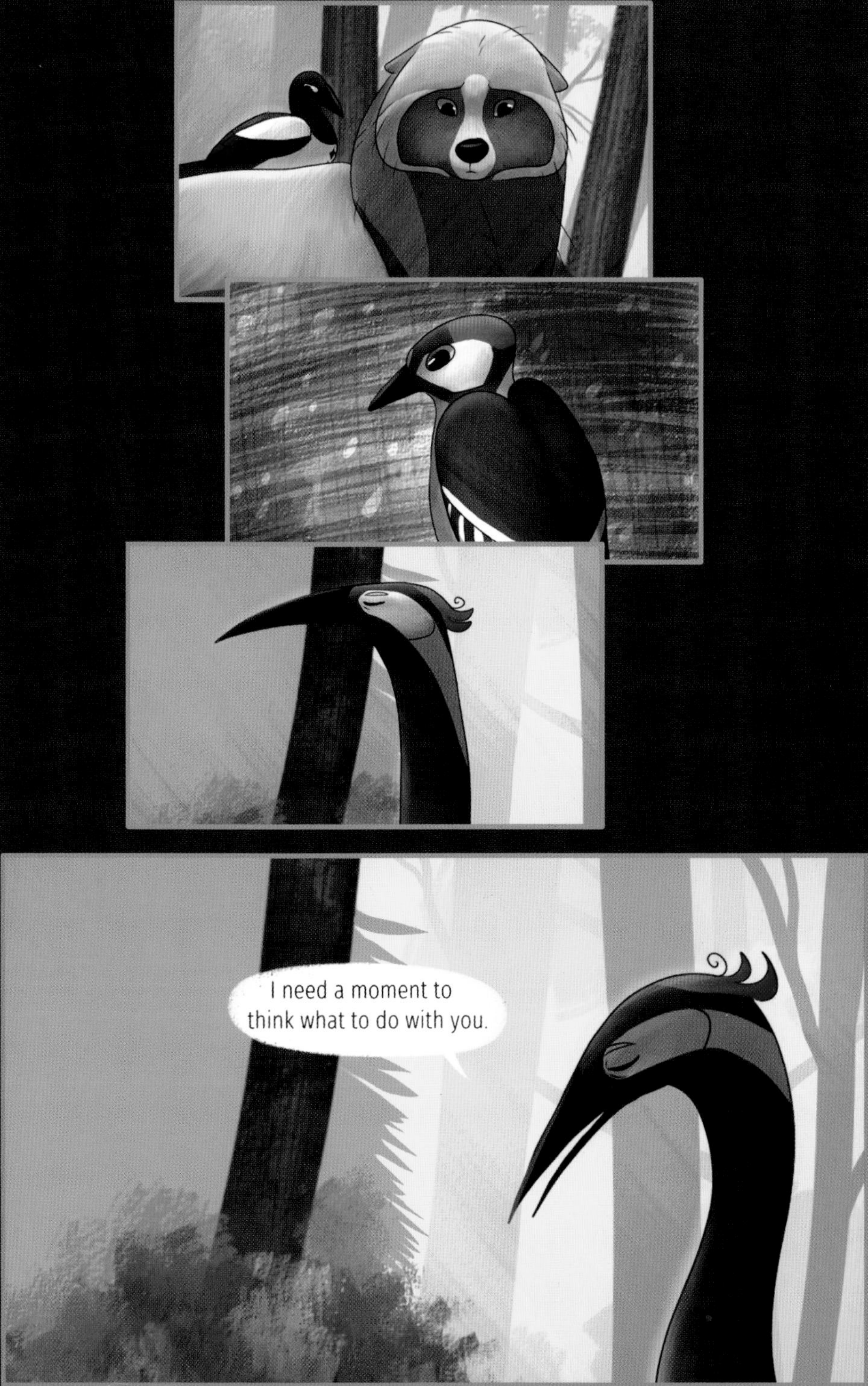
I need a moment to think what to do with you.

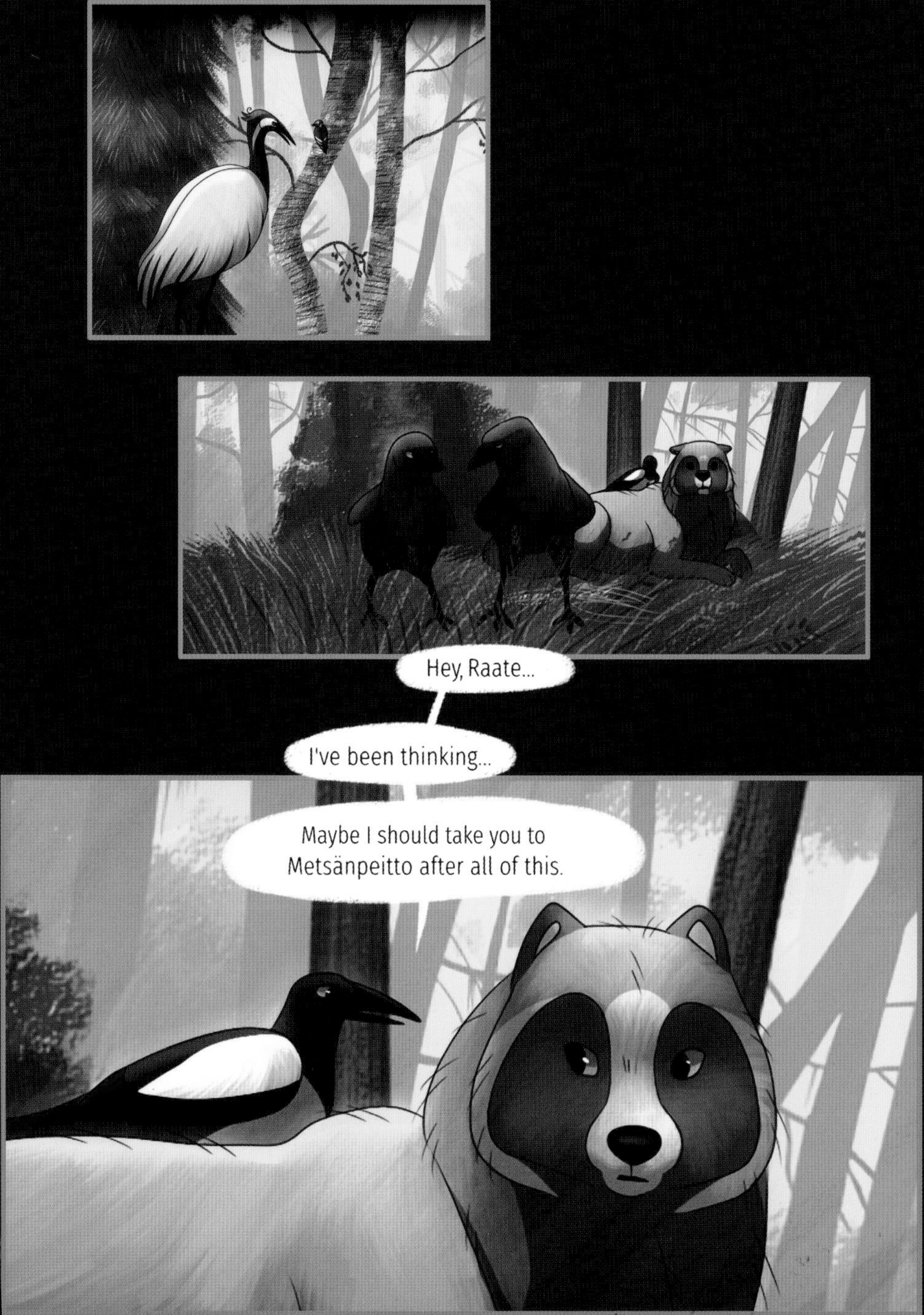
Hey, Raate...
I've been thinking...
Maybe I should take you to Metsänpeitto after all of this.

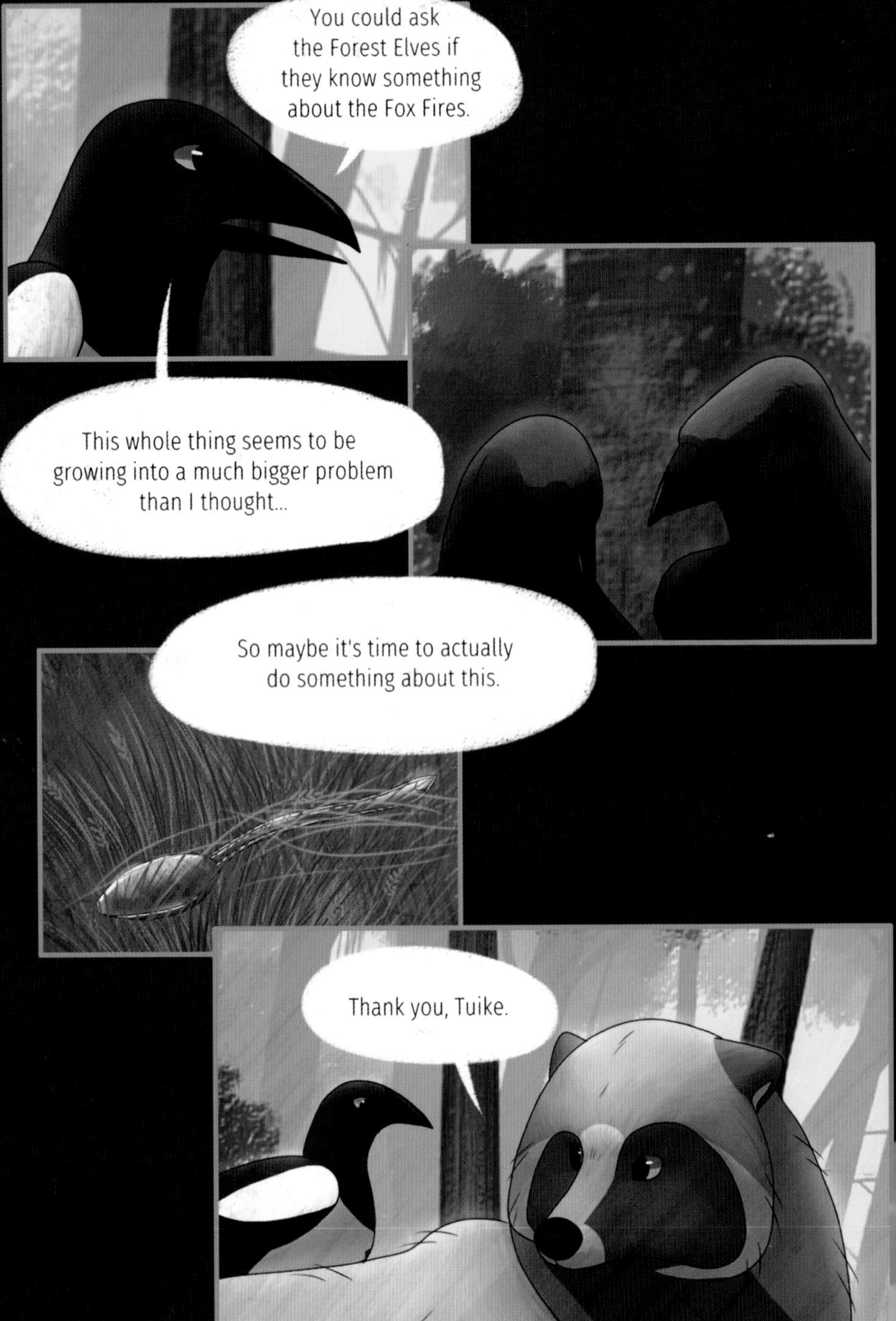
You could ask the Forest Elves if they know something about the Fox Fires.
This whole thing seems to be growing into a much bigger problem than I thought...
So maybe it's time to actually do something about this.
Thank you, Tuike.

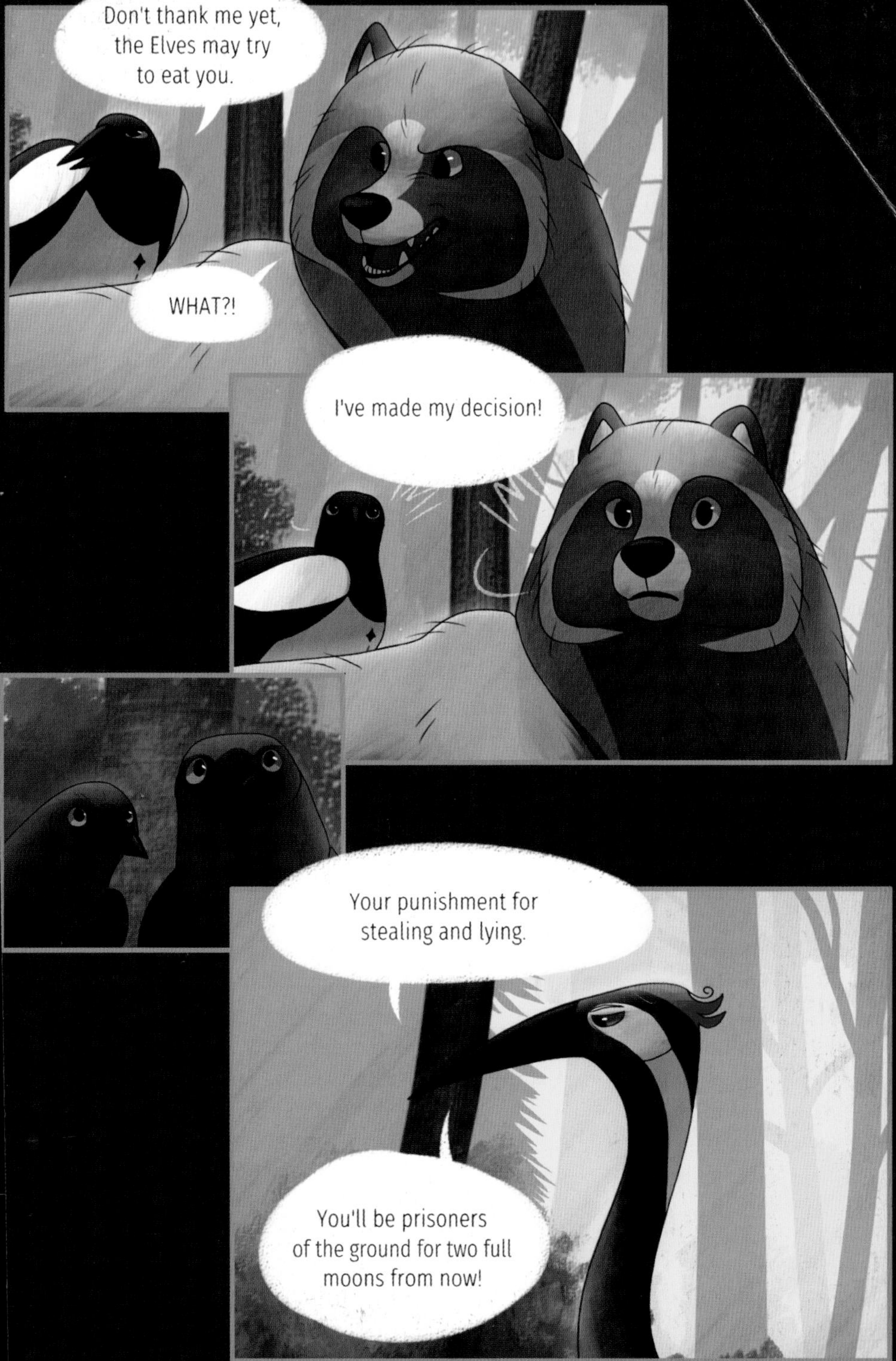
Don't thank me yet, the Elves may try to eat you.
WHAT?!
I've made my decision!
Your punishment for stealing and lying.
You'll be prisoners of the ground for two full moons from now!

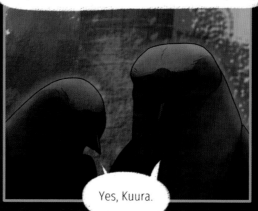

I'm sorry about what happened to your brother, but you still broke the rules, which is unacceptable.

Yes, Kuura.

And then you two!

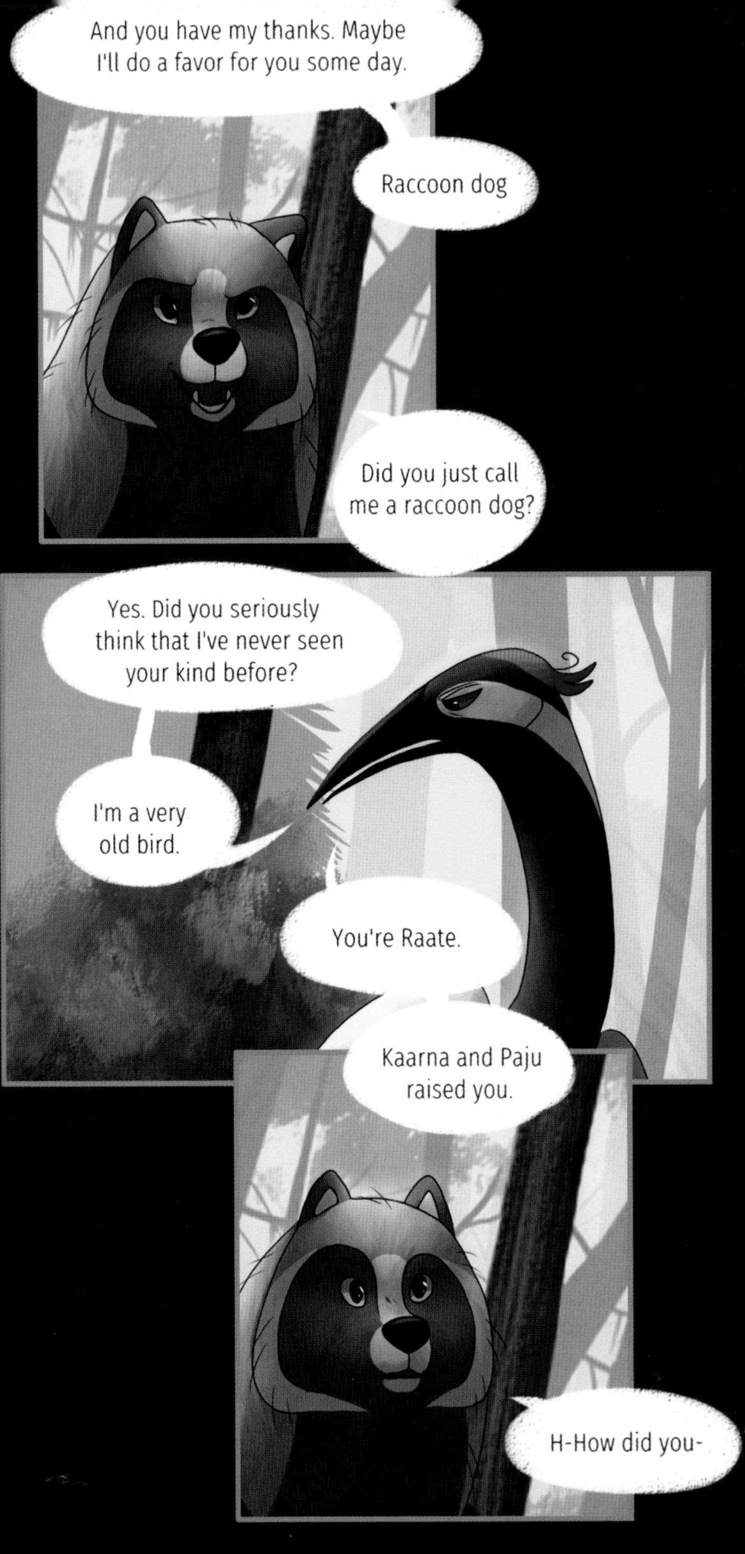

And you have my thanks. Maybe I'll do a favor for you some day.
Raccoon dog
Did you just call me a raccoon dog?
Yes. Did you seriously think that I've never seen your kind before?
I'm a very old bird.
You're Raate.
Kaarna and Paju raised you.
H-How did you-

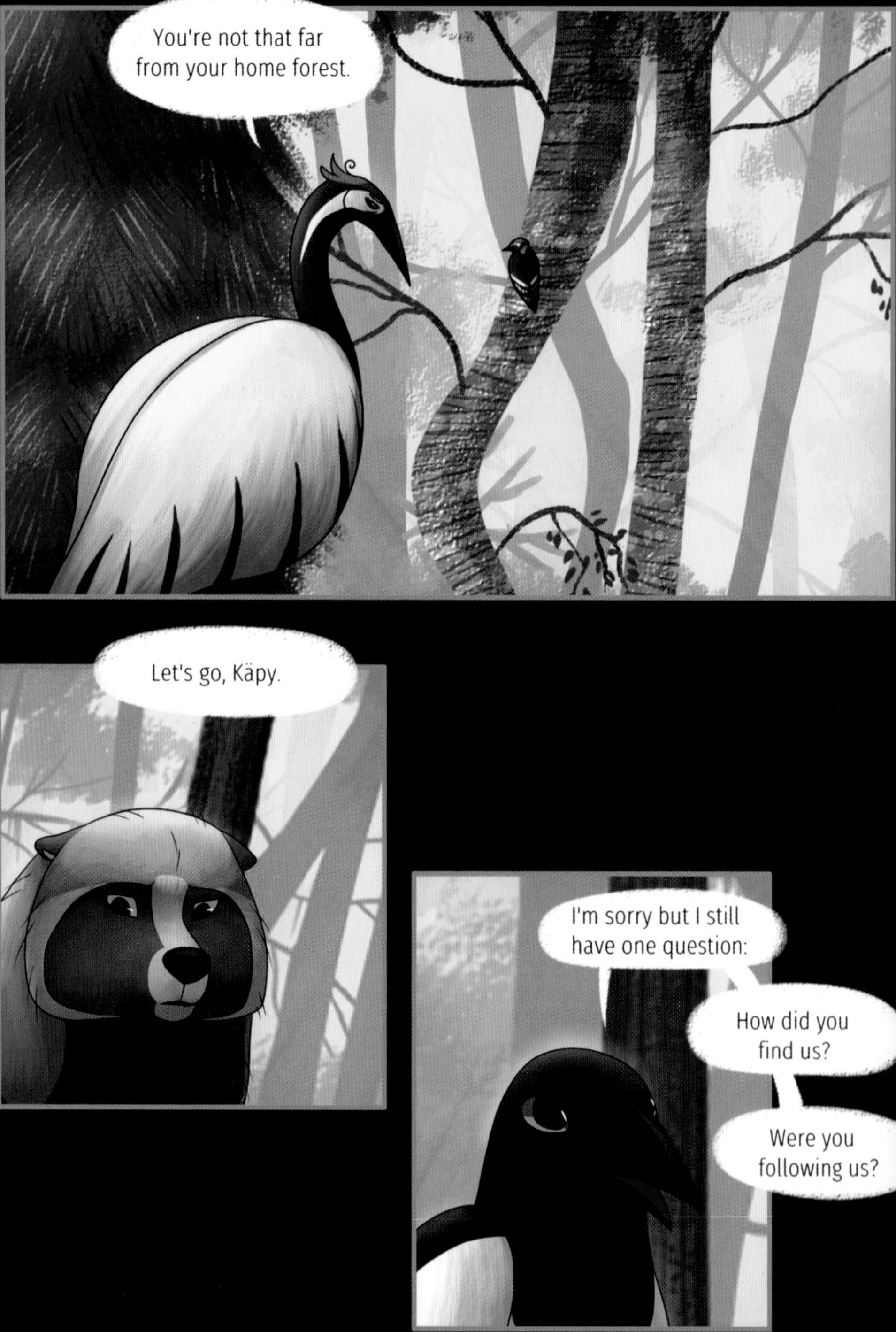
You're not that far from your home forest.
Let's go, Käpy.
I'm sorry but I still have one question:
How did you find us?
Were you following us?

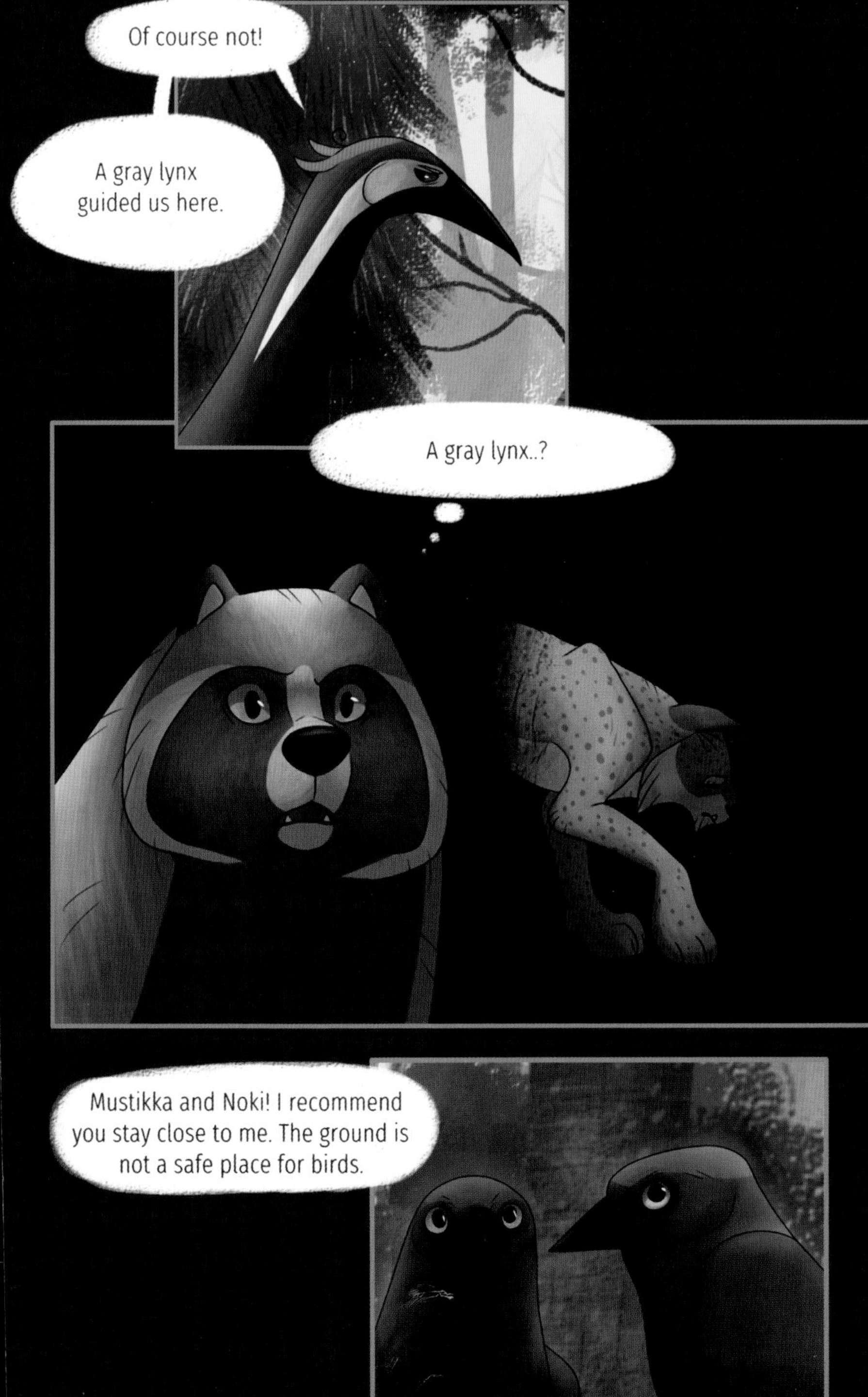
Of course not!
A gray lynx guided us here.
A gray lynx..?
Mustikka and Noki! I recommend you stay close to me. The ground is not a safe place for birds.

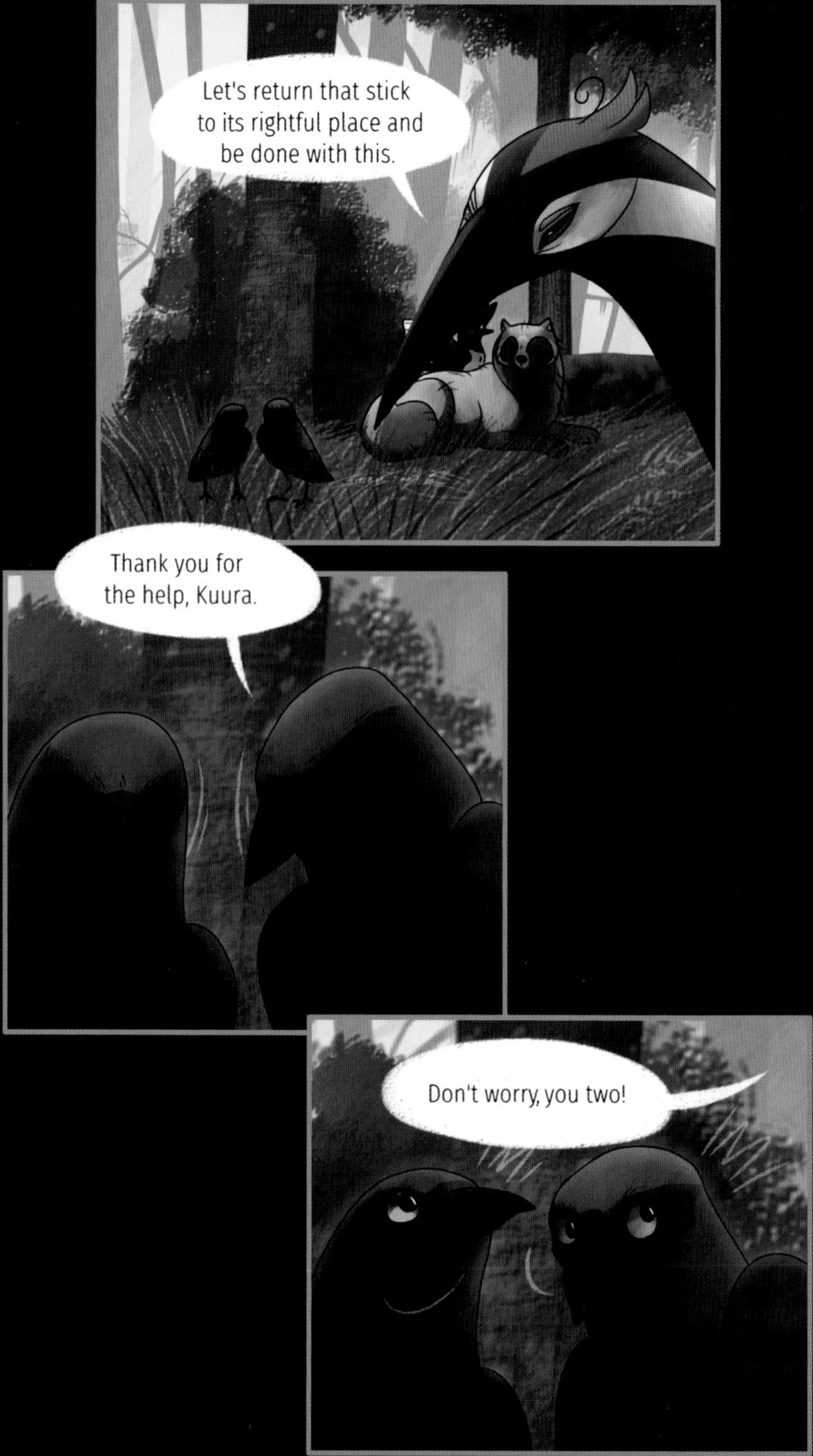
Let's return that stick to its rightful place and be done with this.
Thank you for the help, Kuura.
Don't worry, you two!

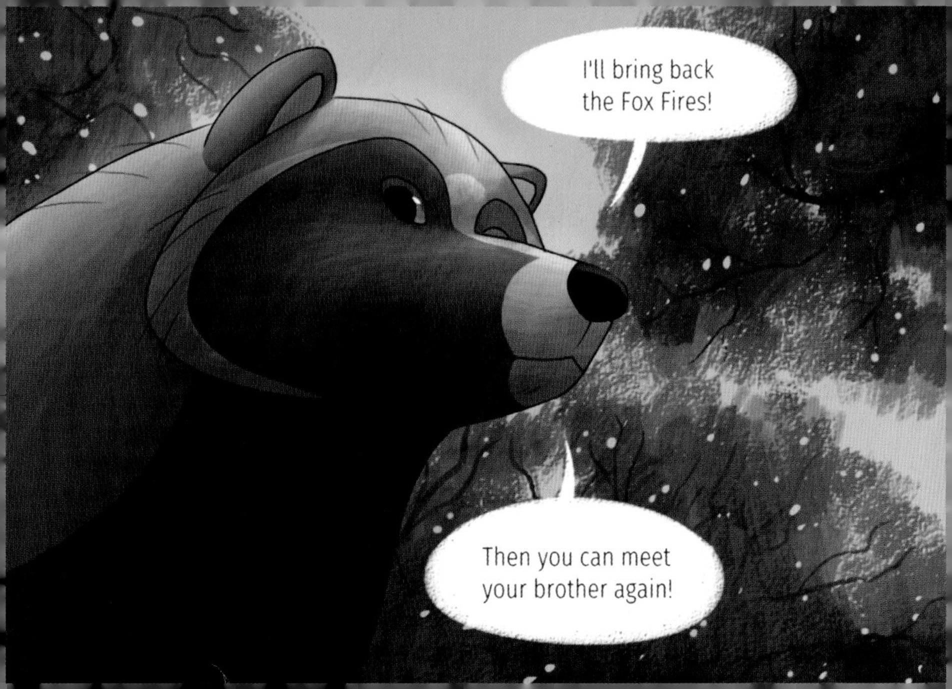
I'll bring back the Fox Fires!
Then you can meet your brother again!

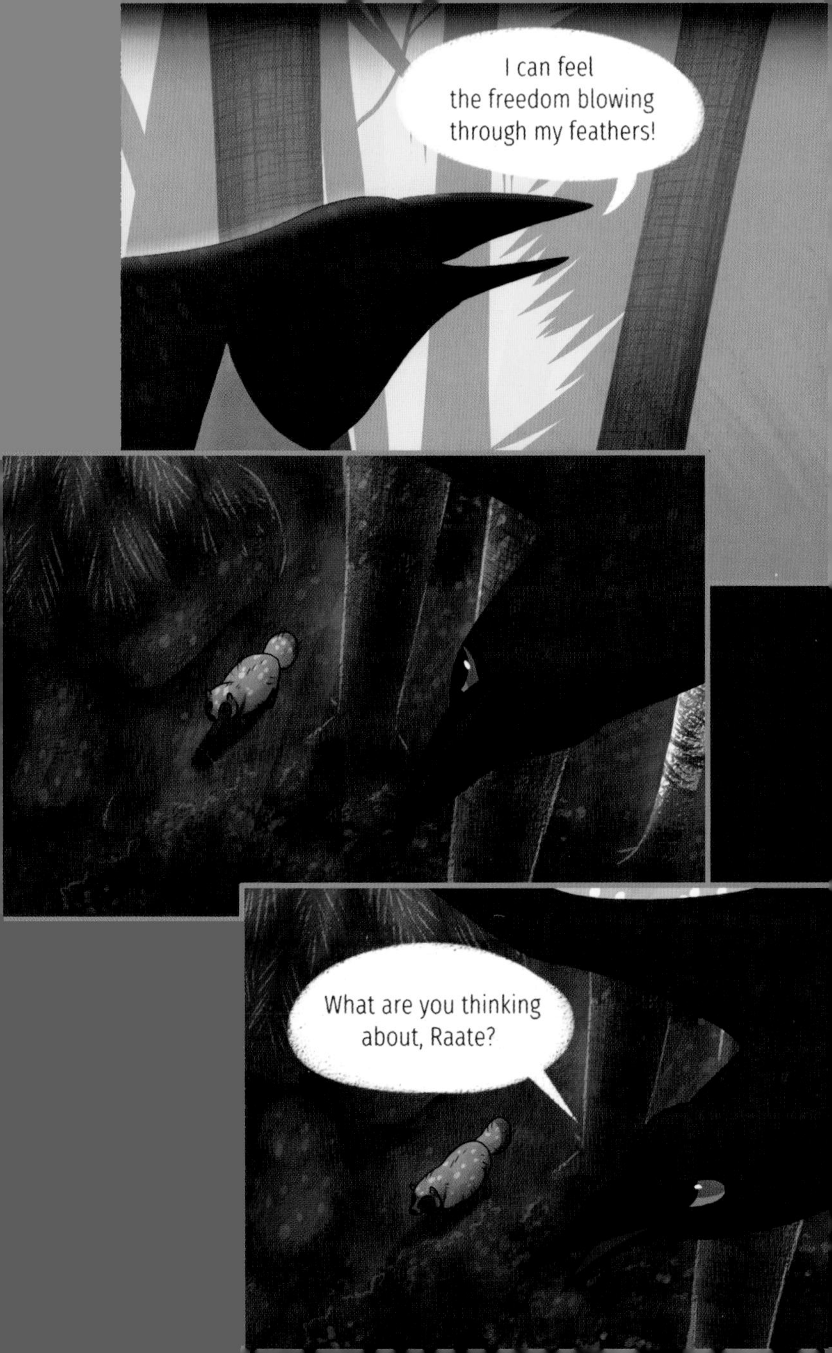
I can feel the freedom blowing through my feathers!
What are you thinking about, Raate?

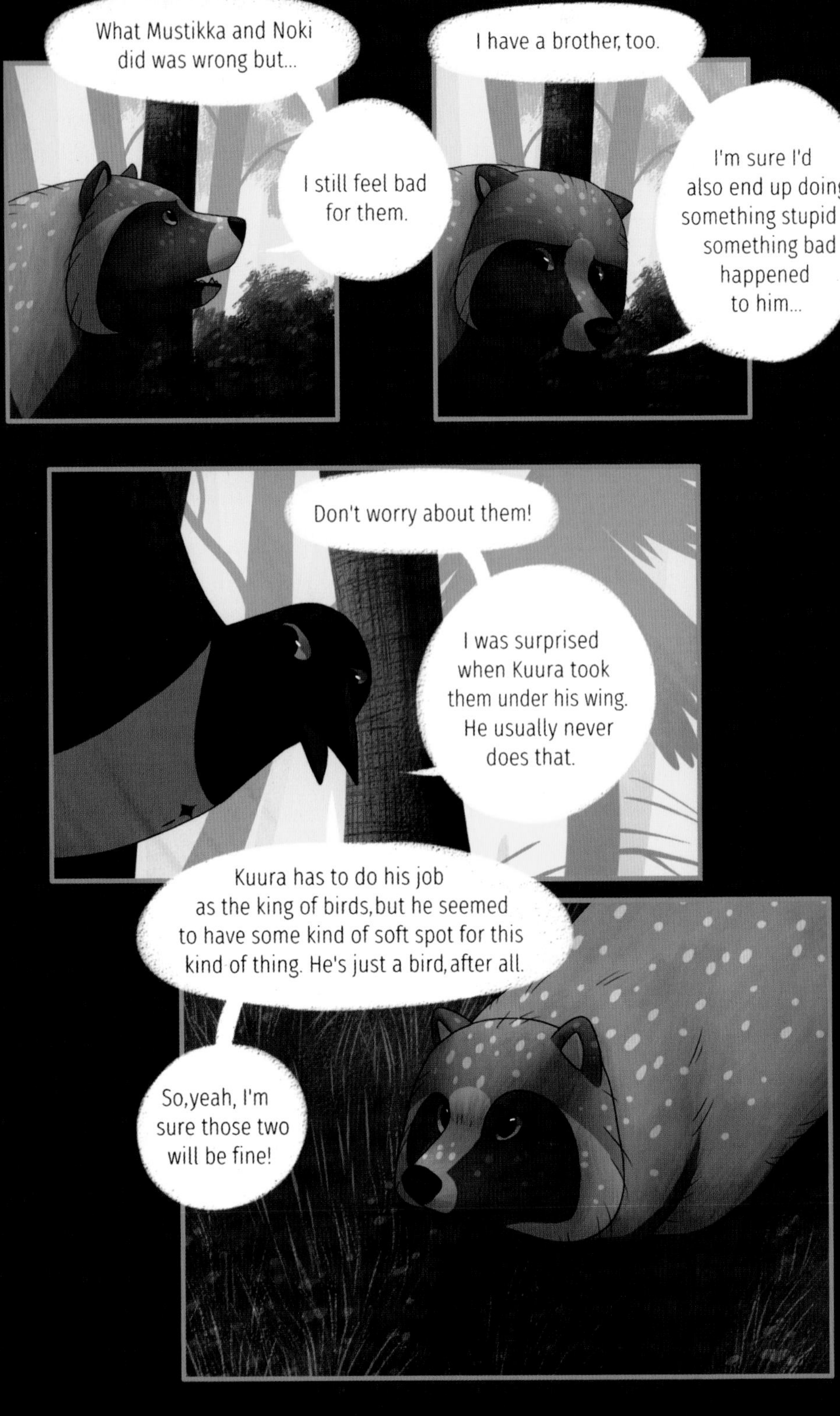

What Mustikka and Noki did was wrong but...
I still feel bad for them.
I have a brother, too.
I'm sure I'd also end up doing something stupid if something bad happened to him...
Don't worry about them!
I was surprised when Kuura took them under his wing. He usually never does that.
Kuura has to do his job as the king of birds, but he seemed to have some kind of soft spot for this kind of thing. He's just a bird, after all.
So, yeah, I'm sure those two will be fine!

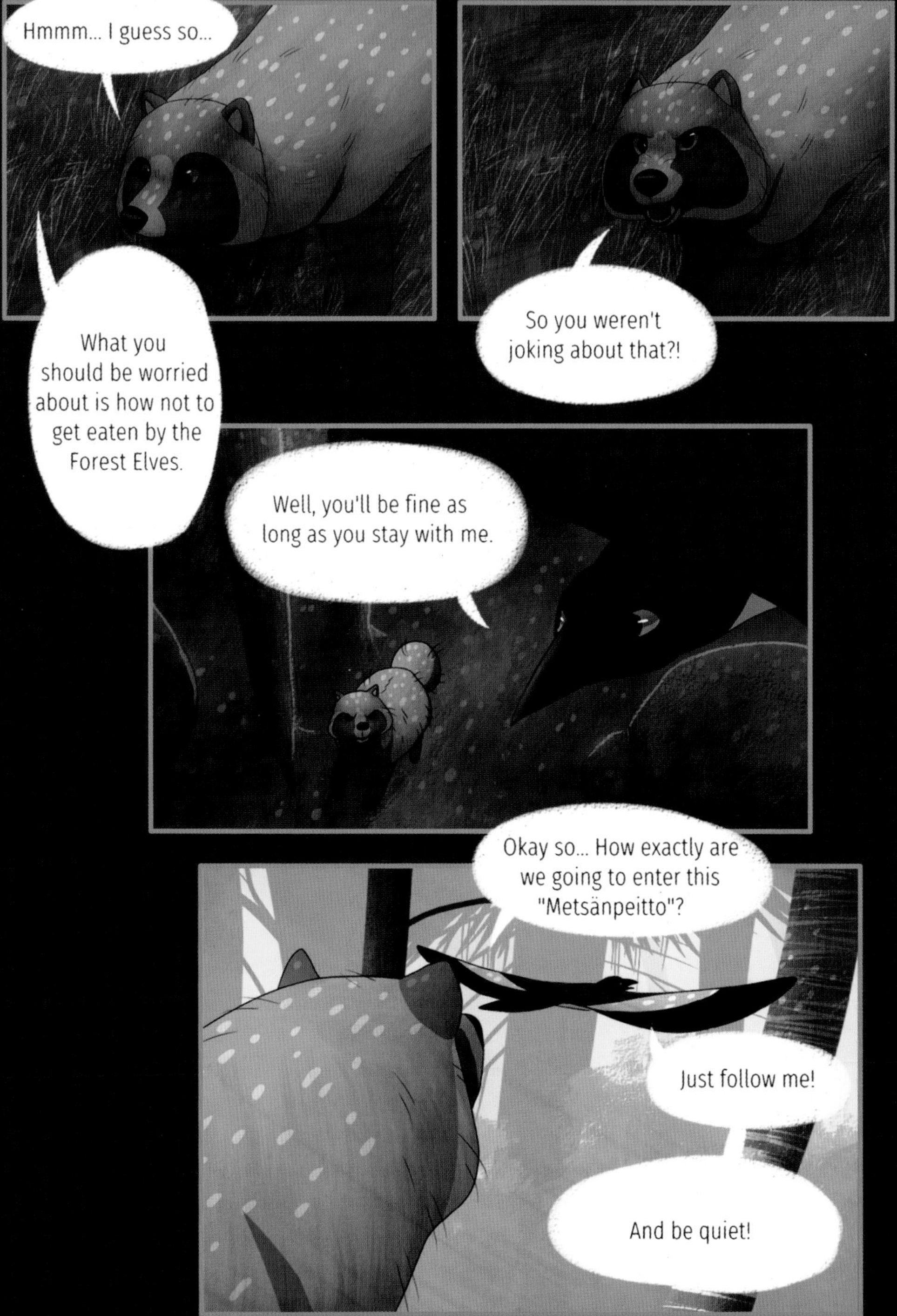
Hmmm... I guess so...
So you weren't joking about that?!
What you should be worried about is how not to get eaten by the Forest Elves.
Well, you'll be fine as long as you stay with me.
Okay so... How exactly are we going to enter this "Metsänpeitto"?
Just follow me!
And be quiet!

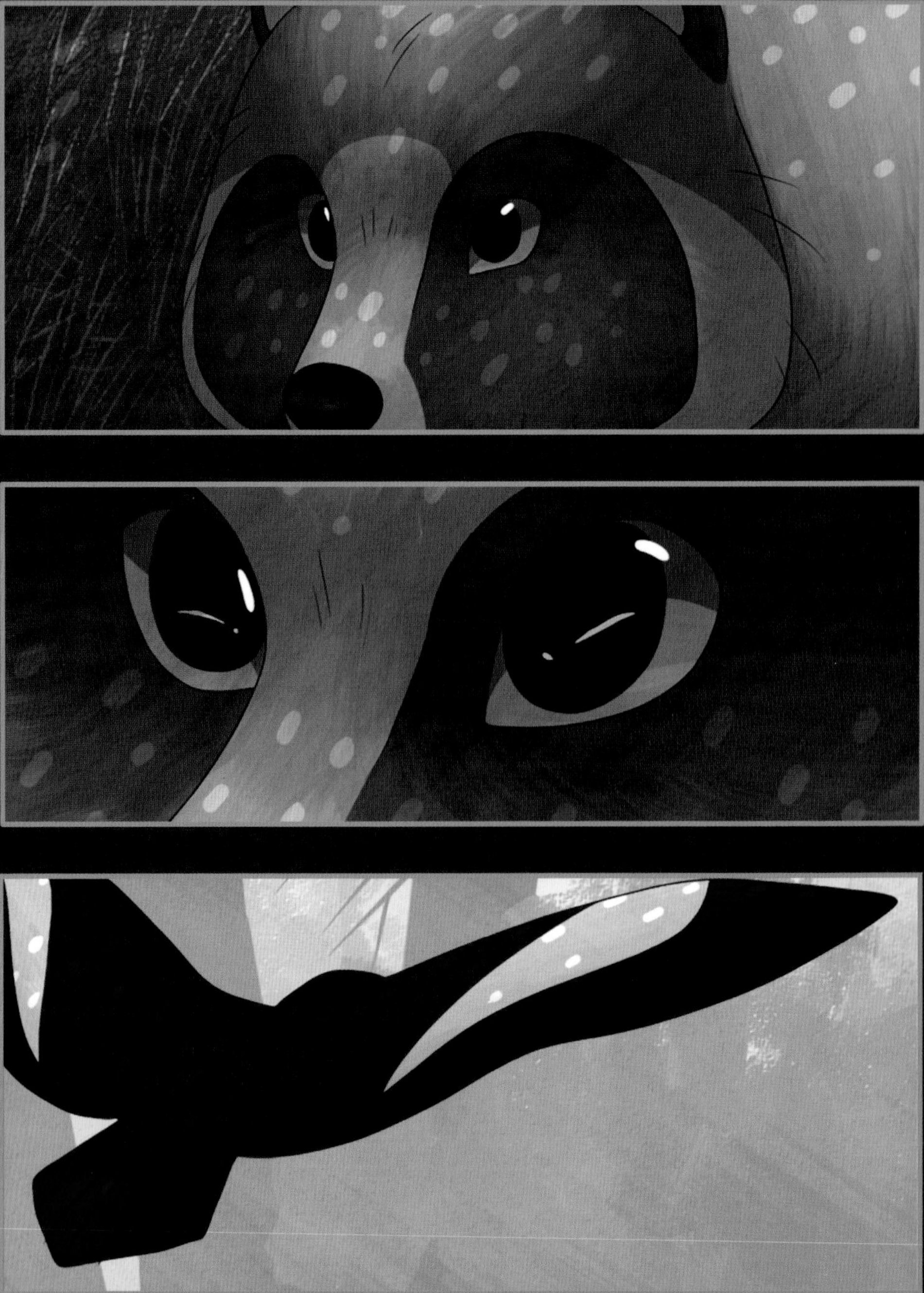

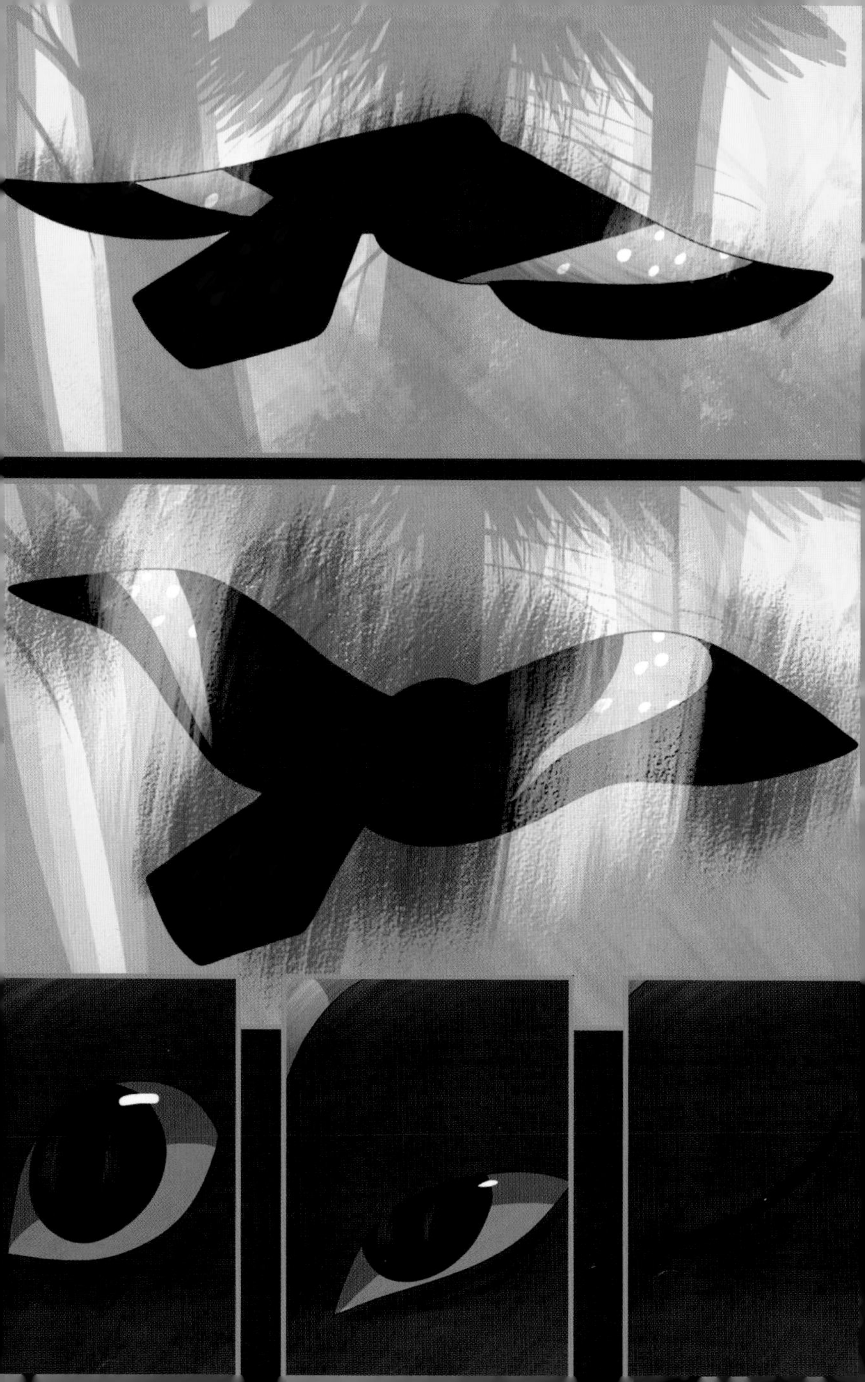

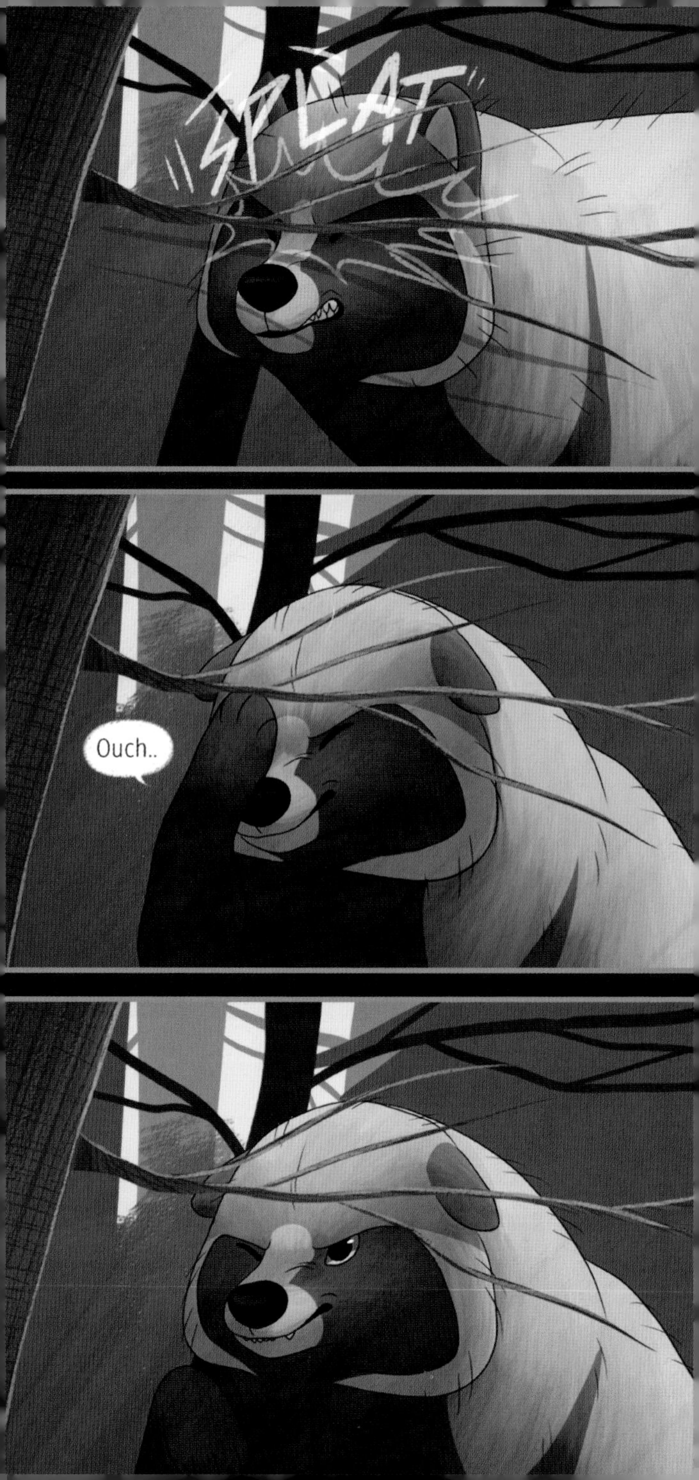
SPLAT
Ouch..

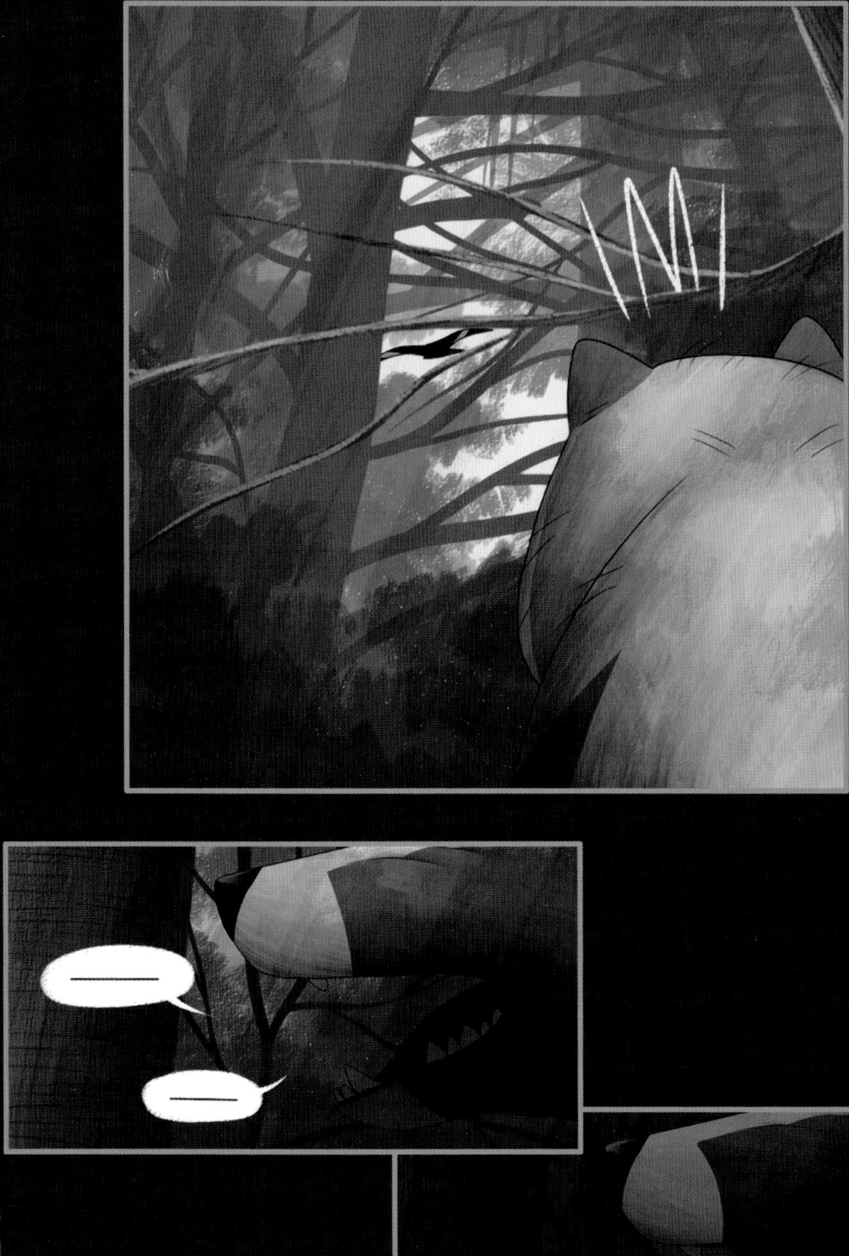

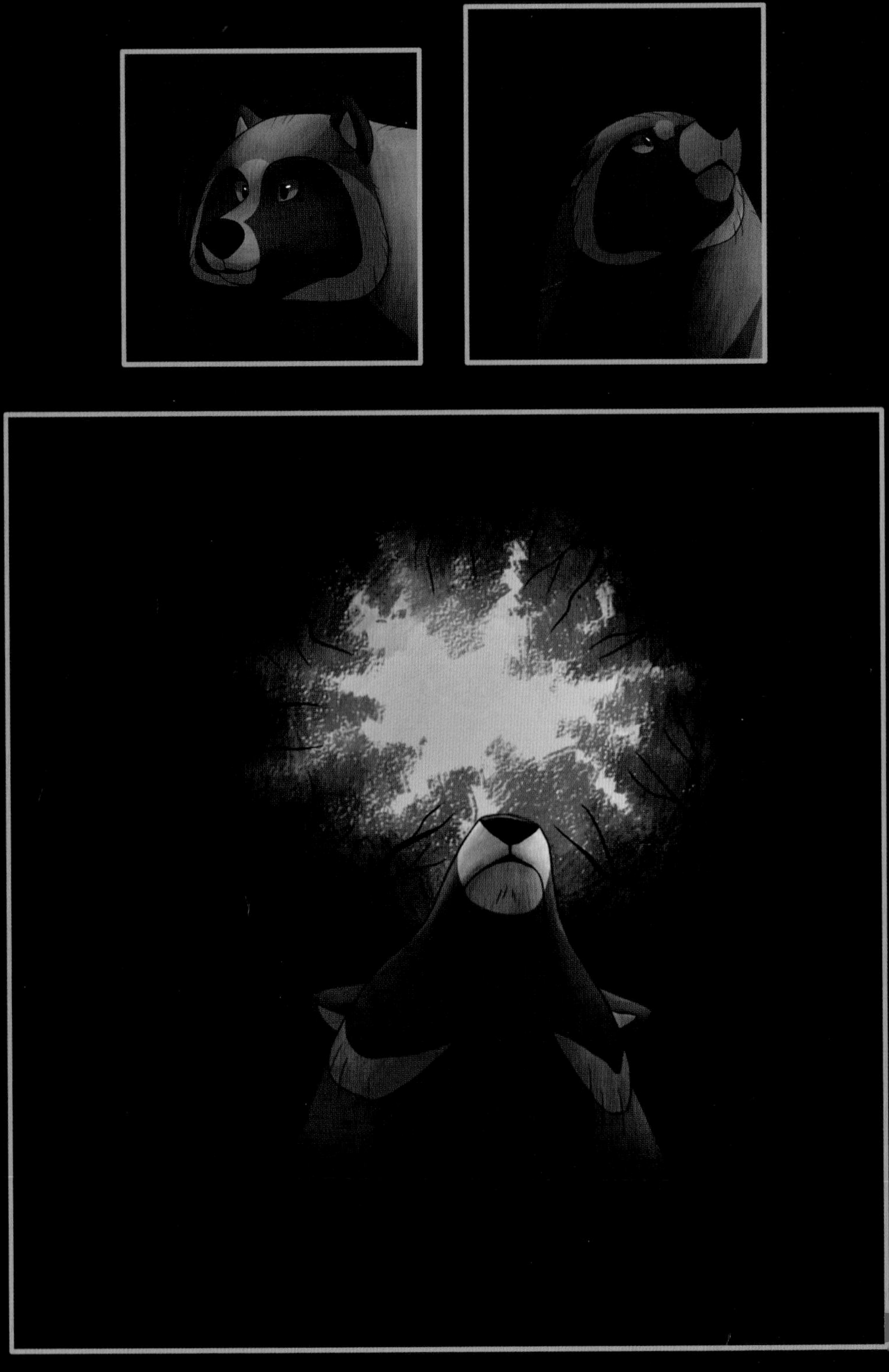

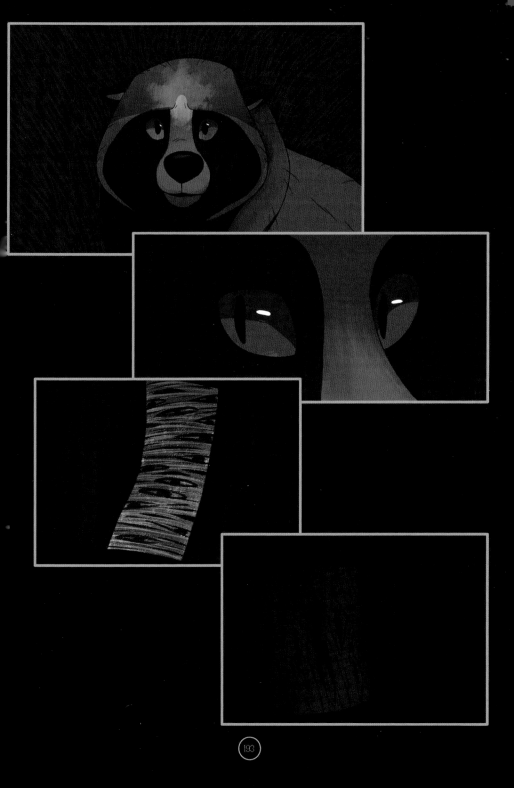

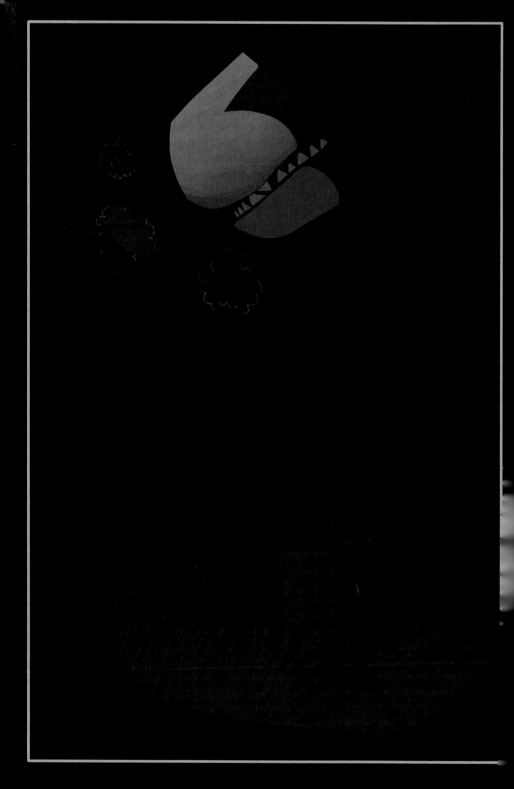

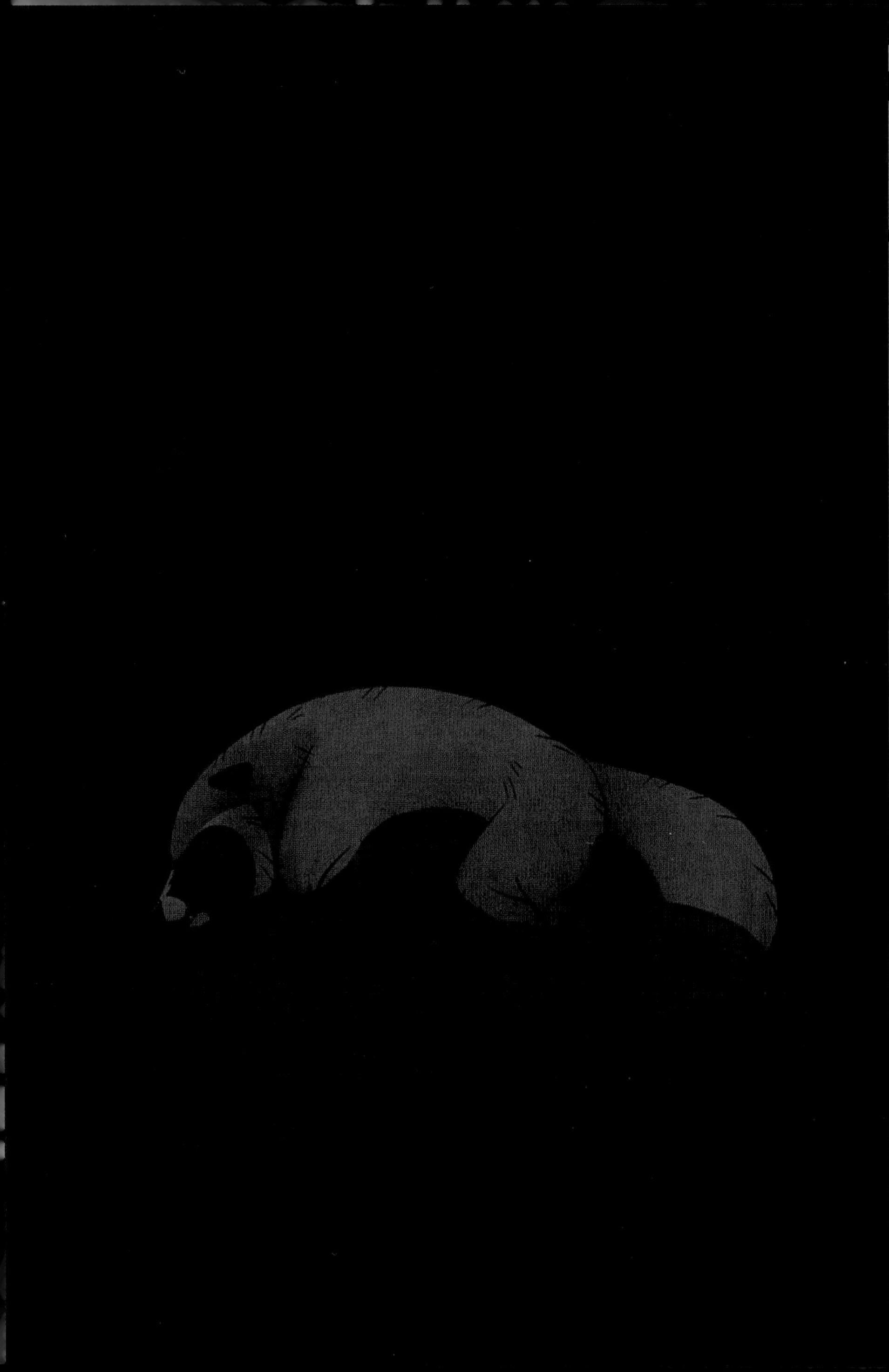

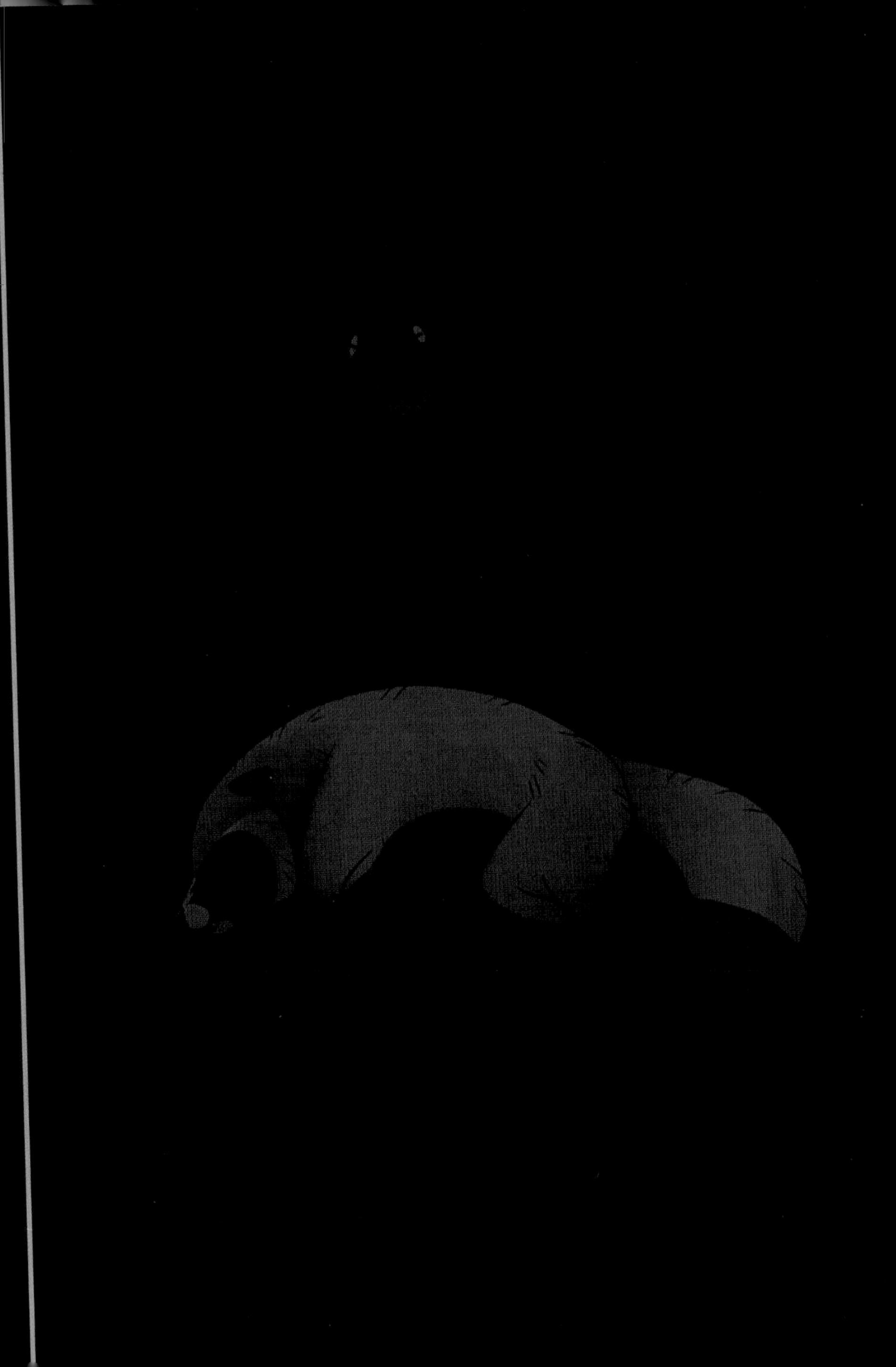

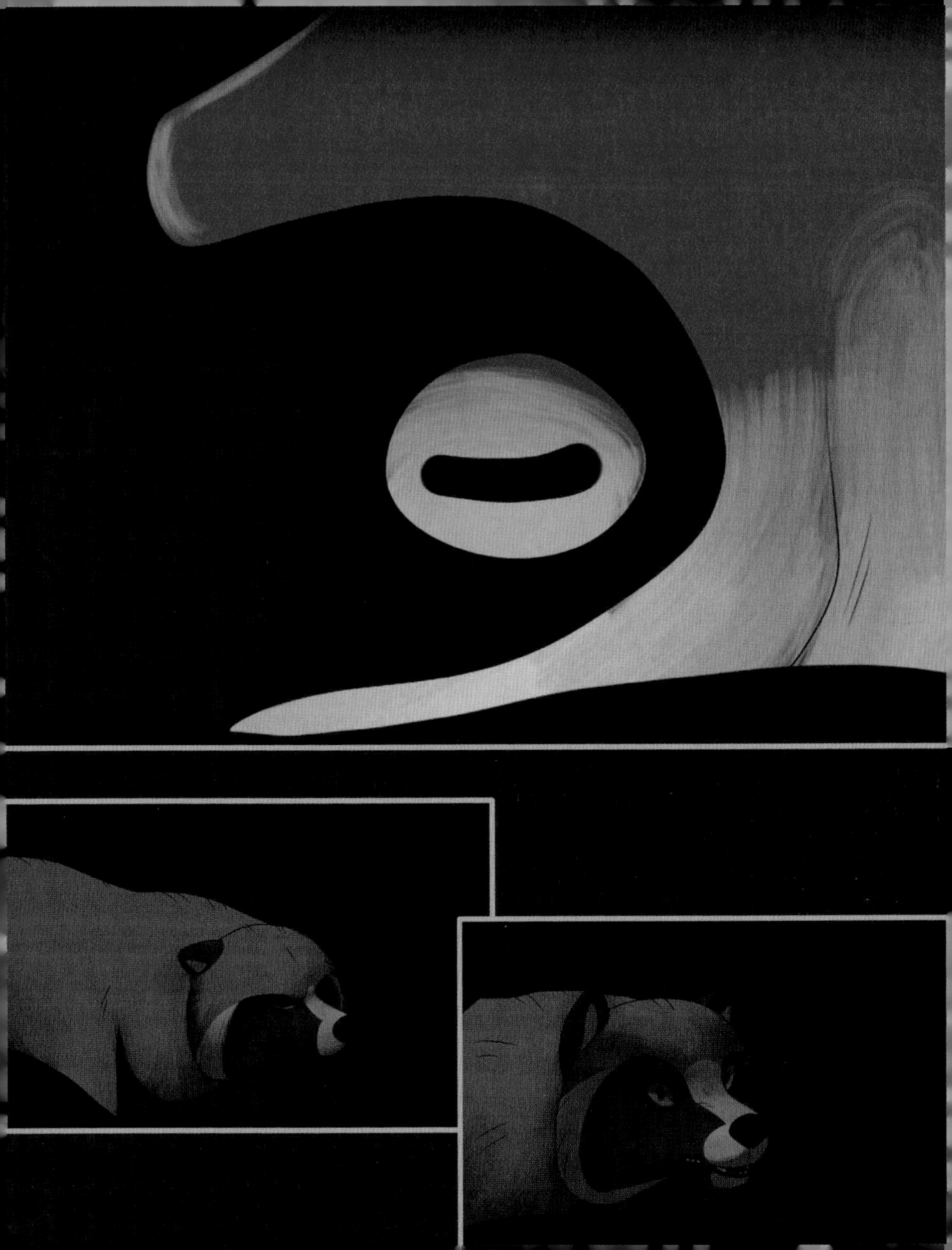

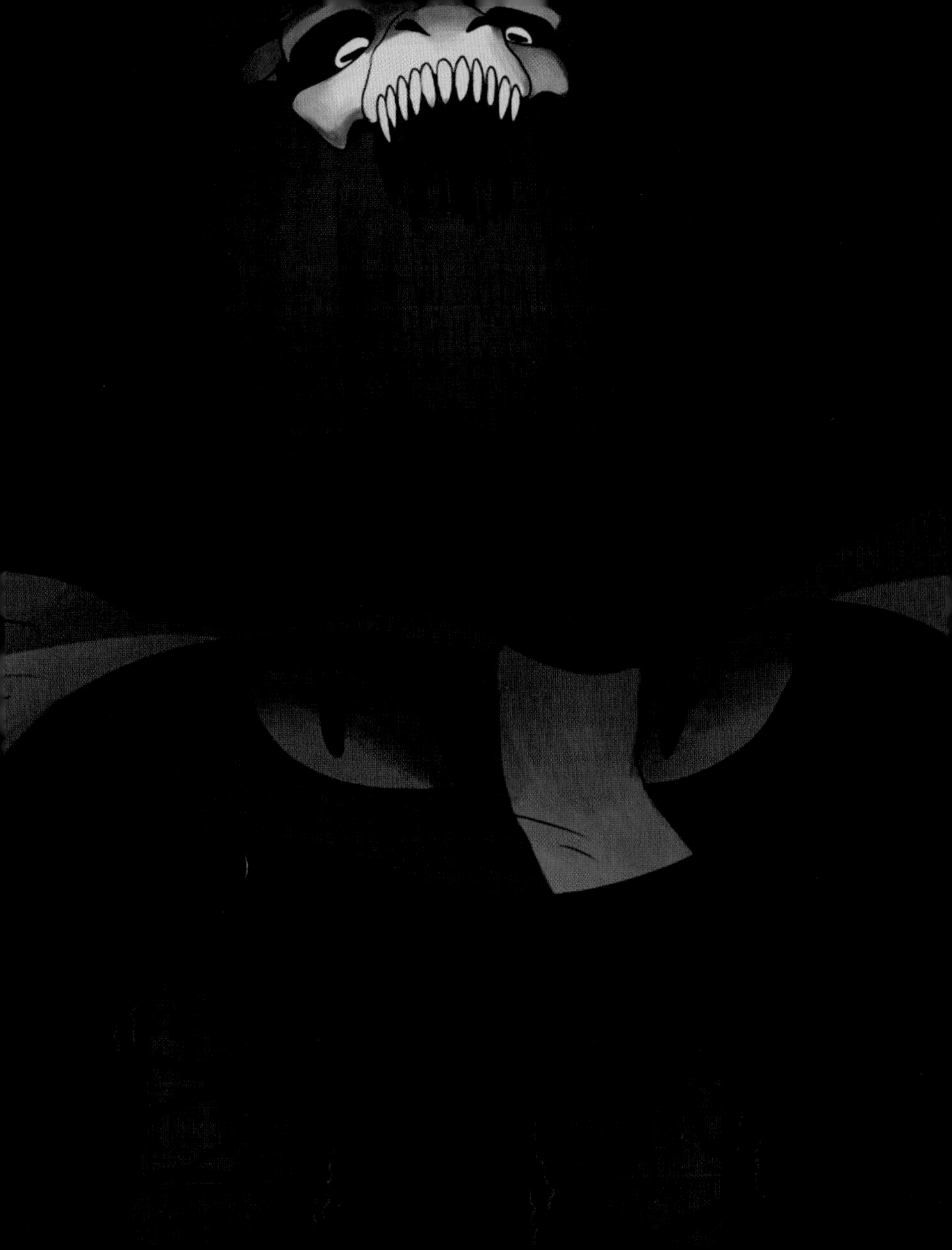

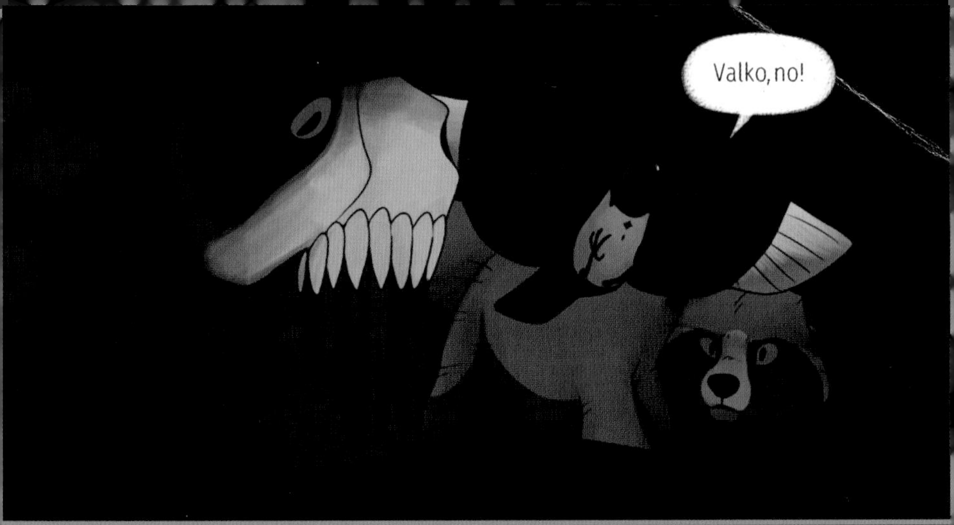
Valko, no!

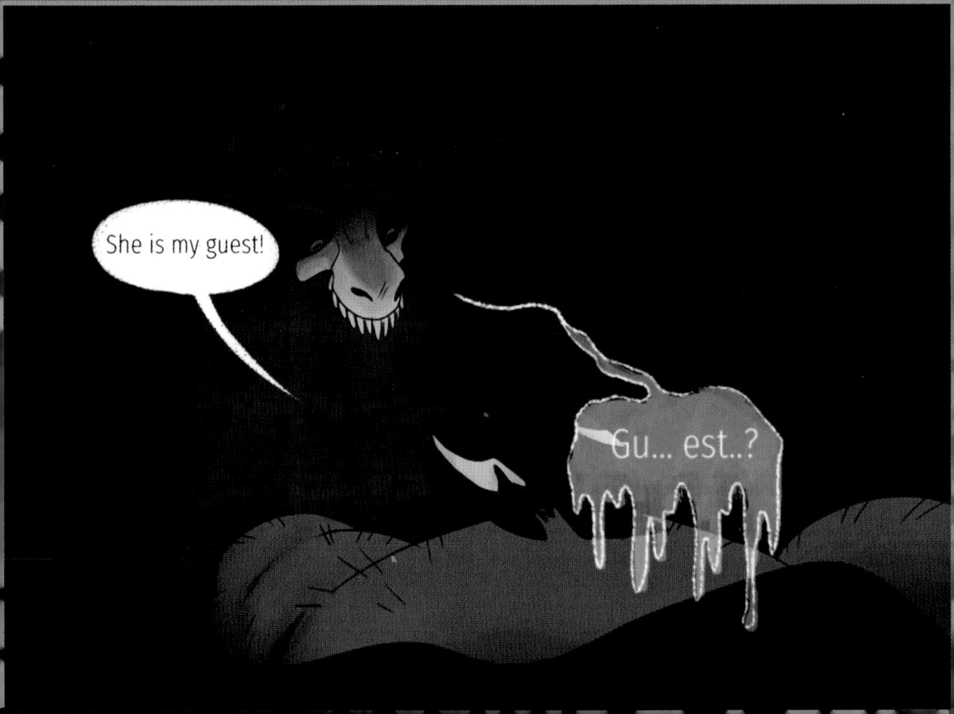
She is my guest!
Gu... est..?

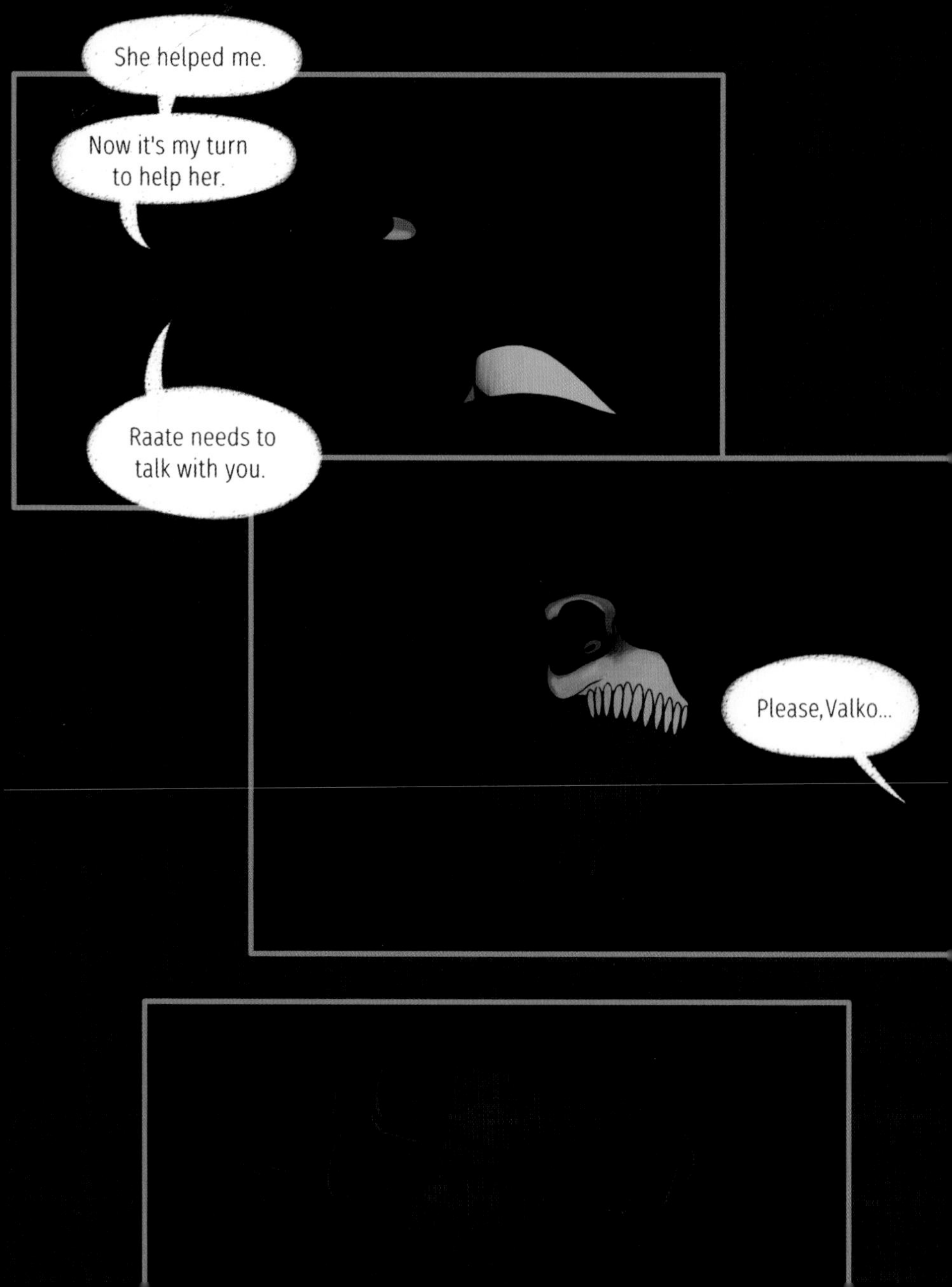
She helped me.
Now it's my turn to help her.
Raate needs to talk with you.
Please, Valko...

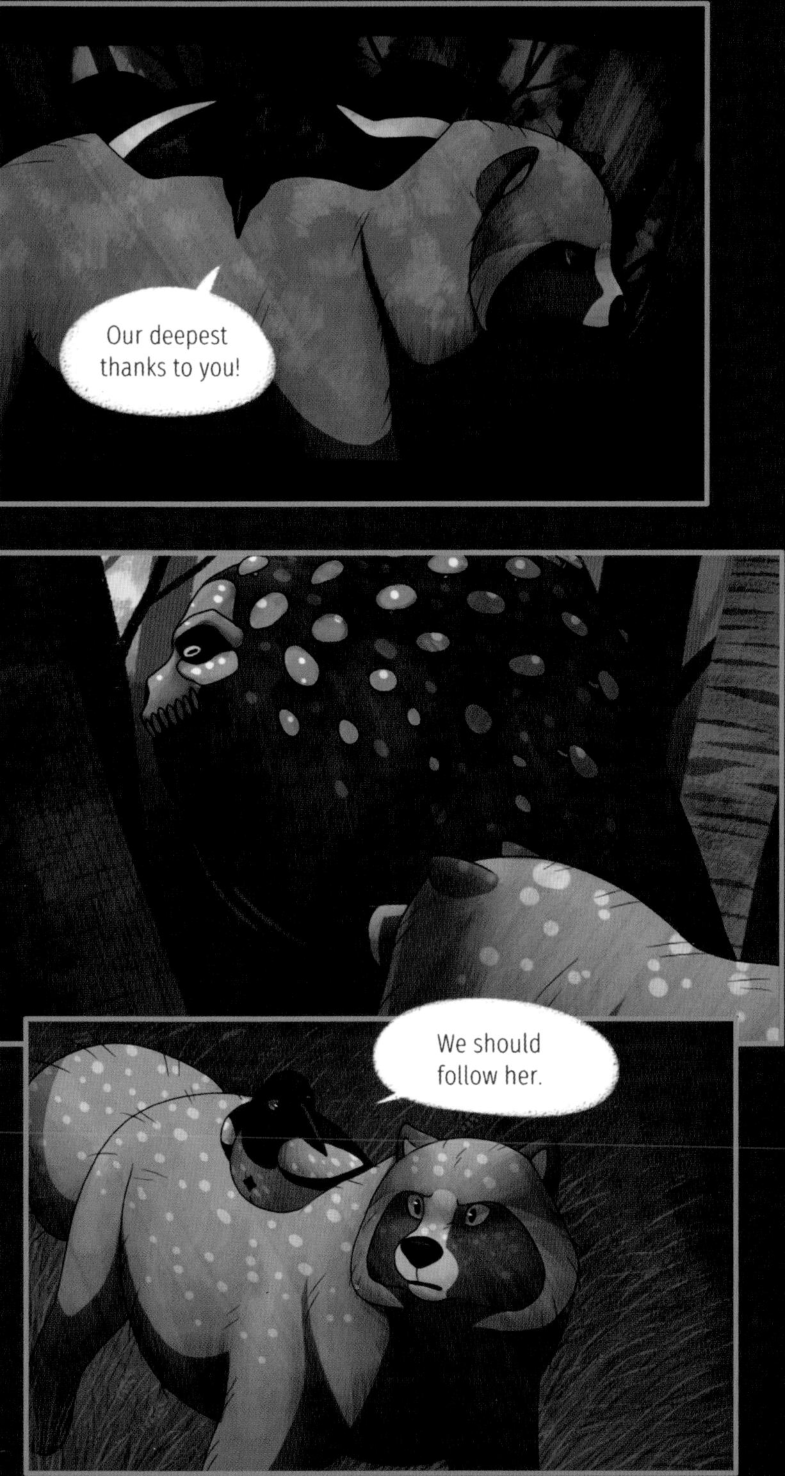
Our deepest thanks to you!
We should follow her.

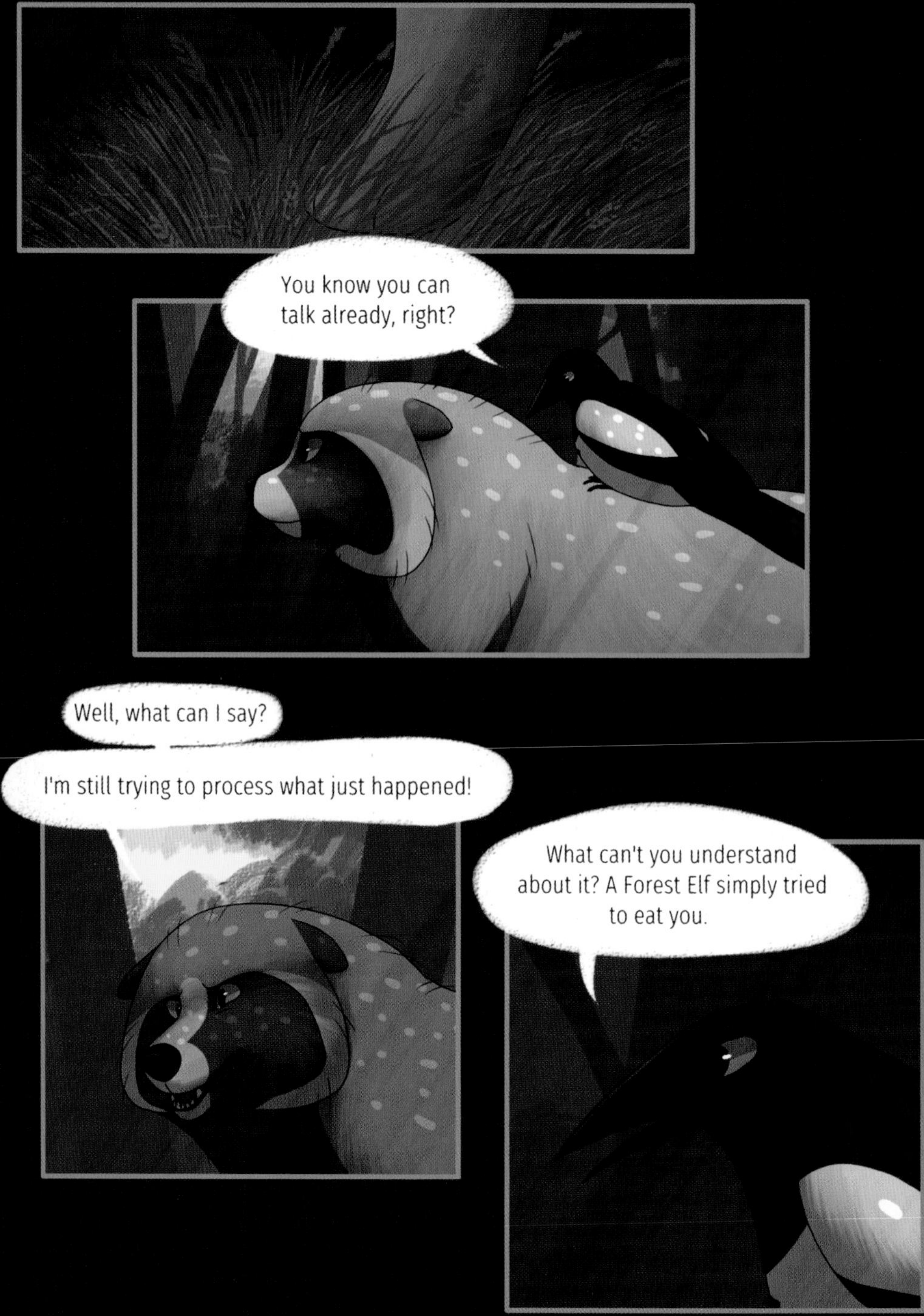
You know you can talk already, right?
Well, what can I say?
I'm still trying to process what just happened!
What can't you understand about it? A Forest Elf simply tried to eat you.

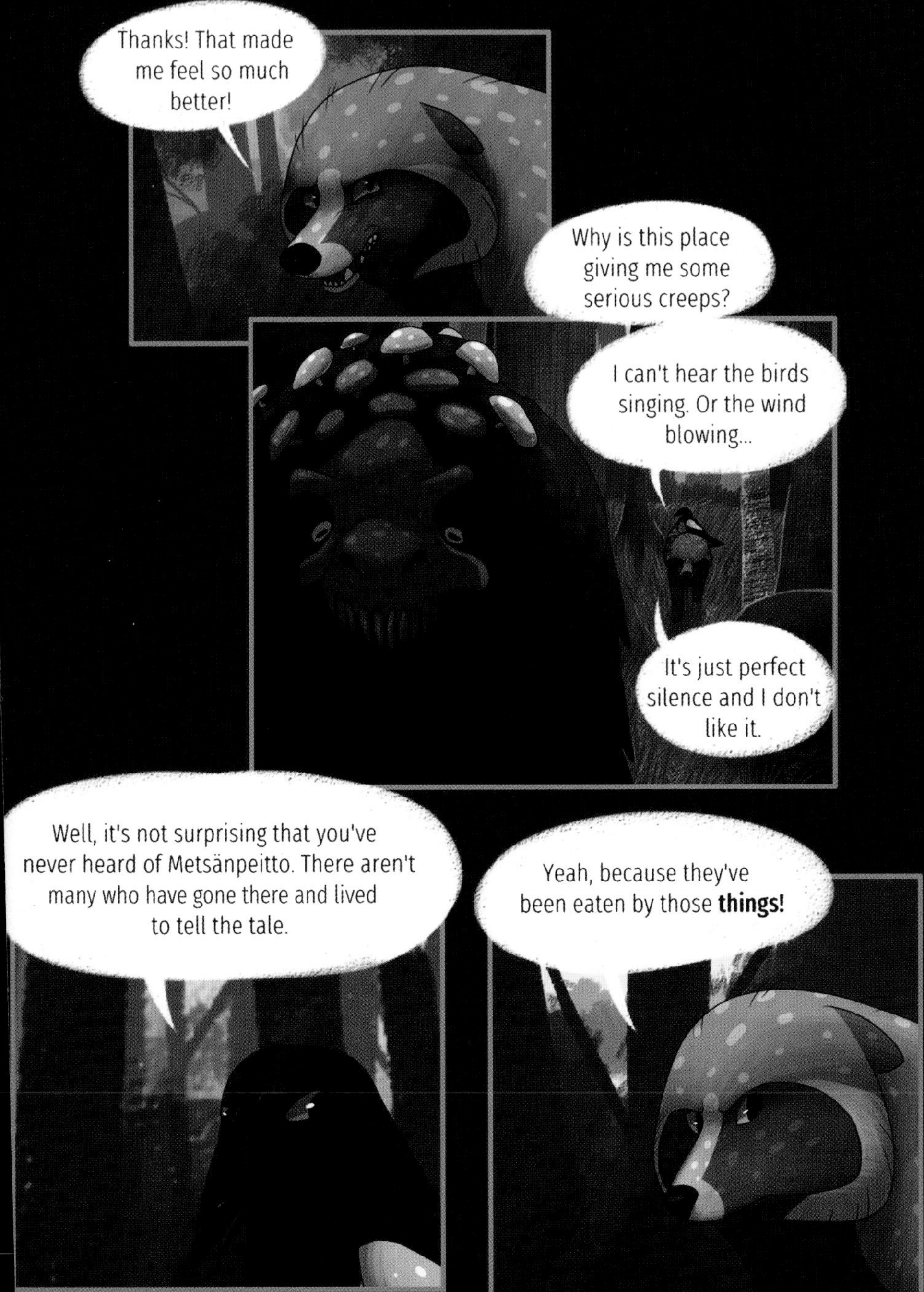
Thanks! That made me feel so much better!
Why is this place giving me some serious creeps?
I can't hear the birds singing. Or the wind blowing...
It's just perfect silence and I don't like it.
Well, it's not surprising that you've never heard of Metsänpeitto. There aren't many who have gone there and lived to tell the tale.
Yeah, because they've been eaten by those **things!**

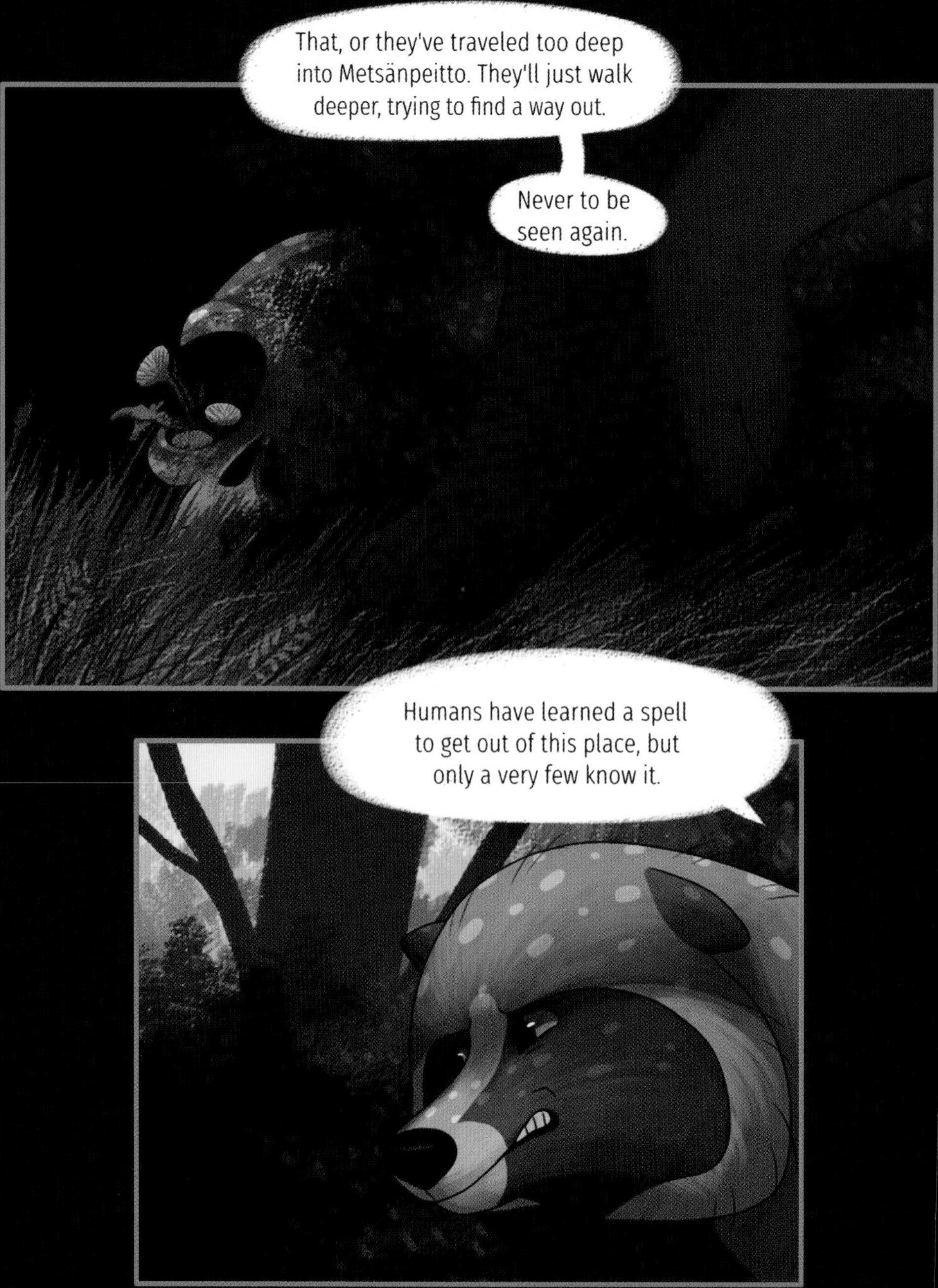
That, or they've traveled too deep into Metsänpeitto. They'll just walk deeper, trying to find a way out.
Never to be seen again.
Humans have learned a spell to get out of this place, but only a very few know it.

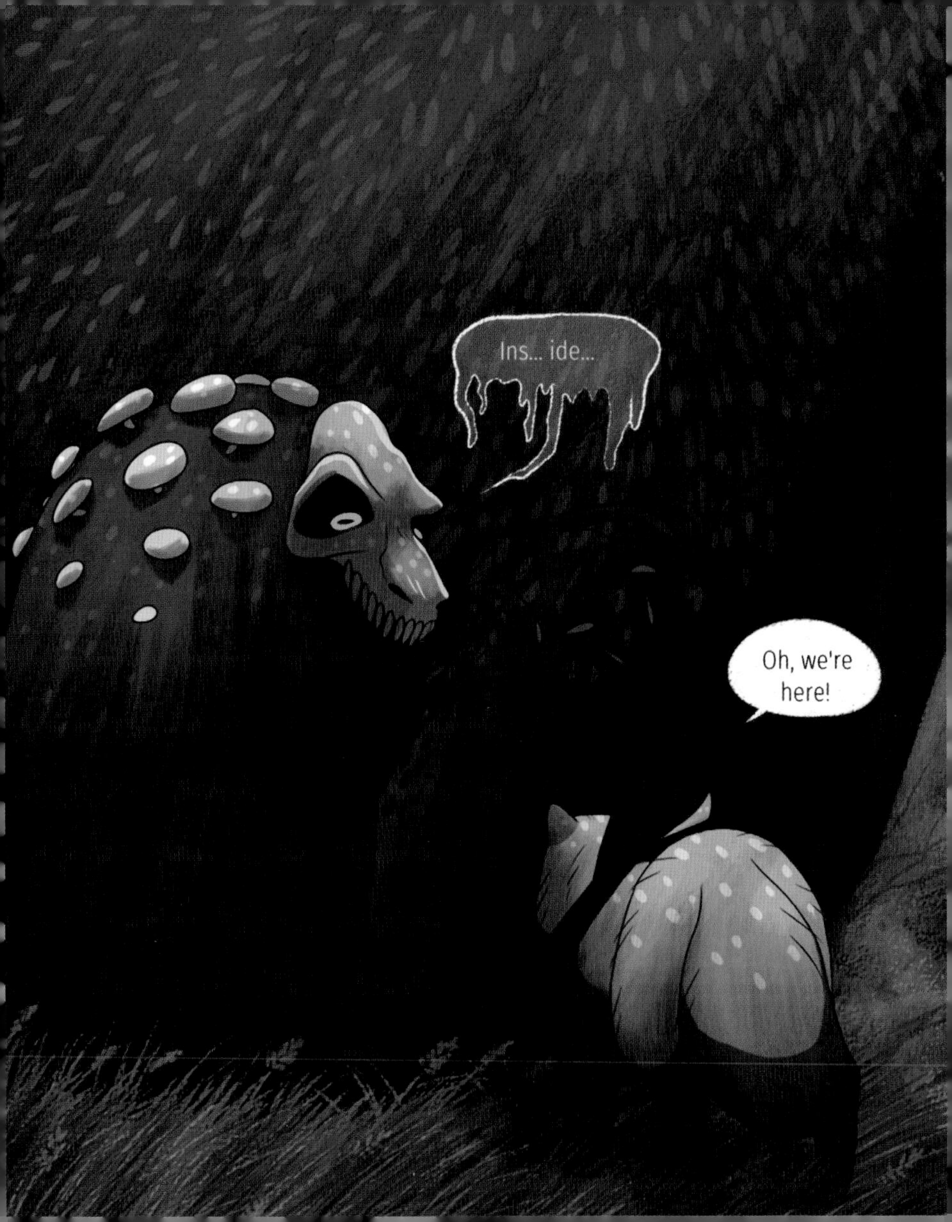
Ins... ide...
Oh, we're here!

Chapter 18

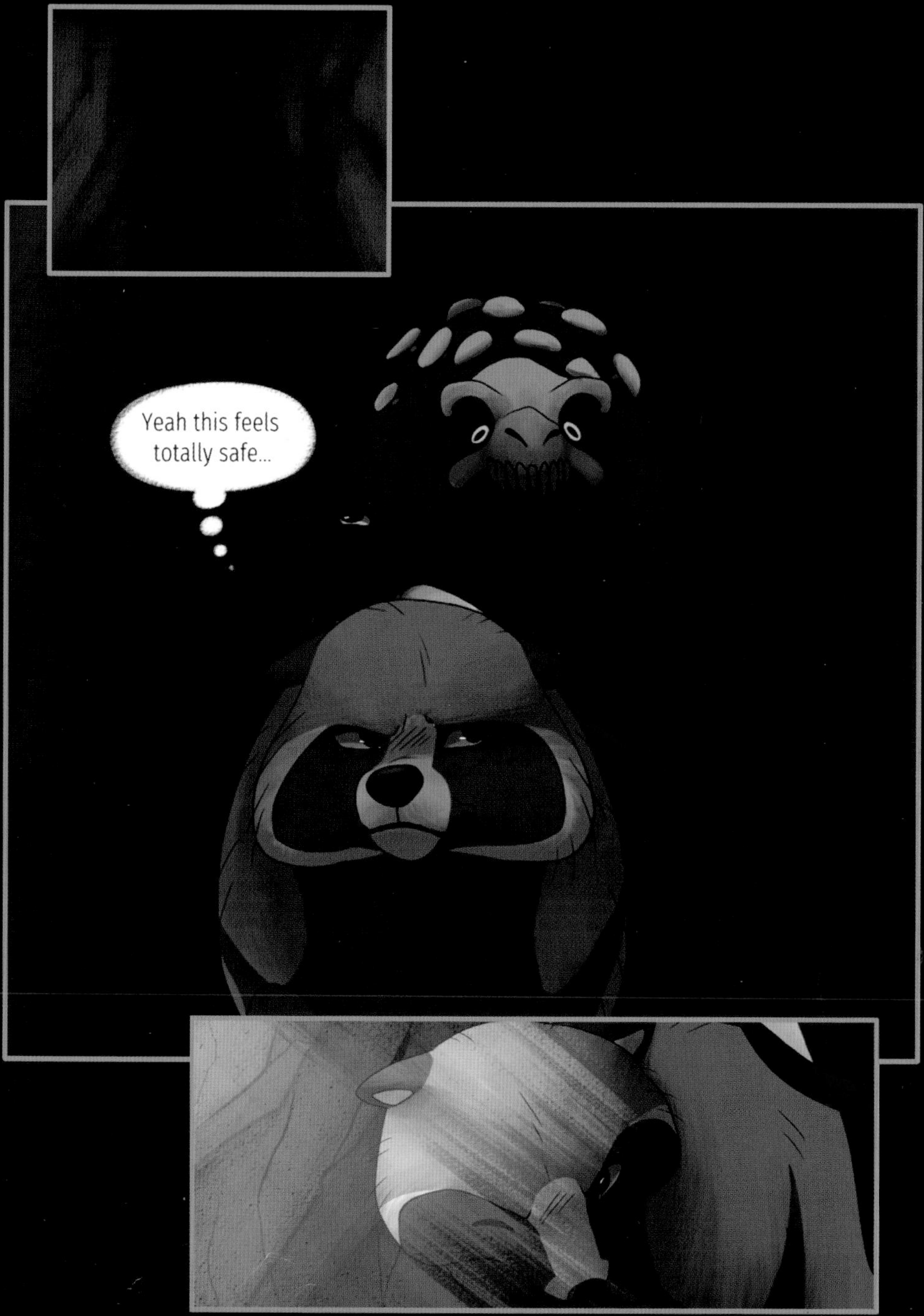
Yeah this feels totally safe...

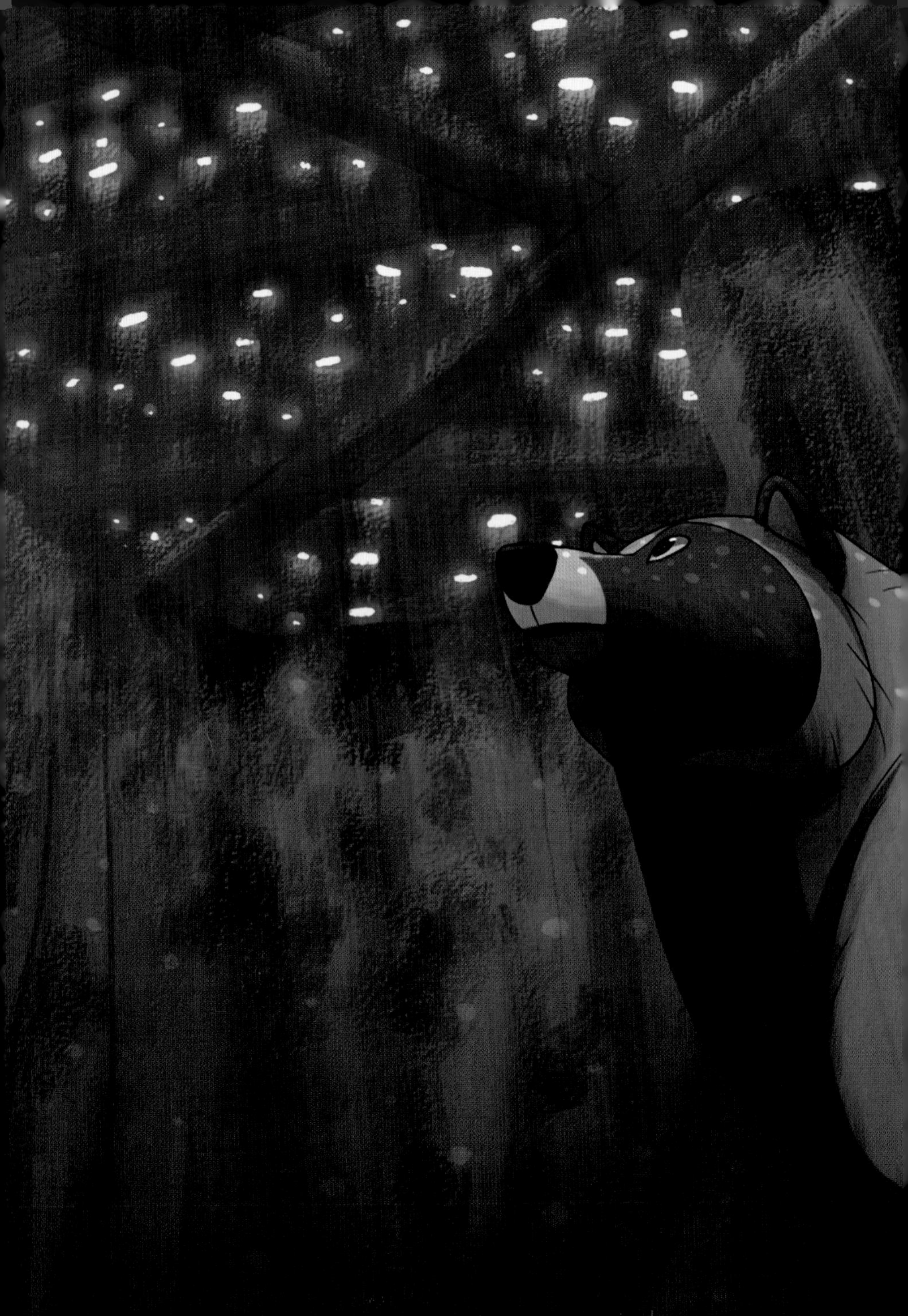

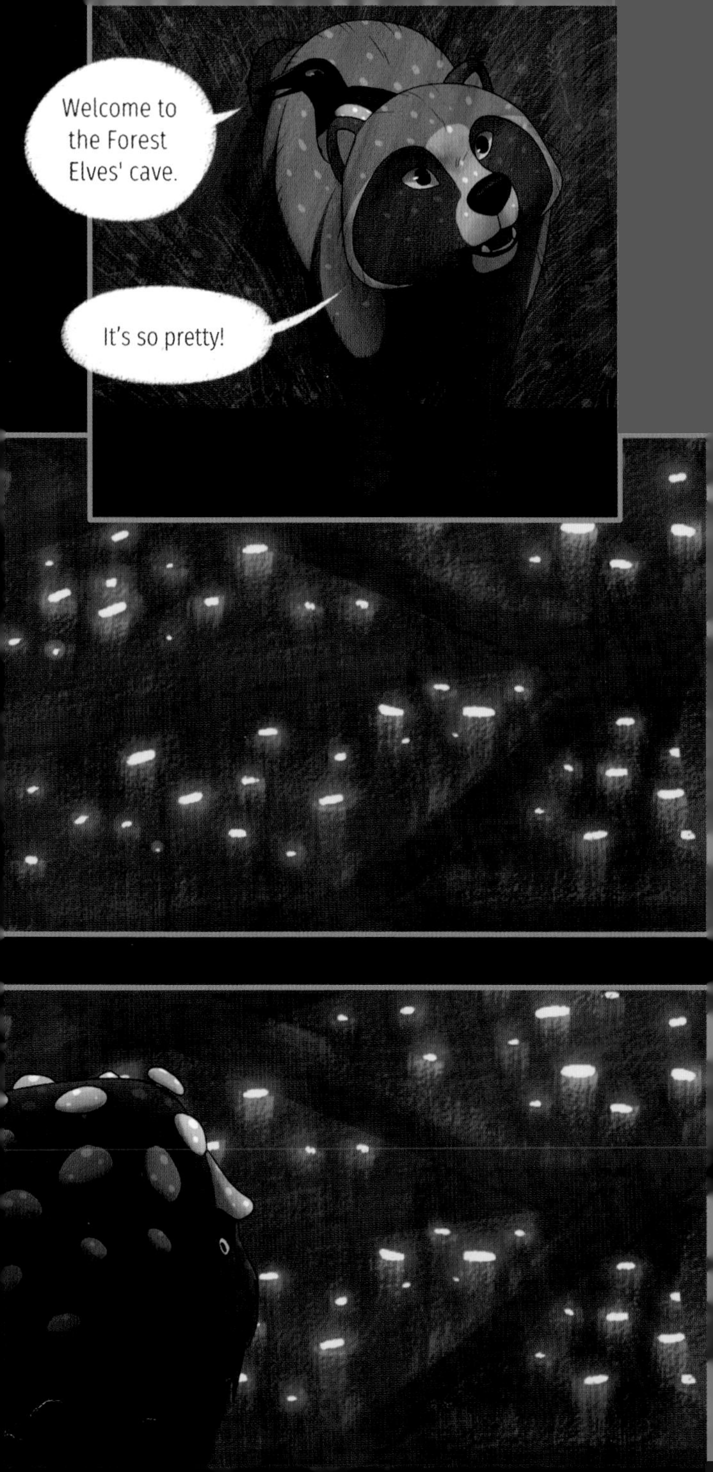
Welcome to the Forest Elves' cave.
It's so pretty!

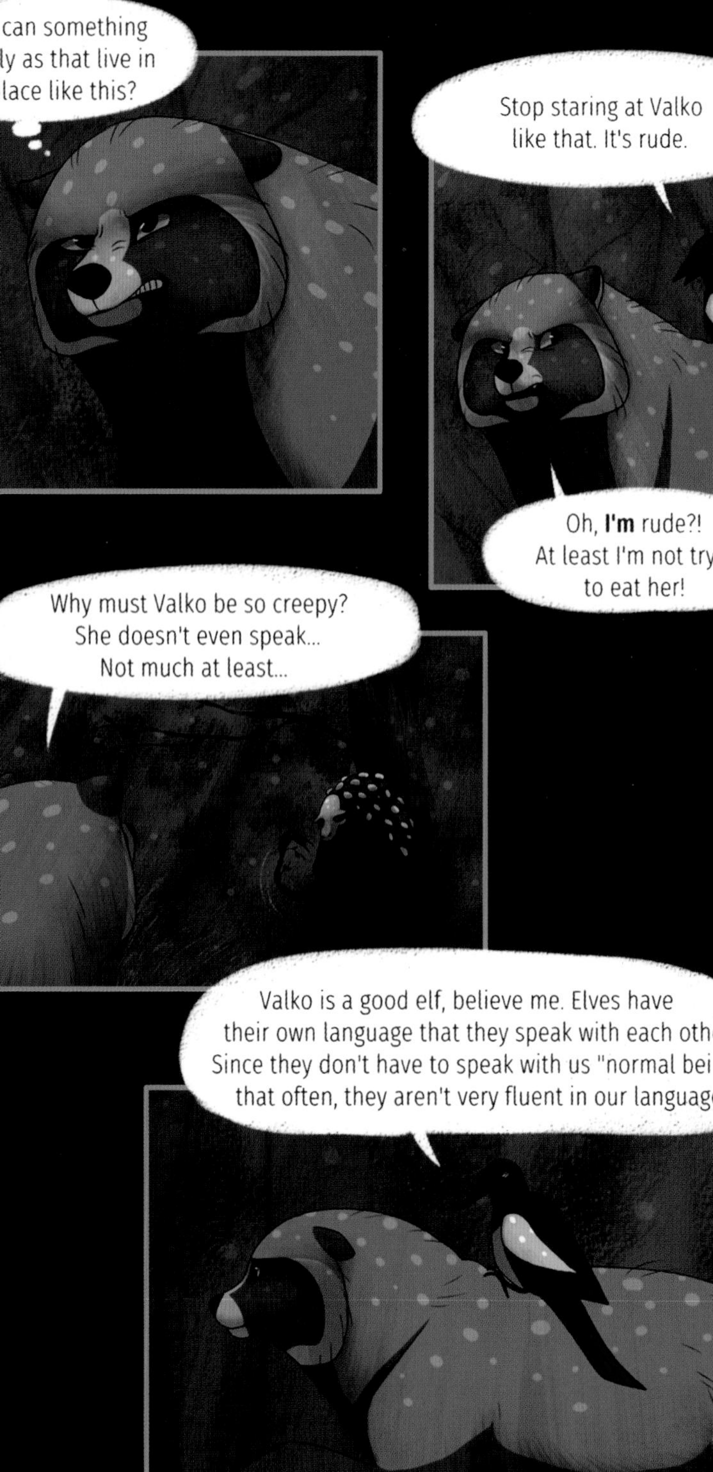
can something
ly as that live in
lace like this?
Stop staring at Valko like that. It's rude.
Oh, **I'm** rude?! At least I'm not try to eat her!
Why must Valko be so creepy? She doesn't even speak... Not much at least...
Valko is a good elf, believe me. Elves have their own language that they speak with each oth Since they don't have to speak with us "normal bei that often, they aren't very fluent in our languag

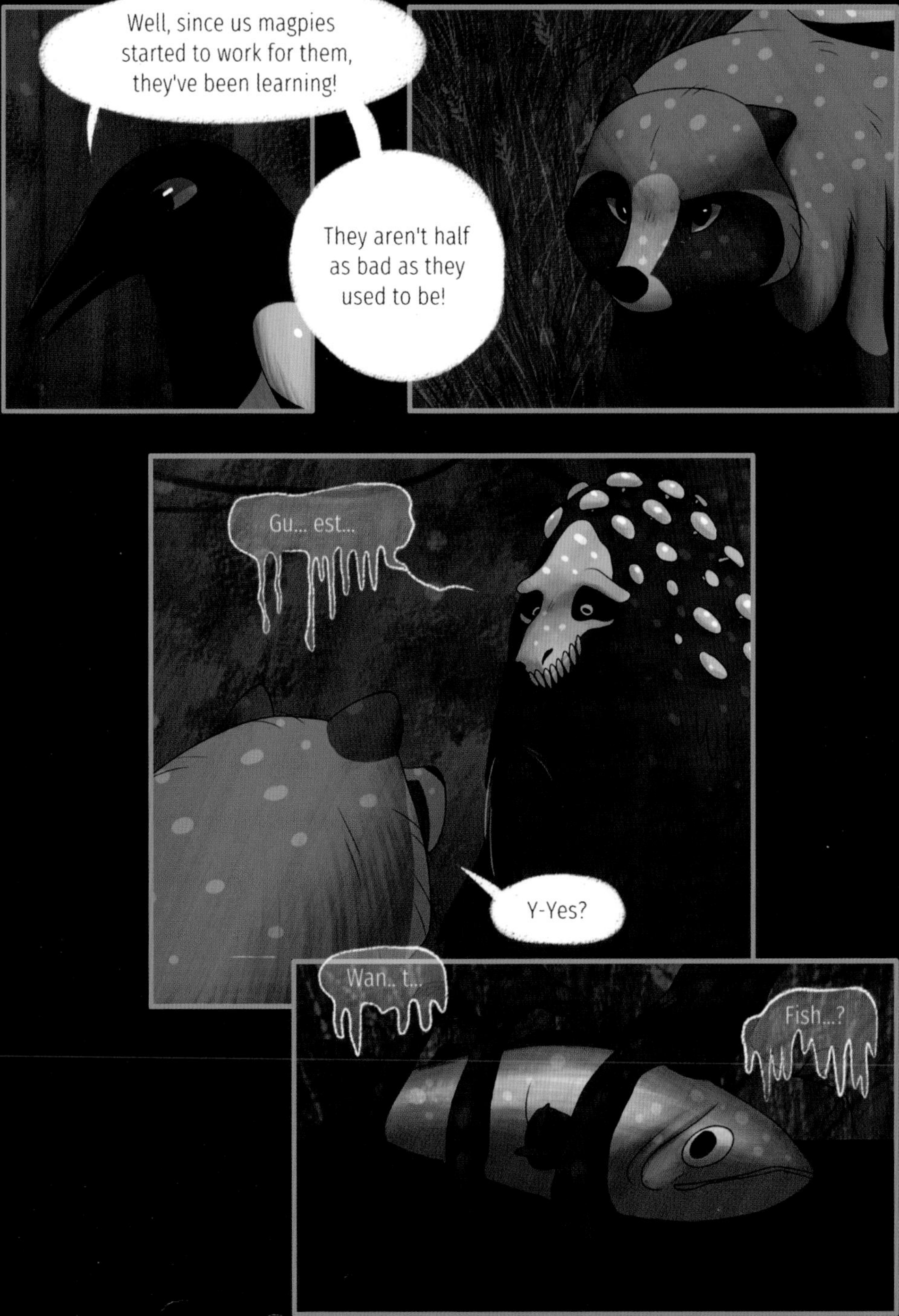
Well, since us magpies started to work for them, they've been learning!
They aren't half as bad as they used to be!
Gu... est...
Y-Yes?
Wan.. t...
Fish...?

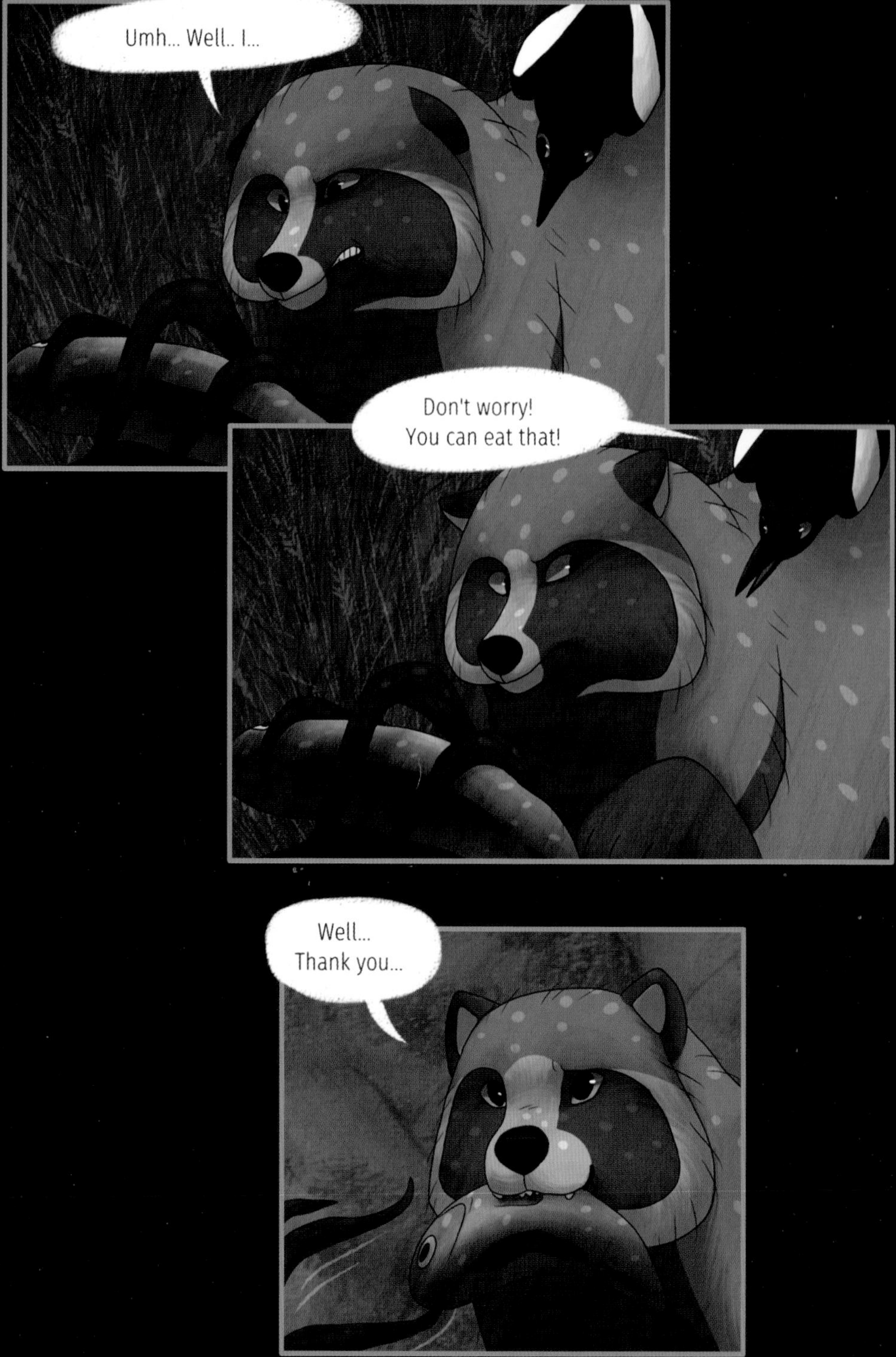

Umh... Well.. I...
Don't worry!
You can eat that!
Well...
Thank you...

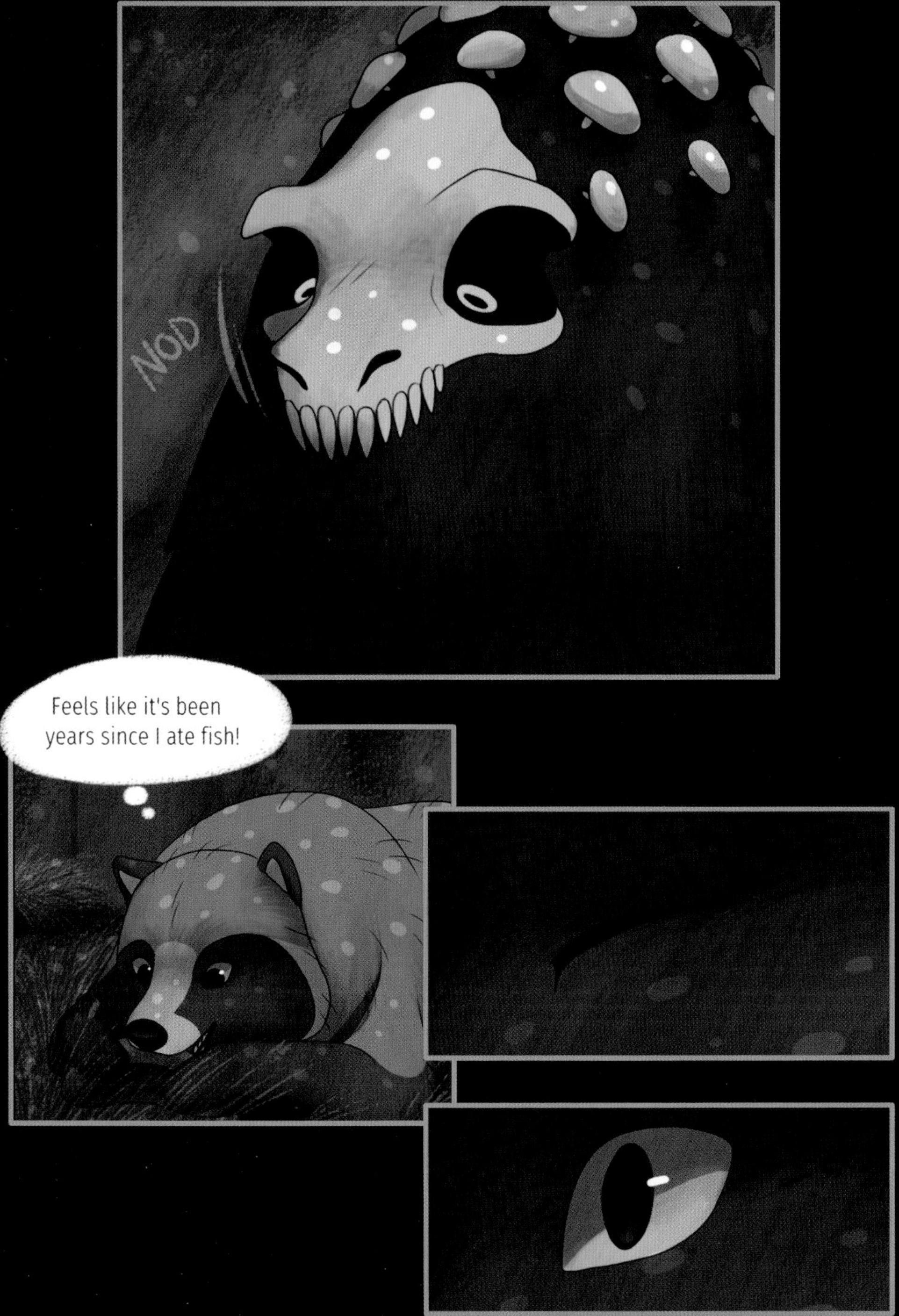
NOD
Feels like it's been years since I ate fish!

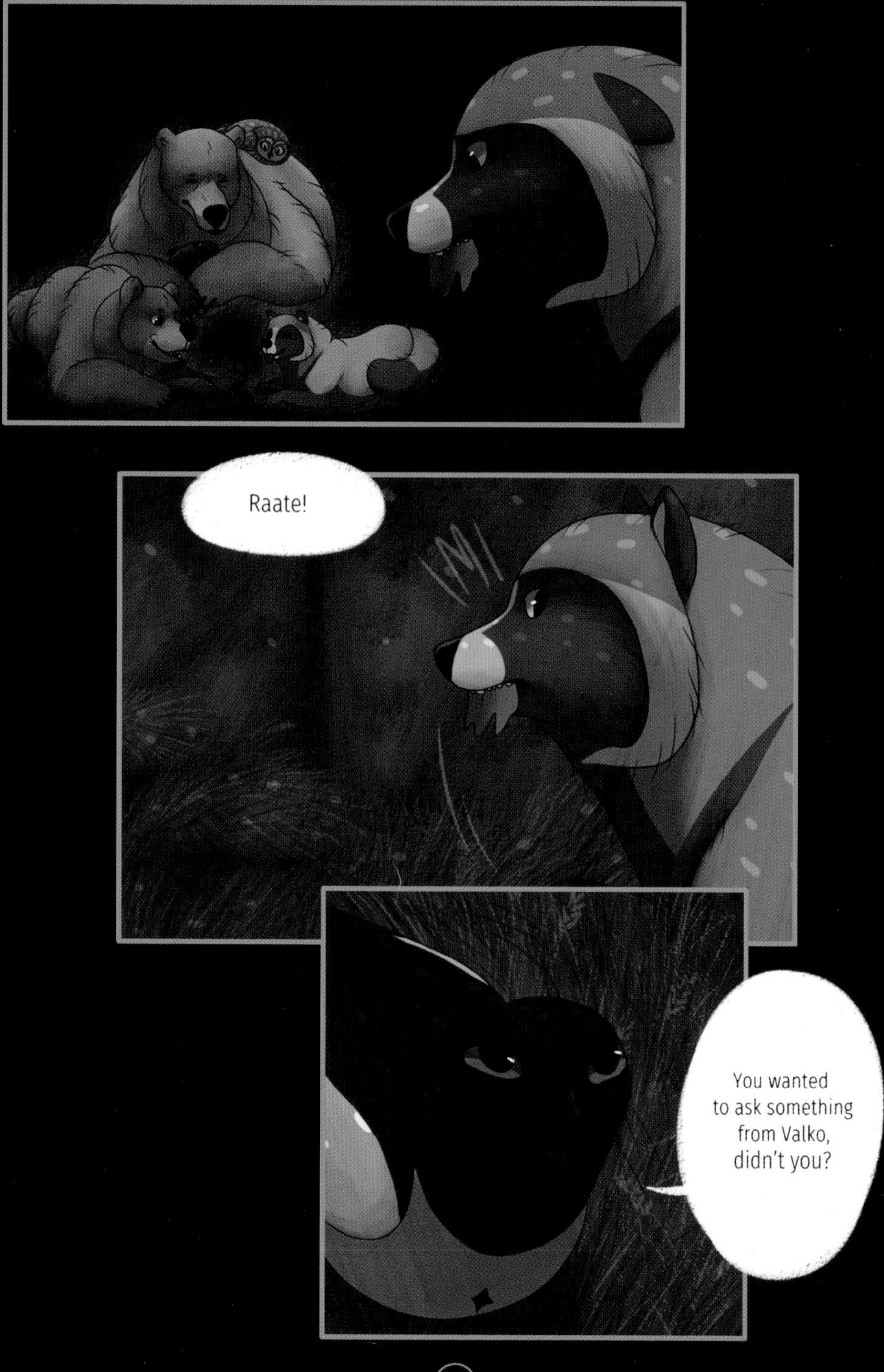
Raate!
You wanted to ask something from Valko, didn't you?

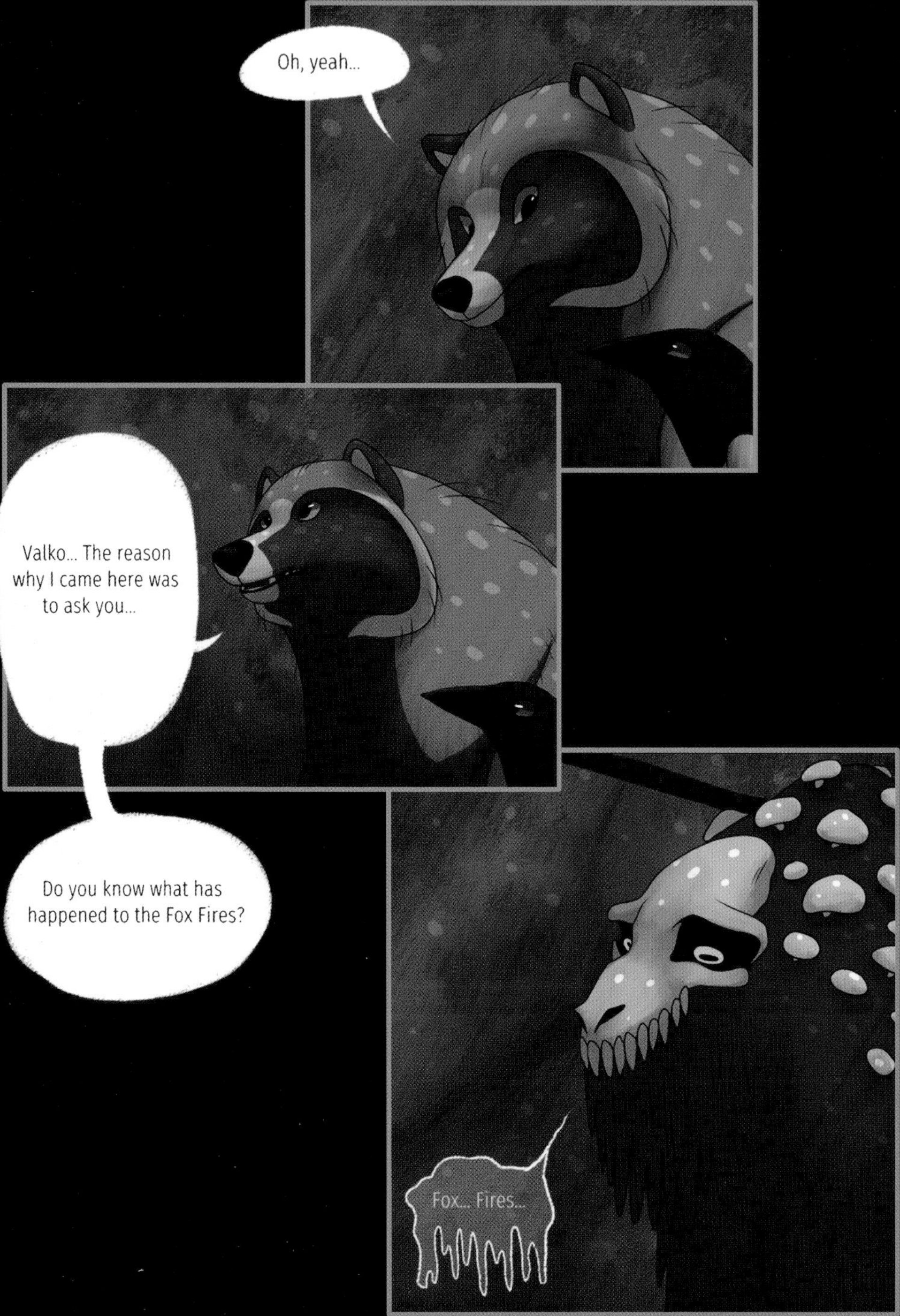
Oh, yeah...
Valko... The reason why I came here was to ask you...
Do you know what has happened to the Fox Fires?
Fox... Fires...

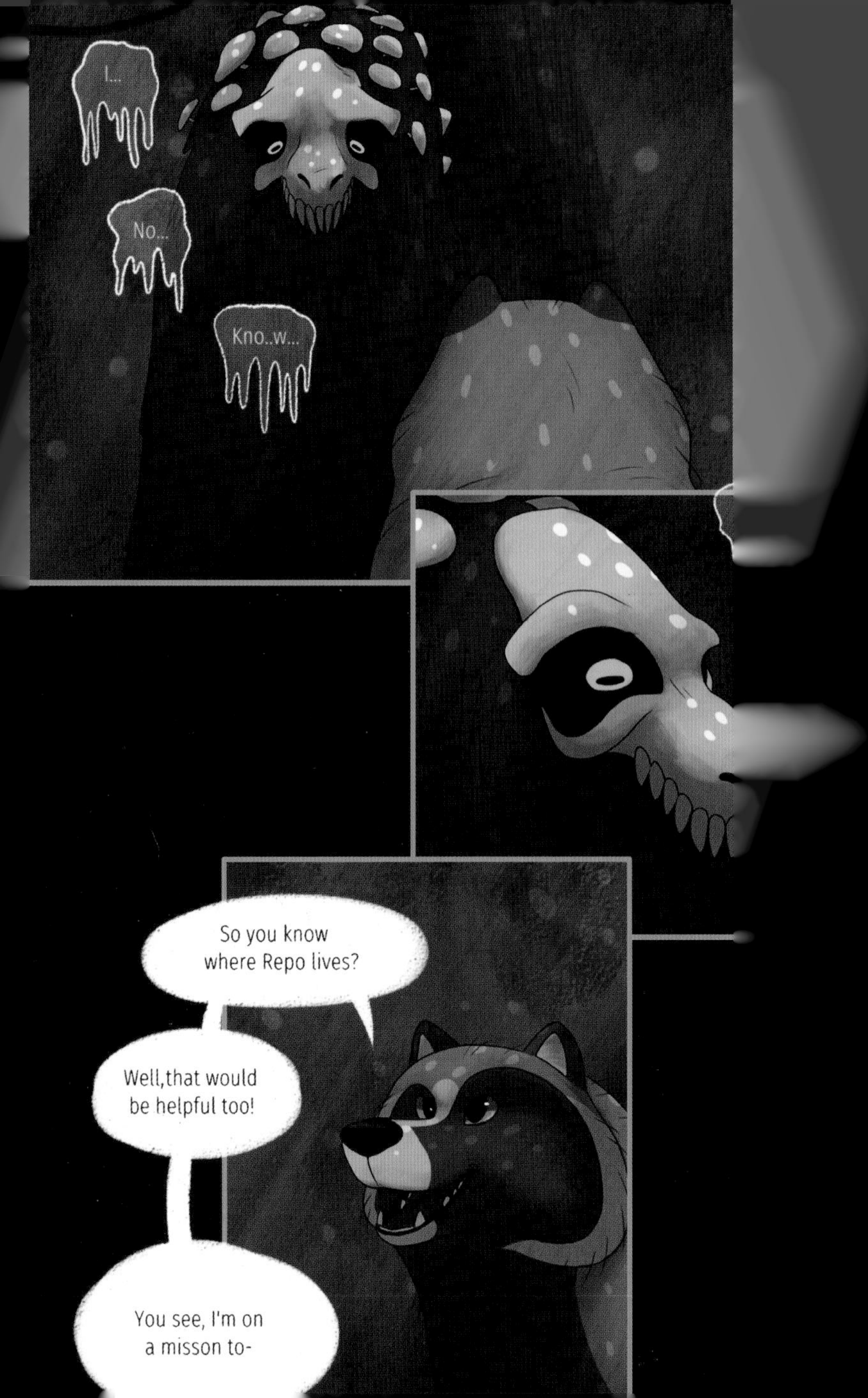
I...
No...
Kno..w...
So you know where Repo lives?
Well,that would be helpful too!
You see, I'm on a misson to-

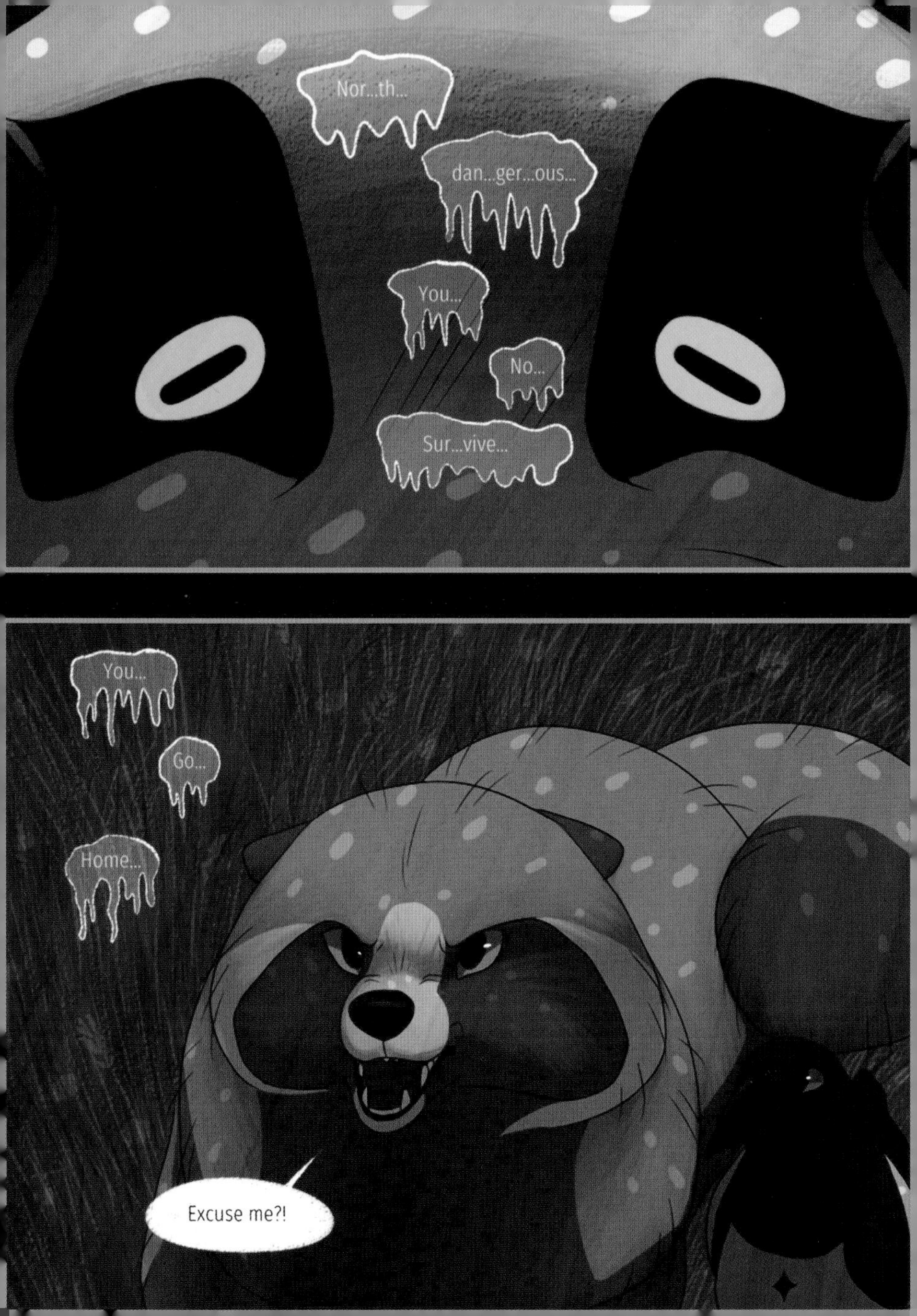
Nor...th...
dan...ger...ous...
You...
No...
Sur...vive...
You...
Go...
Home...
Excuse me?!

Chapter 19

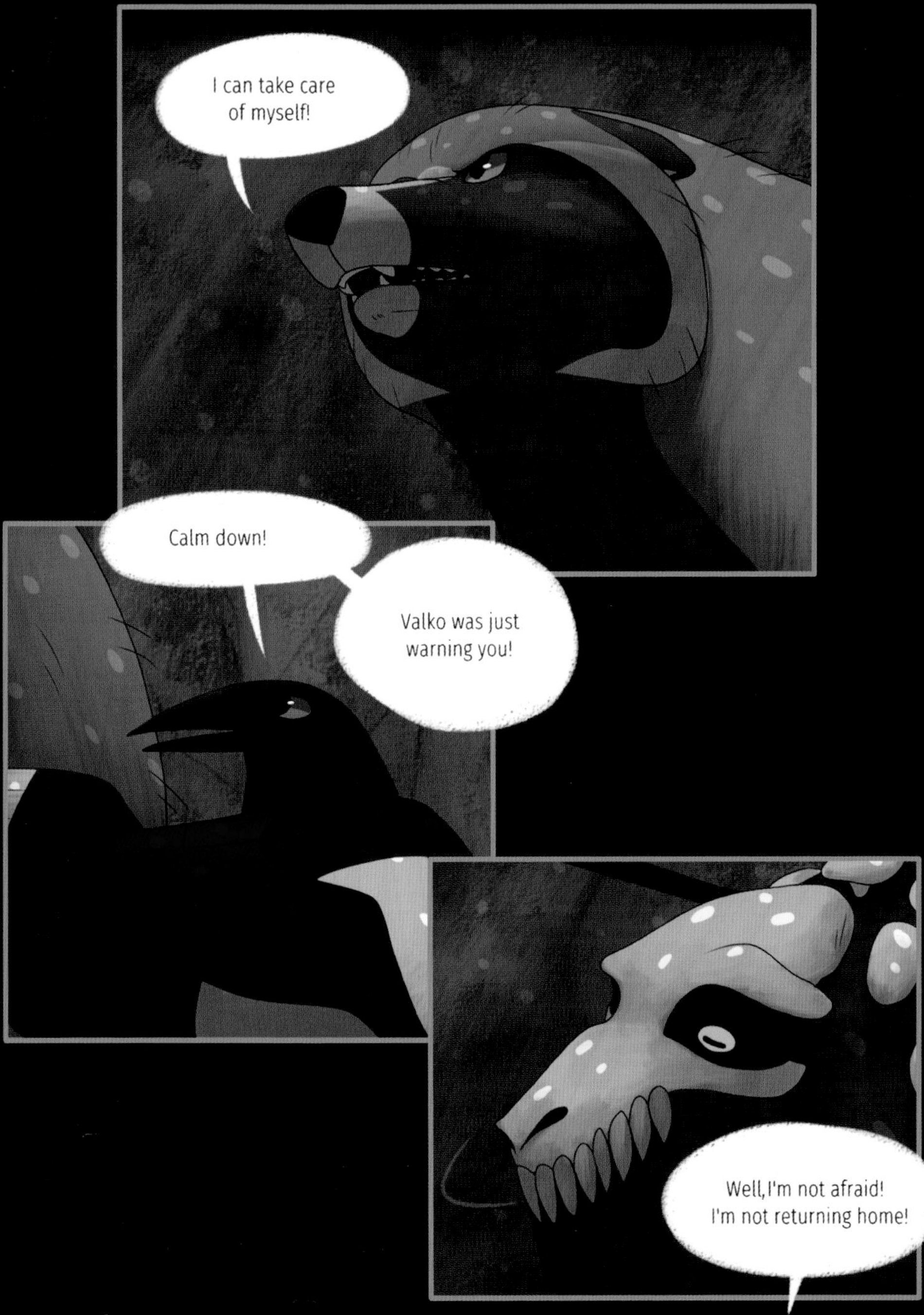

I can take care of myself!
Calm down!
Valko was just warning you!
Well, I'm not afraid! I'm not returning home!

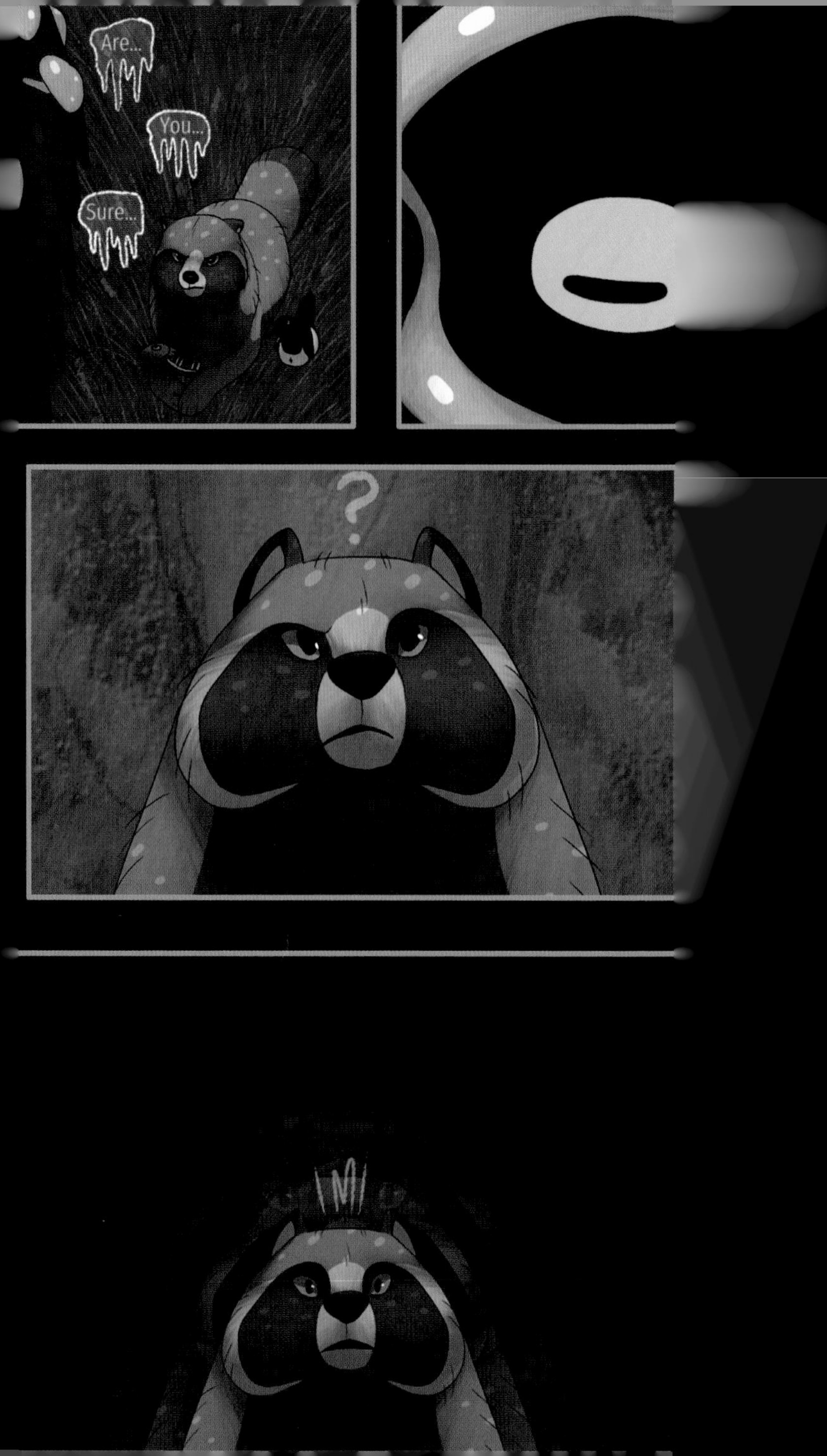
Are..
You...
Sure..

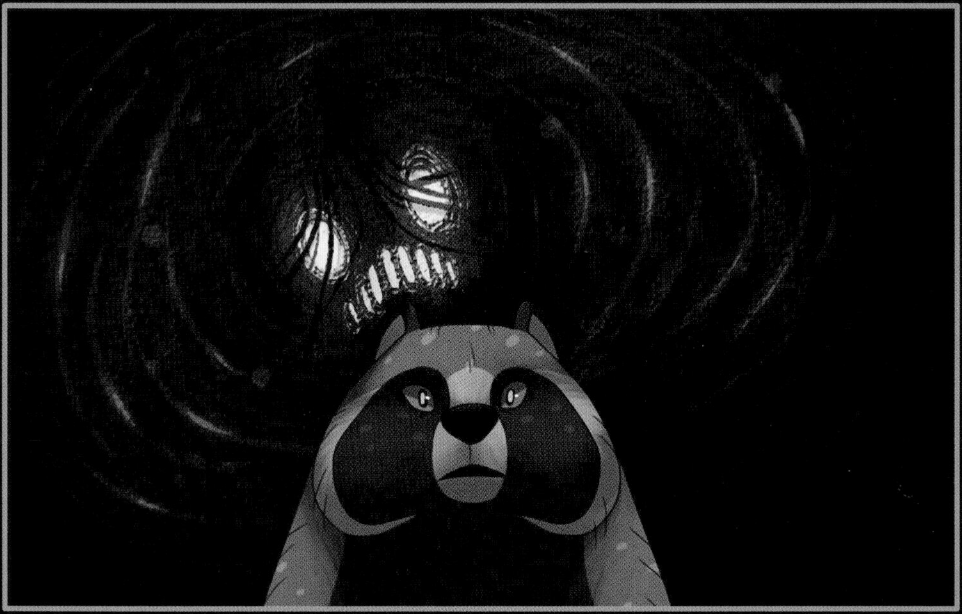

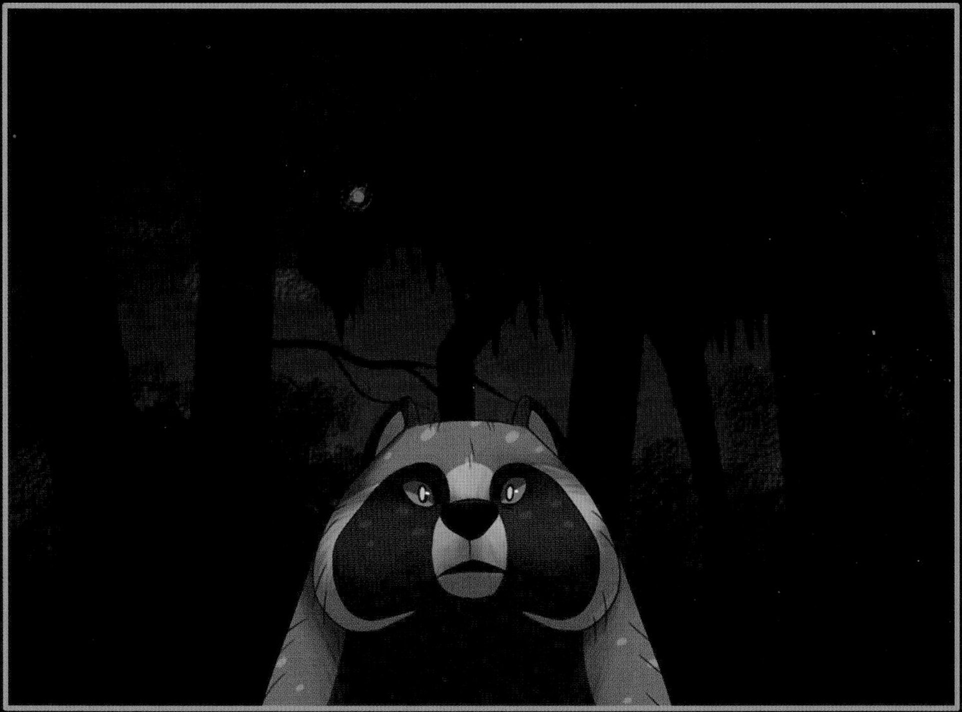

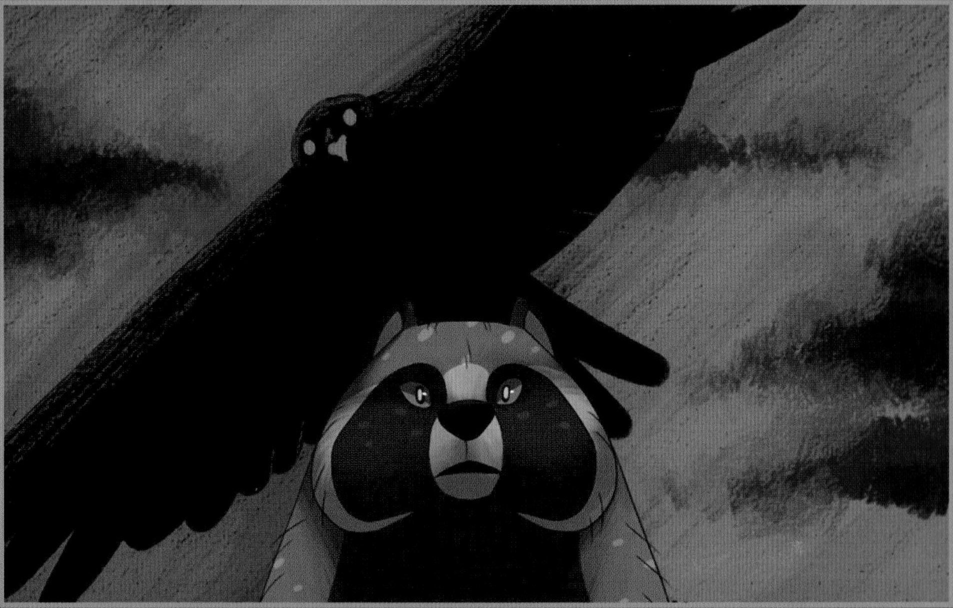

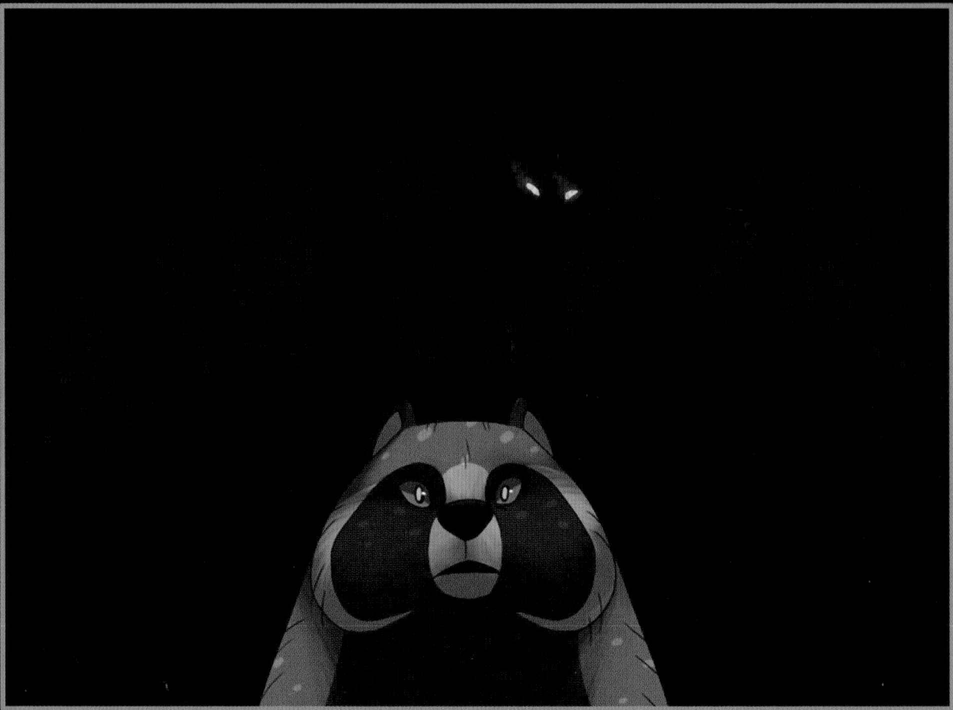

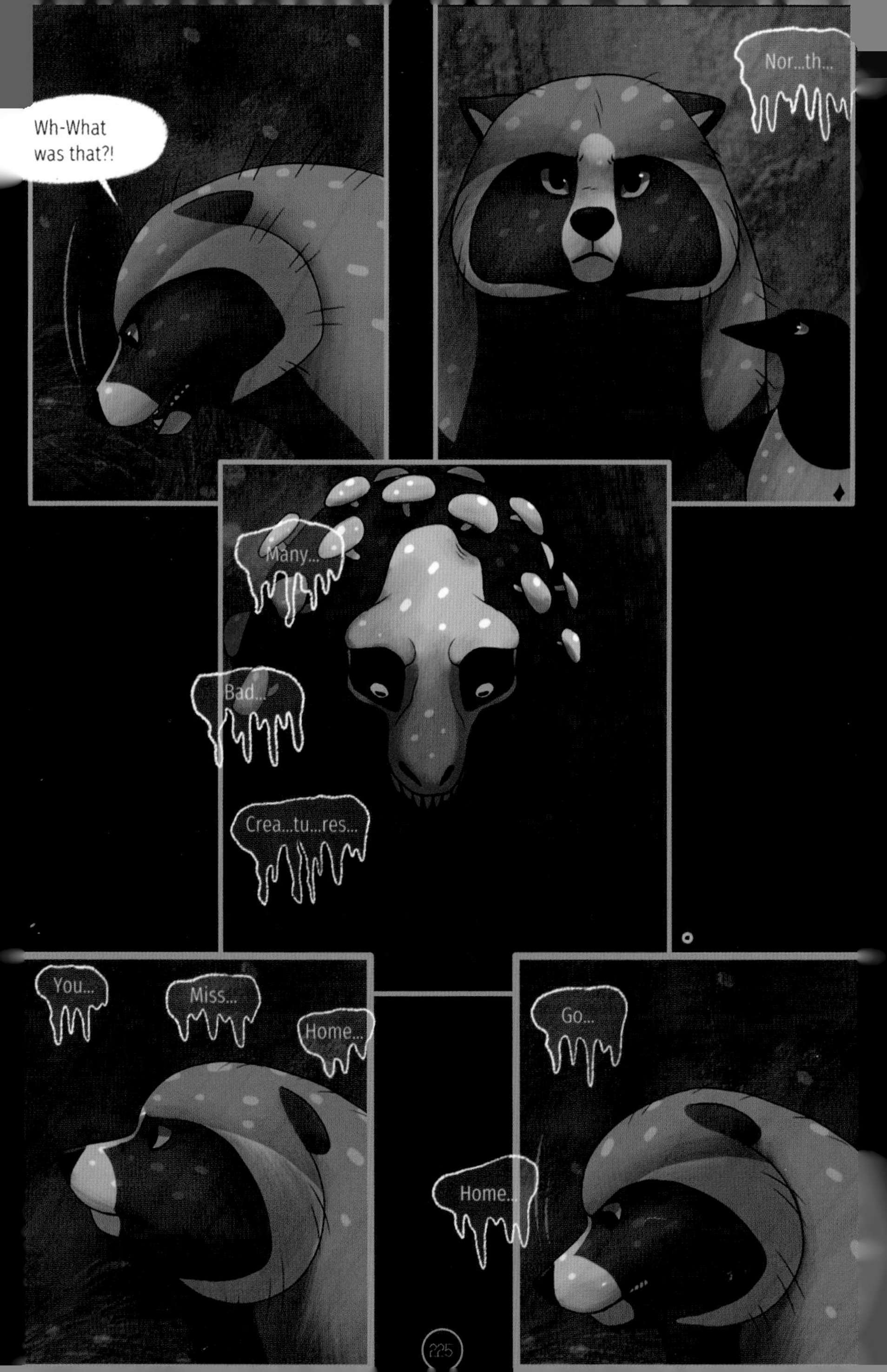
Wh-What was that?!
Nor...th...
Many...
Bad...
Crea...tu...res...
You...
Miss...
Home...
Home...
Go...

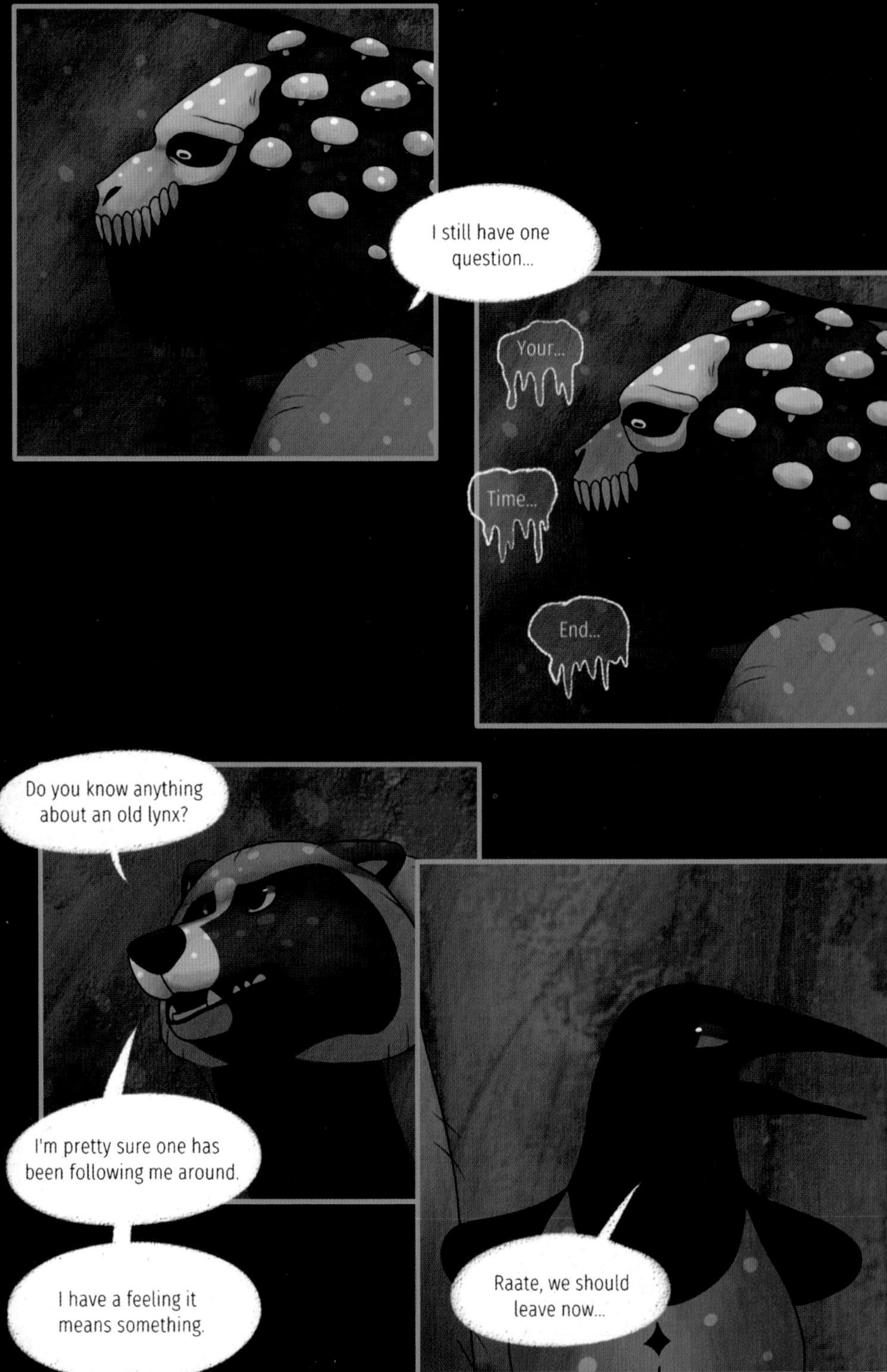
I still have one question...
Your...
Time...
End...
Do you know anything about an old lynx?
I'm pretty sure one has been following me around.
I have a feeling it means something.
Raate, we should leave now...

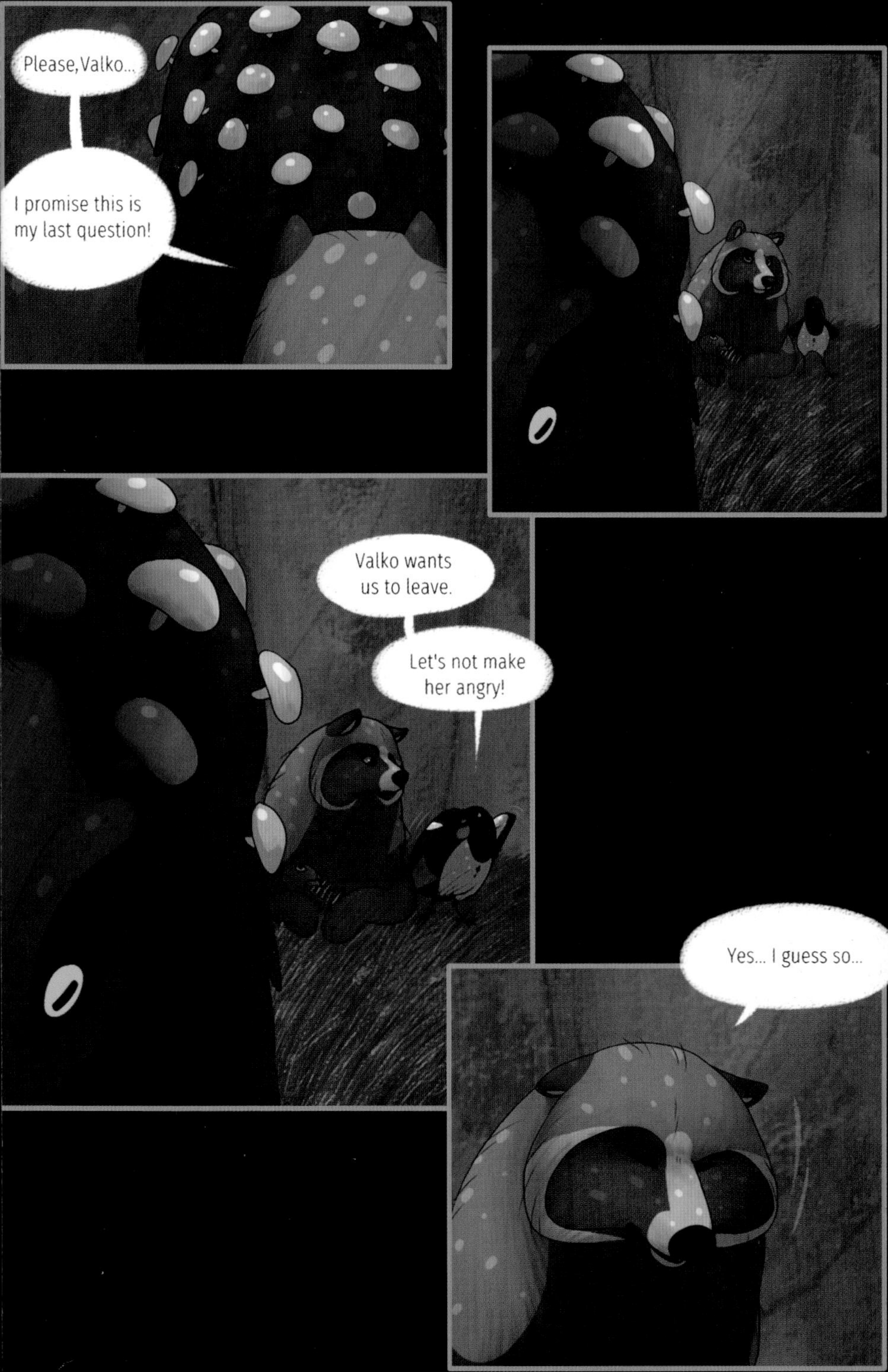
Please, Valko...
I promise this is my last question!
Valko wants us to leave.
Let's not make her angry!
Yes... I guess so...

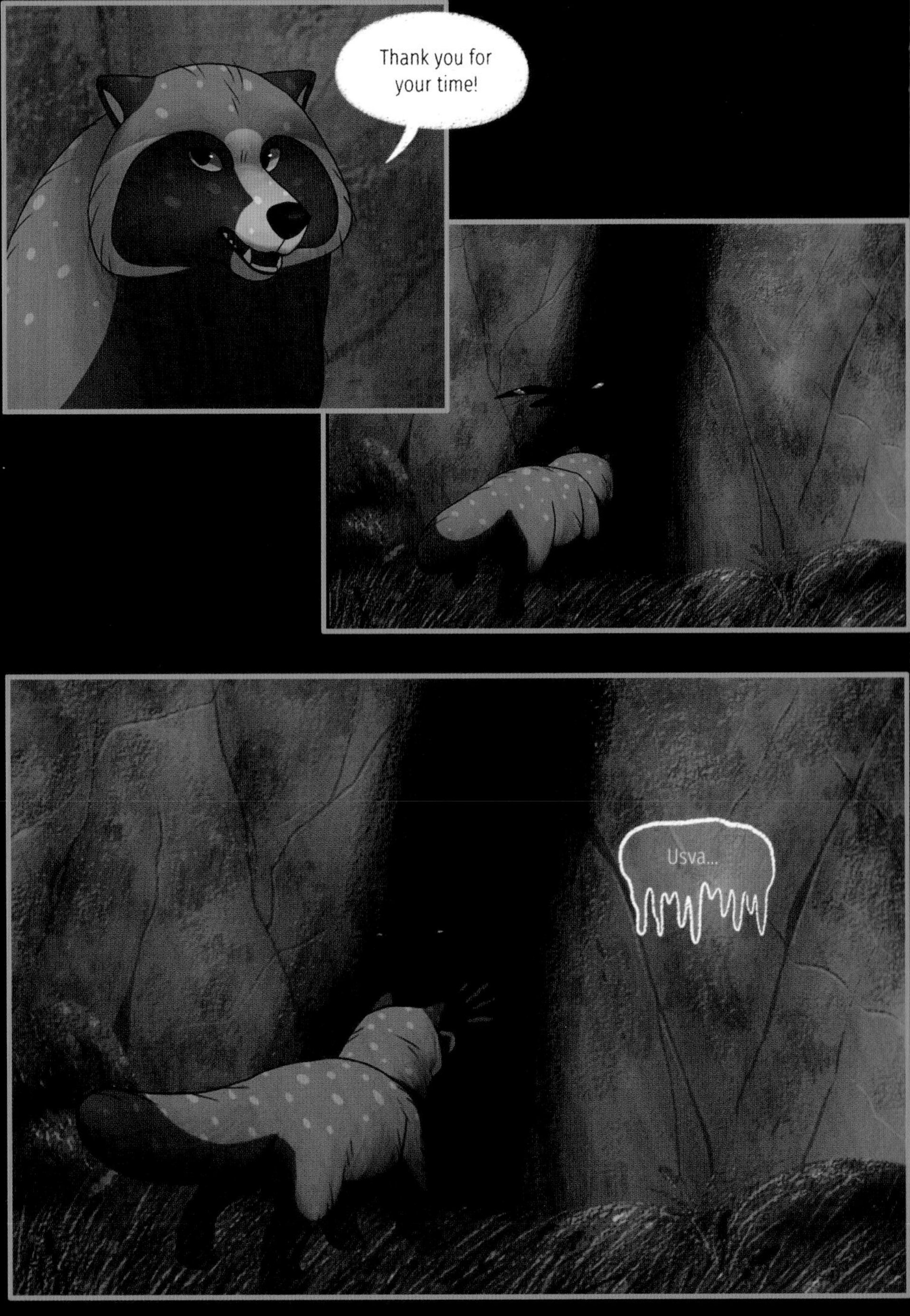
Thank you for
your time!
Usva...

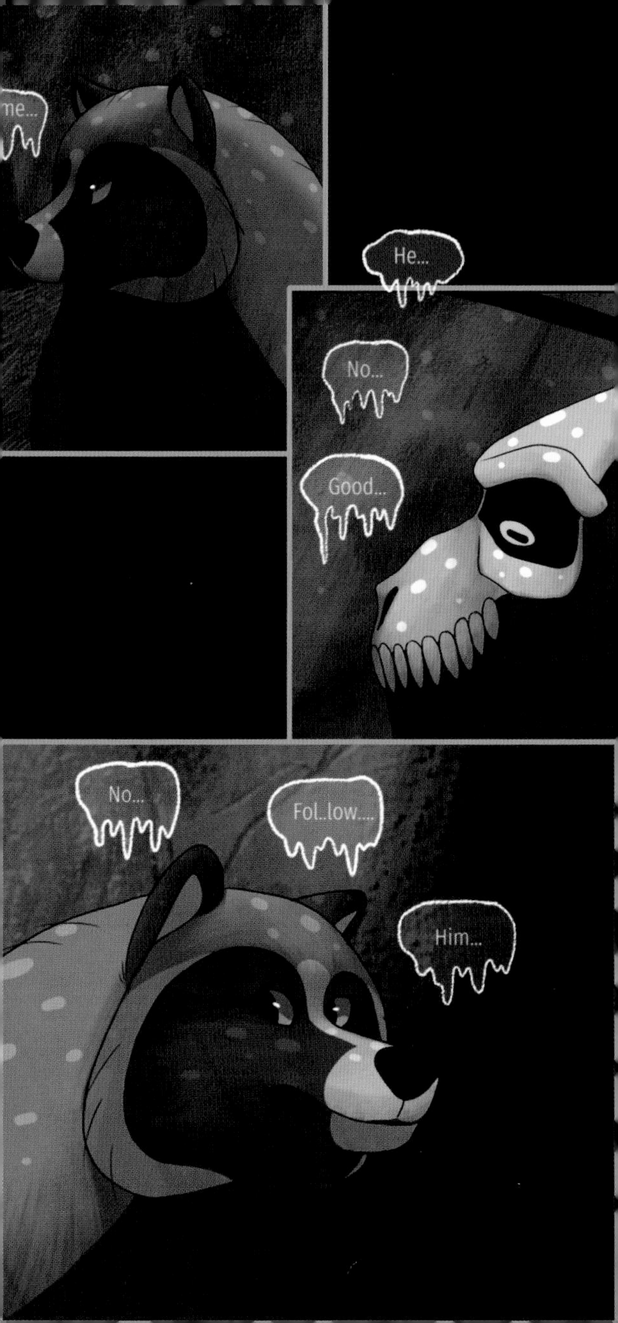

me...
He...
No...
Good...
No...
Fol..low....
Him...

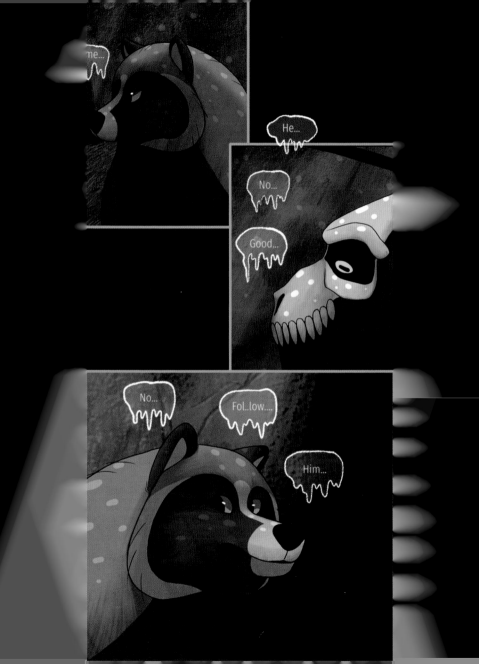

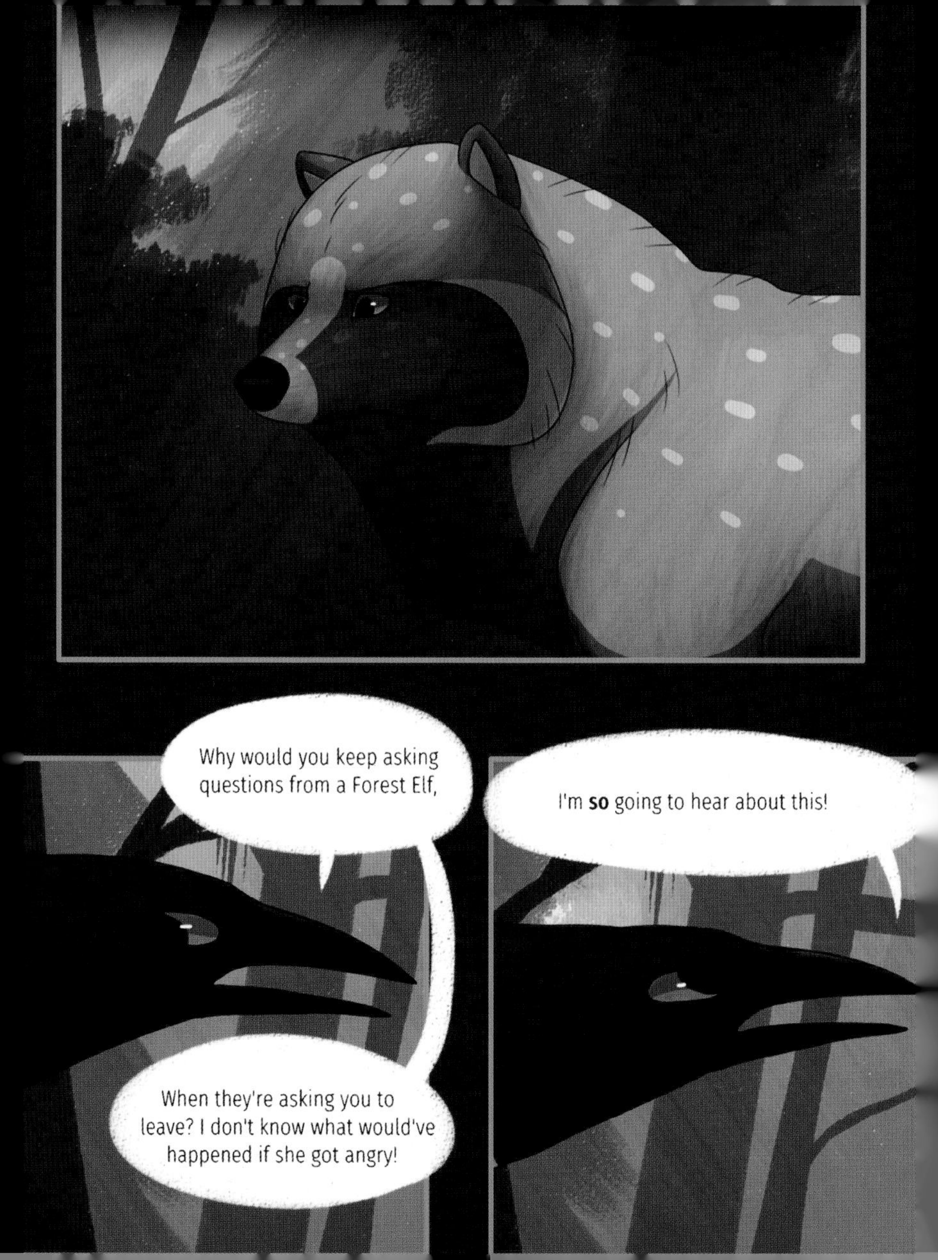
Why would you keep asking questions from a Forest Elf,
When they're asking you to leave? I don't know what would've happened if she got angry!
I'm **so** going to hear about this!

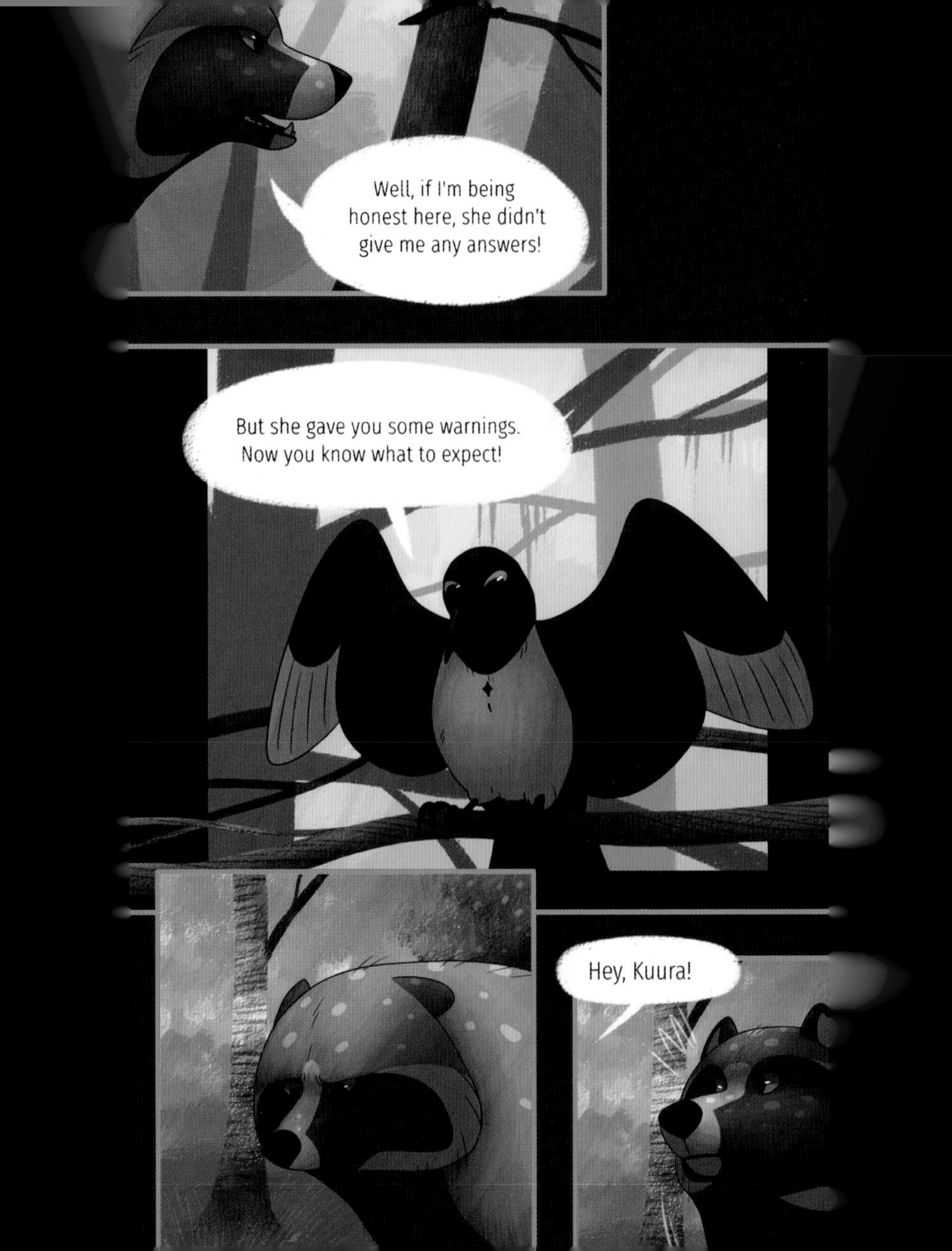
Well, if I'm being honest here, she didn't give me any answers!
But she gave you some warnings. Now you know what to expect!
Hey, Kuura!

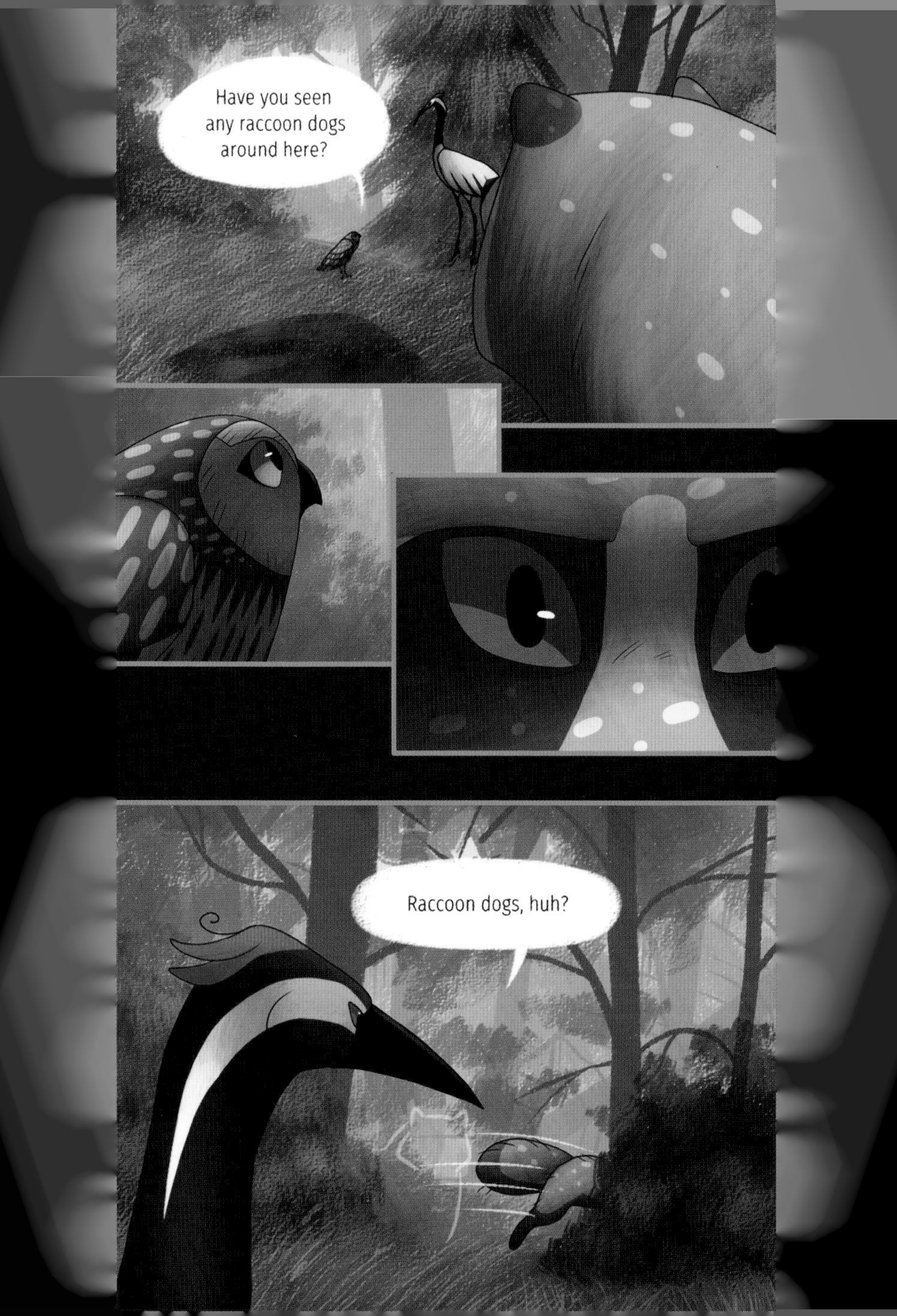
Have you seen any raccoon dogs around here?
Raccoon dogs, huh?

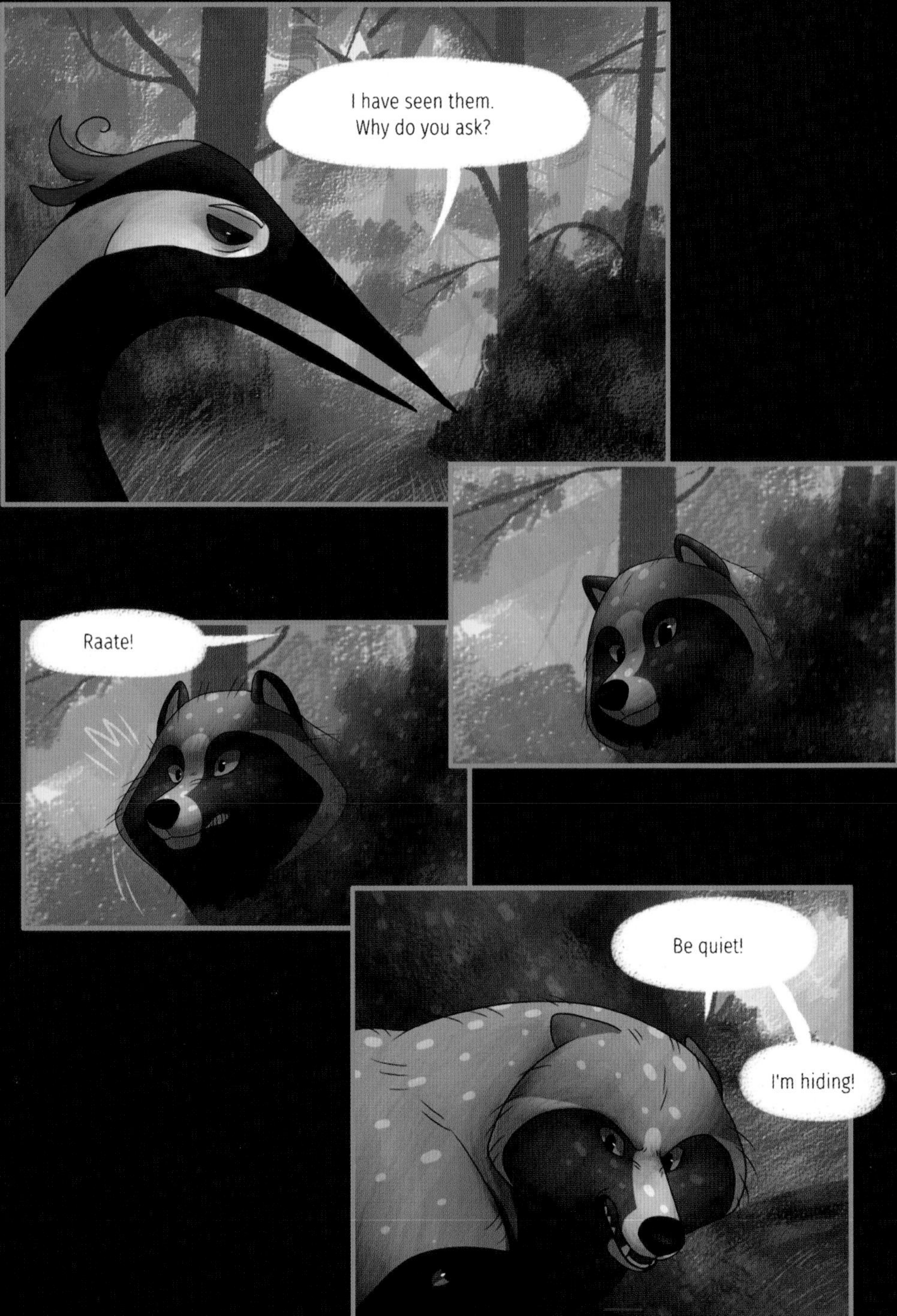
I have seen them.
Why do you ask?
Raate!
Be quiet!
I'm hiding!

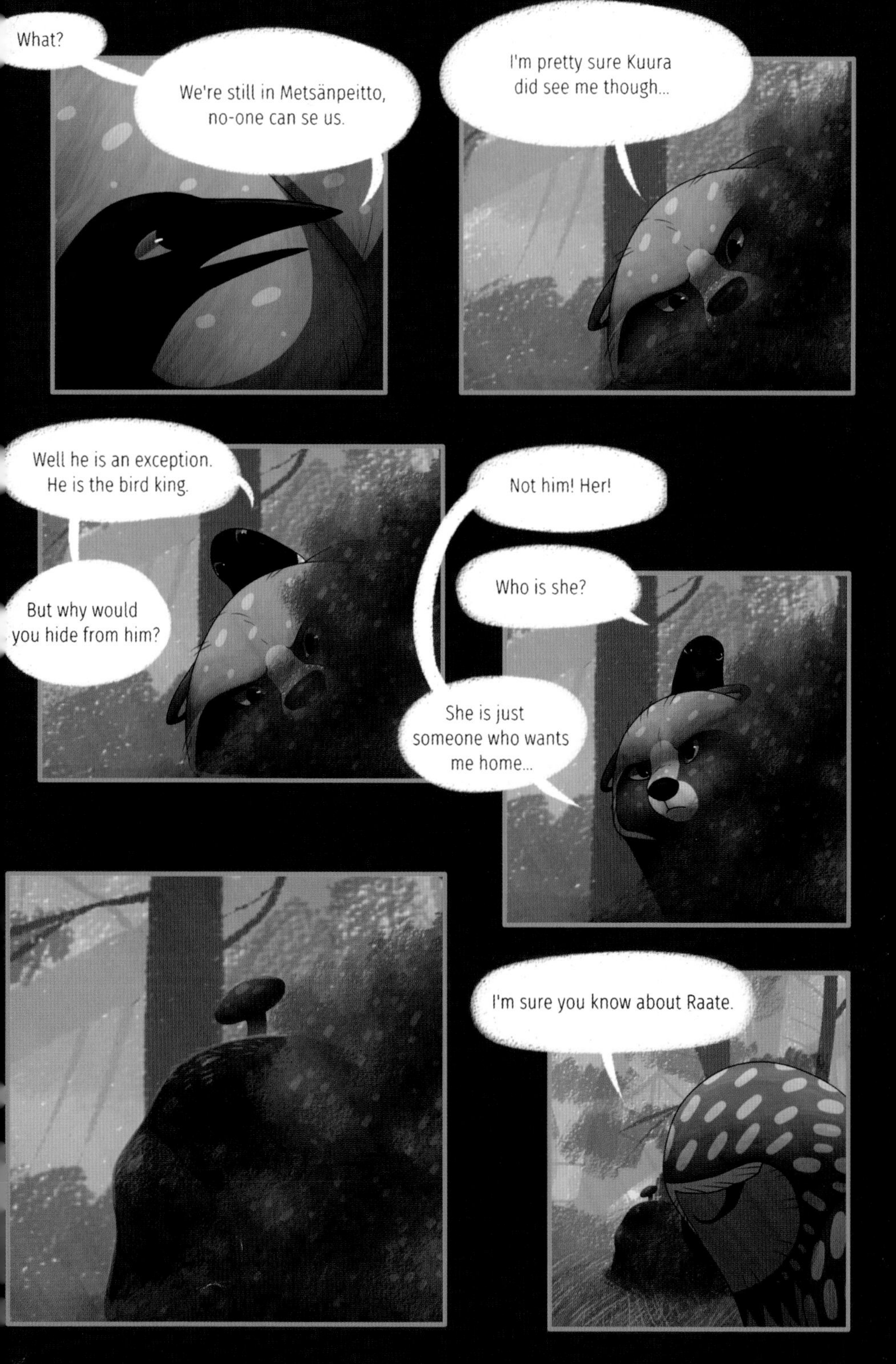
What?
We're still in Metsänpeitto, no-one can se us.
I'm pretty sure Kuura did see me though...
Well he is an exception. He is the bird king.
But why would you hide from him?
Not him! Her!
Who is she?
She is just someone who wants me home...
I'm sure you know about Raate.

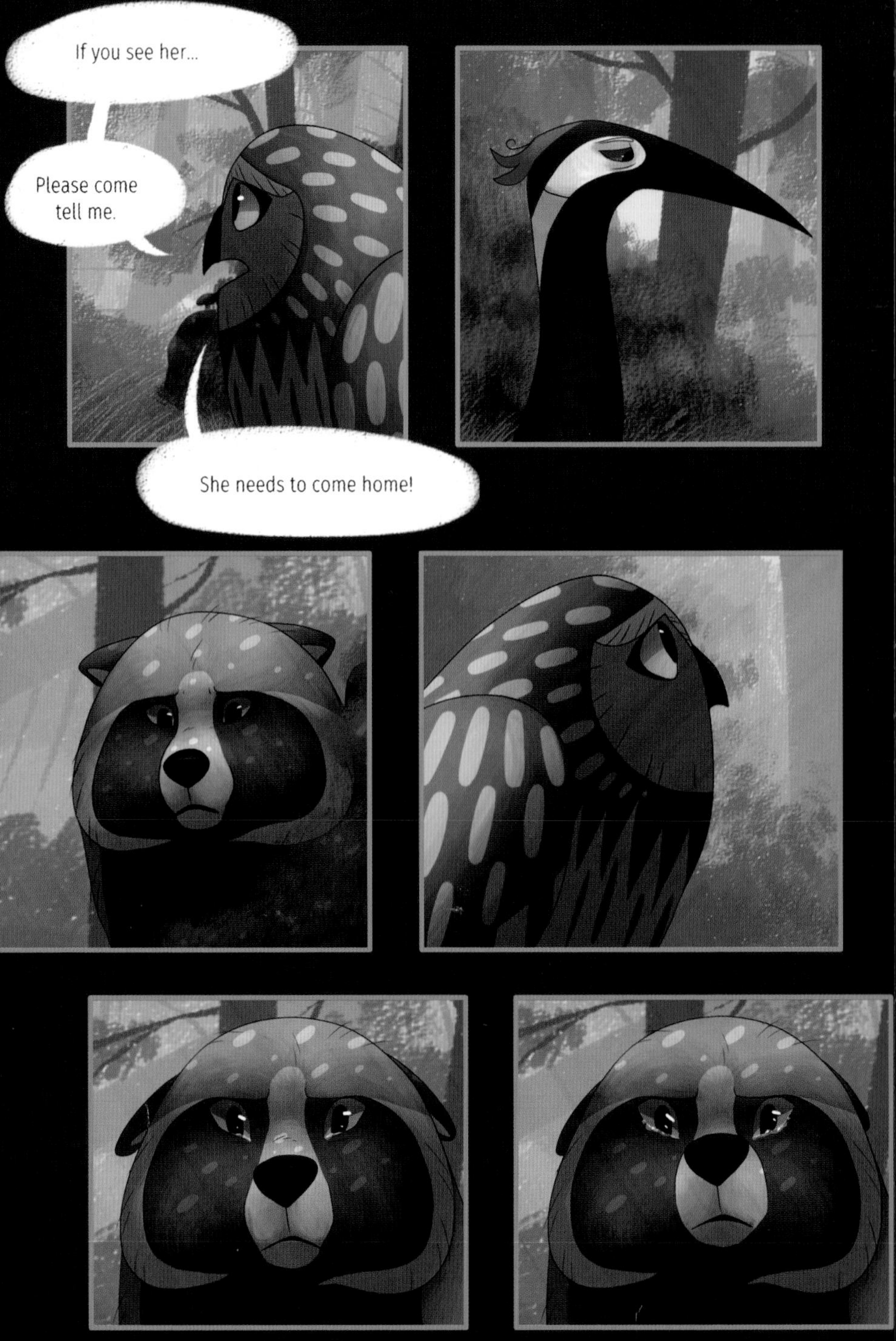
If you see her...
Please come tell me.
She needs to come home!

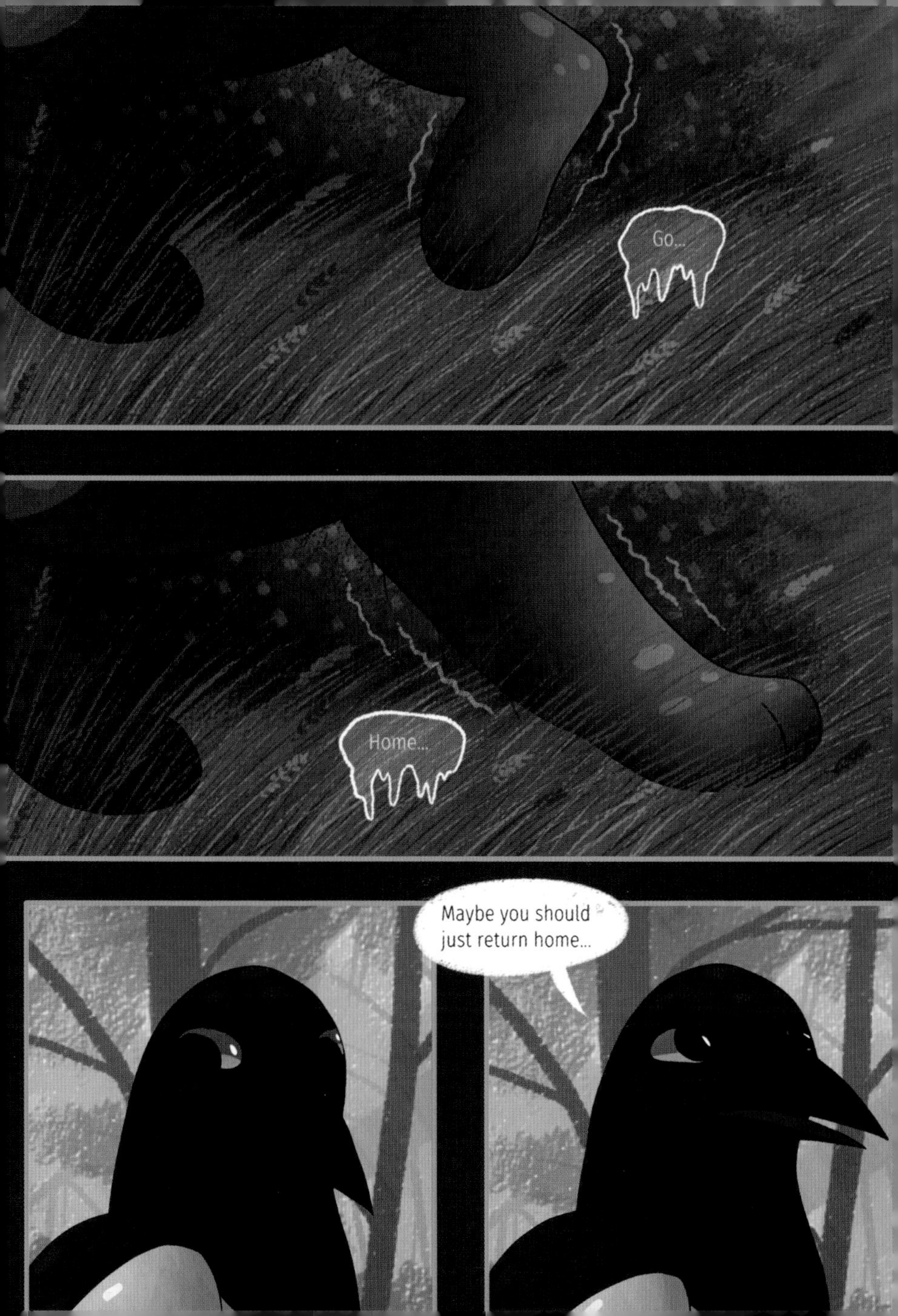
Go...
Home...
Maybe you should just return home...

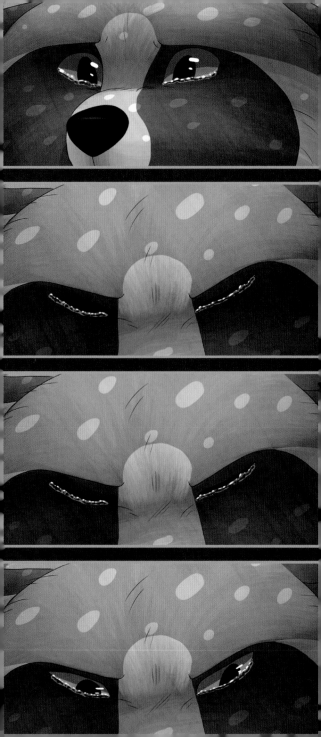

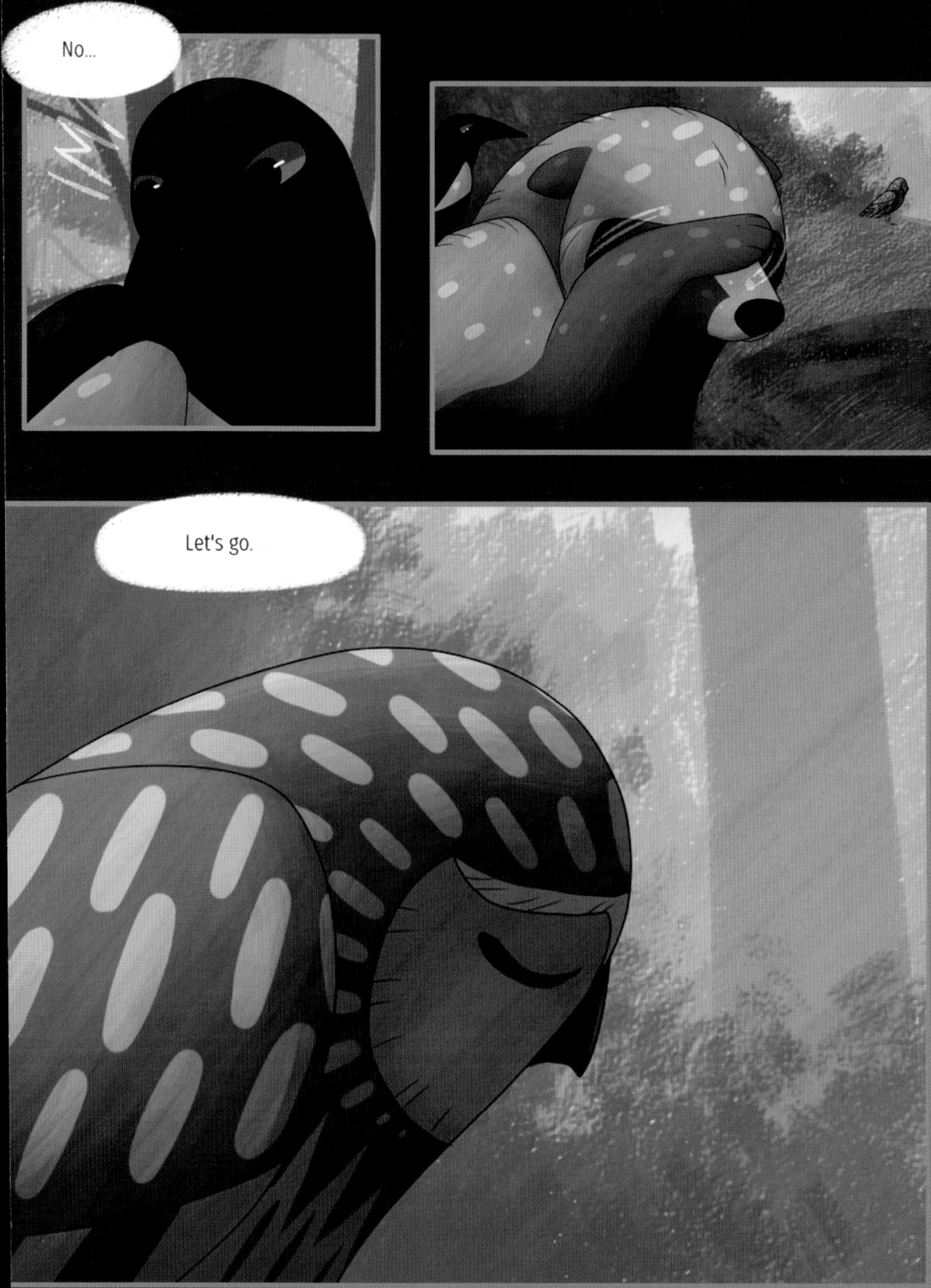
No...
Let's go.

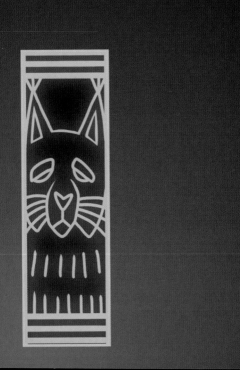

Chapter 21

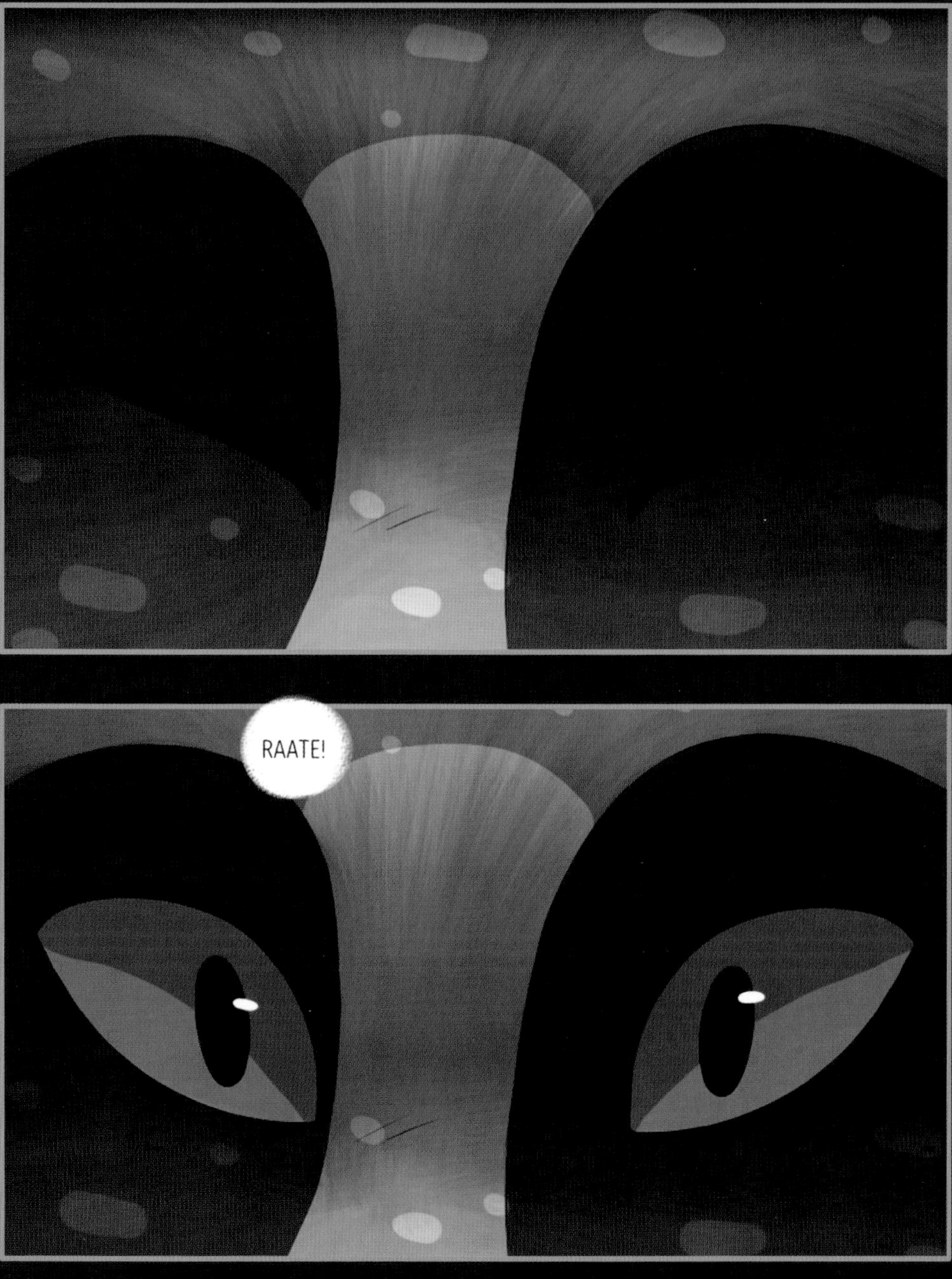
RAATE!

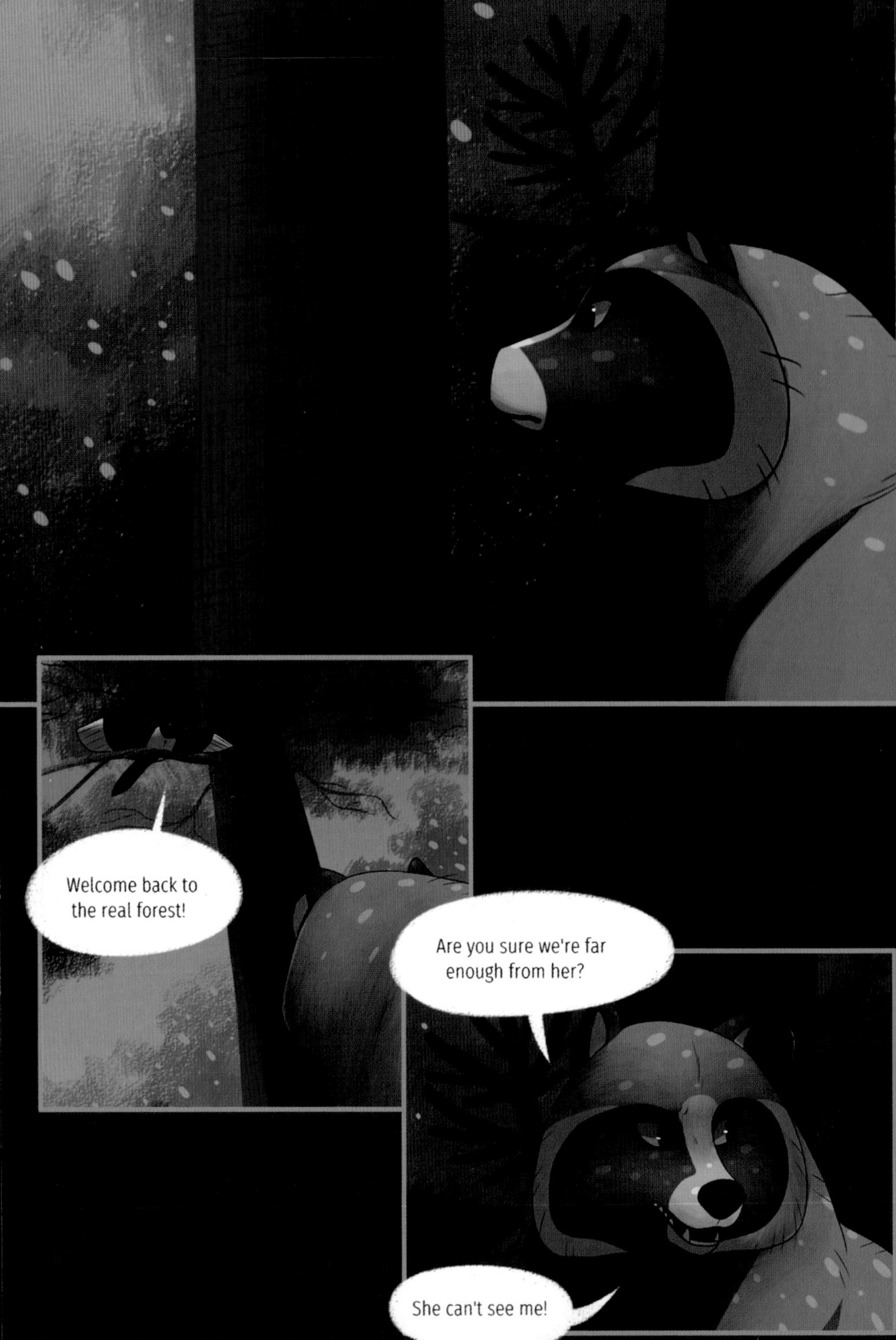
Welcome back to the real forest!
Are you sure we're far enough from her?
She can't see me!

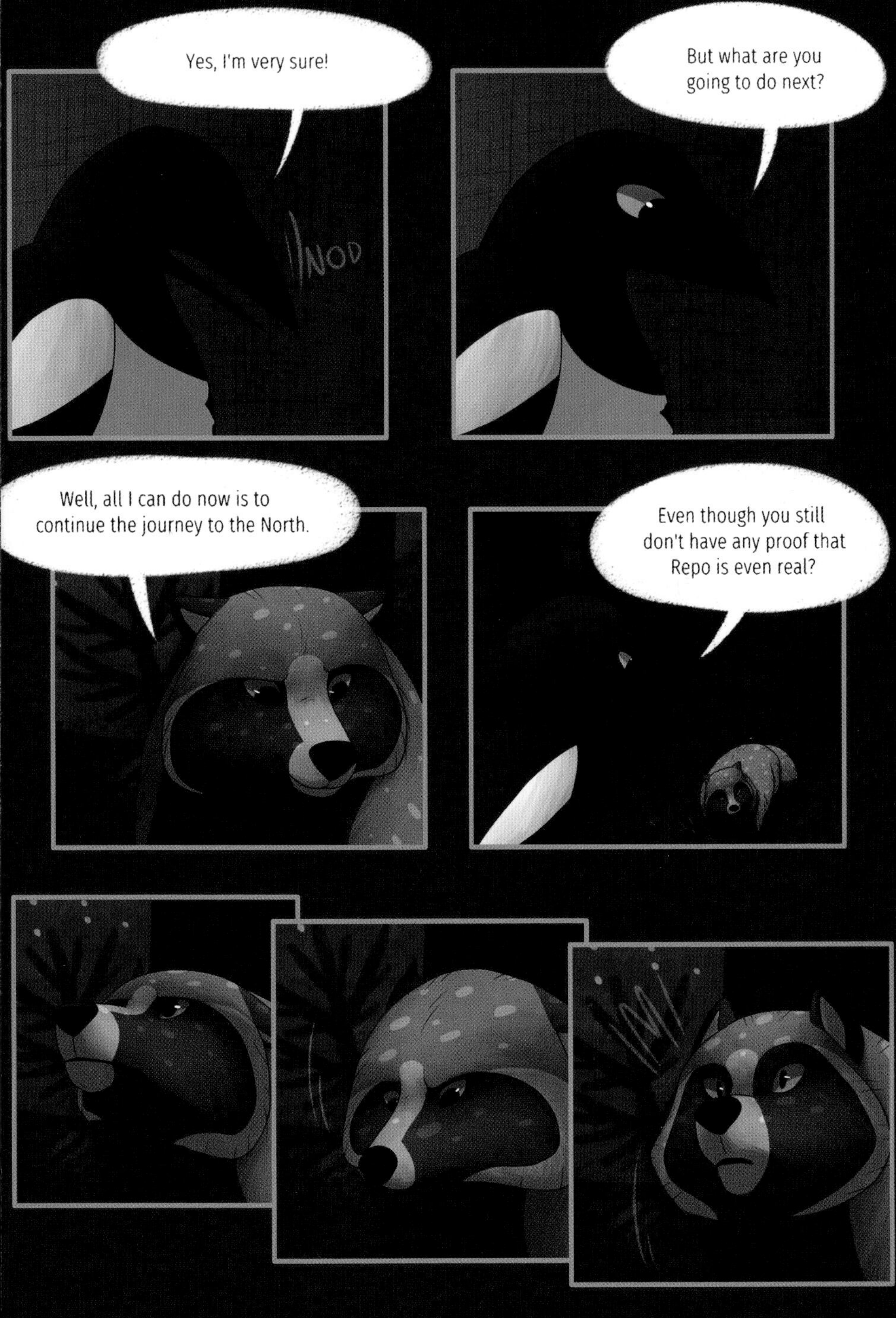

Yes, I'm very sure!
NOD
But what are you going to do next?
Well, all I can do now is to continue the journey to the North.
Even though you still don't have any proof that Repo is even real?

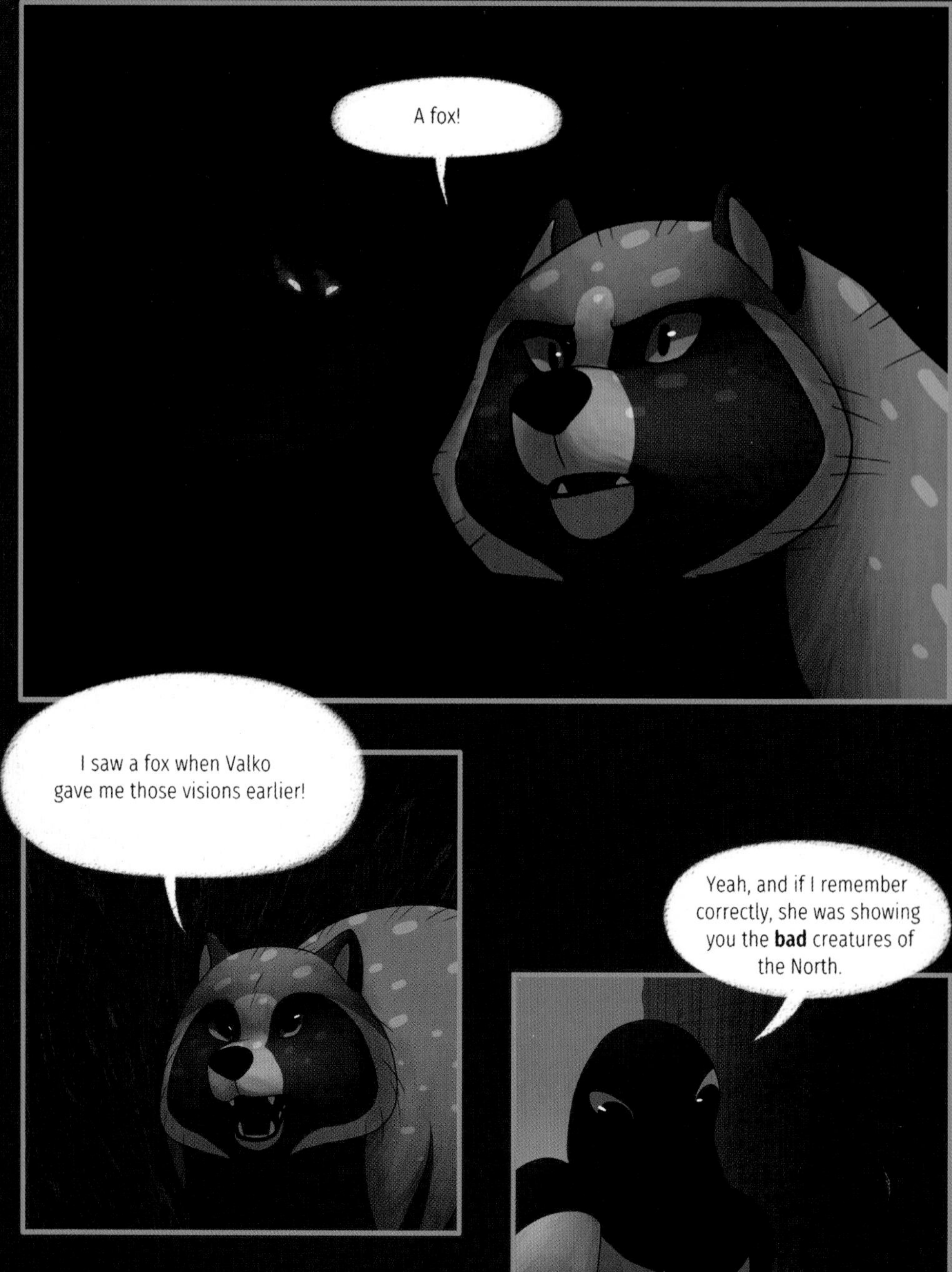
A fox!
I saw a fox when Valko gave me those visions earlier!
Yeah, and if I remember correctly, she was showing you the **bad** creatures of the North.

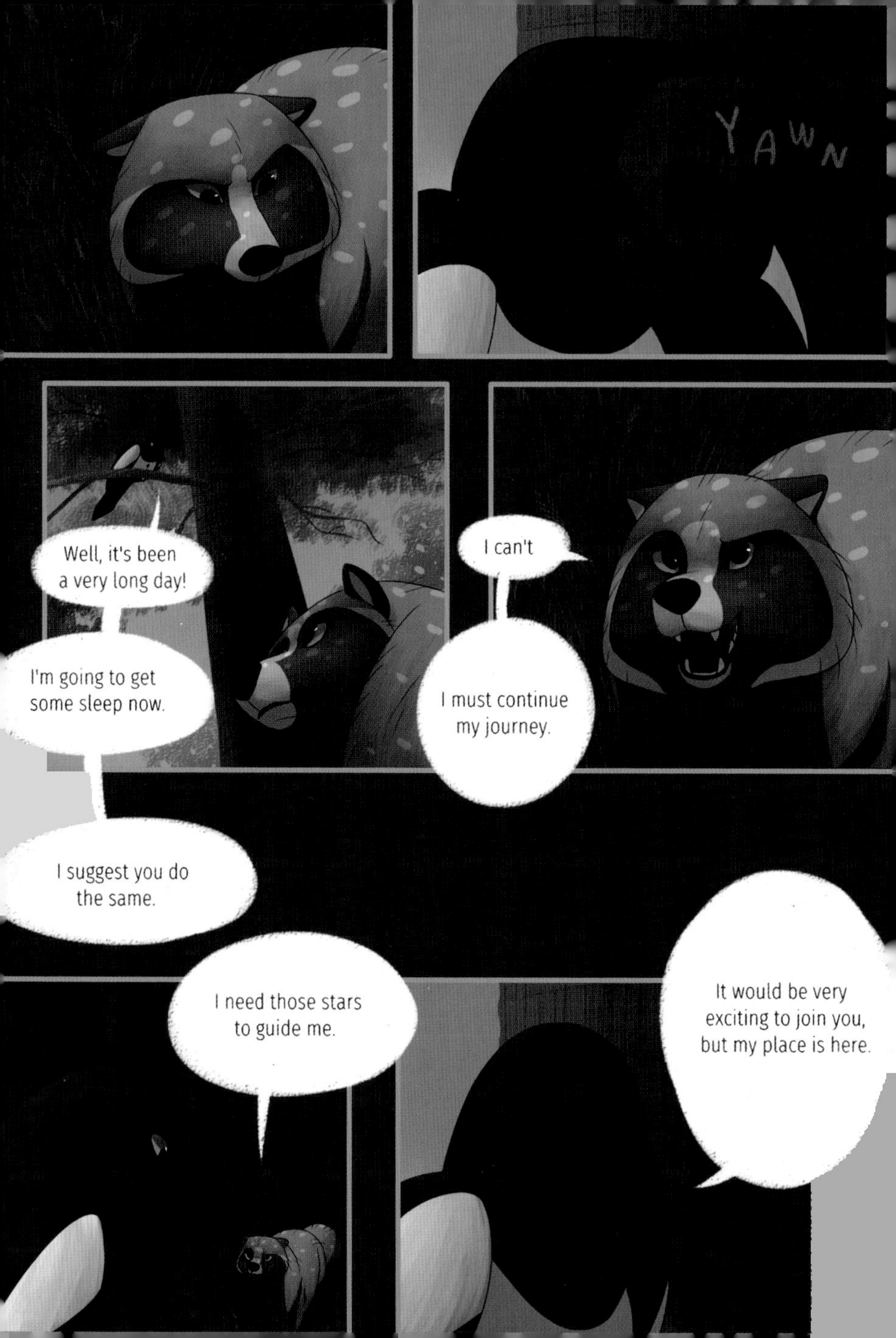
YAWN
Well, it's been a very long day!
I'm going to get some sleep now.
I suggest you do the same.
I can't
I must continue my journey.
I need those stars to guide me.
It would be very exciting to join you, but my place is here.

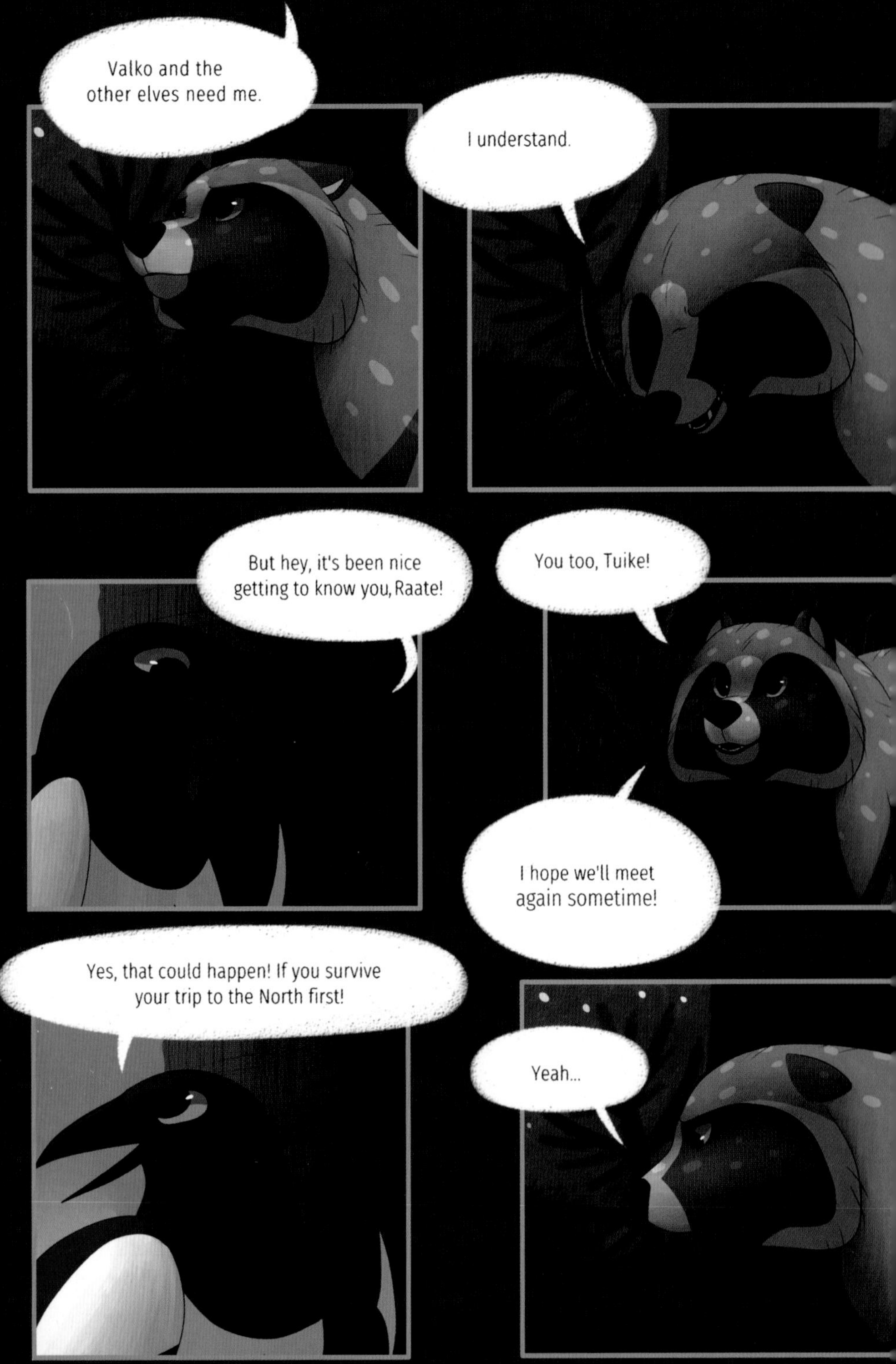
Valko and the other elves need me.
I understand.
But hey, it's been nice getting to know you, Raate!
You too, Tuike!
I hope we'll meet again sometime!
Yes, that could happen! If you survive your trip to the North first!
Yeah...

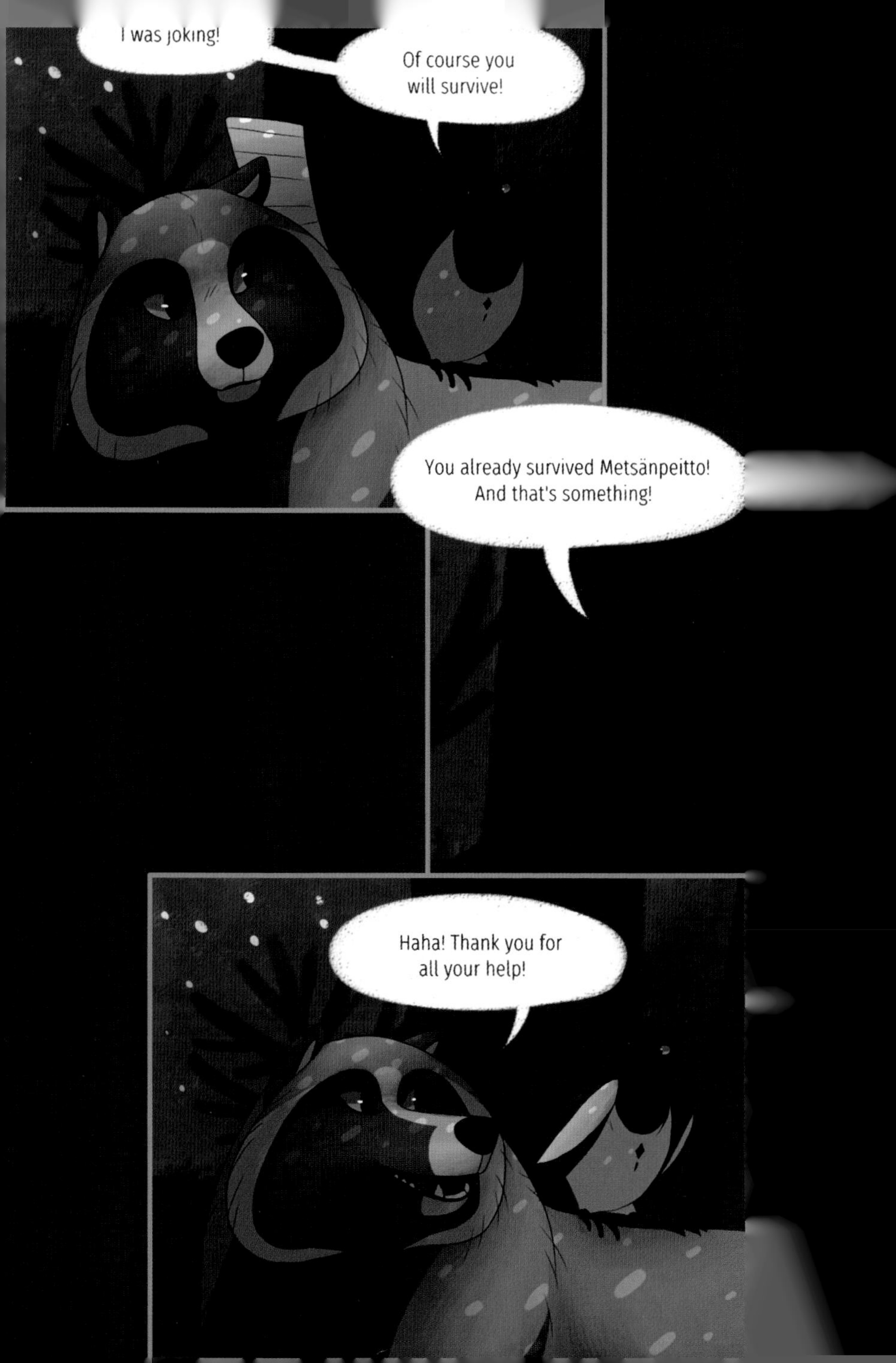
I was joking!
Of course you will survive!
You already survived Metsänpeitto! And that's something!
Haha! Thank you for all your help!

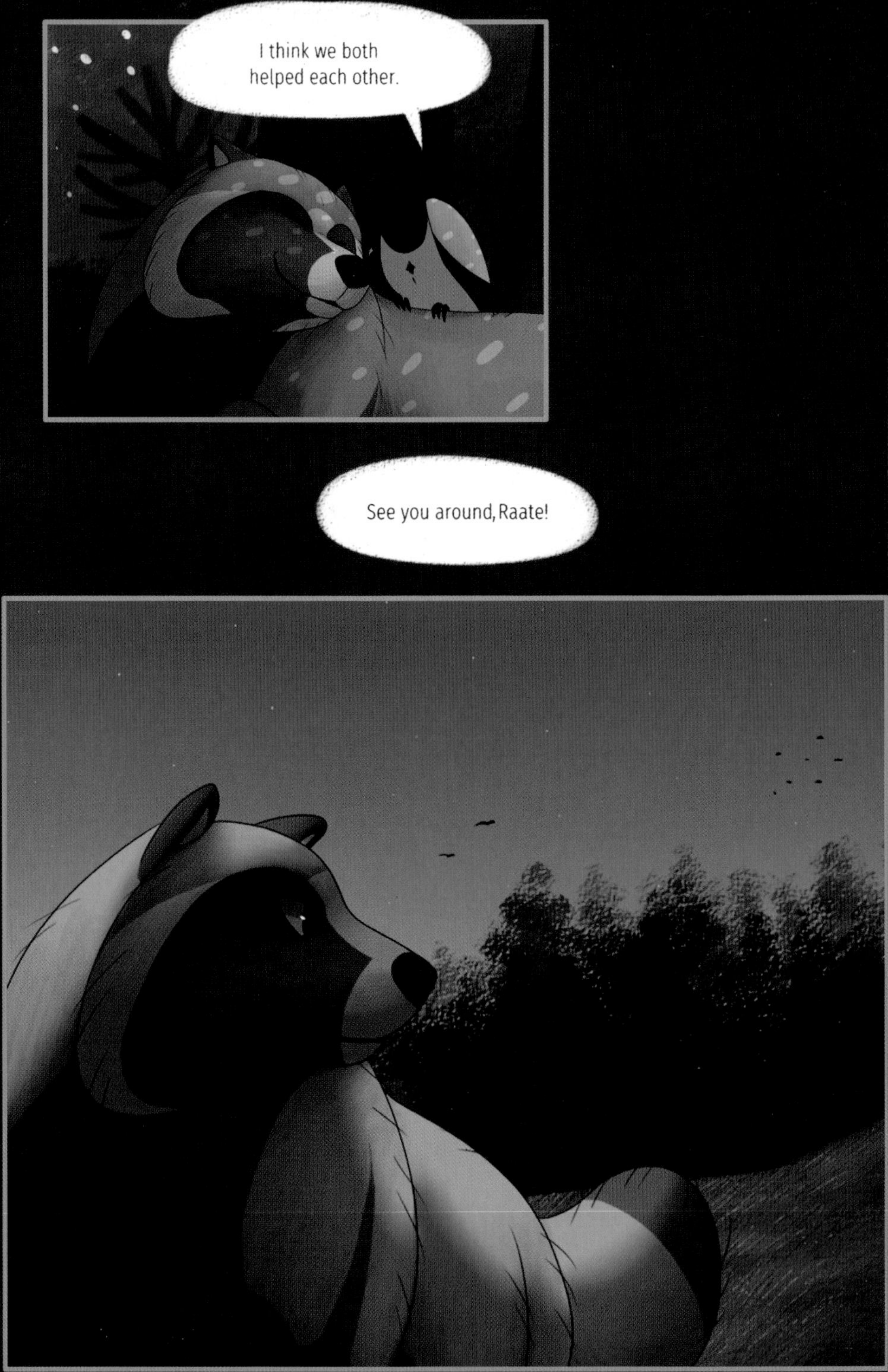
I think we both helped each other.
See you around, Raate!

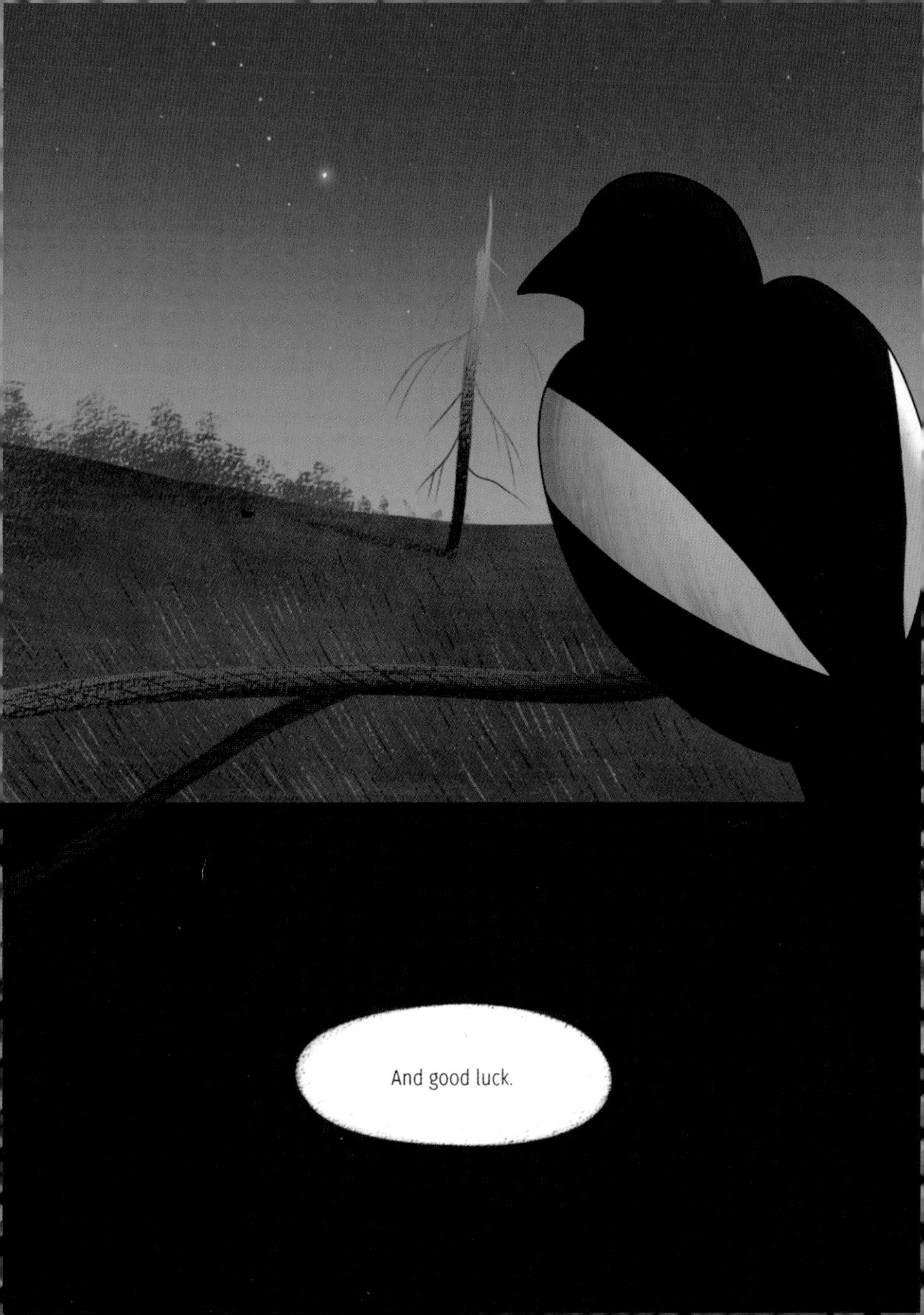
And good luck.

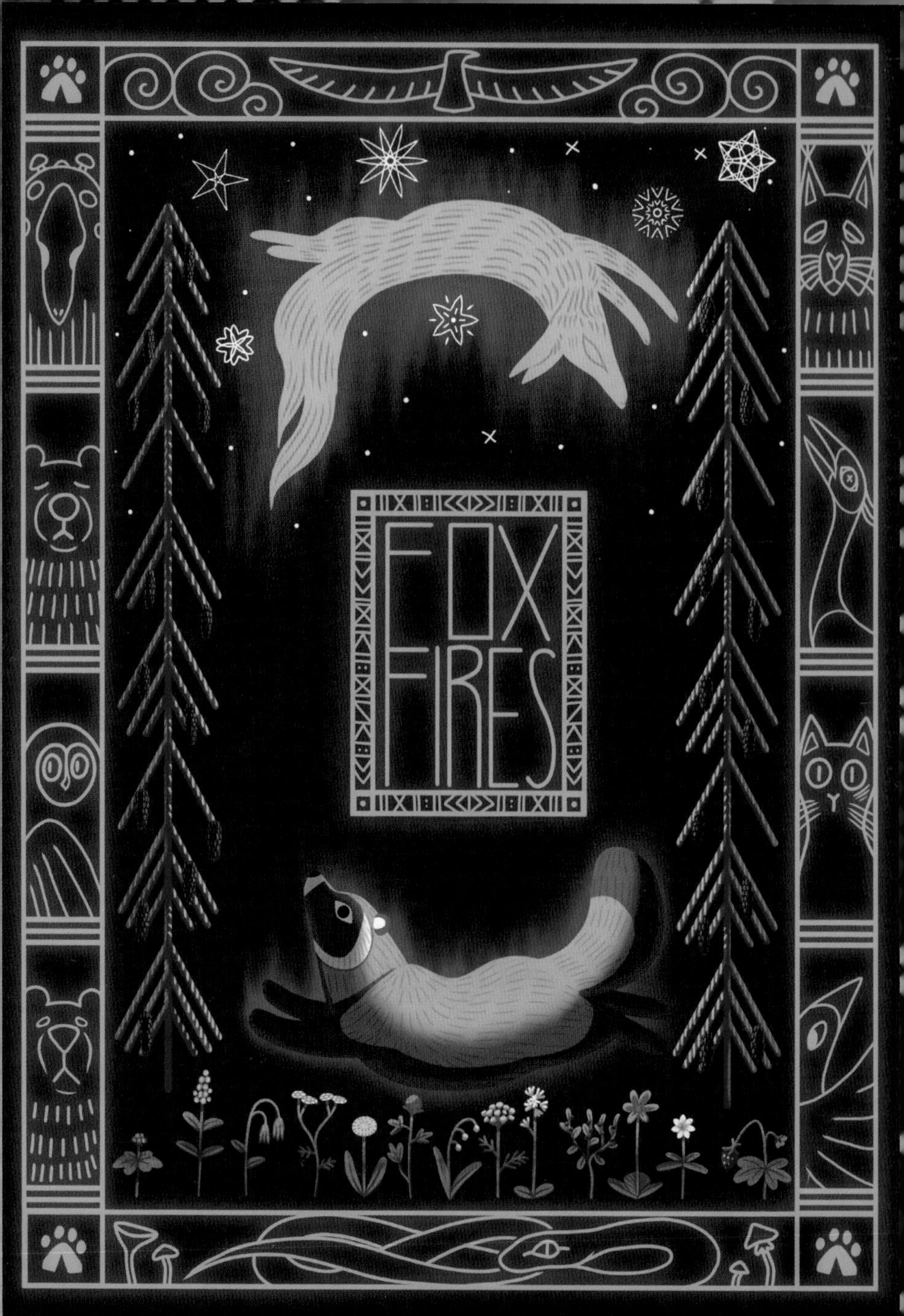
FOX
FIRES

Emilia Ojala, also known as "Pipilia", hails from the small, cold country of Finland. A self-taught artist with a degree in graphic design, Emilia had always dreamed of writing and illustrating folk stories (while also owning many pets, of course!). Her passion for storytelling, art, and animation led her to develop her own stories at a very young age. Even back then her stories centered around animals, typically the adventures of her family pets.

The small, Finnish towns she grew up in, with their close proximity to the fields and forests, provided Emilia with many opportunities to spend ample time in nature. These experiences have driven her creative process for tales about what might happen within nature when people aren't around to see it.

A fan of folklore and mythology, it was while Emilia was reading Finnish tales one afternoon she was inspired to create *Fox Fires*. Since Finnish myths are somewhat lesser known she felt Fox Fires could be a wonderful opportunity to open them up to the rest of the world.

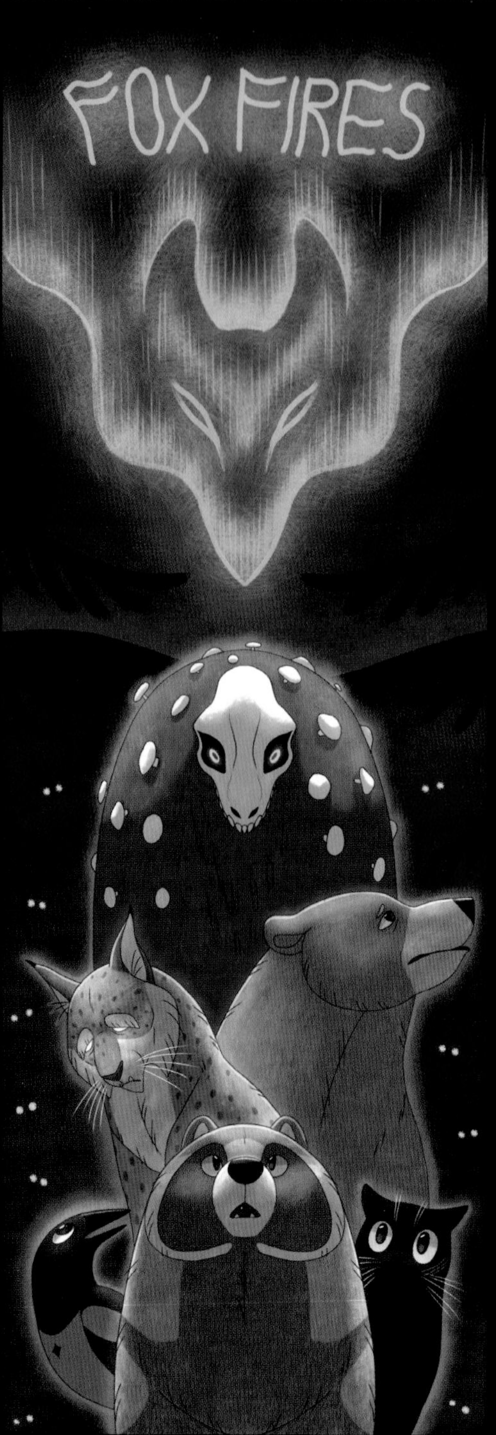
FOX FIRES

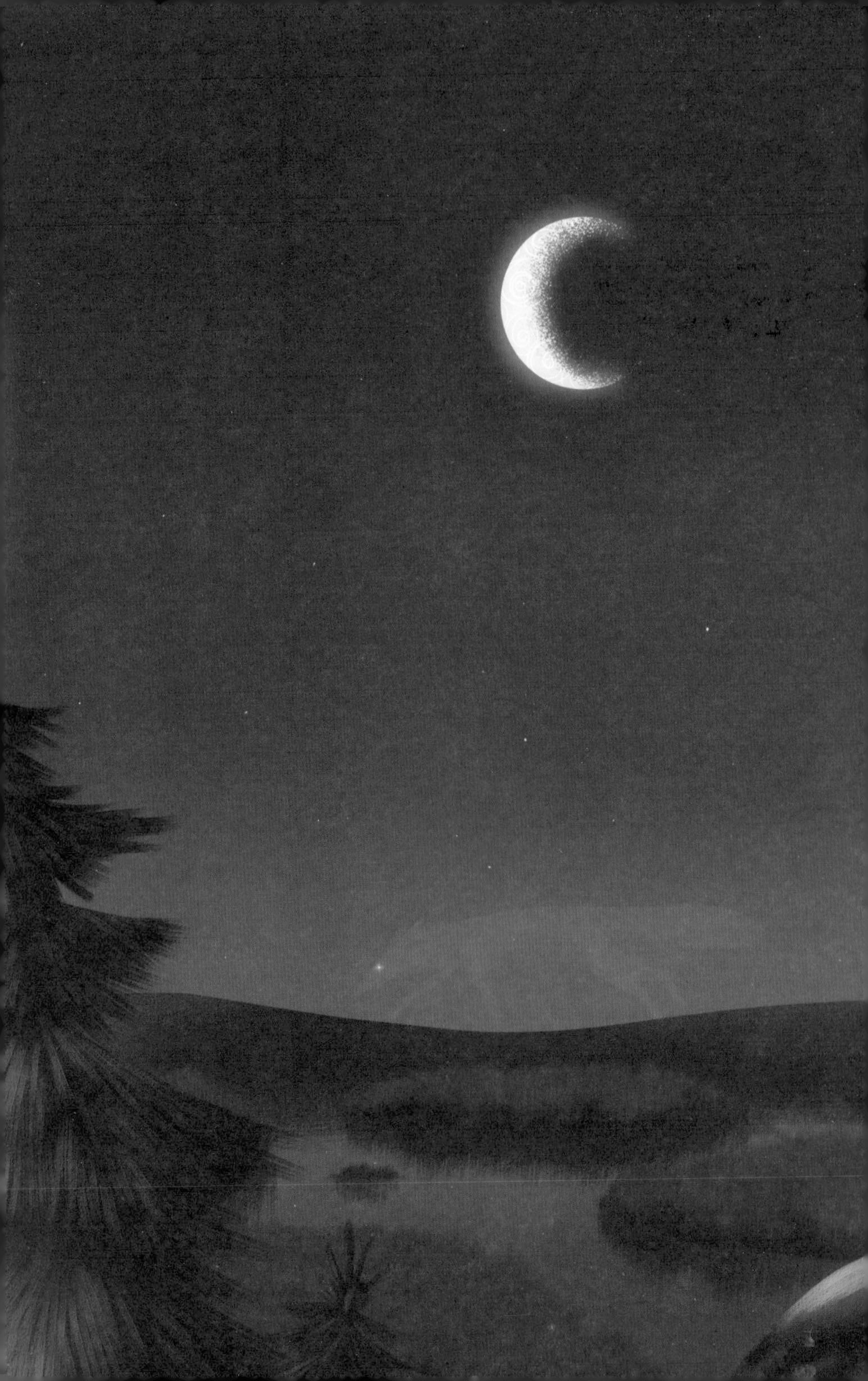